KRIMSON

THOMAS EMSON

snowbooks

Proudly Published by Snowbooks in 2010

Copyright © 2010 Thomas Emson

Snowbooks Ltd.
Kirtlington Business Centre
Oxfordshire
OX5 3JA
Tel: 0207 837 6482
email: info@snowbooks.com
www.snowbooks.com

British Library Cataloguing in Publication Data
A catalogue record for this book is available from the British Library.

Hardcover 978-1-906727-27-7
Paperback 978-1-906727-35-2

Printed and bound in the UK by J F Print Ltd., Sparkford

KRIMSON

PART TWO OF THE
VAMPIRE TRINITY

THOMAS EMSON

In memory of Griff (1993–2010)

PART ONE.

RESISTANCE.

CHAPTER 1.
SLAVE SHIP.

KWAN Mei, eighteen and with her dreams of a better life shattered, cowered on the deck of the yacht.

The girl she cradled in her arms was crying and begging to go home. But home was gone. It had been left behind. Their villages in northern China abandoned for the cities of Europe. For one city in particular.

London.

"We pay for you to bring us, and you treat us like slaves," said Mei to the man.

He wore black – leather jacket, roll-neck jumper, jeans, Doc Marten boots. Acne scars pockmarked his face.

He snarled at her and raised the machete, threatening to chop her up and toss her overboard with the rest of the dead unless she was quiet.

His voice trembled as if he were nervous.

But this man hadn't been scared of anything during the whole journey. What did he have to fear? Not the authorities. They'd passed through many countries that were more unwelcoming than England.

The captain, a Frenchman who spoke Mandarin, told the man in black, "We're coming into Ramsgate soon, so you need to keep them quiet."

The captain licked his lips. His knuckles were white on the wheel. Sweat poured from beneath his baseball cap. He took a sip of water from a jerry can.

The yacht, a forty-footer, rocked over the English Channel. Mei had never been to sea before this journey. She never wanted to go again.

The girl in Mei's arms whined. The child was only twelve or thirteen. Her parents had died on the journey here. After that, Mei had looked after the youngster. It was difficult. The kid cried a lot. She wanted to go home. She was constantly in hysterics, and the traffickers threatened to get rid of her unless Mei shut her up.

"You're still not shutting her up, are you?" said the man in black. He sweated and paced the deck.

"She is upset, can't you see?"

"I don't care."

"We pay you, and this is how – "

"Shut your mouth. We are nearly in England. This is what you wanted, yes? You wanted England. England is here. We give you England, and you complain. I don't care, girl. I don't care if I kill you here, when you are this close to your England, because you are – "

He trailed off. He was going to say something.

"What?" said Mei.

"Nothing. Shut your face. I don't want to get caught, okay? I've not seen my family in three months because of you, and if we get caught, I won't see them for years. I'll go to prison. So you be quiet. Or I will cut you into pieces and feed you to the English fish. All of you."

"You're not scared of prison," Mei said.

"Shut up," he said.

"You're scared of something else."

"Be quiet."

The girl in Mei's arms cried again, and Mei told her it would be all right. But it wouldn't be.

She'd known that soon after they'd left Shanghai.

She knew it when the men smirked and slammed the truck's back door, casting her and the other fifty-seven migrants into darkness. She knew it when they shoved them on the boat in Hong Kong and ignored their cries for help when the hold became so chilly that frost glittered on their skins.

She knew it when the men came down to take the dead away, and when she asked what they would do with the bodies, the men said they'd be fish food and she'd join them if she didn't stop asking questions.

She knew, but she still told the girl, "It'll be all right."

By the time they got to Spain, twenty-one of the migrants had died. Men, women, and children.

In Spain, the traffickers herded the survivors onto this yacht, cramming them below. There wasn't much room, so Mei and the girl found themselves on deck with the captain.

Hunger gnawed at Mei's belly. She was so thirsty she could barely speak to comfort the girl.

They'd not been given water since they got on the yacht, and that had been at least twelve hours ago. Moans and cries wafted up from below, where most of the migrants were stowed. It was cold, and the rags they wore were the clothes they'd been dressed in when they left Shanghai three months previously. Their luggage had disappeared by the time they reached the Philippines. Stolen by pirates, said the traffickers. Mei didn't believe them.

Is this the price of freedom? she thought.

She wasn't sure it was worth it.

England had been a dream since she was a little girl. Her dad, a schoolteacher, had shown her a tattered old book called *Teach Yourself English*, and she'd learned the language.

The captain told the man in black, "Find me VHF channel 14 on the radio, so we can contact port control."

The man in black grumbled. He fiddled with the radio. Static burst from the console. He handed the mic to the captain, who spoke in English:

"Good morning, Ramsgate, this is the *Bloody Mary*, requesting permission to enter the harbour."

A crackle came over the radio, then a voice saying, "You have permission, *Bloody Mary*."

A shudder went through Mei. At last, after a murderous journey across the world, they were in England.

She said to the man in black, "Where do we go? You said there'd be work. You said you'd give us contacts."

The man said, "I have told you to shut up."

"But this was what we paid for also. We paid for contacts, for work. You said – your friends said, they – "

The man slashed with the machete.

The captain said, "Not here, not now."

The yacht bobbed. Mei wondered how the refugees below deck were coping. The journey had been difficult. They had been sick. There had been deaths. This was no way to be treated after they'd paid so much money for freedom.

Mei peered towards the harbour. Light beamed from the port control tower, showing the entrance to Ramsgate, to England.

Her heart raced.

"We're here," she told the girl in her arms. "We're safe – England."

The girl cried. Mei realized she'd have to look after her in this new country. The child had no parents. Mei was her family.

The feeling of seasickness that had been with her all the way faded as the yacht drifted into the harbour. Mei saw masts reach into the sky. She gazed up. Dark clouds filled the night, hiding the moon and the stars.

It made her think of what her mother had said:

"England is a land of monsters, Mei. Our government says it is a dangerous place. They have a plague there, a plague spread by fanged demons."

But Mei didn't believe. She was trying to escape superstition. She'd heard about the monsters and tried to find out about them on the internet. But Beijing blocked or censored most websites. The only news you got was what they wanted you to get. And it was all bad news about England. That's why she didn't believe it.

The yacht bobbed into a berth and stilled.

Only the whining of the refugees below broke the silence.

The man in black tensed. The captain's gaze flitted around.

"Are – are they here?" said the captain.

"They said 3.00am," the man in black answered.

Mei furrowed her brow. Tension filled the deck. The men were anxious about something.

"What is happening, Mei?" the child asked in a whisper.

Mei stroked her hair. "Waiting for friends to come for us."

"We have no friends, Mei. We have nothing."

"Shut it," said the man in black. His eyes were wide, and Mei saw fear in them.

The captain said, "Get your boys down below to shut that lot up."

The man in black started to walk away, but the captain grabbed his arm, and the men froze, staring out.

"They're here," said the captain. "There's the truck."

"It hasn't flashed its – "

Headlights beamed from the harbour.

"Yes it has," said the captain. He crossed himself. "Mother Mary protect me."

"Shut up," said the man in black.

Mei trembled. "What is it? Why are you frightened?"

The man in black stared at her. "You're free. Go. Take your little friend. Go." He took a walkie-talkie from his belt and spoke into it in French. The yacht rocked. Cries came from below. The man in black hooked the walkie-talkie back on his belt. "Go," he told Mei, "go now – up along the walkways, to the gate at the far end. Someone will open them for you – go!"

Mei rose.

The captain, staring ahead, said, "Oh my Lord – the dead, the dead."

Mei grabbed the machete and slipped it inside her jacket.

CHAPTER 2.
FEEDING TIME.

A MINUTE after Travis had flashed his headlights, the Chinese immigrants started to pour out of the *Bloody Mary*. They raced along the jetty. The wooden landing stages shook under their feet.

Travis said, "Oh fuck, here they come."

He raced around to the back of the lorry. He checked that the piece of leathery material the employers had given him was tight around his wrist. He sweated and trembled. He fumbled with the keys, managing to unlock the trailer.

Inside, they hissed and clawed.

Travis nearly pissed himself. He always did. He knew he'd be okay, protected by the red rag around his wrist. But that didn't make him feel better.

"Open the door, you cunt," said a voice from inside. "We're fucking hungry."

Travis moaned. The voice felt like acid going through him. It was filled with hate, tainted with evil.

Travis's legs shook. "I'm doing it, I'm doing it."

He eased the door open, and the smell of death drifted out of the trailer. They didn't give him a chance. They clambered up the door as Travis lowered it to the ground.

He whelped. He let the door go and stumbled backwards. The door crashed to the ground. They poured out, a dozen of them. They hissed and bared their fangs.

Travis, on his backside, screamed.

"Open the gate, open the gate!" he said.

"All right, give me a chance," came the voice.

Travis looked. Les unlocked the gate leading to the jetties. The Chinese immigrants flooded towards him.

"Hurry, Les," said Travis as the vampires ran past him.

Les opened the gate just in time. The vampires piled through, shoving him out of the way, hissing at him. One of the creatures fancied a bite and went for him. But when it saw the red rag pinned to Les's boiler suit, it baulked and followed the others onto the jetties.

The vampires headed straight for the immigrants.

They're having a Chinese, thought Travis, and he laughed nervously.

"Let's get out of here, Les – before the feeding starts."

As he hopped back into the cab, Travis heard screaming.

It made him sick. He shut his eyes, blanking it out. This was a job. He got paid to do it. What happened to those people wasn't his business.

As he started the truck, a growl came from the distance.

Engines, he thought. He ignored the sound and drove away, trying not to think about the refugees getting killed by the vampires.

CHAPTER 3.
YOUR ONLY HOPE.

MEI clutched the girl tightly.

The others raced along the jetty. It wobbled, and a few people fell into the water. Everyone was screaming. The spotlight from the port control tower swept over them. A siren blared in the distance.

A group of men and women raced towards Mei and the others along the jetties. These people had pale faces and angry expressions.

And as they came closer, Mei saw their teeth.

She screamed.

The fanged demons.

Shrieks filled the air. The refugees panicked. The girl tore herself from Mei's arms, and Mei said, "No, come back," but the girl ran down another jetty, following a group who were clambering across a berthed yacht in an effort to escape.

Four fanged demons broke off from the approaching pack. They went after the girl and her group.

Mei screamed. She brandished the machete. Refugees poured past her. Some leaped into the water. Others tried to run back towards the *Bloody Mary*. But the yacht sailed away, leaving the harbour.

"No, please," said Mei, unable to move.

The fanged demons leaped and sailed through the air. They fell on the fleeing immigrants. One creature swooped on the girl. Demon and child dropped off the jetty and into the water.

Mei ran towards them. Ahead of her, the demons killed the refugees. They tore out their throats and when blood spurted out of the wounds, they drank it. They held some people down and bit into their necks.

In the water, the demon held the girl and sank its fangs into her white neck. The creature was female. Its long, dark hair hung wet over its shoulders. A red glint sparkled in its dark eyes.

The child shrieked. Mei reached for the youngster.

The feeding demon snarled at Mei and pulled the girl under the water.

Mei went on her belly and hacked at the water with the machete. She screamed for the girl.

The noises of dread were all around. Horror and pain and death everywhere. The demons laughed as they attacked the Chinese. They killed them like predators killed prey.

The girl bobbed to the surface of the water, dead.

Mei said, "No, please, no," and she stretched out her arm.

The demon reared up out of the water, springing back onto the jetty. It landed behind Mei. She rolled on her back and slashed the air with the machete.

The demon dripped water on the walkway. It laughed at Mei and showed its bloody fangs.

Mei gazed at the creature. Once it had been a beautiful woman, for sure. The striking face remained. But it showed hate and cruelty now.

"I like Chinese," said the demon. "And the girl there was a good little starter. But I'm still hungry, sweet one. You can be my main meal."

The female demon came for Mei.

As it closed on Mei, the sky behind the female demon lit up, and a roar filled the air.

The demon wheeled. "No," it said, "no, not them."

The motorbike landed on the jetty. The wooden stage jerked. Another bike sailed over the fence that surrounded the berths. The bikes roared along the walkway.

The riders wore red leather.

They stopped their machines and vaulted off them and barrelled into the demons without fear.

One of the riders brandished short swords made of bone. They looked like elephant tusks to Mei.

The other rider looked like a woman from her movements, her body lithe and long. A quiver of wooden stakes was strapped to her back. She whipped out a stake and slashed at a demon.

The first rider came at the fanged female threatening Mei. The creature bristled, hissing. It seemed fearful, shrugging its shoulders and making itself small, like an animal cornered.

"Hello, Nadia," said the rider.

"Don't kill me," said the demon.

"You're already dead," the rider said.

He stabbed the demon in the chest with one of the tusk-swords. The demon screeched. The air seemed to fill with fire. Mei smelled burning. The demon cried out, clawing at the weapon buried in its chest.

The rider drove the sword deeper into the creature's breast. Sparks flew off its body. Fire raced up its arms and its neck, into its hair. The scalp burned. Flames burst from its body, and then it disintegrated into a cloud of ashes that flapped away on the wind.

The rider leaned forward and whipped off his helmet.

Mei stared into the steel-grey eyes of a man who looked to her like a god. Scars peppered his face, but they took nothing away from his beauty. His crow-black hair fell to his shoulders. He wore a red handkerchief over his face in the style of a cowboy.

Nothing else mattered to Mei now except for this man. She couldn't take her eyes off him. The noise of carnage surrounding her faded away.

He removed the handkerchief from his mouth and offered Mei his hand, and with an iron will in his steel-grey eyes said, "My name is Jake Lawton. I am your only hope."

CHAPTER 4.
THE HOUSE.

JACQUELINE Burrows fingered the red brooch pinned to her jacket and rose. A murmur went through the House. She waited for quiet and then said, "It is a tragedy that another group of immigrants were murdered in the early hours of this morning in their desperate, but illegal, attempt to enter the UK... "

The MPs roared. Shouts of, "Shame, shame," mingled with, "She wears the trousers," and, "Firestarter, she's a firestarter," as members on both sides of the House of Commons hollered.

Burrows raised her hand to quieten them.

"Order... order," said the Speaker of the House, who was responsible for keeping control of this rabble.

They hushed.

Burrows, at the dispatch box, glanced at Graeme Strand, the Prime Minister. He sat to her left. He scowled, his arms folded.

Burrows thought, *You've been told not to fold your arms, Graeme, because it's a defensive posture.*

She continued to speak:

"People do feel strongly about the issue of immigration, but this kind of vigilante violence is unacceptable."

"Hear, hear," came the chorus.

"The vast majority of immigrants to this country – both legal and illegal – are honest, good people – "

"Rubbish... Criminals... What about the gypsies?" said a tangle of voices from the Conservative side of the House. Other voices from both sides of the chamber responded to the calls with yells of, "Shame... sit down, sit down... "

Burrows went on:

"They are only seeking a better life for themselves and their families, but they come here and find death."

The MPs muttered.

Burrows fixed on the Opposition benches, scanning their faces.

She glimpsed the PM again. He looked like a sulking child. *Cheer your face up, Graeme*, she thought, and then: *Oh, but you can't. Your days are numbered, and I'm flavour of the month.*

The Speaker called on a Tory MP to ask a question.

The man rose, and his jowls followed a while after him. He huffed, and Burrows knew the old man had spent a little too much time at the Commons bar, supping red wine.

The MP cleared his throat and said, "Is the Home Secretary not at odds with the Prime Minister over immigration control?"

"Here, here," came the calls from the Opposition benches.

The MP continued: "Would the Home Secretary like to comment on the e-mail leaked to the press this morning claiming that she supports tougher controls on immigration, while the Prime Minister supports the status quo, which is to allow any Tom, Dick, and Hare Krishna in?"

Roars erupted in the house. "Shame, shame," called the MPs.

The Opposition leader Jayne Monson grimaced. Members of her front bench team groaned. MPs like the jowly fellow were the black sheep of the Tory Party these days. Inappropriate noises regarding race and sexuality had been drowned out by the roar of modernization. But the sexists, the racists, and the homophobes were still lurking in the organization's dark corners.

"Apologize, you racist," said a left-wing Labour MP

19

positioned further down the bench from Burrows.

"Order, order," said the Speaker.

Another Labour member said, "Our NHS would crumble were it not for nurses and doctors from all over the world. And who would clean the Honourable Member's toilet if we didn't allow him his Thai maid?"

The House erupted in laughter. The jowly Tory fell into his seat.

The Speaker said, "Order, order... " and the House quietened. He continued: "I am asking the Honourable Member to apologize for his comments, as they might be perceived as racist."

The jowly MP stood again and said, "I apologize to Hare Krishnas, of whom there are many in my constituency."

The Speaker indicated to Burrows that she should continue, so she stood up again.

"I would not wish to comment on leaks," she said, sitting down straight away. She glanced across at Strand. He gave her a look, quick and sharp, his lip curling a little.

The Firestarter strikes again, she thought.

The jowly Tory, an MP called Shackleton, had been a plant. His question was supposed to make the Government, of whom Burrows was a senior member, feel uncomfortable. Of course, it was she who'd leaked the e-mail the previous night. It further undermined Strand. It made him look weak in the face of continuing attacks on immigrants.

Another Tory rose and said, "When will the Right Honourable Lady be moving?"

The Tories stood and waved their papers, pointing at the PM.

Burrows knew what they meant: when would she be moving to No.10 Downing Street to replace Strand as Prime Minister?

Quickly to her feet, she said, "I like where I'm living."

But only for a few days more, she thought.

She glanced across at Strand and grinned at him. He nodded and unfolded his arms before rising to the dispatch box to howls and jeers from both sides of the House.

Calls of "Resign! Resign!" echoed through the chamber.

CHAPTER 5.
GET LAWTON.

BURROWS said, "What happened at Ramsgate?" She threw down her bag and slammed her file on the desk. She took the brooch off her jacket and held the trinket tightly in her hand. "I want to know," she demanded.

Superintendent Phil Birch flinched. He shut the door of Burrows's office at the House of Commons. He fingered the red ribbon attached to his clipboard. He swallowed, his throat dry.

He said, "Lawton again. And Aaliyah Sinclair."

Burrows sat and struck the desk with her fist. Rage coloured her face.

"Jacqueline – "

"Home Secretary," she said. "Address me as Home Secretary."

"Home Secretary," said Birch, "they destroyed every vampire, every single one."

"All right, but how many did we infect?"

Birch swallowed again. "We... we don't know."

She glowered at him for a moment before swivelling her head to stare out of the window. Birch followed her gaze. A grey sky looked back. Rain spattered the window.

Birch looked at Burrows again. He took a seat opposite her and laid his clipboard on the desk.

Firestarter, he thought. Her nickname. The flame-red hair. The blazing temper.

And then she said, "The fire," which made him flinch, thinking for a second she'd read his mind.

But she hadn't. She was asking about the previous night. That bastard Lawton and his bitch, Sinclair, killing the vampires.

He said, "Yes, the fire. They burned the bodies. They burned the dead. Ramsgate harbour lit up like on bonfire night, apparently."

Burrows grimaced. "Evil."

"Lawton and Sinclair do this all the time. They kill the vampires and then destroy anyone the vampires killed. It stops the dead rising. They're cutting vampire numbers, Jacq– Home Secretary."

She sighed. "I don't feel very well protected by you, Superintendent Birch – "

"What –?"

She struck the table again. "I got you this role in SO1 so you could be at the heart of the action, Philip. Got you transferred to Protection Command. Had them assign you to me. I had to pull a lot of levers, push a lot of buttons, threaten to reveal many secrets, you know."

"I know, thank – "

"And this is how you repay me?"

"Jacq– Home Secretary, I don't understand?"

"You're not protecting me, are you."

"I think I am. Nothing's happened to you."

"But the whole project is in danger, Philip."

"The whole – "

"Why are Lawton and Sinclair out there, alive?"

"Give it time, Home Secretary. We are doing everything. We plant stories in the press. He's a villain to them. His reputation is in tatters. He's seen as some crazy vigilante who attacks immigrants. Kills them and burns them."

"I regret to inform you, Philip, that people mostly do not believe what they read in the newspapers. Most people these days would rather believe what they read on the internet. And Lawton is a folk hero to all those geeks who should be out looking for a job – not spending their days glued to a computer screen, trawling unsavoury websites."

She leaned back in her chair.

"I want him dead before I'm Prime Minister," she said. "And considering Graeme Strand's reputation, that could be a job I acquire sooner than we'd imagined."

"Lawton's like a ghost. The vampires call him Lord of Hell. Because of the fire. Because he's the only one they fear. They're more scared of him than they are of their own gods."

"He did kill one of their gods, Philip."

Birch nodded. It had been three years ago, at the Religion nightclub in Soho. The night was meant to have been a celebration of a new Britain – a vampire nation.

But Lawton had destroyed the newly resurrected undead prince, Lord Kea.

Birch rubbed his nose. Lawton had broken it that evening. It still caused him headaches.

Burrows said, "I don't understand how it can be so difficult. Lawton is a disgraced solider with a big stick and a bitch of a girlfriend, Philip. You're a high-ranking police officer with the powers-that-be *and* the powers of hell at your fingertips. Why can't you find him? Why can't he be killed?"

Birch leaned on the desk and said, "Jacqueline, there is an assassin on his trail. He will be dead soon. Just give it time."

CHAPTER 6.
HE'S THE MAN.

THE Chinese girl asked, "Who is he?" She stared at Lawton. He'd fixed his body in a neck bridge. He'd lain on his back before lifting himself, using his head and his legs. His body arched. His arms were folded across his chest. He bent his neck back so his nose touched the mat. He'd been in that position for five minutes, still and quiet.

Aaliyah said, "He's the only man who could ever get me to make tea." She poured boiling water into the teapot. "You want tea, Mei?"

The Chinese girl nodded. She looked around, her nose crinkled.

Aaliyah noticed and said, "Sorry about the smell. And the damp. And the peeling wallpaper. And the rotting furniture. You just can't get the staff these days."

"You live here?"

"Not all the time. We come and go. We go more than we come. It's one of many safe houses we have."

"You need safe places?"

"You saw that we need safe places."

"Those demons, they chase you?"

"No, we chase them."

Aaliyah leaned against the sink. She glanced at Lawton. He bridged on a mat in front of what had been the fireplace. It was now just a hole in the wall.

The council had boarded up the flat months ago after evicting the tenants. Lawton learned about it from one of their supporters, the loners who spent most of their lives surfing the Web. Those people were outsiders. They helped Lawton and Aaliyah when they could, providing information about safe houses and vampire outbreaks, even warning them if the authorities were on their trail.

"This is a good place," Aaliyah said. "There's a workshop downstairs. Equipment still works. We're lucky our contacts found it for us. We need all the help we can get, since most people are against us."

The Chinese girl said, "You burn the bodies."

"They were infected."

"With what?"

"A sickness."

"The fanged demons kill them, then you burn them all. They say about this at home, but I didn't believe."

Aaliyah said, "Why come here?"

"Freedom."

"No freedom here, lady."

The girl said nothing.

Aaliyah stirred the tea in the pot.

Mei said, "How you know the man?" and gestured towards Lawton, who was still holding the bridge.

Aaliyah touched the choker around her throat. "Three years ago, vampires came to Britain. They invaded. They infected. They tried to take over. Lots of people were involved. High ranking. Important people. It was a conspiracy. Do you understand?"

The girl nodded. Her English was good.

Aaliyah continued:

"They want to make England like ancient Babylon. A vampire nation. Ruled by vampire gods and their human allies. Everyone else is food and slaves."

Aaliyah found it difficult to believe the words coming from her mouth. Three years ago she wouldn't have said them. Not

25

until she and her boyfriend J.T. were attacked on the Tube by three vampires. They'd killed J.T. and taken her away. They caged her with other humans in catacombs beneath the nightclub, Religion.

"They were going to feed us to the vampire god to make it rise up," she said. "Jake saved me. He saved loads of people. There was a fire. The club burned down. We thought we wouldn't escape, but we did, and he killed the monster."

Aaliyah wondered if Mei believed any of this. She didn't care. She wanted to tell the story. She didn't get a lot of opportunities to talk about what had happened.

She and Lawton rarely met anyone for long enough. They were moving all the time. They lived from day to day. But at least she was with him, the best man she'd known. He made her heart burst. No one else had done this to her. Not J.T., not the ones before J.T. They were just bling. They were window dressing. She was into the flash cars and the gold back then.

But now she knew those things meant nothing. Now only survival mattered.

"It's a wild story," said the girl.

"Yes, wild."

"My mother, she say England has fanged demons. She heard stories. I say they were superstition. My mother, she was very superstitious."

"You could've seen all this on the internet."

"Our government didn't let us see all of internet. I wanted freedom. That's why I come here. That's why they all come. All the people with me. And now they are dead."

"You should've stayed in China. No vampires there."

The girl looked at Aaliyah, her eyes bright. "You and Mr Jake, you look after me?"

"Whoa! No. No way. We don't take in waifs and strays. We're not Barnado's. What we do is dangerous."

"I can fight."

"You can't fight."

"I can make food."

"We manage, catering-wise."

"Please, Miss Aaliyah."

26

"No, Mei. And don't call me Miss Aaliyah. I ain't your teacher. Aaliyah, that's all."

The girl cried.

"Oh, stop that. It'll get you nowhere. There's very little sentiment around here. I'm as hard as nails. You won't get past me with tears, honey."

Mei looked up. Her eyes were wet. "I am scared."

"I am scared, too. We're all scared. This is a scary place. This ain't Twilight, you know. No veggie vampires here. No human-loving vampires."

"Lawton scared?"

Aaliyah looked at him holding his bridge. He'd been in that position for nearly ten minutes.

"Yes, he's scared, too," she said.

CHAPTER 7.
A JOB FOR KWAN MEI.

MEI said, "I want stay with you."

Aaliyah said, "You can't."

Mei looked over at Lawton. He sharpened stakes on a lathe. Half an hour earlier, he'd risen from his bridge and said, "I'm going downstairs," and said nothing else. Aaliyah and Mei had followed him down into the cellar. A 60-watt bulb cast a dim glow over the basement. Dust coated wooden crates. The lathe hummed as Lawton sharpened the stakes on it.

He'd stopped for a few minutes to drink the tea Aaliyah had brought down, but he'd said nothing. He looked at the floor. The goggles resting on his forehead made him look like a pilot to Mei.

She felt awkward. They were all quiet. Lawton sipped his drink, sitting next to the lathe. Aaliyah studied a Macbook that stood open on a crate.

Lawton had then returned to his work.

Now, Mei pointed at him and said, "He and you, Aaliyah, you save my life. I help you. I serve you. I owe you."

"We don't need owing," said Aaliyah.

"I help you... please."

Aaliyah shook her head.

The smell of sawdust filled the cellar. The lathe hummed as Lawton ran the ash poles across the blade. He tossed another weapon into the pile. The stakes were two feet long. Wood shavings speckled him.

Mei said, "I kill vampires with you."

"You're not Buffy," said Aaliyah.

Mei knitted her brow.

Aaliyah said, "What I'm saying is, it's not like films or cartoons or Manga or whatever you got over there."

"Manga?"

Aaliyah grunted and shook her head. "It's not safe for you to stay with us; that's what I'm saying, right?"

"What is safe?" said Mei. "I travel across world in boats and trucks. Men put knives to my neck. Men throw the sick and dead into the sea and off mountains. Men take girls, like, like me, and… " She trailed off, memories flooding back and overwhelming her. She put her head in her hands, trying to block out her ordeal. She steadied her breathing. Her recollections faded. She wiped her eyes and looked at Aaliyah. "I came for hope," she said. "I get nothing."

Aaliyah looked over at Lawton and mouthed something that Mei couldn't understand, but he shrugged and went on with his work. Wood chips and sawdust sprayed from the lathe. The machine crooned. Stakes piled up.

Mei went on:

"This country is not good. Where do I go? The men I pay, they say, 'You be safe, you go here, you go there.' But where I go? I should be dead, burned, like the others. I should be dead."

Mei felt shattered. She wanted to lie down in a corner of this dark, dusty cellar and sleep – sleep and not wake up.

Aaliyah said, "I don't know what to say to you, Mei, but – "

"Tom Wilson."

The lathe stopped buzzing. Lawton lifted the goggles. He spat sawdust from his mouth.

He said the name again:

"Tom Wilson."

Aaliyah said, "Tom?"

"Tom needs a carer," said Lawton. "His granddaughter's ill. We're going up tomorrow. She can come with us."

Mei looked from Lawton to Aaliyah. "Where I go?"

He said, "Get a job. Be safe. A friend of ours. Brave man."

"I want to fight vampires."

"Tom Wilson fights vampires," said Lawton. "He's king of the vampire fighters. Here... " He picked up a stake and tossed it over to Mei. "You start learning today. There's a lot of killing to be done. We have many enemies."

CHAPTER 8.
MAKING MONSTERS.

AFDAL Haddad, his hundredth birthday only a few years away, laid his trilby on the table. A scrap of red material flapped from the band around the hat. The old man wheezed and placed a hand on his chest, sitting down at the kitchen table.

George Fuad put the glass of orange juice on the table in front of Haddad. George scratched his beard and considered the old man. "You look tired, Afdal," he said to him. "Too many late nights, eh?"

Haddad grumbled.

"You should slow down, old fella," said George. "Man of your age. Coming up to your big birthday. Telegram from the Queen and all that."

George couldn't believe that this frail figure had been running the organization for decades. The old man had been on his own since the 1920s, when British soldiers killed his brothers and stole treasures from the Haddad family.

Since then, Haddad had travelled the world, tracing his allies, those who carried the bloodline of the Babylonian king, Nebuchadnezzar. A sound broke George's concentration and he looked over his shoulder.

The cleaner fussed. She scoured the oven, really going for it
– some proper elbow grease for a change.

George glared at her. She was English, which is why he'd
hired her. You didn't find many English birds wanting menial
jobs in Spain. They usually came to retire or to hide from the
law. This one was in her forties and looked all right. Dark, curly
hair and a decent figure. She said her husband had dumped her,
and she needed work.

"Toddle off, love," he told her now.

"But, Mr Fuad, I haven't – "

"Yes you have, sweetheart."

She scurried out of the room. He watched her go, swivelling
his thick neck.

After she'd shut the door, George looked out of the window.
It was grey, not the kind of weather he and his brother had
hoped for when they bought this villa. He shrugged, not really
caring. *Even the Med got winter*, he thought.

He looked at Haddad. The old man sipped the orange juice.

"You okay, Afdal?"

Without looking at George, the old man said, "Nadia Radu."

George nodded. Nadia Radu. A hot, nasty bird George
would've loved to bed. She'd been Haddad's companion. She'd
been killed by Lord Kea at Religion. An accidental death when
her protective symbol, a scarlet choker, had been torn away.
Radu became a vampire. But early yesterday morning, she'd
been killed again while leading a planned raid on a batch of
food arriving in England.

Jake Lawton had killed her this time. George shook with
rage.

Lawton used to be a doorman at Religion, the Soho club
owned by George and his brother, Alfred.

Skarlet, a drug created by Haddad from the ashes of Kea,
had been distributed in the club. The drug was a killer. It was
a vampire drug. It sucked up your blood and withered your
organs. But twenty-four hours later, you'd wake up again – as
a vampire.

It was all going so well. Skarlet would make vampires, then
those vampires would make more vampires. London would
crawl with the undead. And the bloodsucking army would help

Haddad and his allies to resurrect Kea. They would bring live prey back to Religion. The human quarry would then be cut open over Kea's remains, and the blood would bring the ashes to life.

That was the plan.

Then Lawton had interfered.

He was meant to take the fall for distributing the drug that killed the first twenty-eight at Religion. And everything got off to a cracking start when he was arrested. It diverted attention away from what was really going on at the club.

But Lawton had spirit. They thought he was broken, since he'd been booted out of the Army in Iraq. But no. He had backbone and guts, and he spoiled everything.

And now Lawton was out there, slaughtering vampires.

"Nadia will live on," said Haddad now. "I have her blood. I took a sample when she was made undead."

"What've you got up your sleeve, Afdal?" said George. "Where's your brother?"

"Messing with his mistress again."

"I wanted to tell you both."

"Tell me. We're twins. We share a psychic link. And all that sort of bollocks."

"I am going to create a monster."

"Okay."

"I am going to forge Kakash, Kasdeja, and Nadia into one creature."

George furrowed his brow. "Kakash and Kasdeja are separate."

"No. They are two parts of a trinity, with Kea. They came out of the same body, thousands of years ago. They're one. And they can be one again."

"You can't shove Nadia in there."

"Yes I can. Nadia will live forever. She led our crusade, George. She can't be forgotten. She can't be lost to the wind. She's not just any vampire. She has a place with the high priests of our religion."

Randy old git, thought George.

Haddad said, "We'll feed it. The blood of migrants. Those we traffic. It will grow while it travels to England. And when

33

we reach London, it will be unleashed. Lawton will not stop us. No one will. Not this time. The city is ours."

The old man dribbled.

George said, "What about Skarlet? That's getting us nowhere. Lawton and his bastards are buggering that up as well."

"Don't worry, George. My mind works well, you know – for an old man. We'll turn London into a vampire Babylon yet. Lawton cannot fight what I am about to resurrect. Now, wheel me down to the sea, so I can enjoy some winter air."

CHAPTER 9.
OLD FRIENDS.

LAWTON said, "I can't do this anymore, Tom."

"You have to. You're a soldier. Who else is there?"

"What difference does it make?"

Tom Wilson shrugged. "Maybe none."

"I can't fight them forever."

"Do it till you die, then. That's all we can ask, lad."

Wilson shuffled in his armchair and grimaced. Lawton knew better than to ask him if he was okay. The old man would usually swat any concern away.

"When you were in Mesopotamia all those years back," said Lawton, "did you think of giving up?"

"Christ, yes – every day. Didn't you, when you were in Iraq? We all do that, Jake, lad." Wilson leaned forward and stroked the weapon lying on the coffee table. It was the Spear of Abraham. A two-horned spear made of what appeared to be elephants' tusks, joined together with a leather-bound handle. "When Jordan and me were trying to escape with this and the ashes, and we were surrounded by those heathens, I thought of giving up. Putting my head down and letting them hack me to pieces."

35

In 1920, Wilson had served with the British Army in Mesopotamia — modern-day Iraq. With his commanding officer, Jordan, he'd stolen three urns containing the ashes of the vampire gods, Kea, Kakash, and Kasdeja, and also the Spear of Abraham, the only weapon that could kill them.

Wilson said, "You've not come to bring this spear back to me, have you?"

Lawton said nothing.

The old man went on: "You can't just give in, Jake."

"Why not? The papers call me a murderer. They say I desecrate bodies. They call me racist and say I kill immigrants."

"What do you care about papers? They pissed on you in the past. You should be used to it."

"I'm not made of steel."

"No, they just say you are."

"I'm not."

"I know. It's hard to be hated. I can understand. But you've got to know that the people around you, they all depend on you, son. They revere you, respect you. Without you, they'd be nothing. And you know, there are thousands of people out there who believe in you. They know there are vampires in Britain, and they know Jake Lawton's the only man with the guts to kill them. The Government can hide the truth if they want, put a coat on it and call it something else, but the people know, Jake. The people know."

"I'm exhausted. I don't have a life anymore, and I never will."

"I'm a hundred and eleven, Jake. I've had a life, I tell you. And it's not much cop. I wish I could fight with you. But I can't. I'll die here in my chair, that's the sad truth. You still doing the bare-knuckle stuff for cash?"

Lawton nodded.

"When's your next fight?"

Aaliyah entered from the kitchen. She said, "The fool's fighting tonight."

Kwan Mei followed Aaliyah into the living room. The Chinese girl carried a tray laden with biscuits and mugs. She laid it down on the coffee table.

"Shall I be Mother?" said Wilson. "Or what about you, love?" he asked Mei.

She smiled and bowed and scuttled over, and began to serve up the tea.

"You'll be all right with her?" asked Aaliyah.

"She knows where everything is, now, does she?" said Wilson.

"I've given her the guided tour," Aaliyah said.

"She'll be fine – won't you, miss."

Mei said, "I be fine – thank you."

Aaliyah asked Lawton if he was all right.

"I'm hunky dory, darling," he said.

"Needed a pep talk, that's all," said Wilson.

Lawton said, "I suppose I won't face anything more bastard than what I faced in Religion, that night. What can be worse than a seven-foot, red vampire?"

CHAPTER 10.
CONCEPTION.

Los Monteros, Marbella, Spain – 1.26pm, February 11, 2011

THE container was twelve feet long by six feet wide and had a depth of five feet. It lay in the basement of the Fuads' villa and had done for months. It was made of clay and decorated with images of red-fleshed monsters slaughtering humans. Scaffolding surrounded the casket, and from the rafters above hung manacles and leather straps.

"It's beautiful," said Haddad. He slid off the stairlift and into his wheelchair. He wheeled himself over to the container and ran his hand across the surface. "You'd think it's old."

"I'd make a good forger, don't you think?" said Alfred Fuad. "Here you go." Alfred laid a briefcase on a table next to the container and flipped it open. Two vases sat in the foam inlay. Unlike the container, the vases actually were old. Babylonian. And priceless. Like the container, they showed images of humans battling monsters.

Haddad looked at Alfred. Unlike his brother, he was clean-shaven and had long hair tied into a ponytail. But they were similar in many ways. They were identical twins who were identically cruel. They were both squat and powerful. And they were both ambitious and successful.

"Thank you," said Haddad.

The twins were over sixty years of age, but Haddad regarded them as young. He'd known the family before the boys had been born. The Fuads took him in when he fled Mesopotamia in 1920, after the British soldiers had killed his family and stolen the artefacts.

At least now he had the vases. He removed one from the briefcase.

"Roll yourself on this platform," said Alfred.

Haddad obeyed. Alfred pressed a button on a unit set in the wall. A churning noise started up. The platform lifted. Haddad smiled. Alfred nodded at him. The platform raised Haddad till he was level with the lip of the container.

"It will do," said Haddad.

Alfred pressed another button, and the platform stopped.

Haddad pulled the stopper out of the vase and looked into the vessel.

The ashes of the vampire god, Kakash. The other vase in the briefcase contained the remains of Kakash's brother prince, Kasdeja.

Haddad poured the ashes into the container. They rained into the dark pit.

"The other vase," said Haddad.

Alfred handed him the second jar.

Haddad opened it and poured out the dust. He stared into the abyss. He thought about the ashes mingling in there.

"Together for the first time since they were created nearly five thousand years ago," he said. And then he felt sad, thinking of Kea, the third brother. A spark of anger ignited in Haddad's chest.

Jake Lawton, he thought.

God-killer. Murderer. Lord of Hell.

Haddad reached into his pocket and took out a glass vial.

"What's that?" said Alfred.

Haddad stared at the blood in the tube. "My Nadia."

"When you mix that up, what's going to come out of this container?" said Alfred.

Haddad looked down at his friend. "Are you worried?"

"No, just wondering."

"It will do you no harm. You wear its skin."

Alfred fidgeted with the length of scarlet material ponytailing his hair. He said, "I just want things to be right, that's all."

"They will be right."

"It's that bastard Lawton."

"That bastard Lawton has met his match, Alfred, I promise you." Haddad uncorked the vial and poured the blood into the casket. "There," he said. "Done. Now, shall we feed our new creation?"

"Sure," said Alfred.

He went to a cupboard set in the wall of the basement and opened the door.

The girl cried out and covered her face. She cowered in the cupboard, shaking.

Haddad turned away. He didn't want to enjoy these rituals. They were necessary. It wasn't murder: it was sacrifice. A life given for something greater.

"Come on, you little tart," said Alfred. He grabbed the girl by the hair and yanked her out of the cupboard.

She screamed.

It didn't matter. They were underground, and the basement was soundproofed. It had been designed to conceal suffering.

"Is she the immigrant girl?" said Haddad.

"That's right – a little peach."

"I read it in the paper. Bring me down, Alfred. And then chain her over the casket."

Alfred gripped the girl. She struggled and cried, but he was strong. She was fifteen, according to the newspaper stories reporting her disappearance. The authorities would show half-hearted concern for a while. But the child came from a refugee holding centre a few miles away. No one would care about her for too long.

"Shall I kill her now?" asked Alfred.

"No," said Haddad, rolling his chair off the platform, "bleed her slowly – it's fresher."

"She's a bloody livewire, ain't you, doll."

"Hit her, then."

CHAPTER 11.
FIGHTER.

LAWTON parried the right hook with his forearm and skipped to the left, and his opponent wheeled after him.

Blood splashed from the cut above the man's eye, a wound caused by Lawton's elbow.

The crowd bayed. They rose and stomped on the wooden benches. The barn shook. Sawdust lifted off the ground to the rhythm of the spectators' feet.

Lawton's opponent growled. He was named Stoke John. Sweat and blood smeared his face. Scars guttered his scalp, the marks of previous battles.

Stoke John shifted forward, kicking up sawdust. He clenched his fists. They were bandaged to protect his knuckles. Lawton's blood stained the wrapping, and seeing it on Stoke John's hands made him lick his cut lip.

He tasted his own blood. His teeth hurt. But he had stamina while his opponent wheezed.

Stoke John stood six-four and weighed nearly twenty stone. He had tree-trunk arms and cannon-ball shoulders. His belly heaved, hanging over his belt.

Lawton wiped his brow and readied himself. Perspiration lathered his body. His heart raced, but his breathing was steady.

The crowd blared.

Stoke John advanced with south-paw stance – leading with his left. He stepped heavily on his left foot, coughing up sawdust.

Lawton feigned a left jab. Stoke John's right elbow rose to fend off the blow. His right foot lifted inches off the floor.

Perfect for Lawton. He kicked his opponent in his left knee – the knee that was momentarily bearing all the man's 280lbs.

And it was too much for the joint.

Stoke John's face screwed up.

His knee buckled.

He toppled over.

The crowd screeched.

Lawton swung a right that whipped past his opponent's chin as he fell. If he'd connected, the fight would've been over.

The crowd whooped. They cursed Lawton and the bookie.

Lawton threw a left hook and clipped the staggering fighter's temple.

Stoke John's eyes rolled back in his head. He keeled over. He hit the ground.

Lawton skipped back as the referee came forward, swinging his arms. The ref sweated, too – as if he'd been fighting. But he'd been doing nothing. Just loitering near the fence, waiting for a knockdown.

There were few rules here for him to keep. You couldn't kick or punch a man when he was down, that was all. So all the ref had to control were the knockdowns.

"Second knockdown," he said, holding up two fingers.

The crowd bellowed.

"Are you getting up?" the ref asked Stoke John, who was now on all fours, shaking his head. "Are you getting up?"

The crowd hooted. They booed. They cursed. They urged Stoke John to get up.

The man got into a crouch and looked at Lawton, whose knuckles throbbed.

He hoped they weren't broken.

He looked at the crowd. He wondered where Aaliyah would be.

"Never worry about me while you're in the ring, David Haye," she'd tell him.

But he always worried. Places like this were hostile, dangerous. They could be in a barn like this one, or an old warehouse on a derelict industrial estate. They could be in the basement of a dodgy pub, or in a forest. But wherever they were, it tended to be unfriendly.

That night, it was an abandoned farm in Lincolnshire. The crowd looked wild, with their blazing eyes and their grimy faces. Sweat and dirt caked them. They drank extra-strong lager and smoked weed.

There were kids and women there, too. The youngsters were scrawny and mean. The women were full-bodied and had "don't-mess-with-me" eyes.

Aaliyah had driven here from Manchester and sat in the car with him while he strapped his knuckles. She didn't like him fighting. She was worried he'd get hurt and wouldn't be able to kill vampires with her. But it was their only source of income. They couldn't go on the dole or get a job, because the authorities would trace them. And he only had to fight once every six to eight weeks. So she just had to deal with it.

When they'd got out of the car, Durkham, with his one eye and his one tooth, had led them into the barn. Durkham promoted these bare-knuckle brawls in the north of England. He was a former boxing manager, banned for letting his fighters compete in illegal tournaments.

The barn had been converted into a fighting arena. Five tiers of benches hemmed a ring that was carpeted in sawdust. The place was packed. It reeked of sweat, booze, tobacco, and dope.

Bones had been broken here. Blood had been spilled. Men had probably died here, too, their bodies buried in the fields or dumped into the lake a few miles away.

Stoke John got to his feet.

Lawton's gaze wandered, looking for Aaliyah. His concentration drifted. He realized he'd made a mistake.

The yell startled him.

The sawdust hit him in the face, blinding him.

He staggered, flapping his arms.

Something heavy and hard thumped him in the belly. The

blow knocked the air out of him. He was flung backwards. He bicycled his legs to keep himself upright.

You didn't want to hit the floor when you were tangled up. The ref wouldn't protect you. If you were grappling with your opponent and you both fell, the fight continued. And if Lawton found himself under this heavyweight, he'd be pummelled.

His eyes burned. Tears streamed down his cheeks. He spat sawdust from his mouth.

He continuously elbowed Stoke John in the spine, right between the shoulder blades. But the big man pumped his legs, forcing Lawton backwards.

The pair slammed into the fencing. Lawton's head snapped back and cracked against the wood. Stars erupted before his eyes. Stoke John rammed his shoulder into Lawton's guts. It was agony, and Jake almost passed out.

Stoke John reared back, ready to slam into Lawton's guts again, but Jake drove up his knee.

Crack!

Stoke John jerked and reeled back, shaking his head. His face blanched and blood poured from his nose.

Lawton gritted his teeth. Pins and needles raced up his flanks. The pain was like fire.

He hobbled after Stoke John and smashed a right hand into the man's jaw – right on the sweet spot.

The jawbone snapped, the crack echoing.

The impact caused Stoke John's brain to switch off for a second, and the lines of communication to the body were cut off.

Stoke John's legs gave way. He toppled. Lawton just missed with a haymaker left. But it didn't matter. His opponent was unconscious before he hit the deck.

From punch to ground, it took less than a second.

The ref crouched over Stoke John.

Lawton's eyes burned. He wiped them. The sweat from his arms singed his eyeballs and made it worse. He wept. His vision blurred.

The crowd howled. They stamped their feet on the benches. The whole place shook.

The referee said to Stoke John, "Are you getting up?"

But he wasn't.

The referee waved his arms over his head, indicating the fight was over.

Stoke John's seconds strolled into the ring, scowling.

They stood over their fighter. One of them nudged Stoke John with his foot and told him, "Get up, you fucker," but the unconscious man didn't move.

One of the seconds glowered at Lawton.

The ref came over and raised Jake's arm.

Lawton looked for Durkham. He wanted his money and wanted to get out of here. You had to, after the fight was over. Most of the spectators tended to be aligned with your opponent. And if, like Lawton, you won your fights, you weren't the most popular man in the house. Not because you'd knocked out their man, but because you'd cost them a lot of money.

Where the hell was Aaliyah?

He heard, "You fucker," and from the corner of his eye saw the glowering second hare towards him.

He wheeled away from the referee and swung a boot.

CHAPTER 12.
DANCING WITH DURKHAM.

DURKHAM said, "I gotta say, Mr Lawton, Stoke John's brother was out of order, and you were within your rights, there, to kick him in the head."

They were sat in the back of Durkham's motor home. A striplight hummed on the ceiling. Lawton drank from a two-litre bottle of water. His body ached.

Aaliyah unwrapped his fists. Christ, they hurt. He flexed the fingers of his right hand and grimaced.

She caught his eye. Irritation flared on her face. Broken bones, injuries of any kind, meant Lawton was a liability.

But he had to fight. And fight in places like this.

"I'd sell my body if anybody'd buy it," he'd said after a bout in the cellar of a Nottingham pub a few months previously. He'd won, but suffered a broken rib.

"I'll give you a quid," she'd said, licking him from neck to navel.

She'd offered to do the same, sell herself.

He'd said he couldn't allow a man who touched her to live.

She was angry and had sat up in bed saying, "You don't own me; don't think you do. Men have thought that before, and they weren't men to me."

He'd apologized and said, "You can kill them yourself, then."

And she'd lain back in his arms.

"I have to fight," he'd said. "Sometimes, you have to fight."
Sometimes, you have to fight.

The words triggered a memory.

Sassie Rae stepped forward into his mind's eye. She was always there, idling. But occasionally she'd come centre stage, and he'd ache.

He recalled telling Sassie three years previously that *sometimes, you have to fight.*

She'd complained about the conflict in Iraq, where he'd been fighting, and declared her disgust at war in general.

Sassie couldn't see that she was fighting a war herself at the time – a war against vampires.

And where had it got her?

Dead.

Or undead.

In the back of the Transit now, Durkham said, "Stoke John's brother will get a hiding for what he did. There are rules."

"Are there, fuck," said Lawton.

"All right, maybe not. But we try to keep it clean in there – 'least before and after a bout."

Shouts came from inside the barn. Aaliyah looked at Lawton. Her eyes said: *Let's get the fuck out of here.*

"Five grand, Durkham," said Lawton.

"Well... now... let me just say... I'm not sure... "

Lawton glared at Durkham in the dimly-lit van.

The promoter flinched. "All right, Mr Lawton, all right. How's about two-five?"

Lawton pulsed with rage.

The Remington Model 870 shotgun appeared on his left, pointing at the promoter.

Lawton said, "Aaliyah never misses, Durkham. Especially not from this range. Five hundred to fight Stoke John, that was the deal. He was undefeated, so it was five grand if I beat him. I fought him. I beat him. You pay."

"I hate to say this, Mr Durkham," said Aaliyah, "but it really is our money or your fucking life."

Durkham said, "Miss Sinclair, guns and girls, they just don't – "

"Don't push your luck, Durkham," said Lawton. "One of these days, we just won't bother with this little dance. She'll just pull the trigger, and we'll take every penny you've got stashed in this bank-on-wheels of yours. Don't try to deny it, mate – I know these panels hide a fortune in used notes."

The shouts increased. Another fight. The rage growing.

"The dogs are getting angry," said Durkham. "You keep turning up, beating their favourites."

"They have to put up someone better, then – pay up."

Aaliyah pressed the Remington into Durkham's cheek.

He reached into his pocket and brought out a wad of notes. Fifties. He licked his thumb. "I count better when I don't have a gun in my face, Miss Sinclair."

She withdrew the gun.

"Thank you," he said, and began to count: "One, two, three… "

He counted ten fifties, ten times.

It took a few minutes.

Lawton kept calm.

The anger mounted in the barn. Another favourite decked. A riot would kick off before the end of the night.

Durkham counted the last fifty. Lawton snatched the money. He kicked open the motor home's door. "We'll dance again soon, Durkham."

He hopped out and grimaced when he hit the ground. His vision blurred momentarily, and when it cleared again he saw them.

"Fuck," he said, and Aaliyah standing next to him said, "Shit."

Four men blocked the way to their vehicle. The men had two pitbulls on leashes. The dogs were up on their back legs, snarling.

Aaliyah and Lawton strode over.

She held the Remington up, barrel pointing skywards. They stopped in front of the men and Aaliyah rested the gun on her hip.

"You must be Stoke Danny," said Lawton to the bloke who looked like the ringleader. A scar ran across the fellow's throat. He was six-two, eighteen stone.

"You decked two of my brothers in there," said Stoke Danny.

"You come at me, you'll find bad luck comes in threes," said Lawton.

"I want some payback."

The dogs slavered and growled. They reared up on their hind legs.

Stoke Danny said, "I'll let the dogs go, how's that?"

"Do that," said Aaliyah, "and I won't shoot the mutts, I'll shoot you bitches – blow you away before you can say 'sit'."

Stoke Danny indicated to his mate not to unleash the pit bulls.

"You want to let us pass, pussycat?" said Aaliyah.

Stoke Danny said, "Should keep your bitch on a leash, Lawton."

It took one step for her to reach him and one swipe of the shotgun to knock him out.

"Anyone else want some?" she asked the other men.

CHAPTER 13.
ENGLAND MUST FALL.

THE men sat in the dark library. Only the moon gave them light. A bottle of red wine stood empty on the table. The men clinked their glasses.

"To your father," said Haddad, "who took me in when I was a child. Six years old, when I came to England as a refugee after the soldiers had killed my brothers. And to you, my brothers, for taking me in once more, now, in my last days."

George Fuad said, "Our granddad came to London from Syria in 1900 to escape the Ottomans. Our father was born in London, and he married our mum there. My granddad brought with him the knowledge of who our family was. He passed that on to his son, who passed it on to us."

Alfred Fuad took over:

"We're grateful to you, Afdal, for choosing us."

"I didn't choose; I was six," said Haddad.

"You chose," said Alfred. "You could've chosen many, but you came to us. You knew what you were doing. My dad said so. You chose us. And we thank you for that. It's given us an opportunity to do something worthwhile. To do something remarkable. It's given us the opportunity to forge a nation, a new country."

The three men drank.

Haddad noticed George watching him with narrowed eyes, but he didn't say anything. Fuad's brain was obviously churning something up.

Eventually, George said, "Why England, Afdal?"

"Why England?" said Haddad.

"There's just a lot of crap going on there. That Lawton bastard popping up everywhere. We just thought, there has to be somewhere better. Here, perhaps. Spain."

Haddad said nothing. He wondered how long he had to live.

He drank again. And then he said, "It's fixed that England will be the place for New Babylon. It is apt. The British, the bastard colonizers, killed my family. They stole the ashes of our gods, and they stole the Spear of Abraham. And it was a British colonist returning from modern-day Mesopotamia who destroyed everything the last time."

He didn't say Jake Lawton's name. It was like poison in his mouth. He continued:

"It must be England. She must be the seat of power. She must be."

"That's good," said George, "but we were thinking, why not —"

Haddad held up his hand. "No more. It's settled. This is how it was going to be, from that day over ninety years ago when they killed my brothers. The sword has fallen. England dies. Its throne shall be a throne of blood."

They fell silent.

After a few minutes Haddad asked, "Is the truck ready?"

"Ready to roll," said Alfred.

"The goods," said George, "will be transferred to England in the lorry."

Haddad said, "There will be food?"

Alfred said, "We've got another batch coming over from Hong Kong. There won't be any left alive by the time we reach Dover. We've got pit stops on the way, too. Picking up some extras, you know."

Haddad nodded.

A noise outside the library door drew his attention.

The door opened and the lights came on. They blinded Haddad.

George said, "What the hell are you doing?"

Haddad's vision adjusted. The cleaning woman stood in the doorway. He narrowed his eyes and looked at her.

She said, "I... I'm sorry, Mr Fuad, I just – "

"Get out," said George, "and come back when we're done."

She left the room and shut the door.

Haddad said, "Do you think she heard any of that?"

"Shouldn't think so," said George. "She's as thick as bricks."

"It's best that you get rid of her," said Haddad.

"We can't give her the boot now, there – "

Haddad interrupted George saying, "No, I mean she has to be got rid of."

The Fuads looked at each other.

George shrugged as if to say, whatever you want.

"Throw her in with the refugees," said Haddad. "They're all as worthless as each other."

CHAPTER 14.
CATCHING UP.

LAWTON, wishing he could be lying in a hot bath, said, "What do we know about the truck?"

Aaliyah drove. They were going back to London. She said, "One of our friendly geeks is searching using the partial number plate I e-mailed him. He'll text me the minute he knows. Aren't they clever?"

"You shouldn't mock them. They're worth their weight."

"I don't mock them. I'm just in a foul mood, that's all."

"Why are you in a mood?"

"Look at the state of you."

"What's the matter with me?"

"Jake, you're a fucking jigsaw. When we get back, I'm going to have to put you back together, but I'm not sure I've got all the pieces."

"I'm all here. Just a bit frayed at the seams, that's all."

"You've got to stop fighting."

"How else are we going to make money?"

"I don't know; I'd rather rob banks."

"Too risky."

"And being in the middle of nowhere surrounded by three hundred people who want your blood isn't risky? We nearly didn't get out of there tonight."

"We always nearly don't get out."

Aaliyah said nothing. She stared ahead. They shared the A1 with very few cars. The clock on the dashboard said 3.42am. It would take another two hours before they were home.

"Where shall we stay tonight, darling?" said Lawton.

"Don't take the piss."

"I'm not – I'm serious. Which one of our holiday homes is more practical? Have we got anything outside London?"

"Why?"

"Because I'm dying, babe."

"You're what?"

"I hurt, that's all. Need a bath."

"You should stop fighting."

"That's what I told Tom."

"What?"

"Told him I didn't know if I could do this anymore."

"Oh." Aaliyah kept her eyes on the road. "You mean fighting vampires. You don't mean the fighting in sheds. You mean... "

"I sometimes think, *How many of them are there?*"

"How many what?"

"Vampires."

"Jake, we've kept their numbers down. You and me. You and me and the others. We're the vampire hunt. Like the fox hunt, just not with red jackets and beagles, that's all."

"And the sherry."

"Yeah, and the sherry – and the posh accents."

"But how many, Aaliyah?"

"We kill and we burn – it works. Don't be like this, Jake. Don't hesitate. I can't stand it when you hesitate, man. You're my foundation, you understand? I need you to stand strong, or I can't do this. No way. And if we don't do it, who will?"

He blew air out of his cheeks.

Aaliyah said, "I'm sorry, but you've got to think of other people. You've got to think of me. You've got to think of Christine, of Fraser."

Lawton looked out of the window.

Aaliyah drank cola. She felt his burden. He was responsible for them all. They couldn't function without him. He gave them strength, and he encouraged them when they wanted to give up. If he stopped fighting, then Aaliyah would too.

She felt tired and wanted to sleep and not wake up for a long time. And maybe when she did wake up, all this would be finished. Britain would be normal again. There wouldn't be vampires and a conspiracy to make this the age of monsters.

She looked at Lawton.

Would he be there when she woke up?

If this hadn't happened, Jake wouldn't be in her life. And what kind of life would that be? She would be with J.T. or someone like J.T. They would spend their days rowing. She'd be questioning him about a text he'd received from a girl, or the earrings she'd found under the bed. He'd accuse her of being paranoid, which obviously stemmed from guilt over something she'd done.

Great fun, she thought. *Not half as much fun as killing vampires.*

Lawton said, "When did we hear from them last?"

Aaliyah was confused. "Who?"

"Fraser and Christine."

"With Fraser, it's been a few days. He hasn't been in touch since he told us about the Ramsgate delivery. I guess he's still up in Nottingham, digging up some more dirt."

"He's a good little digger, is Fraser."

"He enjoys it, traipsing around the bars, meeting up with the low-life – his kind of people, ain't they."

"And Christine?"

Aaliyah said nothing.

Lawton said, "How long's it been?"

"Months, Jake. I think she's dead."

"No."

"They must've got to her."

"No, Aaliyah."

"But once they get your family, they get you."

CHAPTER 15.
MURRAY'S CHOICE.

"RUN," Richard Murray told his wife. "Take the boys and run."

"No," she said, and the boys were saying, "No, Dad, no."

"Christine, take them," said Richard again as the vampires poured along Wellington Road towards them.

"They can't touch me, Richard. I've got the ring. You take Michael and David."

Michael and David shouted, urging their parents to hurry.

The Murrays were leaving their rented house in the village. The property looked out over the North Sea. Waves crashed against the shore. Murray smelled salt on the air.

She screamed for Richard. The car was down the road. They'd packed a few belongings. She didn't know where they would go, but they had to leave.

"They're coming for you," Fraser Lithgow had told her over the phone two hours before.

Lithgow knew things. He heard things. He lived in an underworld of rumour and myth. You couldn't know what he knew if you lived a normal life. The mainstream acted like the three wise monkeys when it came to vampires – hear no evil, see no evil, speak no evil.

But under the surface, conspiracy and secrets bubbled.

A community thrived on the internet, warning against the vampire plague that first hit Britain nearly three years before. Lithgow was tapped into that community.

"How do you know?" Murray had asked him.

"You know that I just *know*, Chris," he said.

Lithgow lived a risky existence. He mixed with dodgy people. He traced rumours of Skarlet, the pill that had triggered the plague.

There was always someone on the message boards and forums suggesting that the drug was being sold in this town or that town.

Lithgow tailed the tittle-tattle.

Murray admired him. She had been the same when she worked as a reporter – chasing a story and refusing to stop until she'd filed it.

Murray had known they had to leave. If they stayed, they would die. She carried the rucksack while David and Michael dragged suitcases behind them.

Richard faced the vampires. A dozen of them hurtled down the country lane.

"Get to the car, Christine," said Richard, brandishing two stakes.

Murray looked at Michael. "You can drive, can't you?"

Michael was fifteen. He said nothing.

"I know you can," she said. "I know you've been stealing cars. I'm sorry." She dropped the rucksack and handed Michael the car keys. "Take your brother."

"Mum, no – "

"Don't argue, Michael."

The boys ran down the road and into the darkness.

Murray opened the rucksack and from it pulled a handful of wooden stakes, and then ran to join her husband.

"The boys," he said.

"They can come back for us."

The vampires came at them.

"I... I'm scared, Chris."

"Leave, Richard. You're not protected. Go with the boys."

He backed up a few steps. Murray chilled, wanting him to

be safe but not expecting him to abandon her. But then he said, "I'm not leaving you," and came to join her again.

The vampires flocked towards them.

"Oh my God," said Richard.

"Go, Richard, go," said Murray.

When the vampires approached her, they bristled. They saw the ring she wore. A man called Ed Crane had once worn it. He had pretended to be an ally of Lawton's to begin with. But Crane was part of the vampire conspiracy. The ring, like all the protective marks, was made from the flesh of Kea, Kakash, and Kasdeja.

The vampires turned their attention to Richard.

She joined her husband in the fray, slicing and stabbing with her stakes. But she was not a vampire killer like Lawton or Aaliyah, and her attacks didn't bother any of the creatures.

The vampires surrounded her and Richard, and Murray was aware of him crying out. And then they dragged him away, and she called out his name, but a voice made her freeze:

"Look at me, Christine."

Murray became very still and there was silence. The vampires encircled her. They bared their fangs. She turned slowly towards the voice that had called her name.

She nearly fainted. She tried to speak, but no sound came from her throat.

Two female vampires held her sons.

"Hello, Christine," said the blonde vampire.

"S-S-Sassie?" said Murray, her throat dry.

"The one and only," said Sassie, her arm snaking around David's throat. Her fangs were inches from his jugular. The boy struggled, but the vampire was strong.

Murray looked at the creature holding Michael. She had long, dark hair as black as coal. She was beautiful. Or had been when she was human. Her long, white fangs brushed Michael's throat.

"Remember me, bitch?" said the vampire.

Murray remembered. The creature had been Nadia Radu.

Now Radu ran her fangs across Michael's neck and squeezed his crotch.

The boy whelped and jerked.

Murray groaned at the sight of her children being assaulted. A scream made her jump, and she turned.

Vampires sank their fangs into Richard's arms and throat. They drank his blood. He twitched and screamed. His veins emptied.

Murray shouted his name and went to him, her heart tearing.

"Stay where you are," said Radu. "Or we rip your children's throats out."

Murray stood frozen between the sight of her husband being murdered and her sons molested.

Richard whined and said her name:

"Christine... "

It was the last human sound she'd hear from him.

Her heart shattered. She fell to her knees, sobbing.

Richard arched his back, and his face showed pain.

"You bastards, you bastards," said Murray, tears burning her eyes.

Richard would become a vampire anytime in the next twenty-four hours. He would join the night hunters in their search for blood.

"Choose," said Sassie.

Murray looked at the blonde. The vampire held David tightly. Radu continued assaulting Michael, stroking his groin and licking his throat.

"Leave my children alone!"

"Choose, Christine," said Sassie.

"This one?" said Radu, kissing Michael's hair.

"Or the baby?" said Sassie, rubbing her cold face against David's cheek.

"Please, please let them go. What do you want?"

"Choose."

Murray initially didn't understand what Sassie was saying. But now it became clear.

Choose.

Murray tried to beg for her sons, but she couldn't speak.

"Choose, Christine," said the Sassie-vampire again.

"You take one and we take one," said Radu.

Sassie said, "A ten count, Christine, or we take them both."

Murray looked around. Richard lay dead. The vampires

surrounded her. They couldn't do anything to her because the ring gave her protection. But they had her children. And that was worse than death.

"I am counting down," said Sassie, "in my head."

"Me too," said Radu, "and I'm at five."

"Mum, save David," said Michael.

"Brave boy," said Radu.

"No," said Murray, "No… "

"I'm down to three," said Sassie. "Three, and they're both ours. We take them, and there's nothing you can do."

"I'll kill you, you bitch."

"I'm already dead," said Sassie.

"I'll kill you again. Jake will hunt you down."

Sassie's face darkened and she hissed. The other vampires flinched at the mention of his name.

"Don't say that," said Sassie. "He is Lord of Hell. He brings fire. He will suffer more than all of you."

Radu went on counting. "… two… one… time is up, Mummy. Which boy do I eat?"

Murray screamed.

Sassie's fangs brushed David's throat. Radu's incisors pressed into Michael's flesh.

"Last chance, Christine," said Sassie.

CHAPTER 16.
CURSED.

"WHO would you have chosen?" said Aaliyah.

The A1 began to fill with early morning traffic.

Lawton said nothing.

"Jake, did you hear me?"

"I didn't have to choose."

"I'm only asking. Who would you choose?"

"I don't have sons."

"But think about her – "

"I do, all the time. Her and Lithgow. And you."

"I wouldn't have chosen," said Aaliyah.

"Then they both would've died."

She thought about something and decided she wouldn't say it. But then she changed her mind:

"If you had to choose between me and Sassie – "

"Christ, Aaliyah – "

"No, listen – when she was human, when she was living."

Lawton shook his head. She blushed, cursing her stupidity.

"I'm sorry, that was a bit needy," she said. "But a girl does think about these things."

"At a time like this?"

"Especially at a time like this."

He said nothing.

Aaliyah said, "It wasn't you fault, Jake – her death."

He looked ahead, but Aaliyah knew he wasn't seeing the road.

He said, "I can still see her look at me, her eyes full of terror."

Aaliyah remembered. The vampires dragged Sassie down into the pit where both women had been held captive. She and Sassie were meant to be a meal for Kea, the vampire god. But Jake and his friends came to the rescue, although he couldn't save Sassie.

"I could do nothing," he said. "I failed. And I could fail again."

"Shut up," she said. "You're whining. Jake Lawton doesn't whine. You've saved my life a thousand times in the past three years."

"And you've saved mine." He looked at her and smiled, and it sparked a desire in her. She wanted to stop and find a motel where they could be together. But his smile faded, and he turned again to face the road ahead.

"What is it?" she said.

"Sassie's a vampire. Murray's husband and son are dead. The other boy's missing. We're cursed, Aaliyah."

She said nothing. It did feel like everything was against them. The fight against the vampires was endless. Aaliyah knew the undead's numbers had dwindled over the years, and that was mostly down to her and Jake. But they were still out there. Hundreds of them. And their human allies seemed to be organizing themselves again.

The Home Secretary, Jacqueline Burrows, had been more prominent in the past few months. After the incident at Religion, she had been out of the public eye.

But now she was in the newspapers and on television every day. They said she was disagreeing with the Prime Minister over immigration. Incidents like the one in Ramsgate had been occurring regularly.

Refugees were being attacked and murdered. Newspapers demanded that Britain's borders were shut. Politicians urged the Prime Minister to act.

But he did nothing. All the members of the Cabinet, except one, disagreed with shutting borders.

And that one, according to the newspapers, was Jacqueline Burrows.

"What's Burrows up to, do you think?" Aaliyah asked Lawton. "Why does she want to shut the borders?"

"They're flexing their muscles again," he said. "The descendents of Nebuchadnezzar. The vampires' pimps. They're getting ready for something. It's been on the cards for a while. Since these attacks started."

"But why would they attack immigrants? And how do they know where they'll be arriving? Who's trucking the vampires around?"

"Let's hope your geek can tell us."

"But why the immigrants?"

"Anything to do with foreigners gets people in this country excited. It makes them mad, makes them froth at the mouth. You know why I think she wants to shut the borders? They're going to blockade Britain. There's an invasion coming. They're planning a takeover, Aaliyah. They're arming themselves. A war's coming."

CHAPTER 17.
WHEN I'M QUEEN.

JACQUELINE Burrows grinned into the camera and said, "I've repeated this many times: I am not interested in challenging the Prime Minister. We are only a few months into this parliament. There is work to do. I am committed to the manifesto upon which we were re-elected. I am committed to the Government and to the voters of this country."

"But not to the Prime Minister," said the presenter.

Burrows was sat in Studio 2 at Millbank Studios, which were based opposite the House of Commons. It was a single-camera studio used by broadcasters to carry out "down-the-line" interviews with politicians.

"The Prime Minister is part of this Government, is *head* of this Government."

"That's all very well, Home Secretary, but will you say, unequivocally, that you support Graeme Strand?"

"I have just said that."

"You said you support the Government."

"And I've explained that the Prime Minister heads the Government and – "

"But do you support him personally, Home Secretary?"

She smiled but inside she was thinking, *I'll have you skinned alive when this country falls*.

She said, "I think I've answered your question."

"Home Secretary, thank you."

Another voice came on the line: "Home Secretary, it's Gail."

"Yes, Gail," Burrows said to the producer, keeping her voice light despite the rage in her chest. The producer thanked her for doing the interview so early on a Saturday morning, but Burrows didn't pay much attention. She was thinking about other things.

Five minutes later, in the back of her ministerial car, she was on the phone to Birch.

"I want them all dead. Do you hear me, Phil?"

"Yes, Home Secretary, but we won't be able to do that just yet."

"I know, but when we're in charge. When I'm queen. When we are on the throne, I tell you, Phil, there's going to be blood."

"I've spoken to George Fuad, Home Secretary."

Burrows sat back in the seat. "Yes?"

"Haddad is ready again."

Burrows looked out of the window. London swept by. She dreamed of this city being hers.

She said, "He's ready?"

"The plague's coming back, Jacqueline. And this time they won't stop it."

CHAPTER 18.
PREPARATIONS.

EIGHT men loaded the container into the van. It was so heavy that the vehicle's suspension dipped when they heaved it into the trailer. The truck's rear bumper hovered only a few inches above the drive.

The men were done, and they came over to where Haddad and George waited. The men sweated and panted, but it wasn't a hot day. The sky was grey and the temperature cool.

Their leader spoke to George in Spanish, and George laughed and said something back in the same language.

He reached into his pocket and took out a wad of euro notes. He handed them to the leader of the men, who licked the tip of his finger and counted off the money.

After the men had gone, George wheeled Haddad back towards the house.

Haddad said, "Is everything else in place?"

"Our lorry will meet this van in Madrid. The container will be transferred. We'll be there, and we'll travel with it from the capital. Me and Alfred'll share the driving. And then it's England next stop."

Haddad nodded. He didn't have much time left. He was nearly 100 years old, and living sometimes had been difficult. But he wanted to see his dream fulfilled.

"What about the cleaner, George?"

"What about her?"

They entered the house.

"She was listening to our conversation the other night?"

"She was polishing the door handle, Afdal."

"You are too trusting."

"I trust no one, pal."

"I think you should bring her. Does she have family?"

George said, "I don't think so."

"Find out. Kill them all. We can't have any mishaps this time."

George wheeled him into the kitchen.

"Oh, and the men you just paid... " said Haddad.

"What about them?"

"Kill them too."

CHAPTER 19.
CREMATION.

MURRAY kneeled over her husband's corpse. The body lay on the side of the road like an animal struck by a car.

Murray cried, and memories of their life together reeled through her mind. She nudged him and said his name, but she knew he was dead. Bite marks rutted his throat and his arms. His skin was pale, bloodless.

They'd emptied his veins of blood. Within a day, he would rise again and be hungry, and he would kill and feed.

"Mum, what are you – "

She turned, and the son she had chosen stood in the road.

Seeing the boy filled her with shame, and she let out a cry before turning her back on him.

But the boy came to her and said, "Dad... Dad... "

Murray stood up and eased the boy away, saying, "He's dead, now."

Her son cried, and she wrapped her arms around him.

She stared out across the sea, and her mind cleared, a thought coming to her:

Should I have saved the other one?

The words seared her brain, and she cringed. How could she have made the choice? But she'd had to, and she'd chosen –

68

"David," she said, looking into his eyes, "David, there's something we have to do."

Fifteen minutes later in the car, David asked, "Where did they take Michael?"

Murray said nothing. She drove along the coast road. It narrowed, becoming no more than a track as they headed south.

"They'll make him a vampire, won't they?" said her son.

"They will."

"Where are we taking Dad?"

"Don't think of him as your dad, now."

"What? He is my dad."

"Not anymore."

They'd lifted Richard's body into the boot of the car, crying while they did it. It sickened Murray that a son had to be doing that to his father's corpse.

It sickened her that a wife had to do it to her husband's corpse, and she remembered now how cold and clammy his body had felt when she'd heaved it into the boot.

She stopped the car and threw open the door and puked.

"Are you okay, Mum?" said David.

She looked around. A gate led to a field. "This will do," she said.

They dragged Richard's body out of the car. David cried again. "Are we burying him?"

"No," said Murray.

She opened the gate and with David she dragged the corpse into the field.

"Mum, I'm scared."

"So am I, David."

"What are you going to do?"

"We have to take him into the field."

"Mum, please... it's my dad... Dad... " David trailed off and began to wail. He knelt over his father's body.

Murray's grief mounted. Madness threatened to splinter her mind. She could feel it creeping up on her.

"We'll do it here," she said.

She went to the boot of the car and removed a jerry can and a length of hosepipe.

"Mum, what... what are going to do?"

She unscrewed the car's fuel tank and fed the hosepipe into it.

She said to David, "Your dad, he's... David, he's going to become a vampire... "

"No... no, we can help him... "

She put the hose into her mouth and sucked, and petrol syphoned up from the tank. When she tasted the fuel, she pulled the pipe from her mouth. Petrol gushed out of the hose, and she quickly fed it into the jerry can.

"Mum, Mum, no."

David was beginning to understand.

"David, he'll turn into a vampire. He'll come after us."

David stared, his mouth open. Tears streaked his cheeks. "No," he said, barely audible. "No," he said again, this time louder.

When the jerry can was half full, Murray pulled the hosepipe from the fuel tank. She stood up and said, "Move out of the way. I have to burn the body." She couldn't believe what she was doing, but she had no choice. "David, get out of the way."

He shook his head. "You can't, Mum."

"He will become a vampire. David, get out of the way."

"He's my dad. You can't. He was always there when... when you weren't. You were never there. You don't understand."

His words wounded her, but she took the pain.

David went on:

"You were always with your newspapers and your work, and he was at home – he was Dad *and* Mum – you weren't Mum."

Murray shivered. She stood still. She waited for David to finish and to realize that this was the only thing they could do.

David's face twisted with rage.

"You can't do this. I'll... I'll kill you... I'll kill you, Mum."

Tears rolled down her face. How could her life have come to this? What decisions did she make in her past that delivered her to a field in Aberdeenshire where she was about to burn her husband's corpse?

She looked at Richard.

He sat up behind David.

His eyes sprang open. They were stained red, the vampire DNA written into his own.

The Richard-vampire hissed, his mouth opening to reveal his fangs.

Murray screamed.

"Get out of the way, David."

David turned. Murray shouted, "No," lunging forward, shoving her son out of the way and raising the can, ready to strike at the vampire.

She froze.

"Mum, what are you doing?"

Richard's corpse lay on the grass. He hadn't got up. The resurrection had happened in Murray's mind. She'd seen the future. She'd seen tomorrow. She'd seen her husband rise again as a vampire.

Murray poured the petrol over Richard's corpse. Tears came. Memories swam through her mind. The night they met. His proposal moments before they skydived out of a plane over Kent. Their wedding day in Jamaica. The boys being born.

She made a trail of petrol from the body to the gate.

She looked at David. He knelt in the grass.

Murray told him, "I'm sorry, baby."

The boy cried.

The air smelled of petrol. Murray dropped the can. She found a lighter in her pocket, but when she tried to light it, her hands were shaking.

"Oh my God," she said. "I love you, Richard. I'm so sorry."

She tried the lighter again and it worked, the flame quivering in the darkness.

"Mum, please... " said David.

She squatted and touched the lighter to the petrol on the grass and it ignited with a whoosh and she felt the heat on her face.

The fire raced towards Richard's corpse.

The heat made her turn away.

David screamed while his dad burned.

The odour of burning flesh made her queasy. But not any flesh. Her husband's flesh.

Flesh of my flesh.

David attacked her, punching. The assault surprised her. She reeled away, trying to protect her head and face.

He fell in a heap, crying.

Murray found her feet, and for a second she felt angry and was ready to scold him.

But then she calmed down and said, "I'm sorry, David, but we had to. This is how we live, now, darling."

David glowed in the flames engulfing his father's body.

Murray reached out for him, but when he looked straight at her, she stopped.

He said, "Mum, I... "

"Darling, come on – let's go, now."

"I... "

"I know, David – it's all right."

"I hate you," he said.

"David."

He stood and walked to the gate and climbed over it into the road. He turned back to look at her and said, "I hate you, and you are not my mum anymore – I don't have a mum."

He turned and ran.

"David."

Murray panicked. She clambered over the gate. She stumbled when she landed on the other side.

"David, come back."

His shape faded into the darkness. She screamed after him, but her throat hurt because of the smoke billowing from her husband's corpse.

She looked into the darkness, but her son had ebbed away, and she fell to her knees on the road and wept for all that she'd lost.

CHAPTER 20.
TIME TO ACT.

THE cleaner hurried out of the Fuads' villa, holding her breath. She never looked back, because she expected one of their thugs to be coming after her, dragging her back into the house.

She always worried about being found out.

After leaving the compound, she relaxed and reached her car. Once inside the Peugeot, she blew air out of her cheeks and shivered, all the fear rippling out of her.

She took a photograph from her bag and looked at it, and her eyes filled with tears. She blinked and named those pictured in the image.

She returned it to her bag and cried.

"Bastards," she said, "You bastards."

She started the car and drove away.

It took her fifteen minutes to get home, a rented apartment above a pharmacy near the centre of Marbella.

She pulled off her curly black wig and tossed it on the couch, before going into the kitchen and making herself a coffee.

While drinking it, she stared out of the kitchen window. Commuters hurried through the streets. Car horns blared as the rush-hour traffic battled its way through the avenues.

Across the road stood a construction site. Someone was building another nightclub. Locals had protested, claiming the town had enough venues where tourists could get drunk. But the planners gave permission.

She toyed with the pay-as-you-go phone in her hand. She'd bought it the previous day. It was a cheap Nokia, and she could toss into the ocean after making the call without worrying too much about wasting her money.

Leave no trace, she thought. *I am no one. I do not exist. Without you I am nothing.*

She looked at the photograph again.

She removed a crumpled piece of paper from the pocket of her jeans and unfolded it. She laid it on the worktop and flattened out the wrinkles. It had been in her pocket a long time. Months had passed since she'd called the number. After her loss, she had nothing but revenge on her mind and she'd abandoned her friends.

But she was ready again. Things were happening, and it was important that she played her part in stopping them. And there was no reason she couldn't still have vengeance.

Her heart raced and she dialled the number on the paper.

The phone rang and she licked her lips, trying to moisten them so she could speak.

A woman answered, her voice like silk.

The cleaner said, "Hello, Aaliyah. It's me. It's Christine."

CHAPTER 21.
BACK IN TOUCH.

AALIYAH sat up in bed and said, "Why haven't you called us, Christine? We've been bricking it. He thinks you're dead."

"I couldn't. Not after… " She trailed off.

"You should have."

"I wanted to kill them. My rage poisoned me."

"So you got a job as their cleaner? Jesus, woman. They know you. Haddad's seen you before. There were pictures of you all over the newspapers after Religion burned down."

"I wear a wig."

"You wear a wig? Just a wig?"

"And I've lost weight."

"Yeah, you sound like the master of disguise, lady."

"Is he there with you?"

"He's gone out foraging."

"How is he?"

"He finds it difficult."

"What?"

"Don't worry, he's still got the fight in him. That's in his genes. But he can't see an end to this. He doesn't know what can stop them. We fight, we kill, but still they keep coming. He's a soldier, so he's used to the enemy either dying, going home, or giving up and begging to talk. None of that's happening."

"Does he sleep now?"

"Very little."

"Where do you live these days?"

"Anywhere we can. This morning I've woken up in a bedsit with no furniture or central heating. It's freezing."

Murray said nothing.

Aaliyah said, "Are you there?"

"I am."

"You know that whenever a vampire kills someone, we burn their body – we burn the bodies of the dead."

"You have to."

"I think that gets to him."

"I burned Richard."

"Oh shit, yeah. I'm sorry, Chris. I'm really – "

"It's okay." Murray sighed and then said, "Haddad is here with the Fuad brothers. The place is called Los Monteros. Fifteen minutes from Marbella. Very pleasant. They have a villa there. I want to kill them. But yesterday something happened. I saw something."

Murray told Aaliyah about a casket and men carrying it to a van and the vehicle leaving Los Monteros.

"Where was it going?" said Aaliyah.

"One of the men who carried the casket into the van said it was headed to Madrid, but he didn't know what was in it. He didn't ask, he said."

Aaliyah chilled. She wanted to ask what Murray thought was in the container. But she could guess. And she said, "It's one of those things, isn't it."

"I think it might be," said Murray.

Lawton came into the flat. He carried a Tesco bag. He looked at Aaliyah and she handed him the phone.

"It's Christine," she said.

Lawton gasped and lunged for the phone and said Murray's name like it was a word that had been lost for years but now it had been found again.

He listened to her for a while, nodding.

After a few minutes he said, "You listen, see what they're up to. Be careful. They're devils. They might be on to you. If you think that, get out of there. Don't get hot, Christine. Hot's no good. Hot'll get you killed – or worse. We do this with ice in our veins, right? You speak to Aaliyah now. I'm glad to hear your voice." He handed the phone back to Aaliyah and told her, "I'm done. Talk to her."

He went out of the room and into the kitchen.

"He hasn't changed much," said Murray. "Brief and to the point."

"We wouldn't have it any other way."

"What's happening in the UK? I keep seeing stories in the papers here about Burrows making noises."

"They're up to something again," said Aaliyah. "Re-grouping. And it makes sense, with what you said about the casket. They're coming again."

"If Jacqueline Burrows became Prime Minister, they'd have what they wanted."

"Not quite. They want a vampire nation. They ain't getting that while we're still kicking. It's good that you're back, Christine. We need you, you know."

"Thank you. I'm sorry."

"Don't say sorry. That's just crap. And David will come back, you know. You'll find him, or he'll find you."

"Oh my God… "

"It'll be okay."

"No it won't, Aaliyah, don't lie to me."

Aaliyah slumped in the bed. "Okay. It might not be. But we've got to hope."

From the kitchen came the smell of toasted bread.

Murray asked, "Do you know anything about Fraser?"

CHAPTER 22.
LEMON BARLEY.

THE girl, in her late teens with white-blonde hair, said, "So you know this guy Jake Lawton, then?"

Fraser Lithgow popped a sweet into his mouth and grinned. "He's my good mate."

"They say he's a murderer."

"He ain't a murderer, man. He's mean, yeah. He's really mean. When they made Jake they got all the 'mean' and shaped it like clay and put it into the Jake-pot where Jake was being baked, you know?"

"Baked?"

"Yeah, when they made him, you know?"

"Who made him?"

"It's a metaphor."

She nodded, but the look on her face told Lithgow she didn't understand.

"So why are you friends with him?" the girl asked.

"Because he'd die for me, and no one would ever die for me. I'm not worth dying for. I'm a waster. But he'd die for me."

"Is that a, uh, metaphor?"

"No, that's, like, truth."

They sat in a Starbucks on Bridlesmith Gate. Shoppers trudged along the street, wrapped up against the cold. Earlier, Lithgow had gone into Lacoste around the corner to buy a hoodie, because he was shivering.

The girl pecked at a muffin. She'd not touched her Frappuccino. She wore a short, canary-yellow raincoat over a red mini dress. Her legs were goosefleshed because of the cold.

They'd been here an hour. Lithgow was drinking his second Americano. He put another sweet into his mouth and sucked. He was slowly getting rid of the taste of cheap wine from his mouth. They'd been drinking till 4.00am at Tantra on Victoria Street, where they'd lounged on a sofa, drinking, kissing.

He didn't feel like kissing her now. She didn't look much like she wanted to be kissed.

"Why do they call you Lemon?" he asked.

"It's my name."

"It's not really your name, is it."

"My surname's Barley, yeah? So it was my big sister who started calling me Lemon – Lemon Barley, see."

"What kind of Barley is your sister?"

"She's not a Barley. She's a Capstick."

"You can't do much with that, can you."

"You could if you were bothered, but I'm not bothered, me."

She tore a piece of her muffin and put it in her mouth. Her mascara had smeared. Lipstick smudged on her chin. She looked rough. Lithgow ran a hand through his hair. It felt greasy on his fingers. He wanted to sleep, but he still hadn't got what he came for. He looked around Starbucks, making sure there was no one close enough to hear what he was going to ask.

But then Lemon spoke:

"Is it true, all that stuff about vampires? I mean, like, I believe it. I believe everything like that, me – psychics, angels, UFOs. I believe. But the Government, they're like, 'No way,' they're like, 'It's bullshit.' But you know, Fraser. You know the truth, yeah?"

"Yeah, I know the truth."

"Is it a conspiracy, yeah?"

"Yeah, it's a conspiracy. The internet's full of bollocks, but there's truth in there, too. Firstly, Lawton ain't no murderer.

He's more like a messiah, or something. He's the saviour of mankind. And they hate him."

"Is he like a superhero?"

"He fucking is."

"But, like, didn't he kill a kid in Afghanistan or something?"

"Iraq. The guy wasn't a kid, he was a terrorist. Lawton shot him and got drummed out of the Army. Now he's killing vampires, and he's getting drummed out of society. He's a prophet, man. He's a legend. And I'm his mate."

Lemon frowned. "I don't know. My fella, yeah, Max – "

The Max you were so concerned about last night, when you had your tongue down my throat, thought Lithgow.

" – he says this vampire stuff is all, like, bullshit and bollocks and just a disease the Government is spreading to control us. All these immigrants are killed, ain't they, and that's wrong and all, but they shouldn't be here. If they didn't come here, they wouldn't be dying, would they. Not so much murder."

"Yeah," said Lithgow, not caring what she thought. He leaned across the table. "Lemon, remember last night you told me about something you might have for me."

She twirled a strand of hair around her finger and pursed her lips around the straw, sucking on the Frappuccino.

Lithgow said, "Where'd you get it, babe?"

"Max got it."

"You said you had some."

She shrugged. "Yeah."

"Can you show me, now?" he said, and thought, *Since I spent loads of money on you, keeping you in wine all night, and even got off with you.*

She reached into the pocket of her raincoat and brought her hand to the table in a fist. She uncurled her fingers. A red pill lay on her palm.

Skarlet.

The drug Lithgow had sold to twenty-eight people at Religion three years previously, killing them all.

And then, twenty-four hours later, all the dead had woken up as vampires.

Whenever he saw the pill, he felt guilty. He'd started all this by distributing the drug in the first place. But in his defence, he'd say he'd been set up – by his own dad, who was in on the conspiracy.

When Lithgow realized what he'd done in planting the seed for a vampire plague, his dad had said, "You should feel proud of this, Fraser. In fact, it's the one worthwhile thing you've ever done."

Thanks, Dad, he thought.

He recalled his father's words:

"Our bloodline goes back thousands of years. Back to royalty. To kings. And great kings, Fraser. Not these tree-loving hippies ruling over us these days. Kings who led their armies. Kings who died on the frontline. Kings who built cities of gold."

And then his dad had given him a choice:

Join us or die.

He chose death – or the possibility of death.

Now he asked Lemon, "Do you want to tell me where you got it?"

She pulled a face. "Do I get paid?"

"You know you do. It says so on the website, doesn't it."

"Is this, like, helping Jake Lawton?"

"Yes, this is helping Jake Lawton. How many of these do you have?"

"I have to call my boyfriend, yeah?"

"Where did he get them?"

"I'll ring him, right. It's two-hundred quid, yeah?"

"Lemon."

"Yeah?"

"You haven't taken one have you?"

"Why?"

CHAPTER 23.
ASKING QUESTIONS.

"BECAUSE they make you into vampires," said the boy.

"How do you know that?" said Bill.

"Because this is how it all started."

Bill put the red tablet back in the plastic bag with his other medicines. He stuffed the bag into his pocket.

"How what all started, son?" he said.

The boy bowed his head.

"Are you going to cry again, son?" said Bill.

The boy shook his head.

"Your eyes look a bit damp, there."

"I'm not going to cry."

Bill offered him a rag. "Just in case."

The boy looked at the rag. "No, thank you."

Bill blew his nose on the rag and stuffed it back into his coat pocket. "Nice of you to buy me dinner." He bit into the cheese and ham roll. He was hungry. He'd not eaten since twelve hours ago, when a commuter had tossed him a Snickers bar. He should've kept half for later, but he wolfed it all down straight away. "You're a kind lad, ain't you. Kind to old tramps like me."

"I'm not that kind."

"I think you are, son. You look hungry yourself. A bit pale. Scrawny, too. Do you eat?"

"When I can." The boy licked his lips. "When I'm hungry."

Speaking with his mouth full, Bill said, "These vampires, they never got me, you know. I probably stink too much."

"They can only smell blood. Blood smells the same."

"You know a lot about them. You're not one yourself, are you?"

The boy grimaced as if he were feeling pain.

Bill said, "You seen any ever?"

"I've seen plenty of them."

"I heard things on the street. There was some business right here a few years back. Vampires bursting out of the Empire cinema over there. Look at all these people, though. Be a feast here for bloodsuckers, eh?"

"It would be. Can I ask you, now?"

Bill chewed on his sandwich. "Wait till I'm done eating, son."

"I need to know."

"Everyone wants to know things, but sometimes you just got to wait – be patient. How old are you, boy?"

"I'm thirteen."

"Big man, eh?"

"No, not really."

"I remember being thirteen. Jesus. Long time ago. Tell you what, you just don't know how life'll turn out."

"No, you don't."

"Right, I'm done with my evening meal – ask me what you want to ask me."

The boy said, "Where did that pill come from?"

"I get pills from all sorts. Pills for this, pills for that."

"Don't take it."

"You're a doctor, now."

"Don't take it. I told you why. Don't take it."

"I never take 'em, son. I just keep them. Pills ain't no good. My mam took them when she was hurting. Painkillers. They caused her more pain. I don't touch 'em. Now, was that your question?"

"No."

"Right."

"They told me to come looking for you because you were a soldier. You were in the King's Regiment."

Tears came to Bill's eyes, and now he bowed his head.

"Are you going to cry, too?" said the boy.

"No point in tears, lad. Too late. Yes, I was a Kingsman."

"I'm looking for a Kingsman."

"Are you? Jesus. Northern Ireland, son. Terrible place. Seventy-two, I went there first with my regiment. I was twenty years old. Just a kid. Things I saw, son, the things I saw. Spent ten years in the uniform before I came back to Civvie Street. It wasn't easy. You go from danger to dole queue, from blood to beer. No one knows what it's like, so they leave you alone to manage – and some of us don't. Some of us end up here."

"Jake Lawton."

"Jake Lawton?"

"You know him?"

"I see a lot of the boys, still. All the regiments. They come to visit me here on my street corner. I hear stories."

"You've heard stories about Jake Lawton?"

"Why are you asking, son?"

"I have to find him."

"Why's that?"

"I just have to."

Bill shook his head. "He's everywhere, I hear. I never met him, but there's tales of him. They said he died in a fire."

"I was there."

"You were there?"

"It was near here. Soho."

"Oh yes. And did he die?"

"No, he lived. Do you know where he is?"

"Like I said, son, he's everywhere. What's your name?"

"David Murray. I have to find him. He's the only one who can save my brother."

CHAPTER 24.
THE PROMISE.

"YOU can save us all, David – me, Dad, and Mum, too," said Michael.

"Please let him go," said David. "Please let my brother go."

"Do as they say, David," said Michael. "Please do as they say, or they'll kill me."

"Please," David said again.

The man grabbed David by the collar and shook him. "Look at me, you scrotum, look at me," and David looked. "Do you know who I am?" said the man.

"I... I... "

"My name is Bernard Lithgow. You know Fraser, don't you? I'm his father. I can help you, boy. I shouldn't be doing this, but I can help you."

He shoved David into the chair. "Is my brother a vampire?"

Bernard Lithgow said, "Yes he is, but he can be human again. Or he can be like that forever, hungry and in pain. Missing his family."

David looked at his brother. Michael had a collar around his neck. A chain led from the collar and was attached to a large, rusted ring pinned to the wall. They were in a cellar. It was old, made of stone. Moss covered the walls. Water dripped from the ceiling.

The vampires had brought David here. He'd been part of the crowds packing the Quayside that night, waiting for the new year.

David hadn't been celebrating. He'd been trying to stay alive. It was safer around people. The vampires tended not to attack crowds, these days. But when David went to pee down an alley, three of them pounced on him – including Sassie Rae.

"Let me drink from him, Mr Lithgow," Sassie said now. She prowled the cellar like a panther. "Sink my teeth into his little neck and suck him dry."

"Keep away," said Mr Lithgow, and flashed a scarlet handkerchief at the vampire. Sassie hissed and reared away.

Mr Lithgow looked at David again and said, "I can't protect you for long. They're hungry. They want to feed."

"Does Michael want to feed?"

"Michael hasn't had blood yet. That's why you can change him back to human."

David looked at his brother. Michael looked pale. His fangs were sharp and white. "Is that true, Michael? You haven't killed anyone for blood?"

"That's true, David," he said. "I'm really starving, as well. It hurts very, very badly."

"You don't want your brother to suffer, do you?" said Mr Lithgow.

"Why... why are you doing this?" said David.

"Because I love my son. And although he thinks I'm evil, and you probably think I'm evil, too, because I'm helping these vampires, I want to show that there's good in me."

David thought about what Mr Lithgow had said.

"What about my dad and my mum?"

"Do you believe in magic?" asked Mr Lithgow.

"There are vampires in the world. I believe everything."

"Good fellow, David. So I'll tell you. If you spill blood with this" – he took something wrapped in a cloth out of his pocket – "knife, this very special knife" – he unwrapped the package and showed David a six-inch blade with an ivory handle – "you can defeat death and bring back the lost."

"My dad?"

"Your dad, yes," said Mr Lithgow.

"And me, too," said Michael.

"Yes," said Mr Lithgow. "Michael will be human again."

David stared at the knife. "Is this true?"

"Take it," said Mr Lithgow. "Take the knife."

David accepted the weapon from Mr Lithgow. Having a knife made him feel like a man. He could protect himself if anyone attacked him. He looked up at Mr Lithgow. "Is it true?"

"It is true."

"How do I spill blood?"

"You have to kill someone."

"Kill... no... "

"To bring your brother and your father back, David."

"No, I... I can't... "

"Don't you love them?" asked Mr Lithgow.

"Yes... yes, I do..."

"David, please," said Michael, clanking the chain. "Mum would tell you to do it, because she'd want us together again as a family. Please."

"Who... who do I... do I kill?"

Mr Lithgow smiled at him. "You kill Jake Lawton."

* * * *

After David had left, Michael said, "Unchain me, unchain me," and Bernard Lithgow released the vampire. He scurried over to where Sassie waited. "Was that a magic knife?"

Bernard Lithgow wrapped up the chain. "No, of course not. It was something I picked up today at an Army and Navy store."

"Will he do it?" said Sassie. "Will he kill Jake for us?"

"If he believes that it will bring back his brother and his father – and grief makes you believe anything."

"I'm hungry," said Michael.

Bernard Lithgow turned to face the vampires. "Go eat, then. There's plenty of blood out there tonight."

The creatures hurried up the stairs, laughing.

"Happy new year, monsters," said Bernard Lithgow. "And Jake Lawton, I hope this is your last. A child is coming to kill you."

CHAPTER 25.
FOLLOWING ORDERS.

THE warehouse stood on the edge of an industrial estate.
Lawton slowed the car to a crawl and drove into the car park.
"There it is," said Aaliyah.
"Our friend was right."
The text containing information about the Ramsgate truck
had arrived soon after they'd spoken to Christine that morning.
It had been good to hear her voice again. Lawton was relieved
to know she was alive.
Losing her son and her husband had scarred Murray deeply.
But Lawton knew that the only way to get over such tragedies
was to move forward.
You couldn't dwell on things, or the pain would fester and
poison you and drive you mad.
Lawton stopped the car and switched off the lights.
"That's the one, isn't it?" said Aaliyah.
"That's the truck," said Lawton.
The vehicle they'd seen at Ramsgate harbour stood in a
parking bay.
A light shone from a window near the warehouse's main
entrance. The blinds were drawn, so they couldn't see inside.
But then a shadow moved inside the room.
"Looks like someone's working late," said Aaliyah.

"Ready, princess?" he asked her.

"Always."

They got out.

"Let's do this the hard way," said Lawton.

"You're not planning to use the door, then."

"Shock and awe, darling."

Lawton sprinted towards the warehouse. The blinds flickered. The lights dimmed. Lawton dived at the window, shielding his face with his arms.

The glass shattered.

Shards sliced through his leather coat. He crashed through into the office and smashed into a tall lamp and rolled and kicked out in case someone had decided to attack him and then leapt to his feet. His threw punches at the air, fending off any potential attackers until he got his bearings.

And then he clocked the room: a girlie calendar hung on the wall. There was a desk with a laptop on it. A chair lay upturned against a filing cabinet.

And in the corner, a man slumped.

He was thin and tall, his arms covered with tattoos. He tried to get up. Lawton pounced on him and grabbed him by the collar and helped him up before throwing him against the wall.

The man bounced off the wall and fell in a heap into broken glass. He groaned. Lawton pulled him to his feet and rammed him against the wall again and this time held him there.

The man said, "What the fuck do you think – "

"Ask nothing. Just answer."

"You – "

Lawton pressed him against the wall and the man huffed.

Lawton said, "What's your name?"

"Cunt – "

"Okay, Cunt – "

"I meant – "

Lawton headbutted him.

Aaliyah barged through the door.

"You're covered in glass."

"Hazard of diving through windows. Give me that." He indicated a shard of glass on the floor. Aaliyah handed it to him. He pressed it to the man's cheek, an inch from his eye.

He told the man, "You'll be seeing things from the perspective of your cheek unless you get all the answers right, my friend."

The man groaned. Blood poured from his nose. Lawton let him fall.

"Question one: your name. It's an easy one."

"Travis," said the man."

"I'm Jake Lawton."

"Yeah, I fucking know that."

"You know us?" said Lawton.

Travis said nothing. He made to get up. Lawton's boot stopped him, forcing him down on his back. Lawton stood with one foot on Travis's chest.

"I'll crush your ribcage," said Lawton.

Travis's face reddened. He struggled for breath. He grabbed Lawton's ankle, trying to lift it off his chest.

"I... I can't... "

Lawton smelled fags. "Smoking's bad for you."

"You're – you're fucking bad for me," said Travis.

Lawton pulled his foot away. "Tell us or I'll set her on you – and she's not as nice as me."

The man looked at Aaliyah.

"What do you want?" he asked

"We were at Ramsgate the other night."

"Yeah? Did you have some fish and chips?"

"We couldn't stop," said Lawton. "Maybe next time. You drove vampires to the harbour so they could feed on those migrants."

Lawton allowed him to sit up.

Travis said, "They... they'll kill me."

Aaliyah said, "We will, too."

"Tell us," said Lawton, "or I will use you as bait the next time we go hunting vampires."

The man groaned.

Lawton said, "You can go after we're done here. We don't care what you do or say, you can go. All we want is information. Who paid you?"

"You promise to let me go? You're ex-Army aren't you? You've got honour and bollocks like that, haven't you, lad?"

"I got bollocks, mate."

Aaliyah said, "Who paid you?"

The man shook his head. "We get hired by a firm called F&H Wellbeing. I think they're based in Spain."

Lawton glanced at Aaliyah. Her eyes sparkled.

The man continued:

"They ring us – "

"Who rings you?"

"Some chap. London accent. Tells us where to go, like. We go. It's fucking scary, man. Fucking pant-wetting, it is. Usually it's some derelict building or a barn in the middle of nowhere, and I'm fucking bricking it. The vampires are there. Fucking hungry and eyeing us like we're food. We load 'em up, and we go where we've been told to go."

"Who's we?"

"Me and my right-hand man, Les."

"And then you let them loose."

"Aye, we do that."

"And watch them kill women and children," said Aaliyah.

Travis looked away. "I can't say anything about that." He narrowed his eyes as if he were thinking. Then he said, "They're foreigners, though. They come here, take our jobs. There's too many of the bastards – "

"So let's kill them, yeah?" said Lawton.

"No. It's not what I meant, man. We just do as we say – following orders, that's all. Why should we fret about them? They choose to come here – they know the dangers."

"I don't think they expect to be killed by vampires, mate," said Lawton. He looked at Aaliyah and then turned back to Travis. "When's your next job for this bunch of bastards?"

CHAPTER 26.
LITHGOW'S APPOINTMENT.

LITHGOW arrived at the tower block at the time arranged with Lemon Barley.

He stared up and shivered. It didn't feel right. But nothing did anymore.

Lemon had called her boyfriend Max from the Starbucks that morning, and Lithgow had to listen to her arguing with him. He finally agreed for Fraser to come round.

"You're joking. Ten o'clock tonight?" Lithgow had said to Lemon.

"Max is busy all day."

"He's unemployed."

"Yeah, well, he's busy."

Lithgow spent the day idling around Nottingham. He had time to think – far too much time to think. That never did him any good. And when the time came for him to catch a bus to the Radford area of the city, where Max lived, he'd worked himself up into a panic.

He stepped into the stairwell. It stank of piss. He screwed up his face. Graffiti covered the walls. Needles, beer cans, pizza boxes, and McDonald's containers littered the stairs.

Voices echoed from above.

"Bollocks," he said.

He went up the stairs. His legs felt weak.

Lemon and Max lived on the fourth floor.

After she'd told him what time he should come to the flat, Lithgow had asked her again where Max got the drugs. She said nothing.

The voices grew louder. Lithgow's throat felt dry. He wished Lawton were here. Lawton never cowered. If only he could be as brave as Jake. Footsteps echoed. Sounded like three or four people.

In the end, there were five.

They came down the stairwell towards him.

They were teenagers, about fifteen or sixteen years old. They wore hoodies or baseball caps. One of them glowered at Lithgow, and he snapped his eyes away. The youth shoved into him.

"What you fucking doing, queer?" said the boy.

"S... sorry, my fault," said Lithgow.

"Cunt," said the boy. His mates laughed. They didn't stop. They kept walking down the stairs. Their laughter dwindled. Their voices faded.

Lithgow panted, his heart pounding.

You're such a fucking coward, he told himself.

He came to the fourth floor. The walkway was dim and many of the flats were boarded up.

He scuttled along the passage and glanced down into the car park below. The youths he'd passed in the stairwell loitered there. They leaned on a couple of cars. Lithgow wondered if the owners ever told them not to.

He came to the door marked 12 and knocked.

The door snapped open.

Lithgow flinched. A man in his twenties with red hair and dark circles around his eyes glared at him.

"What?"

"I'm Fraser, I met Lemon last – "

He looked Lithgow up and down. "So you're the fucking vampire killer, yeah?"

"Not really."

The man gestured with his head for Lithgow to enter the flat.

The smell of damp hit him. The hallway was gloomy. One bulb dangling from the ceiling illuminated the living room. Mattresses were scattered everywhere. He smelled cannabis.

"So these pills," said the man, "they're deadly, yeah?"

"Deadly," said Lithgow. "You're Max?"

"Yeah, I'm Max."

"Where – where's Lemon?"

Max's eyes widened, and Lithgow recognized a look in them. He recognized it because he'd seen it many times during the past three years.

It was fear.

"She's not in," said Max.

"So… so you've got the pills?"

"You got the cash?"

Lithgow nodded. Two hundred quid was stuffed into the empty sweet packet in his inside pocket. He hated carrying cash, especially in a place like this.

Lithgow said, "Get me the Skarlet, mate."

Max looked at him for a second, and then he went through a door on the right, shutting it behind himself.

He returned after about half a minute and held out a plastic bag containing red pills.

Lithgow's mind found a memory and played it back.

He saw himself in Religion three years previously, selling Skarlet to clubbers for a tenner a pill. A few minutes after taking the tablet, the victim would collapse. He or she would twitch and froth at the mouth. They would die in minutes – and twenty-four hours later they would wake up hungry for blood.

Lithgow shuddered at the images, and he shook his head to get rid of them.

Max said, "You look pasty, mate."

Lithgow ignored him and said, "Give them to me."

"Cash first."

Lithgow handed him the money. The man counted the notes.

"There's only four fifties," said Lithgow. "It doesn't take much counting."

"Counting money's my favourite thing."

A cold sweat broke on Lithgow's back. Max still hadn't handed the pills over. And now he shook his head and smiled at Lithgow, saying, "They're mine."

"I've just bought them off you."

"I'm not selling."

"Give me back the cash, then."

Max held out his chest. "Try taking it off me, buddy."

Lithgow panicked. Someone hammered at the door. Max said, "What the fuck… " and then he called out: "Who's that?"

"It's me, babe."

"Lemon? What are you doing here, stupid tart?"

"Open the door, babe," she said.

Lithgow sweated. He looked at the money in Max's hand. He wondered if he could snatch it and escape the flat.

But then Max walked out of the living room and down the dimly-lit hallway. "I told you to come back tomorrow morning," he told Lemon.

Lithgow heard the front door open. Max swore. Screaming and shouting came from the hallway. Lithgow held his breath. A scuffle appeared to have broken out. Max yelled and Lemon screamed, while another man cursed.

And then Lemon screamed, "Max, come back – don't fucking leave me!"

Lithgow was shaking.

He backed up into the living room. He looked around, wondering how he was going to get out.

The front door closed and someone came in, shoving Lemon ahead of them. She whimpered and staggered into the living room, her face stained with tears.

"Oh shit, we're in trouble," she said.

A man with a gaucho moustache entered the living room behind her. He lifted his right hand, and he had a gun in it. He brought it down like an axe across the back of Lemon's skull. The crack made Lithgow jerk. The girl fell in a heap. Blood matted her white-gold hair. Lithgow fell to his knees and shouted for mercy.

"Get up, Fraser," said the gaucho.

Lithgow said, "How the fuck do you know my name?"

Another man appeared behind the gaucho, stepping out of the gloomy hallway and into the living room. The man stood tall and lean.

Lithgow said, "No, not you."

The tall man said, "I'm afraid it is."

* * * *

LEEDS – 9.52PM

"Open the van," said Lawton, as he slammed Travis against the vehicle. "Open the fucking van," and he threw him against the side again.

"I can't, I can't," said Travis, his voice a squeal.

"Open the fucking van."

Lawton tossed him against the vehicle for a third time, and the panelling buckled. Travis fell to the ground, whimpering. Lawton panted. Rage flared in his breast. He was going to kill this guy unless he opened the van. He was going to run him over.

He said, "Last time, Travis: fucking open the van."

Travis cried. "I can't, Lawton, I fucking can't."

"Jake, wait."

Lawton turned. It was Aaliyah. For a few seconds, he'd forgotten she was there. He ran a hand through his hair. It was greasy and thick. He blew air out of his cheeks. They were in the car park outside the warehouse. They'd forced Travis to show them the van that had just arrived.

She said, "Why don't we take it and follow the plan."

"Yeah, yeah, follow the plan," said Travis.

"Get up," said Lawton and hoisted the man to his feet.

Travis screamed and begged Lawton not to hit him again.

Lawton said, "How does it work?"

Travis said, "I give this fella a ring. Me or Les – or usually the both of us – we drive the consignment to an address where the fella's waiting with another vehicle, then… then we open up whatever we got in the back… "

"You said you couldn't open the van."

"Usually, it works like this – I get delivery of the keys to the other van – the one that's waiting wherever. The other bloke gets keys to the back of this one. That's the way they do it. Means you can't just fuck off down a road somewhere and... and let 'em go."

"Let who go?"

"Oh Christ, you know."

"Who, you fucking puddle of piss, who?"

"Oh Christ, the fucking refugees, man – you can't get all sentimental and let them go and then tell the bosses the job's done when it's not done. You've got to see it through. Jesus, Lawton, leave me alone."

"Never. That's not how it worked at the harbour."

"No... well, it's different sometimes."

"Different when, Travis."

"When... when they... the foreigners... when they're brought in on boats. Then, we just... we just take the... the fucking vampires to them. Jesus, Lawton, leave me alone."

"I said never."

"Fucker."

Lawton ignored the insult. He looked at the van in the car park. And then a cold feeling came up from his belly and spread across his chest. Without taking his eyes off the vehicle, he said, "What's in this van?"

"Oh, please," said Travis.

"You better tell him, mate," said Aaliyah.

"It's human cargo, Lawton," said Travis.

"Let them out."

"I said, I can't."

"Cut the fucking thing open."

"It's rigged. Like a fucking security truck, man. Try to cut into it and some kind of gas is released, kills everyone inside."

"Jesus," said Aaliyah.

"And you do this for money," said Lawton, his face in Travis's face.

"I got five kids and two ex-wives, man."

Lawton stepped back. He tried to relax. Travis slumped in a heap on the car park.

"Travis," said Lawton, nudging him with his foot. "Travis, you spineless fuck, phone your bloke and tell him the delivery's on its way."

"You what?" said Travis. "It's not expected till – "

Lawton kicked Travis in the thigh.

Travis screamed.

"Phone your fucking friend, Travis, or I'll pin you to the bullbar of this van and drive it against that building – back and forth till you're pus."

CHAPTER 27.
CAR CHASE.

THE A-7 AUTOVIA DEL MEDITERRÁNEO BETWEEN
LOS MONTEROS AND MARBELLA, SPAIN – 11PM, FEBRU-
ARY 12, 2011

AFTER finishing her evening shift at the Fuads' villa,
Murray drove home. Her heart pounded and sweat poured into
her eyes.

She looked in the rearview mirror. Behind her, the road was
dark. No one followed. She relaxed.

But then a car swept around the curve in the road, and its
headlights lit up the gloom.

Murray cried out.

They were coming for her.

She pressed down on the accelerator. The Peugeot didn't
have much power. The engine groaned. She urged the car to
speed up.

The chasing vehicle got closer. The headlights' glare grew
stronger. They were on the main beam. They momentarily
blinded Murray. Her eyes watered.

She stared ahead, watching the road. It curved around the
Mediterranean coastline. The hills rose up to Murray's right,
and to her left, the slopes fell away.

Her pursuer accelerated. The car's headlights filled the night. It made it difficult for Murray to see.

A horn blared. The car swept past her. The driver waved his fist at her. He swerved into the lane in front of her and shot off down the highway, the engine whining as he rammed through the gears.

Murray blew air out of her cheeks and slowed the car down.

"Oh God, oh God," she said, shaking.

She stopped the car on the side of the road and leaned her forehead on the steering wheel.

"Oh God, oh God, oh God," she continued to say.

She raised her head and looked ahead. In the distance, the lights of Marbella glittered. She glanced in the rearview mirror. The road was empty.

No one was following her. No one *had* followed her.

Not tonight, at least.

But she knew they would come.

The way they'd been looking at her for the past couple of days made her think they'd recognized her. And even if they didn't know who she was, she'd heard them talk – and they *knew* she'd heard them talk.

Murray drove on, and during the last few miles of the journey her nerves slowly uncoiled.

In Marbella, she parked outside the pharmacy and got out of the car. She looked around, the tension rising again. The street was quiet. She walked from her car to the building. Her heart quickened. She was about to put the key in the lock to open the door when a voice called, "Hola."

Murray froze.

She swivelled her head to see behind her.

Her heart stopped.

Two men in hard hats and orange bibs stood near the construction site across the road.

They waved at her and smiled, and one of them said something in Spanish that she didn't hear.

The hairs on the back of her neck stood on end. She opened the door and went inside. The slammed the door shut and raced upstairs.

Once inside her apartment, she ran over to the phone and dialled and waited.

"Come on, come on," she said.

"This is Aaliyah," said the voice.

"Aaliyah, listen – "

Feet tramped up the stairs.

Murray couldn't speak.

Aaliyah said, "Christine, is that you?"

The apartment door flew open.

Murray screamed.

CHAPTER 28.
TORTURING KITTENS.

"YOU leave a trail like a pissing dog, Fraser," said his dad.

Lithgow's belly trembled. The gaucho grinned at him. Lemon huddled on a mattress. Blood tinged her blonde hair.

Lithgow's dad sat opposite him on the couch and now looked around the flat with his nose turned up.

"This is dreadful. Do people live like this?" he said.

"We got no choice," said Lemon.

His dad ignored her. "This is what we would put a stop to, Fraser. There would be no slums. No dereliction to tarnish this nation. We would be great again. Greater than we've ever been. We would be Babylon."

"C-can I have my money?" said Lemon.

"Mr Norkutt," said Lithgow's dad, speaking to the gaucho, "if the trollop opens her mouth again, cut her tongue out."

Lemon's eyes widened in terror.

"This place has a dreadful stench to it," said his dad. "It is as if the corruption is laid into the brickwork. As if the talentless town planners who designed this monstrosity layered the structure with sleaze and vice."

Lithgow said, "Have you come to talk about architecture, or is there something important that you want?"

His dad smiled. "You know what I want, Fraser."

"I don't – I really don't."

"I have a shopping list, but let's start with Lawton and that Amazon creature he runs around with these days."

"I don't know where they are; I never do."

His dad said, "You remember – you must have been ten, eleven maybe – I'd mislaid my golf clubs, and you were such a scamp. I was convinced you'd taken them. Do you remember, Fraser, how I made you tell me where they were?"

Fraser winced.

His dad said, "That's right. I can make you tell me. Of course, you don't have a kitten, now. But I'm sure I can improvise." He looked over at Lemon and smiled.

"I hadn't taken your fucking clubs," said Lithgow, the memory bright in his mind. "I *guessed* where they were – I had to."

His dad shrugged. "Well, fear focuses the mind. You guessed well, didn't you. You might have to guess again – unless you already know."

"Who are you people?" said Lemon. "You said you'd give us money, and then you –"

His dad glanced at the gaucho called Norkutt, who strode over to the girl and slapped her across the head.

"Leave her, Dad," said Lithgow.

His dad said nothing. Norkutt grabbed the girl by the hair and lifted her off the mattress. She shrieked.

Norkutt pulled a pair of pliers from the inside pocket of his jacket, and he forced the girl to the floor.

She struggled, but he was too strong. He straddled her and forced his hand into her mouth, opening it.

"Christ, no," said Lithgow. His bowels chilled. "No, Dad. No. Tell him to stop, for Christ's sake."

"Would you hold on for a moment, Mr Norkutt," said Lithgow's dad. "My son is displaying that dreadful failing again. It's called compassion. I shall never understand it. But it was useful to me when I tortured his kitten all those years ago, and it will be useful today."

Norkutt paused but kept his hand in Lemon's mouth to stop her from screaming. Beneath him, she writhed and bucked, but he was big and strong, and she was small and weak.

"Just let her go, Dad," said Lithgow.

His dad tutted. "I can't do that. We'll have to get rid of her. But we might just do it quickly. Not cut out her tongue. You tell me where you've hidden Lawton and his bitch."

"I told you, I don't know."

His dad looked over at Lemon. "These chavs are the plague of Britain, aren't they. Our welfare state has enabled them to breed and multiply. If we were any other animal, the strongest in the group would've killed them. They serve no purpose. They do not benefit the species. But we allow them to thrive. I'm telling you, son, once we have Babylon again, this will not happen. They will be slaves and food."

Lithgow said, "You're off your head."

"Fraser, I gave you an opportunity at Religion three years ago to atone. I opened a door for you and asked you in. Back then, I don't know why, you rejected my fatherly overtures. But because I am a loving dad, I am giving you another opportunity."

"To do what?"

"To inherit your birthright."

"My birthright – "

"You are the scion of a magnificent family, Fraser. Your bloodline can be traced back to Nebuchadnezzar, for heaven's sake. Doesn't that mean anything?"

Lithgow said, "No."

"Then what does mean anything to you?"

"Here. Now."

"Well, 'here, now' doesn't look promising, does it? You never did think about your future, did you. I always said, 'Plan ahead,' but all you wanted to do was party and waste your life. I've no idea where you got that from."

"Maybe I'm not you son."

His dad's face darkened.

Lithgow gulped.

His dad said, "That should make it easier to kill you, then."

Lithgow's chest grew cold.

His dad said, "Don't you think?"

"Dad... Dad, I – "

"It's 'Dad', now, is it?"

"I was only – "

"You were only showing your lack of spine, eh?"

"Dad, I... "

"What would your heroic friend, Lawton, say?"

"He... he doesn't think I'm a... "

"A coward? He doesn't know you very well, does he?"

His dad rose and went to the window. He looked out across the city in the dark.

"Do you see this country?" he said.

"Every day," said Lithgow.

"And what do you see?"

Lithgow said nothing.

His dad said, "Chaos, that's what you see. The scum spilling out of their ghettos. The corrupt ruling with their bureaucratic ways – so many rules, such petty laws. Pick her up, Mr Norkutt."

Norkutt hoisted Lemon to her feet.

"Sit her down," said his dad.

Norkutt shoved the girl on the sofa next to Lithgow.

His dad went on:

"I've said all this to you, Fraser. Told you three years ago. I'm repeating myself in the hope that you've changed your mind. You've seen more of this country in that time. You've travelled deep into it – into its ugly gut. Travelled for your friend, Mr Lawton. Oh, we know. We know that. We know a lot. We know much more than you think. So I ask you, Fraser: during your travels, have you seen the corruption?"

"I see it, and I've always seen it – nothing changes."

"That's a coward's response – nothing changes, indeed."

"It's always been like this."

"And that's why it needs changing."

"To what, though? Your world would be no better."

His dad removed the red handkerchief from the breast pocket of his suit jacket. He caressed the material in his hands. He brought the cloth to his face and sniffed.

"Fraser, it will be paradise," he said. "It will be pure and clean. It will be ordered, lawful. Everyone will know their place."

"And where will your place be?"

"At the top table, of course."

"And mine?"

His dad smiled. "You only have to say the word, Fraser. Say the word, and you'll be there with me. You can have all the girls you want, all the drugs, the booze – "

"I thought you were cleaning the country up."

His dad shrugged. "This is how empires operate."

"And what about my friends?"

"Friends? You do not have friends. There are no friends. There is only us, Fraser, and them. Us and them. You are either with us, or you are against us. It's as simple as that. What will you choose this time?"

Lithgow said, "Jake Lawton's my friend."

His dad canted his head to the side and said, "Is he, Fraser? Are you sure about that?"

CHAPTER 29.
WHAT CAN WE DO?

LAWTON said, "Jesus Christ."

He kept his eyes on the M1 and stayed in the first lane. They'd left Leeds at 10.07pm, taking the van and ditching the car in a back street. The clock on the van's dashboard said 11.24pm.

It had been a difficult journey. He and Aaliyah were aware of what they were carrying, and the urge was to somehow rip the van open and free the refugees. But that would mean the people died.

Neither of them had spoken since they'd left Leeds. Lawton thought it was the worst situation he'd ever been in.

But then Christine Murray rang.

Aaliyah stared at the phone in her hand.

Lawton again said, "Jesus Christ."

"What should we do, Jake?"

"I'm coming off." He swung the van down the slip road and eased it into the Travelodge's car park. He turned off the engine and switched off the lights, and they sat in the dark.

"She screamed?" said Lawton.

"You heard."

"Okay."

"Okay what?"

"Okay. We've got to assume they've got to her."

"Shit."

"That's what we've got to assume."

"Right. We're assuming that. What now?"

Lawton furrowed his brow. He said nothing.

Aaliyah said, "Come on, Jake, you're the soldier."

"There's nothing we can do."

"You what?"

"Nothing."

"Jake, they've – "

"We don't know." He turned on the engine and the headlights.

"You said – "

"Assumed."

"Yes, you said we have to – "

"Assume, Aaliyah."

"Yes, so?"

"She's taken. There's nothing we can do right now. She's in fucking Spain. We're in fucking Leicester Markfield Services."

"We can't leave her."

"We can." He drove out of the car park.

"Is this what you would've done to a mate in the Army?"

"What you do is sit back and come up with a plan. They won't kill her, Aaliyah. They'll use her to get to us, to me. You sit back, you formulate a plan. Then... "

"Then what?"

"Then you fuck them."

He joined the motorway and picked up speed.

After fifteen minutes of silence between them Aaliyah asked, "Are you trying not to think about her?"

"I'm trying."

"You don't think they'll hurt her?"

He shut his eyes for a second, his mind plagued by an image of Murray suffering at the hands of the people Lawton knew had taken her.

And then Aaliyah said, "What if they kill her?"

"I don't think they will. I think they'll use her. That's what they'll do. That's what I'd do."

"Christ, you're not them, Jake."

"No, but you've got to try to think like they think."

They were quiet for a while.

"How do we stop this?" said Aaliyah.

He said nothing.

She said, "They're back, aren't they — the bastards are back."

He stayed quiet.

"What will they do this time, Jake?"

He shook his head.

"How long do we have to fight?" she said.

"Till there's no fight left in us."

"I'm scared, Jake."

He was silent, his eyes fixed on the road ahead.

"Why can't you speak to me?" she said.

"Because I've got human beings in the back of this van, and it's driving me crazy."

CHAPTER 30.
DOOMED.

Los Monteros, Marbella, Spain – 11.49pm, February 12, 2011

AFDAL Haddad held up the curly black wig and said, "Quite a rotten disguise, Mrs Murray."

Two men had broken into her apartment. They were the construction workers she'd seen outside moments earlier. She'd tried to fight, but they were strong and warned her they'd kill her in the apartment unless she came quietly.

"Where are we going?" she'd asked them, sitting in the back of a Renault.

The passenger had told her, "You know where we are going, Señora Murray."

It turned out she did, because twenty minutes later they pulled into the Fuads' villa in Los Monteros.

The men ushered Murray inside and shoved her into a room containing a table and four chairs. It looked like an interview room in a police station. The walls were painted white. A camera looked down at her from the corner. A striplight flickered on the ceiling.

For a few minutes she called out for them to let her out and made threats, but no one came.

She decided to sit and wait. After an hour George and Alfred Fuad came in, followed by Afdal Haddad.

The Fuads dragged a chair each from under the table and sat against the wall.

Haddad rolled his wheelchair up to the table and was opposite Murray when he slung the wig down in front of her.

"Didn't you think we'd see through it?" he said.

"You're not that bright," she said.

"We clearly are, Mrs Murray."

She shrugged. Inside, dread pulsed through her. But she was determined not to show her fear.

"There were so many photographs of you after Religion," said Haddad.

"Religion? Would that be your" – she pointed at the Fuads – "nightclub, where you" – jabbed her finger at Haddad – "tried to resurrect some ropey old demon, and the whole place burned down, meaning you had to run away? That Religion?"

"Mouthy cunt, ain't you," said Alfred Fuad.

Haddad laughed. His teeth were yellow. Liver spots covered his face. He looked old. He *was* old. Nearly a hundred, Murray guessed.

Haddad took off his trilby and laid it on the table. A red ribbon was pinned to the band. It was the same material that was in Murray's protective ring. But she didn't have it anymore. Her kidnappers had yanked off her finger before pushing her into the Renault.

And now, Haddad placed it on the table.

"You and your allies," he said, "are not deserving of such protection. It was Edward Crane's ring, wasn't it?"

Murray said nothing.

"He was a brave man."

"He was a coward, if I remember – shrieked when your own god tore him apart."

Haddad narrowed his eyes.

Murray said, "And I hear your bitch, Nadia Radu, is no longer alive or undead – Jake got to her, turned her to dust."

The old man stayed very still. His nostrils flared. Murray's shoulders sagged. Her assault had failed to make him angry. And when his mouth started to curl up into a smile, she could tell what was coming and could do nothing to fend it off.

"I hear your son has joined the ranks of the undead, Mrs Murray, and you set your poor husband alight before he had a chance to enjoy his immortality."

For Murray, it was like being hit by a juggernaut.

"Lawton will kill you."

George Fuad laughed out loud. Murray looked at him. Alfred was also smiling.

Murray told the brothers, "He'll kill you, too."

"Do you know where your son, David, is, Mrs Murray?"

Hearing her son's name made Murray's heart break, and she put her face in her hands.

"You have him, don't you?" she said. "I beg you – "

"You're threatening to kill us a second ago," said George Fuad, "and now you're begging us."

"Please – if you have my son, please... "

"We don't actually have him," said Haddad.

"Where is he?"

"I truly don't know," said the old man. "But he is doing us a great favour." He picked up the ring and twiddled it around his bony fingers. "It is such a predicament for us that Lawton and the rest of you have these protective items. Stolen, of course. You are nothing but thieves."

Haddad picked up his hat and studied the scarlet ribbon attached to it, and then he went on:

"These marks are made from the flesh of Kea, Kakash, and Kasdeja. They were gathered by our faithful ancestors after Alexander murdered the trinity. My lords' ashes were stored in the urns you know so well. Their skin was stored, also, and passed down through the ages."

He laid down the hat. He wiped his face. His eyes were red and tired.

"They finally came into the possession of Nadia Radu's father," he said. "Sadly, he had no respect for his bloodline. I claimed them from him when I took Nadia and her dear brother, Ion. Now, they are given to honourable brothers" – he gestured to the Fuads – "and sisters."

"Not fucking reprobates," said Alfred Fuad.

Haddad went on:

112

"They protect us from the vampires. Unfortunately, they also protect you people from the vampires. This is why we need a human assassin. One who can get close to Lawton. The child of an ally, maybe."

"No," said Murray, the horror of Haddad's words chilling her blood. "No, David would never – "

Haddad interrupted her by saying, "You've no idea what a child who has lost his brother, and seen his father burned by his mother, will do with a little encouragement."

He wheeled himself back from the table. The Fuads rose and looked at her menacingly.

"You will all die," said Haddad. "Do you think our lords of night have not faced greater enemies? Alexander the Great – "

Murray shook with terror and shouted out, "Who killed your monsters – "

"They will live again."

"Not Kea."

The old man growled. "Kakash and Kasdeja will rise. This time Lawton can do nothing. None of you can. You will all be dead."

The Fuads pulled her to her feet, and she struggled, but the brothers laughed at her and restrained her without difficulty.

Haddad said, "Alexander, Richard the Lionheart, Vlad the Impaler – they all failed, ultimately. You cannot kill immortality. And Lawton, who is a mouse next to those men, will fail as well. And you, Mrs Murray? You will join your family and live forever and drink the blood of the millions of Britons who will become slaves when we take England's throne. Bring her."

CHAPTER 31.
DELIVERY.

THE fat man told Lawton he didn't like being woken up by Travis, especially since he'd had a curry a few hours before and was desperate for a shit.

"I fancied I could wake up tomorrow" – the fat man looked at his watch – "or later to-fucking-day, as it stands, and toddle off to the bog with my copy of *Bravo Two Zero* for a nice sit down."

"Yeah, sorry we couldn't arrange it around your bowel movements, mate," said Lawton.

"I just don't like getting up a couple of hours after I've gone to bed, and then I need a dump, that's all."

"It's a hard life."

"Not as hard as the lump of shit in my small intestine, mate. It's not primed yet. It's like a rock in my gut, now. At 7.00am, it'll be soft – ready to spool out of my arse nicely."

"Yeah, thanks for sharing."

Lawton tried to control his anger. His mind was focused on the refugees in the back of the van he and Aaliyah had driven from Leeds.

He thought about the people responsible for this barbarity.

I'll kill you all, he thought.

114

Murray was also in his thoughts. He knew the phone call Aaliyah had received while they were driving here meant Murray was in trouble. He couldn't do anything now, but that didn't stop the dread from growing and becoming heavy in his chest.

He cleared his mind so he could concentrate on what he had to do here.

Beneath his long coat, he was armed. He'd taken the Spear of Abraham apart and had each tusk holstered on his thighs, like a gunslinger.

He said to the fat man, "What is this place?"

"Used to be a hospital, but they shut it down."

Lawton looked around. They were in an underground car park. When he'd driven into the compound, he'd stopped the van and Aaliyah had leapt out.

Now he knew she was here somewhere in the dark acting as both look-out and back-up.

The fat man was already waiting for him in the car park when he drove in. He was leaning on his horse trailer, smoking. Another man sat in the driving seat. He was young and had a shaven head and scratches on his face, and he glared at Lawton.

Lawton had got out of the van and the fat man had started moaning about Travis's phone call.

Now the fat man said, "They don't know what to do with the site. Kids come here to fuck and drink. Dealers use it as a spot to buy and sell drugs. I know a few local gangsters who torture grasses here, too."

Lawton said, "Have you got the key to my van, mate?"

"Yeah, you got the key to mine?"

Lawton dug into the pocket of his jeans and took out a key, and he tossed it at the fat man and said, "You now, vindaloo."

"What's up with you?"

"What's up with me what?"

The fat man unclipped a bunch of keys attached to his belt and shuffled through them, selecting one. "You're not who I'm used to, that's all." He tossed the key to Lawton. "I'm used to Travis and Les."

"They've got dodgy tummies," said Lawton and then without a pause added, "Open your truck."

115

The fat man frowned. "We open them together – and then I get the fuck out of here."

"Do you?"

"Oh yes. You should see me move, mate. I might not look like that Usain Bolt fellow, but I can move like him when I have to."

"Open your truck, fella."

"Here, what's going – "

Lawton reached under his coat and whipped out both ivory swords and held them inches from the fat man's face.

The shaven-headed youth gawped. He scrabbled about in the truck as if he were trying to retrieve something – a phone to call for help, maybe, or a weapon.

Aaliyah came like a ghost from the darkness.

Before the youth could find what he was looking for, she had him out of the truck and face-down on the concrete, a knife to his ear.

"You feel the cold steel there?" she said. "Move or make a noise, and I will drive it into your ear-canal and it will pierce your brain and paralyze you – you'll be a vegetable, and you'll have nurses wiping your arse for the rest of your life."

The youth stayed still and quiet.

"What do you want?" said the fat man.

"I want you to open your truck."

"What... what about your truck?"

"My truck stays shut."

"You know what's in my truck, don't you?"

"I know."

"And you want me to open it up."

"You're getting really good at this."

"You... you're protected," said the fat man and pointed at Lawton. "You've got that red thing around your neck. We're not. If we open that trailer, they'll kill us if there's no food."

Lawton thought for a moment. "Give me the key, then – slowly."

The fat man handed him the key again.

"What's your name?" said Lawton.

"Kieran."

"Kieran what, Kieran?"

"Why?"

"Or I'll feed you to them."

"Kieran Wallis."

"All right, Kieran Wallis. I can now find you."

"Eh?"

"You understand me?"

"Oh. Yes. Yes, chief, I understand."

"Good. Now, you and boy wonder over there, get the fuck out of here. Go and have your big shit, Kieran. And if I hear of you being involved in this kind of abomination again, I'll be knocking on your door — and you'll have problems shitting then, I promise you."

After the men had run out of the underground car park, Aaliyah asked Lawton, "What now?"

CHAPTER 32.
ONE OF US.

LITHGOW'S dad walked back and forth in the living room and said, "Money, Fraser. Money and women. More women than you could imagine. You can choose your women." He looked at his son. "Can you imagine?"

Lithgow could imagine. He had a headache and felt tired. His dad had been speaking for hours. Lemon had fallen asleep on the sofa next to Fraser. Norkutt stood by the window.

"What are you thinking?" his father asked.

Lithgow said nothing.

"Are you thinking about Lawton, Fraser?"

Lithgow closed his eyes and put his head in his hands.

His dad said, "I'm sure he's not thinking about you."

Lithgow looked at his father. "Why do you say that?"

His dad sat down. "You appear to see him as a father figure, don't you. I'm your father, Fraser."

"You've not acted like one."

"Perhaps that's true. Perhaps this is partly my fault. But I am here to make amends. I should punish you, of course. I gave you a chance to redeem yourself three years ago. A hand was offered. A place at the table."

Lithgow shook his head, confused.

His dad continued:

"You should have joined us back then. We are your family. We are your blood. And, son" – his dad leaned forward – "they don't care about you."

"Yes they do. Lawton's my friend, he – "

His dad reached into the inside pocket of his jacket and brought out a long strip of red material. He dangled it in front of Lithgow. The fabric was the length of a shoelace.

"Do you see this, Fraser?" said his dad.

"Yes, I see it."

"If they care about you, why don't *you* have one of these?"

Lithgow's mouth opened, but no words came out.

"You don't know?" said his dad. "I'll tell you why. It's because Lawton doesn't regard you as important."

Lithgow's father laid the piece of material across his knee.

"This ancient piece of skin protects against a vampire attack. The undead horde can only recognize their allies by this mark. You know this, Fraser."

He knew.

"Lawton has one, doesn't he," said his dad. "Christine Murray, too. She had Ed Crane's ring. Heavens, Lawton cut the poor man's finger off. And that Aaliyah woman. Lawton's witch. She has Nadia Radu's choker, has she not?"

Lithgow sagged. The truth drained him of strength.

His dad said, "They are protected, son. You are not. You're nothing to them. You're fodder. Had they cared about you, they would have given you one of these."

"They don't sell them at Top Shop, man. They're not available on the internet, you know. It's not like you can pick one up at the pub for a tenner."

"That's true. They are rare. But Lawton could've easily stolen one, like he stole his own, like he stole Murray's ring and Sinclair's choker. But in truth, these marks are only for the chosen. For the Nebuchadnezzars. For us. Not for Lawton, and Murray, and Sinclair. Not for them." He threw the material to Lithgow, and the strip of red fell at Fraser's feet. His dad went on:

"For us, Fraser. For the chosen. Pick it up."

Lithgow looked at the strip of skin, coiled on the carpet.

"Go ahead, Fraser," his dad said.

Lithgow reached down and hooked his finger under the old, leathery flesh.

"There," said his dad. "You are one of us, now, Fraser. One of us. Aren't you, son?"

He looked his dad in the eye.

* * * *

Luton – 1.46am, February 13, 2011

They cowered in the shadows at the back of the trailer. Lawton smelled the dirt and the sweat. They'd probably been in there for days.

"Come out," he said, gesturing.

"Where are they from?" said Aaliyah. "Try another language."

"What other language?"

Aaliyah made a "come out" gesture into the truck. "Out, out, go free… " she said. But the refugees stayed where they were.

Lawton stared at them. Twelve migrants were crammed into the back of the vehicle. Seven of them were men. They were aged between late teens and early seventies. Two of the women were in their twenties, and the other aged about forty. Both of the children looked younger than ten.

"Leave them," he said.

"What?"

"Let them make their own way. They're free, now."

"We can't… "

"We will."

"Where are they going to go?"

"I don't know. Where do people go?"

One of the male refugees came forward out of the shadows. He was in his forties and he had a thick beard. His hair was long to his shoulders.

"Thank you," he said.

"Where are you from?" said Lawton.

"Iraq," said the man.

Lawton nodded.

"Come out," he said to the bearded man.

The man beckoned the others, and they began to emerge from the shadows.

The bearded man came out, head bowed. He didn't look at Aaliyah, but took Lawton's hand and kissed it saying, "Thank you, thank you."

Aaliyah said, "You're welcome," as the man ignored her.

But then he looked at her and said, "I'm sorry," before turning to Lawton again. "They told us we would live forever. There would be pain and fear, and the devils would feed on our blood – but then we would be immortal. What kind of place is England?"

Lawton said, "I don't know anymore."

"Are there more devils?"

"Yes."

"What choice do we have now but to stay?"

The others filed out of the van and as they passed Lawton they touched his hand and bowed to him, while the women crouched to brush Aaliyah's feet.

The bearded man said, "Which way is London?"

"Don't go to London. Go west. Or east."

"Will they welcome us there?"

Lawton said nothing.

The man nodded.

"West or east," said Lawton.

In a line, the refugees started to walk into the darkness of the underground car park. The bearded man waited to join the rear of the line, and while he waited he spoke to Lawton:

"The world is full of devils who make more devils, but you... you are from God."

Lawton shook his head and said, "I'm not. I'm from New Cross, mate."

The man said, "I am Rashid, and I am your brother," and then he turned away and followed his people.

Lawton stared after them until they couldn't be seen.

Aaliyah said, "What now, superhero?"

He said, "Let's teach them something."

"Teach them what?"

For a moment, he thought about Murray and then said, "Teach them that if they think they can get to us, we can get to them, too."

CHAPTER 33.
IT'S ONLY CATS.

HOLLAND PARK, LONDON – 7.15AM, FEBRUARY 13,
2011

BURROWS sat up in bed sipping coffee and flicking through
The Sun.

Immigration was still high on the agenda for the newspapers.
All of them ran stories about the issue. *The Independent* urged
the Prime Minister not to shut Britain's borders "and play into
the hands of the extremists".

What the government should do, the paper said, was try to
find out who was behind the attacks on asylum seekers.

The *Daily Express* called for the borders to shut. "It is only
then that the authorities can focus on investigating the murders
of the immigrants," an Opinion piece said. "The floods of
immigrants arriving in Britain do nothing but fuel the hatred
of those perpetrating these crimes."

Burrows, reading a similar story in *The Sun*, smiled. The
immigration scandal was putting pressure on Graeme Strand.

Although she publicly supported the Prime Minister, all the
papers claimed that Burrows wanted to shut Britain's borders.

She'd leaked information to the press that suggested she and
the PM disagreed on the subject of frontier controls.

When asked about the matter by MPs in the House of Commons, or by a reporter during a press conference, Burrows would smile and say, "I don't comment on leaked information."

She put the newspaper aside and settled back, enjoying the aroma of the coffee.

In the next few days, the pressure on Strand would increase. He would meet with members of the Cabinet and ask them to declare their support publicly. Burrows would refuse and announce her intention to challenge him for the leadership of the party.

Traditionally, Labour MPs would be asked to vote for their chosen candidate. Burrows didn't know if she had enough support in the party to beat Strand in an election.

Probably not.

Her opinion that Britain's borders should be closed was unpopular in the Labour Party.

But it didn't matter. There wouldn't be a ballot. Because Strand was going to die.

After that happened, Burrows would reluctantly accept the leadership of the party and the role of Prime Minister.

Borders would be shut to stop people escaping, and prevent other countries from interfering.

And then, a vampire nation would be forged.

With me on the throne, she thought.

Moans coming from outside in the street made Burrows sit up. It sounded like cats. A lot of cats.

No one round here owns cats, she thought.

It was an exclusive street. The properties were mostly second homes owned by politicians or celebrities.

Afdal Haddad owned a house nearby, but that property now stood empty. Three years before, it had been the headquarters of their campaign. The old man had lived there with Nadia Radu and her brother, Ion. But when their plot failed, Haddad allowed the house to become derelict.

Burrows had bought this property a couple of years ago. She had a flat in Westminster, and her official residence as Home Secretary. But it was nice to have somewhere private, away from all the other politicians.

She got out of bed. Dawn was breaking, and light rinsed into the night sky.

The mewling grew louder. It sounded now as if the animals were in pain.

Burrows put on a dressing gown and tied it at the waist. She hesitated for a moment, but then scolded herself.

It's only cats, she thought.

She strode to the window so she could open it and scare the animals away.

But when she pulled open the curtains and stared out into the new day, she nearly fainted.

The smell of burning flesh seeped into the bedroom.

Burrows screamed.

CHAPTER 34.
SACRIFICE.

THE screams woke Murray up.

She jerked as she came out of sleep and hit the back of her head against metal.

She cringed, her eyes watering. But the screams continued and when her vision cleared, she saw what caused the noise.

A youth hung from the rafters. He was black, aged about eighteen or nineteen.

Murray cried out and lunged forward, but she was yanked backwards.

"Oh God," she said when she saw the manacles around her wrists.

She looked around, not knowing where she was.

An engine rumbled and everything quaked around her.

I'm on a truck.

Her mind began to clear and she remembered being taken out of the Fuads' villa after Haddad had said, "Bring her."

She complained at the time, but Alfred had told her to be quiet. Outside the villa, he'd forced her into the back seat of a red Mercedes and locked her in. She remembered how hot it had been in back of the car, despite the temperature outside being cool.

They'd left her in the vehicle while Alfred and George packed suitcases into the back of a Range Rover. She became thirsty and begged for a drink, but they ignored her.

"Someone turn the heating down in here," she'd said.

After about an hour, Alfred had strolled over to the Mercedes and opened the door.

"What are you complaining about?"

"What's going on?" she'd asked.

"Shut your mouth, you cow."

"What are you going to do?"

"Stop moaning."

"I'm thirsty. It's boiling in here."

"Christ. Fucking women. Always complaining." He tossed a bottle of water into the back seat. "Have it and shut up."

She remembered unscrewing the bottle and drinking the water and feeling tired.

Bastards, she thought and then shouted the word: "Bastards!"

They'd poisoned her. Tricked her into drinking the water. And now – where was she?

A chain led from the manacles around her wrists. It was attached to a bolt in the corner of what appeared to be a trailer that was used to carry cattle or horses.

A large casket made of clay took up the back of the trailer. Scaffolding surrounded the casket. The young man had been chained to the scaffolding. He hung by his arms and his legs, face down.

"I'll help you," said Murray and tried to go to the boy but the chain was too short. "What's going on?"

The youth looked at her. His eyes were full of fear. He said, "Oh Lord, please help me, please help me!"

"What's... what's in the casket?"

"Oh Lord! Oh Lord!"

The young man cried.

Murray's senses were sharpening all the time, and now she started to smell something.

It was decay.

It was death.

"Oh God, no," she said, "not again."

They stopped moving. The engine was switched off. A door opened and closed outside, and Murray heard voices. It must have been the driver and his passenger getting out of the cab, and now they were opening the back door.

Light poured in, blinding Murray.

Two figures entered the truck.

"Morning all," said a familiar voice.

As Murray's eyes got used to the light, she recognized the speaker.

It was George Fuad. His brother was with him.

"Just had to stop to feed our pet," said George.

The youth on the scaffold screamed.

"Let him go," said Murray.

"Shut up, darling," said George.

"What are you going to do?" she said.

They said nothing. She could see properly now. Alfred Fuad wore a butcher's apron. It was stained with old blood.

George carried a plank of wood and he took it over to the container. He lifted it and laid it across the casket to make a bridge. Steps were inlaid on the side of the container, and Fuad climbed up them, and then carefully stepped out onto the plank. He bounced on it to check its strength. It buckled but held his weight. He then looked up at the youth and gave him the thumbs up.

The young man screamed.

George climbed down from the plank.

"Where are we?" said Murray. "What's happening?"

"We are," said George, "about five miles north of Madrid, darling, and what's happening is – well, just keep an eye on my brother, here."

Alfred went to the tank and climbed up the steps and walked out on the plank. He looked up at the young man, who was only about a foot above him.

From the pocket of his apron, Alfred took a knife.

"Don't, Alfred," said Murray.

"Shut up, you slag," said Alfred.

The youth shrieked.

George Fuad laughed.

"What're you laughing about?" said his brother.

"Get on with it, Alfie," said George.

Murray screamed.

Alfred drove the knife into the youth's belly.

The young man bellowed.

Blood rained down.

Alfred cut upwards.

Murray vomited.

The victim squealed.

Alfred gutted him.

Blood and organs tumbled from the youth's belly. His intestine spooled out like a long, grey snake and struck the plank before splashing into the tank.

The young man screamed and twitched and died, his body emptying like a sack.

Alfred turned and smiled, his face and his body covered in blood.

Murray shook with terror. A sour taste filled her mouth. She vomited again.

"Anything happening?" said George.

"Not yet," said Alfred, looking down into the container where the inside of the boy's body and his blood had fallen. And then Alfred's eyes widened. "I stand corrected, brother — here we go."

Smoke rose from the container. A sizzling sound came from inside it.

Murray knew what was coming alive in there. Her dread grew. The stench of shit and blood and death filled the air.

CHAPTER 35.
UNDER OUR NOSES.

THE police had cordoned off the street. Burrows wore an overcoat, the collar turned up. A woollen hat was pulled down over her ears. Sunglasses covered her eyes.

Police and security officials surrounded her. They kept the other residents of the street in their homes.

The press had gathered at the end of the street. Burrows could hear them shout questions at the police and officials. The journalists hadn't recognized her so far, although some of them were asking, "Does the Home Secretary own a property here?"

But they got no answers. No one was saying anything.

A helicopter hovered overhead.

"What's that?" Burrows asked.

"It's a police helicopter," said Phil Birch. "Keeping the television choppers at bay."

Burrows shivered. "How did this happen?"

Birch studied his clipboard. The red ribbon flapped.

"Look me in the eye, Phil," she said.

He looked at her.

"Tell me how this happened."

"Jacq – Home Secretary, I don't – the police are – "

She wheeled away from him and went back towards her house. At her front gate, she stopped and turned her gaze towards the dozen wooden posts rammed into the grass aisle that ran down the middle of the road.

Yellow police tape encircled the poles and officials from the Forensic Science Service looked for evidence. They scraped the stakes with swabs, and they crawled through the grass, picking at it with tweezers.

The posts were about seven feet tall and the thickness of Burrows's arm. The ends had been sharpened to points.

When she'd looked through her window that morning, she saw vampires pinned on the sharpened stakes. Twelve of them staked through their bellies.

The mewling sound she'd heard had been the creatures crying in agony as the sun came up.

Lawton.

His name in her mind sent waves of hatred pulsing through her.

How had he done this?

The bastard had avoided piercing the vampires' hearts, so they were still alive when dawn broke – still alive to burn to death.

"Right under our noses," Burrows called across to Birch, who looked at her with confusion.

Burrows had seen their destruction. As the sky reddened, the vampires charred and burned. Smoke rose from their twitching bodies. Their flesh turned to ash. Fire shot from their corpses. They withered and shrank. Their skins rotted away. Their bones baked and blackened and disintegrated. The remains floated off.

"Did you hear me, Phil?" she called out.

People looked at her. Birch came over.

"Jacqueline, you've got to calm down."

"How did he do this?"

"I don't know."

"Where were they from?"

"They were taken to Luton last night. Travis called our people there to say he was delivering some humans who'd just arrived in the country. But it wasn't Travis."

"It was Lawton."

"Yes, it was Lawton."

"What about Travis? And the Luton people?"

"We beat it out of Travis this morning – Lawton and Aaliyah turned up at his warehouse last night, roughed him up."

Burrows walked up the path and went into her house and Birch followed.

She told him to shut the door and when he did, the light fell away, and it became gloomy, and this made her feel calm.

Five minutes later, they were sitting at her kitchen table.

Birch said, "The Fuads are on their way with the casket. They have Christine Murray. Bernard Lithgow, the last we heard, had tracked down his son."

"Is he going to kill him?"

"I think he'll try to bring him round again."

"It didn't work the last time."

"I think he may put him to good use, Jacqueline. Use him for Haddad's project. And Bernard is keen to keep testing his son."

"What about Lawton and Sinclair?"

"Our assassin is headed their way."

"I want that bastard dead, Phil."

"We all do."

"How dare he do this? How dare he come to my door and leave this? It is appalling. Who does he think he is?"

"I... I don't know."

"I've got to pull myself together."

"Yes."

"Yes? You think I need to pull myself together?"

"Well, I'm just agreeing with you."

She ignored him. "I'm seeing Strand tomorrow. The Prime Minister has called for a private meeting with all his Cabinet. He will ask us directly for our support. My time has come, Phil."

"Our time, Jacqueline."

Somewhere in the house a phone started to ring.

She looked Birch in the eye. "Our time."

CHAPTER 36.
THE MEMORY OF MONSTERS.

HADDAD ate breakfast in his suite and watched the news on the LCD plasma television.

When pictures from Holland Park in London appeared on the TV, his face froze.

He called Jacqueline Burrows and listened when she told him what had happened.

When he put the phone down, the fury in his chest gave him heartburn.

He drank a full glass of orange juice and tried to relax.

Slowly, he mastered his anger.

This does not matter, he told himself.

This is nothing.

Lawton and the rest are nobodies.

They will die like all our enemies.

Nothing mattered except Haddad's purpose in life – what he had been born to do.

After the English soldiers killed his brothers and stole the artefacts, he thought for a while that he had failed.

A six-year-old failure.

But he became a refugee and fled to Britain. The Fuad family took him in. When he grew up and graduated as a chemist, he started to travel. He was searching for the stolen artefacts and tracing his fellow Nebuchadnezzars – and he was also discovering a way to resurrect the ancient vampires.

Three years before, he'd nearly achieved his ambition.

But Lawton became involved.

Babylon had to wait.

But we are stronger now, he thought.

Jacqueline Burrows was about to become Prime Minister of the United Kingdom. The Fuads were fully involved and had enough money to sustain Haddad's project. Other members of the Nebuchadnezzar bloodline were coming forward to offer their support.

They are sick of Britain, thought Haddad. *They see this as an opportunity for a new beginning.*

A new beginning with a new god.

Haddad shut his eyes and imagined how the creature was developing in the container. The Fuads should be nearing France by now. They would be feeding the remains with blood. By the time they reached the UK, a monster would be forming.

A creature forged from three vampires – Kakash, Kasdeja, and Haddad's beloved Nadia.

Haddad opened his eyes.

Nothing would stop this beast. Maybe not even the Dark God himself, buried thousands of feet under the desert.

Haddad wheeled himself away from the couch and through to the bedroom.

On the bed there was a briefcase marked F&H Wellbeing, which was the homeopathy firm launched by the Fuads and Haddad in the 1980s.

Haddad rolled himself forward and lifted the briefcase off the bed and put it on his lap. He rubbed his hands and opened the case.

Three test tubes sat in crimson foam. The tubes contained water. And the water had memory.

The memory of what Haddad had injected into it a week previously.

Before pouring the ashes of Kakash and Kasdeja into the casket that was being transported to London, Haddad had taken a sample of their remains and diluted them with water.

He then continued to dilute the solution, and did this ten times. He then poured the solution into the three test tubes.

Finally, he attached a label to each tube, claiming they contained homeopathic medicine.

If customs officials stopped him and asked to see inside the briefcase, they would quickly allow him through the gates.

Homeopathic remedies did not have to suffer the same tough procedures as mainstream medicines, so the officials would not question him too harshly about the vials.

Haddad picked up one of the tubes now and held it to the light.

Clear water.

And the memory of monsters.

He chortled.

This "medicine" would be more successful than Skarlet at spreading the vampire plague.

What was contained in these three vials would be enough to infect millions. The creature's DNA in the water would kill the humans by devouring their blood. Their organs would shrivel, and their hearts would turn into black, throbbing pulps. They would die. But a day after they died, they would rise again as new creatures.

As vampires.

And they would be hungry for blood.

It would all begin tomorrow. The plague would be unleashed to coincide with Burrows's elevation to Number 10. The Fuads would arrive in England on the same day with their cargo.

Haddad gazed into the tube of water.

The memory of monsters, he thought.

But not a memory for much longer.

CHAPTER 37.
IRKALLA.

THE great hunter's voice boomed through the catacombs deep beneath the tower:

"Kill them all. Kill the children."

His voice went through Ereshkigal like a sword, and she trembled.

The girl had been lain on a stone altar. Her wrists were bound above her head. Her feet were manacled so that her legs were parted. A thin red sheet had been draped over her naked body.

It was so cold and dark. The air smelled of decay. Ereshkigal sobbed. She looked around her. The altar on which she lay stood in a clearing. The area was lit by ten torches, five on either side of her.

The fire showed Ereshkigal where she was being held. The room seemed vast. Darkness spread around her. Columns rose from the rocky ground. They were so high that Ereshkigal couldn't see where they ended. But there were hundreds of them. It was like a forest of pillars. She could see their shapes in the gloom, stretching for miles all around her.

Irkalla, she thought.

The underworld.

They said it existed deep beneath Babel's tower, and it was a place for the dead.

No living thing came out of Irkalla.

Only unliving things.

Two days ago, Ereshkigal had been gathering flowers around her neighbourhood in preparation for her marriage to Haran.

An old woman had stopped her in the street and given her a bunch of red flowers that Ereshkigal couldn't name. She asked what they were, but the woman had gone.

Ereshkigal took the flowers home. They smelled like heaven to her. But the odour made her sleepy. Leaving them next to her bed, she had lain on her blanket to doze.

And she had woken up here, screaming.

"Quiet," a voice had said.

She had craned her neck, and a tall, powerful man with a silver beard and shoulder-length, silver hair stepped out of the shadows.

"Who are you?" she'd said.

He'd answered without looking at her: "I am General Uttu." His gaze was fixed on the darkness, and Ereshkigal saw fear in his eyes. But he was a soldier. He wore the red cloak and the fringed kilt of a Babylonian warrior.

"Why are you scared?" she'd asked.

"Be quiet, now, girl."

"Have you come to save me?"

"Be quiet."

"Please, I am to be – "

A roar had bellowed through the darkness making Ereshkigal quake. The pillars rumbled. The ground shook, and the rocks on it bounced.

Uttu steadied himself against a pillar.

"Lord Nimrod," the general had said, and Ereshkigal melted with horror.

The voice had then boomed from the darkness:

"Kill them all. Kill the children."

The general said, "But Lord Nimrod, the people will rise up – "

"Rise up?" Rubble showered Ereshkigal. She cried out and struggled, trying to avoid the falling debris.

Lord Nimrod spoke:

"They will not dare. I will crush them and raise another slave nation to feed me. Find this child, General Uttu. Destroy him. Kill them all. Every child born these past seven days. Every child still in the womb."

Ereshkigal cried out again.

"Be quiet, girl," said the general.

"Save me, save me," she said.

The general snarled at her: "Don't be foolish. He'll be on you soon enough. You are his, now. May Marduk carry your soul – "

"Her soul is mine, General Uttu."

The voice made the catacomb tremble again.

"Yes, Lord Nimrod," said Uttu, falling to his knees. "Yes, she is yours, as we all are."

"Send out your troops, Uttu. Kill the children. Kill this prophesied son of heaven. He is the one with wounds. My stargazers say he can destroy me, so kill him."

The general rose. He glanced at Ereshkigal. Fear glinted in his eyes. He faced the darkness again. "I will send out my troops, Lord Nimrod, but... but they may be reluctant to kill children – "

"They've not shown reluctance before."

"They will kill our enemies, my lord, but not our own people – not the children of Ur."

"This child will be our enemy, General Uttu. He must be stopped. Kill the children. Kill them, or I shall find me a general willing to kill them. There are many senior troops ready to follow orders."

"Great lord, I am reluctant – "

The darkness hissed. Something lashed out of the gloom. It was red and leathery, like a tail or a serpent.

It flashed past Ereshkigal's face, and the heat from it seared her skin.

The tail whipped around the general's waist.

His face showed terror.

He shot past Ereshkigal as the serpent yanked him into the darkness.

After a moment of quiet, a shriek erupted from the gloom, followed by a slurping noise.

The cries of agony continued.

The general's high-pitched voice pleaded for mercy.

Then he gave a final screech, and silence fell.

Ereshkigal panted, dread spreading through her like a plague.

Something flew from the darkness and landed near the altar.

She twisted to see what it was and screamed when she saw the general's head and torso lying there next to her.

His dead eyes looked at her. His body had been torn apart at the chest. His right shoulder and arm remained, but their left equivalents had been ripped away. His spine tailed out of the shredded body.

Ereshkigal cried.

The ghost stories were true. The legends all said a girl would be in danger until she married. They said that the night before a maiden's wedding, the Great Hunter could always claim her as his wife.

One of his hundred brides.

The unliving she-devils who fed on the children of Babylon after darkness fell.

Ereshkigal writhed on the stone slab.

The first of them appeared.

They hissed like snakes, and their shimmering white shapes came out of the darkness.

White hair, white skin, white gowns. Everything white, apart from their eyes – their crimson eyes.

The wives of the Great Hunter.

The one hundred brides.

Or ninety-nine. One must've died. And Ereshkigal was to make up the numbers.

The brides massed in the gloom. They had come to witness her initiation. They snarled at her, showing their fangs. They were hungry, and with blood so close, they were desperate to feed. But none of them would've dared attack Ereshkigal.

It would have meant death at the hands of their husband, the only creature who could kill them.

"No, please," Ereshkigal cried out.

A growl came from the dark.

Ereshkigal froze.

The earth shook, and the Great Hunter came out of the shadows.

She had heard the stories. He was a monster. A giant. A handsome king. An old man. A child with wings. A goat who spoke. There were many legends. But when he finally appeared, everything she had imagined was nothing compared to what loomed above her.

She screamed in horror.

Lord Nimrod mounted her and came into her and filled her with himself.

CHAPTER 38.
SOMEONE IN THE HOUSE.

LAWTON'S eyes snapped open.

He sat up and held his breath. Next to him, Aaliyah slept. He slid out from the sleeping bag. He grimaced, his body aching. There had been many battles, and each of them had taken its toll.

He was naked and stood still in the dark room and listened.

Shouts came from outside. Kids hanging about the estate. The abandoned council house stood on the corner of a crossroads.

Youths had been hanging around the place drinking at 6.30am when Lawton and Aaliyah arrived after leaving Holland Park.

One of the boys was pissing on the front door of the house. Lawton told him to stop. The boy and his mates squared up to Jake and threatened to assault Aaliyah.

She'd pointed her Remington at the yob's forehead, and he'd taken another piss. Involuntary this time – in his pants.

After the teenagers had gone, Lawton and Aaliyah had broken into the property and gone upstairs. They had been exhausted and rolled out the sleeping bag and slipped their bodies inside. But as usual, he'd found it difficult to sleep properly. He would doze for only a few minutes. Deep slumber never came to him, but at least that meant he could be alert.

Alert like now.

He listened, ignoring the voices outside in the street and focusing on what he'd heard downstairs.

Feet crunched on glass. The glass Lawton had sprinkled on the tiles in the hallway. A floorboard creaked. The one he'd loosened in the living room.

He looked at Aaliyah. She was sleeping.

He bent down and picked up one tusk of the Spear of Abraham. He also got a torch from a bag.

He touched the handkerchief wrapped around his neck. It was the only thing he never took off. And Aaliyah would never take off the choker once worn by Nadia Radu, either. They protected against vampires. They were life-saving.

Lawton crept to the bedroom door and opened it. The hinges creaked, and he gritted his teeth. His own security measures were obstructing him. Whoever was down there would've heard.

He thought about switching on the light. If the trespasser were a vampire, it would see better in the dark. And a sudden flash of light would blind it for a moment, giving Lawton time to drive the spear into its black heart.

A shaft of daylight pierced the wooden planks that boarded up the landing window.

It was day. It couldn't be a vampire.

A sound came from downstairs, as if someone had bumped into something.

Lawton froze at the top of the stairs. His feet were cold on the floorboards. His eyes were getting used to the gloom. He looked down stairs but saw nothing.

A hand fell on his shoulder. He didn't flinch. He knew who it was. She came to stand beside him. She wore his old Army pullover and nothing else.

He pointed downstairs to indicate they had an intruder and mouthed the word, "Human."

Aaliyah tiptoed back into the bedroom, and after a few seconds came out again on the landing carrying her shotgun.

Lawton gestured that he was going downstairs.

With his back to the wall, he moved down one step at a time.

Someone shuffled about in the living room. It sounded as if the intruder were going through their stuff. They'd left a rucksack down there when they'd arrived.

Lawton wasn't worried. The most important gear had been upstairs with them.

Downstairs it was only clothes and some food. The remains of a pizza they'd eaten on the way here. He smelled it, and he could also hear the stranger eating the meat feast.

Lawton quickened his pace. He felt more confident. He didn't think the intruder meant them any harm. Maybe he or she was a tramp or a squatter.

He reached the bottom of the stairs and peered around the corner into the living room.

Lawton saw a shape crouching over the pizza box. The figure stuffed the food into its mouth.

Not a vampire, then.

At worst, a human assassin.

No, not even that.

Lawton strode into the living room and switched on the torch, aiming it at the trespasser's face.

The light showed the intruder.

Lawton raised his ivory sword, ready to strike.

CHAPTER 39.
FRIENDS OR ENEMIES?

THE M1 (WATFORD GAP SERVICE AREA) – 10.30AM, FEBRUARY 13, 2011

FRASER Lithgow leaned against the window of the BMW and shut his eyes. The night had taken its toll.

Only Lemon had slept, while Lithgow, his dad, and Norkutt stayed awake. He and his dad had talked. Or his dad had talked. Talked at him all night. Told him things. Told him Lawton wasn't really his friend.

Lithgow was exhausted. He couldn't think properly. He didn't know what was true anymore, especially after his dad gave him the piece of red, protective skin.

Why hadn't Lawton done that?

He opened his eyes and said, "What will you do with Lemon?"

"Lemon?" said his dad from the front seat.

"The girl, dad."

"Don't fret about her, now."

"I'm not; I'm just asking."

"Mr Norkutt," said Lithgow's dad, turning to the driver, "what did you do with this Lemon person?"

"I squeezed her, sir."

Lithgow's dad laughed. "There you are, son."

"You killed her?"

"Sit back, Fraser," said his dad.

"You didn't kill her?"

"No, Mr Norkutt didn't kill her – just gave her a squeeze."

"What does that mean?" said Lithgow.

"It means," said Norkutt, glancing at Lithgow in the rear-view mirror, "that I *put* the squeeze on her. I told her to never mention what happened in that flat and to forget about us."

Lithgow sat back. "I don't believe you."

"It doesn't matter, does it?" said his dad.

Lithgow thought that maybe it didn't. Perhaps nothing mattered now that Lawton wasn't his friend anymore. Or maybe he'd never been his friend.

I thought we were like brothers, thought Lithgow. But maybe you only got to feel like that if you were a real soldier. And Lithgow would never be one of those.

His dad said, "I have an important task for you, Fraser."

"What do I have to do?"

"You have to show Jake Lawton that you mean something."

Lithgow bristled and stared out at the motorway traffic rushing by in the rain.

His dad went on:

"You have to change the face of this country."

"I'm not a Prime Minister, am I."

"You can be more important than that, Fraser. You can be the most important man in Britain. That will show Lawton. That will teach him your value."

Lithgow's mind reeled. He was so tired. Were they keeping him awake to exhaust him, to make him easier to deal with? He was more likely to agree to things if he was knackered.

His dad said, "Has Lawton ever made you feel important? He didn't even let you have a skin to protect you. You were never part of his team, were you."

Lithgow felt sick. He thought about the times he and Lawton had spoken during the past three years. Not many times. And Jake had always been blunt. But that was Lawton for you. He was mean.

Made of mean, thought Lithgow.

But my friend and my brother.

His dad said, "You've been blind if you thought he cared for you, if you thought you were part of his little army. He doesn't regard you as a fighter, Fraser. Look who's with him. That woman. He thinks a woman is stronger than you. He sends you out to do menial jobs such as scurrying around nightclubs looking for pills. Send old Fraser – that's all he's good for."

"I don't know if he's thinking that."

"Isn't he?"

Lithgow said nothing.

His dad said, "I've enlightened you, Fraser. I've given you protection, too. The vampires can't get you, now. Lawton never cared if they did. Or he would've protected you."

Lithgow pulled the strip of material out of his pocket and gazed at it.

"Okay," he said, "what do you want me to do?"

* * * *

Deptford, London – 10.35am

Lawton barricaded the door after getting dressed. The intruder had damaged it while entering the property.

Aaliyah, fully dressed, came downstairs. "What's he doing here?" she said.

Lawton shook his head and entered the living room. It was gloomy, but their eyes were used to it by now.

Lawton folded his arms and said, "What *are* you doing here, David?"

David Murray looked up at him and then at Aaliyah.

"David," said Lawton. "Tell me what you're doing here."

"I've been following you."

Lawton's skin prickled. He glanced at Aaliyah, and they shared a fearful look.

If a boy could track them, what could professionals do?

"How?" said Lawton.

"I know your people, remember?" said David.

Lawton narrowed his eyes. "You know my people?"

"The people who help you – who help us. I've... I've just found them and asked them. I'm good at finding things."

146

"Where's your mum?"

David bowed his head. "I don't know."

"When'd you see her last?" said Lawton.

"Ages. Not since... you know."

"You've not seen your mum in three months? Why?"

"She burned my dad, Jake. She chose me and let them... let them kill Michael."

"She had to make a choice, David," said Lawton. "And your father wasn't your father, then. He was something else. He would've come back from the dead, just like Michael's come back."

"Michael's not – " David trailed off.

"What?" said Lawton.

Aaliyah said, "What were you saying, kid?"

"N-nothing. Nothing. I – I just... I just don't want him to... to be dead, that's all."

David was blushing. Lawton sensed the boy was not telling him the truth. But Jake didn't pester him. The lad was probably stressed. He'd seen his father killed by vampires. David's mum had then burned his dad's body. He'd also lost his brother to the undead.

Aaliyah told David, "You know she couldn't save you both."

"She's our mum; that's her job."

Lawton started rolling a cigarette.

"Can I have one?" said David.

"You what? You're twelve," said Lawton.

"Thirteen," he said. "I bet you smoked when you were thirteen – and twelve, too."

"You shouldn't follow my example."

CHAPTER 40.
A LESSON.

"AND there will be thousands of them?" said Burrows.

"Millions," said Haddad.

The briefcase Haddad brought from Spain sat on the kitchen table. The old man had arrived an hour before. Phil Birch had gone to pick him up him from Heathrow. Burrows had been excited to see him. It had been three years since they'd seen each other.

"You see it, Jacqueline? The ashes of two gods, combined with the ashes of my angel, Nadia. This is the fuse that will spark my vampire nation into life."

Burrows sat down.

"What is it?" he asked, seeing her glum face.

"It's about this morning. Lawton coming to my door with his... his bloody gift."

The old man shrugged. "He is nothing."

"He is something, Afdal."

"He is a tick. Anything else I should know?"

"Bernard has found his reprobate of a son."

"I understand."

"We'll use him to distribute this," she said, indicating the vials in the briefcase's foam inlay.

"Murray is also ours," said Haddad. "George and Alfred are bringing her. She travels with our new monster. She will be its first feed once it is risen."

"But Lawton… "

"The boy will kill him."

"How can a boy – "

"He is desperate, Jacqueline. He believes killing Lawton will reunite his family. Belief is a powerful weapon. People kill for it – and the Murray boy will, too."

Voices carried through into the kitchen. Burrows's police bodyguards, led by Birch, filled the house. Protection Command, the unit guarding senior Government figures, was nervous after what had happened that morning in Holland Park. As a result, it increased protection on all its clients.

It was frustrating for Burrows to have so many people in the house who were not part of the plot. She'd ordered Birch to get rid of the other officers. But he'd shrugged and said he couldn't: "It's out of my hands, Home Secretary. Senior level at SO1 made this decision – in conjunction with the Prime Minister's office."

Burrows had seethed.

Strand, she'd thought. *Let today be your last day.*

Now she told Haddad, "I want everyone who has ever stood against us gone by tomorrow."

Haddad lifted his eyebrows. "You are giving orders, Jacqueline?"

Her shoulders sagged. "I'm sorry."

"You are not Prime Minister yet."

"I understand."

The old man frowned. "And even when you are Prime Minister, you will be *our* Prime Minister."

She reddened. "Of course, Afdal. I understand. I am doing this for… for us." She looked the old man in the eye. "It was a slip of the tongue."

Haddad looked away and started to speak:

"I have never wanted authority or power. All I've done is serve. Serve and sacrifice. All my family – my parents, my

149

brothers – died for our cause. I've have spent a lifetime in the service of our destiny, Jacqueline. I want for nothing, myself. My glory will come from Babylon. When these streets run crimson with the blood of our enemies, when the throne of England is forged from their bones, when we, the Nebuchadnezzars, reign under the patronage of the great trinity, I shall sleep soundly."

Burrows felt as if she'd been crushed. Something writhed in her belly. It was shame. She'd been caught out. Her ambition had made her arrogant. She felt Haddad's eyes on her, but didn't want to look at him.

"It's all right, Jacqueline," he said.

She lifted her gaze to his. He looked like a father rebuking a child. He was angry, but there was love in his words.

He said, "I would like one thing, though."

"Yes, of course. Tell me."

His eyes narrowed. "Vengeance."

"Vengeance?"

"On the one who killed my brothers."

CHAPTER 41.
A THORN IN THEIR SIDES.

"HE got to them," said Tom Wilson, "he always gets to them." He cackled and slapped his fist in the palm of his hand. "They'll never be rid of my boy, Jake."

He tried to reach for the radio to switch it off, but his bones creaked.

"Mei," he called out, "Mei, come turn this thing off, now. I've heard the headlines."

Kwan Mei came out of the kitchen, drying her hands on a tea towel. "You listen again at five o'clock?"

"Yes, I listen again."

She switched off the radio. "Be same news."

"Good news, though. Good to hear that Jake's kicking their arses. Good to hear he's still a thorn in their sides."

The Chinese girl furrowed her brow. She'd been helpful since Jake and Aaliyah had dropped her off here a few days earlier. But Tom was having a few communication problems. The girl's English was very good, but some things just didn't translate properly.

She said, "He kicking their arses?"

"Not quite, but... ah, never mind. How about some tea and biscuits. You understand that, don't you?"

Mei smiled.

Ten minutes later, they had their brew and shared a plate of Custard Creams, Digestives, and Jammie Dodgers. Mei had never tasted these biscuits before, and she loved them.

"England's not too bad, eh?" said Tom.

"England is very good." Crumbs fell from her mouth. "Very good for biscuits and tea."

"You like it here, love?" said Tom.

"I like."

"Jake was good to bring you."

"I wish I can be with Jake, killing vampires."

"We can't all be killing them, love."

"He say you were a vampire killer."

"Oh, years ago. Jake's the man, now."

"He save my life."

"He saved many lives."

"I owe him my life."

"I see that, but it's best you stay here."

"Will they come here again?"

"Jake and Aaliyah? They come when they can. It's dangerous. There are people looking for them. We've a lot of enemies, Mei, love. We've got to keep our heads down, see."

"One day I will help him."

Tom smiled. "I'm sure you will, lass."

"You don't believe me."

"Pass us another Custard Cream."

* * * *

In the flat in Deptford, David's hand rested on the knife in his coat pocket. Bernard Lithgow had given it to him and said it was a special knife. A knife that could bring back his father and his brother if it were used to kill Jake Lawton.

"You going to help us pack, or do you prefer sitting there?" said Jake to him now.

"Sit here," said David.

Jake grunted.

David watched the man fold clothes and stuff them into a rucksack. He watched him gather equipment together. He watched everything Lawton did, and he felt awe.

He didn't want to kill Jake Lawton. He wanted to be like Jake Lawton. He wanted to *be* Jake Lawton.

Jake was all the comic-book heroes David had read about, all the film heroes he'd seen.

The boy's stomach churned. He felt sick. If he wanted Michael to be human again, if he wanted his dad to be alive, he would have to kill Lawton.

Kill everything he wanted to be.

Aaliyah came into the room. She carried two rucksacks. David stared at her, and she saw and said, "What're you looking at, shrimp?"

David flinched. She was scary and sexy. He felt odd when she was nearby. Odd in a good way. But if he killed Jake, she'd hate him – and she'd probably cut his throat. She already thought he was a nuisance.

David wanted to scream. He wanted to confess to Jake and Aaliyah:

They've sent me here to kill you, because if I do, Michael and my dad will be alive again.

But he bit his lip and kept quiet. He carried on watching Jake and Aaliyah.

"I'll go and get the car," said Lawton and went for the door.

A phone rang. Aaliyah took it out of her pocket and answered it and then handed it to Jake, saying, "Durkham."

Lawton frowned and took the phone and walked out into the hallway to speak to the caller.

David stared at Aaliyah.

"Yes?" she said.

He felt hot and sweaty and tried to speak, but couldn't say anything.

She laughed, and David felt himself blush.

"Don't laugh at me," he said.

Aaliyah looked straight at him and her face softened. "Okay," she said. "I won't. There's no need to be scared, now. You're safe."

David bowed his head.

"You want to kill vampires?" said Aaliyah

He nodded.

"Good," she said and picked up a rucksack. "But you carry bags first. Take your hands out of your pockets."

CHAPTER 42.
GIRLFRIENDS PAST.

LAWTON went back into the living room.

Aaliyah said, "What did Durkham want?"

"He's got a fight for me."

"No way, Jake. It's only been a couple of days. You're still bruised from that Stoke lot."

"We need the cash."

"We don't need cash."

"We... we do," he said. "You never know."

"We'll cope."

"No. Best we have a slush fund. New cars. Gear. Equipment. Everything."

She folded her arms and looked away from him. Lawton glanced at David. The boy stared right back. Lawton held his gaze for a few seconds, trying to work out what the kid was thinking.

I know you've lost your dad and brother, and your mum's missing, thought Lawton, *but something else isn't right with you.*

Aaliyah said, "Where's the fight?"

"Somewhere near Milton Keynes."

"When?"

"Tomorrow."

"Valentine's Day. And there's me thinking we'd have a nice meal together, you and me. Flowers. Chocolates. Champagne. Sex."

David blushed, and Lawton said, "Aaliyah, the boy."

She ignored him and said, "You're not fighting."

"Who are you? My manager?"

"Yes, I am. Your manager. Your… your fucking everything… I'm everything."

Lawton's heart leapt. He said nothing, just looked at her and saw the tears coming into her eyes.

He said, "What's the matter?"

"Don't do this."

"Why?"

"Just… something," she said.

"This'll be the last one for a while."

"What am I to you?" she said.

Everything, he wanted to say.

He thought about Jenna McCall, the ex-girlfriend who'd encouraged him to get a job at Religion after he'd been moping about following his discharge from the Army.

He took her advice and watched her die there, after she swallowed one of those Skarlet pills that Lithgow had been tricked into selling.

Jenna became a vampire and came back for him. He'd let her bite him and take blood from his veins.

He remembered her words:

If I don't have blood, I'll die. I'll die in three days, Jake. I'll wither away, turn to dust.

She asked for his blood, just enough for her to survive – or she would go out and kill someone.

Jake gave her what she asked for. He rubbed his neck, now, thinking about it. His mind conjured her parting her lips, showing her fangs, and canting her head towards his throat. And then the cold, sharp incisors on his skin.

He shuddered, remembering those teeth piercing his flesh and the excitement building in him when she sucked, his head swimming as the blood left him.

She'd only taken a little. Not emptied his veins. Not killed him and turned him into a vampire. And the excitement had quickly turned to disgust. He felt sick, physically and emotionally, after she was done.

155

She'd laughed at him, with his blood trickling down her chin.

But Jenna's spitefulness turned to pain a few days later when Lawton drove a stake through her heart.

And while he killed his ex-girlfriend, the woman he'd got close to over the previous weeks was attacked by vampires.

Sassie Rae.

He shut his eyes and remembered the moment of intimacy they shared.

A kiss in his kitchen.

It would've gone further, had she lived. But Lawton brought death into her life. Her colleague, Ed Crane, who was part of the vampire conspiracy, had kidnapped her.

Lawton tried to save her, but failed. Instead he watched her die. And now she was alive again. Out there somewhere, an immortal hunter.

He'd have to kill her, too.

He looked at Aaliyah.

How long before they got her? How long before he'd have to drive a stake into her breast?

He shook his head to clear his mind, but the dark thoughts had stained his memory.

They would all die in the end. All his friends. And he would be left. He would have to kill the people he once cared for.

Aaliyah said, "You don't have an answer? What am I to you?"

"I have an answer. It's everything. You're everything. We have to go."

CHAPTER 43.
PROPHECY.

THE ground trembled. Dust fell from the buildings and showered the people as they fled through the streets. Screams filled the air.

Terah's grip on his wife's hand loosened. She was gone. He panicked and turned to see if he could find her again. The crowd surged past him. They shoved him against a house. He called for her. Dust and sand swirled in a mist that made it difficult to see. The noise was terrifying. He couldn't hear himself above the din of the stampeding townspeople.

But he raised his voice:

"Amsalai! Amsalai!"

I've lost her, he thought. *She's been crushed. Trampled to death. My wife and my unborn –*

Amsalai came out of the dust like a ghost.

Terah let out a cry of relief. He took his wife's hand, and they were swept forward by the crowd again.

After a while, Terah slipped down an alleyway. He embraced Amsalai. She panted. She was close to giving birth. Sadness and joy mingled in Terah's heart.

He was seventy and had waited all his life for a son. The idols had finally delivered after Terah spent decades making sacrifices to them. But now they were going to take the child away. He would be murdered before he was born.

Amsalai looked up at him. Her tears had made a path through the dust on her face. He felt a yearning in his heart. She was so beautiful. He had watched her grow, and married her four years previously, when she was sixteen. Amsalai was his third wife – and his last, he prayed to the idols. The one who would bear him a son.

"Terah, what is it? Who are they?" she said. "Who's coming from the desert?"

"The armies of Nimrod."

Her mouth opened in shock.

"You have to go," said Terah.

"Go where?"

"To the desert, Amsalai. To the caves."

"We will both go."

"I can't. I must stay."

"Stay? Stay? Why would you stay? The armies of – "

"We must defend Ur."

You can't – they will destroy the city. It's Nimrod, Terah. It is the Dark God. The Lord of Irkalla. He cannot be killed."

"Our son will kill him."

"What did you say?"

"Our son. In your belly."

"Terah – "

"That's why you have to go. Our son must live. He is chosen. The idols say so."

"Chosen?"

"A prophecy. Our son will be as powerful as Nimrod. The one with wounds."

"Wounds? Our son?"

The people of Ur poured past the alleyway. The dust swirled and made the sky dark. The earth shook as the armies of Nimrod stormed through the desert towards the city.

Terah looked his wife in the eye. "They've come to kill our children, Amsalai. The born and the unborn. Nimrod knows the prophecy."

"You come too, Terah. You can't leave me."

"Go to the desert."

"Why do you have to stay?"

"To stop them, Amsalai. To stop them coming after you. The men, we must stand before the armies. We must be a wall. You see?"

"No. You're a fool. Come with me. Be a father – "

"I will be his father. Go. Go with the women. Go with the people. Into the desert. Into the caves." He shook her. "Do you hear me, Amsalai?"

"I hear."

"Do you dare disobey me?"

"No, no!"

He kissed her and shoved her out of the alley, and the river of people swept her up and carried her along.

She screamed, and it pierced Terah's heart, and he fell to his knees, weeping.

* * * *

The pain in Amsalai's belly was terrible. Her waters had broken. She could feel the baby come.

She lay on the ground in the cave and looked out at the night. There were no stars and no moon. It was a bad omen. In the distance, she could hear Ur die. The city screamed. Her children were butchered. All for a prophecy.

The one with wounds.

Amsalai raged against the idols.

My child will not have wounds.

She bellowed, pain and fury racing through her body.

After escaping the city, the people had scattered. They'd spread through the desert like ants. Amsalai followed a group south. As night fell, she grew sick and weak and found the cave. This was where her son would be born. In the dark and in the cold.

She pushed, shutting her eyes. Her body burned. She screamed. She was being cut in half. Something started to come out of her. Her eyes flew open. She froze, a scream locked in her throat.

The wolf snarled at her from the mouth of the cave.

CHAPTER 44.
DO I HAVE YOUR SUPPORT?

No.10 Downing Street, London – 8.07am, February 14, 2011

GRAEME Strand, Prime Minister of the United Kingdom of Great Britain and Northern Ireland, and a liability to his party and his country, said, "I am grateful for your support, Jacqueline. I knew I could count on you."

"I have always tried to give you my support, Prime Minister."

"Let's not be formal here," he said. "Call me Graeme."

She nodded and forked some scrambled egg into her mouth. They were in No.10's breakfast room. It was a simple space, lacking the pomp of other rooms in the building. A waiter had served them breakfast. He didn't stay in the room while Strand and Burrows ate, but was waiting outside the door and would enter when the Prime Minister rang a bell.

Burrows and Strand sat at the mahogany table, which could seat eight people. They sat opposite each other at the far end. Strand looked tired. He had dark rings under his eyes. Grey flecks peppered his crow-black hair, and lines mapped his cheeks.

His face was blotched, the signs of too much alcohol. The press had hinted that the PM enjoyed too many whiskeys. But his spin doctor, Luke Spofford, had threatened editors, saying he'd reveal *their* drinking habits if stories about the PM's boozing were ever published.

But even the brute Spofford couldn't stop all the other bad news about Strand from flowing out of Westminster.

The PM said, "This is a very difficult time for the Government, Jacqueline. We're under great duress. I'm having one-to-ones with all of you, requesting your support. Ralph has backed me, but I think he loves the Foreign Office so much he'd back an envelope."

Burrows grinned.

The PM went on:

"Liz has come out strongly, but then that's expected... " He blushed and fidgeted with his coffee cup.

Chancellor of the Exchequer, Elizabeth Wilson, was rumoured to have had an affair with Strand when they were both elected to Parliament for the first time in 1987.

Strand and Wilson were MPs in the North of England. They were both in their early thirties at the time, two of the very few Labour MPs who'd made it to the Commons that year.

When the General Election campaign began in '87, everyone thought Neil Kinnock would beat Margaret Thatcher. But the Iron Lady sealed a third consecutive victory for the Tories.

Strand became Prime Minister in 2005, and won the 2007 election – but only just. He wasn't going to achieve his dream of equalling Thatcher's hat-trick of victories. He wasn't even going to win two General Elections.

Not if Burrows had anything to do with it.

She had been invited to breakfast at No.10 Downing Street and was enjoying the scrambled eggs and bacon she'd asked for.

Now the PM said, "We have to put up an united front, especially at senior level. So the Foreign Secretary and the Chancellor have agreed to back me publicly. As Home Secretary, Jacqueline, you've been supportive, of course. And I will be eternally grateful for your continued allegiance. These are difficult times. There's a press conference tomorrow morning. I want to confirm that you'll be there. You know – the big guns united."

He smiled and sipped his coffee. He put his cup down said, "So 10am tomorrow at Downing Street – "

"I'm sorry, Prime Minister, but I won't be there."

Strand gawped. He held his cup near his mouth. Coffee dribbled down his chin. He put the cup down.

He said, "Do you have another engagement that I am not aware of, Home Secretary?"

She looked him in the eye. "Nothing at all, Prime Minister."

He swallowed, his Adam's apple bobbing. He looked away for a couple of seconds and then his eyes came back to her and they showed anger.

"Would you like to tell me why you won't be there?"

"Because, Graeme, I can't support you anymore."

He flushed.

Burrows reached into her pocket and brought out the envelope.

Strand flinched.

She placed the letter on a small plate. She continued to eat.

"Whatever that is," said Strand, "I don't want it."

"You're getting it."

"Jacqueline, why are you doing this?"

"It's all in the letter, Prime Minister. The reasons. And my intentions."

"Intentions?"

"Yes. Ring your little bell. The waiter can come in and bring it over to you. Lovely bacon, Graeme. Very crispy."

CHAPTER 45.
BAD NEWS.

A509 APPROACHING MILTON KEYNES – 9.52AM, FEBRU-ARY 14, 2011

THEY had the radio on while they were driving, and the news headlines had just mentioned Jacqueline Burrows.

Aaliyah said, "What was that?" and she turned up the volume on the radio.

The newscaster said, "... but it doesn't appear that all the Cabinet is unanimous in their support of the Prime Minister, with reportedly a senior member telling Mr Strand they would not be supporting him. We have our political correspondent, Richard Newbell, outside No.10. Richard, what can you tell us?"

Richard Newbell came on the radio and said, "It appears that Home Secretary, Jacqueline Burrows, has refused to back the Prime Minister. We saw her leaving about an hour ago with a smile on her face, but the unofficial – and I hasten to say it is unofficial – line coming from Downing Street is that Mrs Burrows – known, of course, as Firestarter – will not back the troubled Mr Strand."

"Any comment from the Home Office?" asked the newscaster.

Newbell said, "They are being tight-lipped at the – "

Lawton switched off the radio. He looked ahead, concentrating on traffic. The weather was grey. Drizzle fell, and it was cold. They were on the A509, headed for Milton Keynes. They'd left Deptford a couple of hours ago in a yellow Fiat bought through the small ads in a local paper.

After leaving the squat the previous day, they had tried to make contact with Fraser Lithgow. He wasn't answering any of his phones. There was no activity on his Facebook page or on his Twitter account. Aaliyah e-mailed him three times but got no response.

Now Murray *and* Lithgow were missing.

Fear gnawed at Lawton's belly. He drove over the Northfield Roundabout. Only a few miles and they would be at their destination. It would give him time to relax before tonight's fight.

The previous day, Aaliyah had continued in her efforts to stop him taking part in the event.

"Things aren't right," she'd said.

It was true. Things were different. Things *felt* different. His gut told him. His instincts alerted him. But he ignored the warnings. If there were danger ahead, he was going straight for it. But that was the best way to deal with threats.

Confront them.

He glanced in the rear-view mirror. David Murray slept in the back seat.

Last evening, they'd returned to the squat and stayed there a second night. David had bunked on the floor in the same room as Aaliyah and Lawton. But Lawton, who rarely slept, knew the youngster had been awake most of the night.

The boy looked troubled. He'd suffered a terrible three years. No child should see what he'd seen. No adult should, either. Lawton didn't know if the kid would ever get over this experience.

And what are we going to do with you? he thought.

David couldn't come with them. It was too dangerous.

Lawton shook his head.

"They're flexing their muscles," he said. "Burrows and her cronies. I bet you Haddad's back in the country."

Aaliyah took out her laptop and opened it. She was checking something. After a few moments she said, "Still nothing from Lithgow."

Lawton bit his lip and thought about things.

"What do we do, Jake?" said Aaliyah. "Both of them are… "

"I know," he said.

Should he follow Lithgow's trail to Nottingham? If he had been kidnapped, he probably wasn't there anymore. But he might be dead, somewhere.

Lawton cringed.

"We do this," he said, "and pick up our money, then we head back to London. Things are kicking off. They're coming. They're here. And we need to be there, too."

"We should kill Burrows," said Aaliyah.

"They'll just put somebody else in her place."

"Kill them, too."

"They'll keep on coming, Aaliyah."

"Okay, so what do we do?"

"I'm thinking about it."

CHAPTER 46.
LUXURY LIVING.

BERNARD Lithgow nudged the curtain aside and looked down over Green Park.

It was busy down there. Lots of people. All of them doomed.

He smiled and went to the couch to sit down. The furnishings in the Deluxe Suite were all antique. He needed to be in luxurious surroundings after his time in Nottingham.

He hated estates like the one where he'd found Fraser. They were depressing places. Symbols of a broken Britain.

But very soon those grim, concrete jungles would be put to good use.

They would become factories where humans would be stocked and harvested, ready for consumption by the vampires.

His phone rang, and a familiar name appeared on the caller ID screen

"Hello, Dr Haddad," said Bernard into the phone.

All Haddad said was, "Do you have your son?"

"We have him."

"Is he ours?"

"He's ours, Afdal."

"Not like before, I hope. When you failed. When he rejected you."

Bernard bristled. "He suffered from a disease. He was obsessed. But my son is now cured. He sees the light. He is on the good path. He's special, and that's what my son has always wanted to be."

"We can't afford for him to go astray this time."

Bernard simmered. "He won't. He didn't go astray three years ago. He distributed those pills, didn't he? Your pills just didn't work as well as they should have."

"They worked perfectly well."

"But the Fuad brothers were careless with their employment process," said Bernard.

"Speak to them about that."

"Had they not employed Lawton – "

"Speak to them. Lawton won't trouble us anymore."

"Can you be sure?"

"I am sure."

"Well, he and his – I don't know what you'd call that women – his… they've been causing carnage."

Haddad said, "Lawton will be dealt with."

"We've been saying that for years."

"You concentrate on your son – "

"Fraser is signed up."

"All right, Bernard, let's not fall out."

"I agree."

"We're under a lot of strain."

"We are."

"But we are close, now. Burrows will be our scythe from the seat of power. I shall be over soon with the materials for your son. George and Alfred will arrive in England later today. London is ours. Britain is ours. Lawton will be dead. They will all be dead. All our enemies. All my enemies."

CHAPTER 47.
THEY'RE COMING.

TOM Wilson gritted his teeth as he watched the television. It was bad news from Downing Street.

The volume was low, and he strained to hear. He looked for the remote. It was usually next to him on the sofa.

"Mei... where's the bloody remote?"

The Chinese girl came out of the kitchen.

"I put away," she said.

"Well, don't put away."

"They on floor. You stand and fall."

"I haven't stand and fall in fifty years, love."

She put her hands on her hips. "I only take care."

"I know, I know. Now where's the remote?"

The girl blew air out of her cheeks. She bent and picked up the remote from the TV stand and handed it to Wilson.

"What's it doing there?" he said.

"It live with TV. You know where it is all time."

He turned up the volume. "I don't, do I."

"Now you do."

Mei looked at the television when the volume became louder. She said, "Downing Street."

"That's right, love."

A reporter said that the Prime Minister was "hanging by a thread".

"By thread?" said Mei.

"Means he's walking a tightrope."

"Walking a tightrope?"

"He's in deep shit, love."

"Deep shit? Oh, deep shit."

The reporter said, "Jacqueline Burrows has not yet announced her resignation, but we understand that it is imminent – "

"You understand nothing, son," said Wilson to the reporter on the TV.

The journalist went on:

"Following her resignation, we expect Mrs Burrows to announce that she is standing against Mr Strand for the leadership."

"That bitch," said Wilson.

"She's bitch?"

"Big bitch. Queen bitch."

"Jake in trouble?"

"We are all in trouble, Mei."

They're coming for us, he thought. *I can feel it.*

The Nebuchadnezzars were attacking democracy. They were planning to steal the country. Only Lawton, Aaliyah, and their few allies could stop the takeover. But the Nebuchadnezzars would never allow that. They made that mistake three years ago. Not this time. And Wilson knew what that meant. It meant death for Lawton, for Aaliyah, for all of them. It meant death for him.

The front door buckled.

He turned and stared as the wood splintered.

He didn't wait for whoever was outside to smash the door again.

"Mei," he said, "get out of here now."

The girl stared.

The door cracked again.

Her face had paled.

"Mei," said Wilson, "you are to leave, now."

Mei said, "What is happening?"

"Get out!" He shook with fear. "Get out now!"

CHAPTER 48.
TRUCK STOP.

ROUTE DE LA MOTTE DU BOURG, TARDINGHEN,
NEAR CALAIS – 11.35AM, FEBRUARY 14, 2011

MURRAY woke up. She was thirsty and ached all over. It was cold and wet in the back of the truck.

She blinked the sleep away from her eyes. She tried to peer through the slots in the side of the trailer, but the Fuads had shut them. Slivers of daylight came through, and although she failed to see anything, Murray smelled grass.

It was better than smelling blood and meat.

The truck slowed and turned, and she swayed in the back. It made her feel sick, her head swimming.

The truck stopped. Murray listened. It was very quiet. But after a while, an engine groaned. The noise came closer until it was right outside the truck, and then it stopped.

Outside the truck, doors opened and voices spoke French. She narrowed her eyes and focused. It sounded like five or six men. She recognized the Fuads by their English accents, while the other speakers spoke with thick, East European twangs to their voices.

Murray looked at the container. Three male bodies hung upside down above it from the scaffolding. Two hours earlier,

Alfred Fuad had cut the men's throats. Their blood had poured into the casket.

How much longer before the monster would come alive? How much longer before she was dead?

She almost didn't care. It would be a relief, if only to be free of the terrible smell in here.

Murray had vomited a few times, but they'd not cleaned it up. It puddled around her legs, and its sour odour mingled with the stench of death inside the trailer.

The bodies dangled. Smoke rose from the container. Something sizzled inside, as if it were cooking. Liquid crept over the side of the tank and corroded the metal.

Whatever was in there was coming alive.

Murray groaned. She tried to stand and stretch her legs, but they buckled under her. She was so weak and stiff.

She fell to her knees, exhausted. They'd not fed her properly since the journey began, only providing water every few hours.

She laid her head against the side of the trailer, and thoughts of David drifted into her mind. She hoped he was alive. An ache grew in her chest. It spread through her, making her bones feel heavy.

We've lost, she thought. *We've lost.*

And she started to cry.

The voices outside got closer.

She didn't know who they were, but they might not be friends of the Fuads.

They might be police, she thought. *They might be strangers stopping to ask for help.*

It sparked something in her and she kicked the side of the trailer and shouted, "Help me!" over and over.

The voices quietened.

The door started to open. The day spilled in. She was blinded by the light.

Murray said, "Save me, please save me," as five silhouettes appeared in the doorway.

* * * *

171

David sat in the toilet with the ivory-handled knife on his lap.

He tried to imagine plunging the blade into Jake's chest. He played out the scenario in his head over and over.

Everytime the knife went into Jake, David flinched. He could feel the pain in his own breast. The blood would pour from his wounded heart and his damaged lungs, and spread through his body.

He would cough it up. It would be hot and thick in his throat. He'd choke on it. The pain would spread and slowly he'd lose his strength and grow tired.

And death would come.

And it would be over.

Lawton dead. Michael and his dad alive again.

He looked up. The toilet was dirty and smelly. It was a hut standing in the corner of the farmyard. Graffiti covered the outside of the structure. Rude pictures had been drawn on the inside of the door, threats scratched into the floor.

They'd got here about forty-five minutes ago. It was a derelict farm a few miles from a village called Salford, just outside Milton Keynes. They were somewhere on the Cranfield Road, but David didn't know for sure. He had no idea how he was going to get away after stabbing Jake. And he had no idea where to go, either.

After I do it, how do I know Michael and Dad are alive again? he thought.

He should've asked Fraser's dad. But he didn't think.

He sighed. Jake was his friend. Jake was his hero. But sometimes you had to do difficult things. You had to make sacrifices.

"For the greater good," the old man Tom Wilson had said once. "We do things for the greater good."

So if Jake had to die so that Michael could be human again, that would be a greater good, wouldn't it?

David thought about that. He wasn't sure about things. He looked at the knife.

Just stick it in him, he thought. *Stick it in him and run.*

It would be over tonight.

I'll wait till after the fight, he thought.

Jake would be tired. He would be hurt. It would be easier.

David ran his finger along the blade. It gave him a cut. He winced, and blood smeared the steel.

CHAPTER 49.
MURDER, MADNESS, AND
BLOOD.

TWO elderly men in wheelchairs faced each other. Tom Wilson, aged 107, and Dr Afdal Haddad, aged 95. Old enemies.

"You owe me blood," said Haddad.

"You got blood." Wilson rolled up his sleeve. Tattoos covered his forearm. He pointed at a scar on his sunburnt skin. "July 23rd, 1920."

"You were a thief," said Haddad.

"I was in the right."

"You were a thief," Haddad repeated.

"You were going to kill people. You *are* killing people. Hundreds have died."

"Hah! And did the famous British Army not kill, too?"

"I never killed no one who didn't threaten me first."

"You killed my brothers, Wilson."

"They threatened us."

"They were boys."

"They attacked us, me and Lieutenant Jordan. And it was him who shot them. Jordan. But I'd have done it, too."

Haddad bristled, his knuckles turning white as he gripped the arms of his wheelchair. He was about to say something, but Wilson interrupted:

"Jordan was right – humanity was in danger. And it still is. You lot, you've got to be stopped. And if I was twenty years younger, you'd be in trouble, chum. You and your cronies."

He coughed. His heart pounded. *What a place to die*, he thought. Some abandoned factory in the middle of nowhere.

Three men had smashed their way into the flat that morning. They were dressed like paramedics in green overalls. Wilson threw teacups and plates at them. But they swatted away the crockery and wheeled him out. They put him in the back of an ambulance and laid him on the cot. They stuck a needle in his arm, and he cried, believing they were putting him down. He faded away, calling out his wife's name.

He woke up babbling. At first, he thought he was in hell – and wasn't surprised. But then he recognized one of the paramedics.

"Welcome to London, Mr Wilson," the man had said.

They'd wheeled him out of the ambulance and into a grey building that didn't have any windows.

"So what is this place?" he asked Haddad now.

Wilson craned his neck to study his surroundings. The room was empty. Striplights purred. The paint on the walls peeled. Empty pizza boxes and copies of *2000AD* were strewn on the floor. Behind Haddad, there was a door with a porthole in it. Beyond the door it looked dark. But Wilson sensed something was alive in there.

"This is called B13," said Haddad. "It's a secret government facility. It is used to house victims of unusual deaths."

"Unusual deaths?"

"Do you know, the first twenty-eight victims of the Skarlet pill were kept here – until they woke up?"

"You must be very proud."

"I am, Wilson. Very proud."

"You won't be when Jake Lawton sticks it up your arse again, you old cunt."

Haddad pulled a face. "You've terrible manners."

"Fuck you."

175

"But what does one expect from the killer of children?"

"And you ain't killed children?"

Haddad ignored him and said, "As for Lawton, he won't trouble us much longer."

"We'll see about that."

"We will."

"You've not got to him yet. He can spot you lot a mile off."

"That's why one his friends will kill him, Wilson."

Wilson opened his mouth. His mind reeled. He hoped Mei had got away. She would try to find Jake. She wanted to save Lawton's life and return the favour. She'd have to, if Haddad was telling the truth.

"You don't look so well, Wilson," said Haddad.

"Wheel yourself over here, you bastard, so I can puke all over you."

Haddad laughed. He wheeled himself the other way, towards the door with the porthole. He was still laughing when he opened the door. "You know the other good thing about this place, Wilson?" he said.

Wilson's heart froze as he stared into the darkness beyond the door.

"No windows," said Haddad.

Wilson tried to roll his chair away, but his hands were covered in sweat, and he couldn't grip the bars properly.

Haddad said, "Leave his head," as undead things came out of the shadows.

* * * *

Route de la Motte du Bourg, Tardinghen, near Calais – 12.11pm, February 14, 2011

MURRAY said, "Help me, please – "

The men walked up the gangway into the truck.

George Fuad said, "This ain't the help, darling."

Fuad turned to the other men. They looked Mediterranean, with dark hair and dark eyes. Two of them mumbled to each other in a language Murray didn't understand. The third stood with his head canted to one side and his arms folded.

Fuad said something in French to the pair, and they sneered at her before saying something else in their own language.

The three men walked away with Alfred Fuad.

George asked her, "Are you enjoying the ride, Christine?"

She tried to say something, but it came out as a croak.

"Best you don't talk, eh?" he said.

He crouched next to her and flapped his hand in front of his face to indicate that she smelled. Then he said, "The Albanians have gone to get you some company."

She groaned.

"It's a very useful way to get our prince here fed, don't you think — refugees, immigrants. I mean, me and my brother, we were immigrants. Well, our grandparents were. From the Middle East. They worked hard, though. Integrated. And me and Alfie, we're Brits through and through. Not like foreigners these days, Christine. They want to abuse the system. They don't want to contribute, make the country great. They want to destroy it. They want to shit on Britain. And Britain lets them do it."

"And... and what will you do to Britain?"

"Found your voice, then."

"You're turning it into a dictatorship."

"That's right," he said. "The age of monsters. An empire of death."

"You count yourself British, and you're destroying your country."

He shook his head. "I'm saving it. I'm making it strong again. Putting the 'Great' back into it. You need to be tough to be strong. You need law and order. You need an iron grip. You need to put people in their places. And this is what we're about."

"You're about... about murder and... and madness... and blood."

He rose. "You think what you like, darling. It don't matter. Me and Alfie, we'll be kings by the time this is done. Fucking kings. And you — well, you'll either be dead, or you'll be a vampire. But you'll be *nothing*."

"If I'm a vampire, I'll come looking for you."

He waggled a piece of red cloth at her. "Untouchable and

you know it, Christine. Anyway, be nice for you to be undead. You can join your eldest."

Rage went through her, and she screamed.

"And then your youngest can join you – after he kills Lawton."

Dread seeped through Murray's veins, making it impossible for her to move. But then the crying of children snapped her out of her condition.

George Fuad said, "Here we are – some new company for you. You can watch them being fed."

Murray's heart grew heavy. She'd seen men and women hung above the tank over the past few hours and watched Alfred bleed them to death. What could be worse?

She knew what could be worse.

Children.

Then the crying grew louder. She blinked, and her eyes adjusted to the glare. The youngsters came out of the light and into the gloom. There were six of them, all aged under twelve.

They were terrified. "No," said Murray, "no, for the love of God – not children so young. How could you? How could you?"

"Everything's food," said George.

The men shoved the children into the truck and came in after them before shutting the door and making the trailer dark.

For a few seconds, Murray couldn't see, and the only sound she heard was the children crying.

CHAPTER 50.
LOOKING AFTER No.1.

FRASER Lithgow sat on the windowsill of the fifth-floor apartment. He picked boiled sweets out of a paper bag and popped them into his mouth.

Beneath his window lay the Thames. The river was grey and dirty. Office buildings lined the far side of the river. Tower blocks rose into the sky. Traffic shuttled by on the streets below. The pavements were packed with people.

What's going to happen to this place? he thought.

And then he curled his lip:

Do I give a shit? Not if they don't give a shit about me.

He looked out across the city and remembered how three years previously he'd driven through vampire-riddled streets.

The creatures had been attacking people. Lithgow even saw one of the undead swinging on Big Ben's hands.

When he saw that, he'd known London was in trouble.

But it didn't stop him trying to help. Driving past Big Ben that night, he'd bombed it to Leicester Square, where he'd saved Jake Lawton.

Lithgow ploughed through his memory. Had his dad been right? Had Lawton really never appreciated him?

He held the red rag his dad had given him. They were meant to protect you from vampires.

Burrows, Haddad, his dad, and all their friends had them. Aaliyah Sinclair wore the choker stolen from Nadia Radu. Christine Murray was protected by Ed Crane's ring.

Was Lawton protected by a mark? Did he have one of those scraps of red material? Lithgow hadn't seen him much in the past three years. He tried to remember. Fraser's dad said he did.

"So why didn't he ever give you one, Fraser?" his dad had said before handing him a piece of vampire skin.

He shook his head and sucked on another sweet.

His dad gave him a mark. His dad, who'd been a bastard all Fraser's life. But maybe dads and mums were the only ones who really loved you, who truly cared.

They shared something with you. Something more than friendship. They shared blood.

And a heritage that spanned centuries.

He lifted himself off the windowsill and padded into the kitchen.

It was a two-bedroom apartment. High ceilings and black-and-white marble flooring. White walls decorated with abstract paintings.

A leather lounge couch dominated the living room. A 50-inch flat-screen TV hung on the wall. It now played MTV with the volume turned down. Beyoncé was doing her "Single Ladies" routine.

"It's yours," his dad had said, dropping the keys into Fraser's hands.

In the kitchen, Lithgow opened the fridge and considered the selection of booze on offer. The four-pack of Stella looked tempting. There was also some Sol and Heineken, but he chose the bottle of white wine. It looked Italian, but he didn't care. He liked wine. Any wine. His dad could've named it and told you the grape it came from. He would've sniffed it and swooned about the bouquet. But Fraser wasn't like his dad.

He found a glass in the cupboard and went back into the living room and sat on the windowsill again. He poured himself a glass of wine and looked out over London, feeling sad and confused.

His dad had asked him to do something. For doing this task, Fraser would have anything he wanted.

All his life, he craved luxury. Fast cars. Cool apartments. Sexy girls. Tons of money.

For the past three years Lithgow had been further from his desires than he'd ever been. But he'd also been happier than he could remember. It had been a dangerous time, but he felt fulfilled.

Doing the right thing was good for you.

Or so he thought.

Now he was back to thinking that everyone was in it for themselves.

I was bait, wasn't I, Jake, he thought. *I was nothing to you*.

"So fuck you," he said to London now. "Fuck you all."

His dad was going to give him whatever he wanted – just as long as he did one thing for them.

They'd tricked him into distributing Skarlet three years previously. He was angry and scared about that. But maybe that's why he'd helped Lawton. Now he wasn't angry and scared. Now he was pissed off.

"Fuck you all," he said again, thinking about Lawton. "You were in it for yourself, weren't you, Jake. Like everyone else."

Lawton was a soldier. He was looking for a war. Any war. He just wanted to fight. When he got kicked out of the Army for killing that terrorist in Iraq, he went sniffing for another battle.

The vampires gave him one.

"And I was just another foot-soldier in your fucking army," Lithgow said.

I was just fodder.

He hadn't seen Lawton in nearly three years. Maybe that showed how Jake felt about him. After all, Aaliyah was allowed to be with Lawton all this time. But she was a girl. And she was hot.

Everyone for himself, he thought.

He gulped down the wine. It went straight to his head and made him dizzy. It also piped some Dutch courage into his veins. He looked around the flat.

Yeah, he thought, *this will be a nice spot. Start living again, stop running.*

That's all he'd done these past three years – run.

He wanted to go to clubs again. He wanted to get drunk, take drugs, have sex.

I haven't had sex in ages, he thought. *Bet Lawton gets his oats, though – with that Aaliyah.*

He poured himself another glass of wine. He stared across the river. Rain fell. Wind lashed the trees on the Embankment.

A storm was coming.

No one could stop it, so why stand in its way?

Why not benefit from the devastation it would wreak?

His dad had said, "You are with us, or you are not with us, Fraser. You live or you die. You are master or slave."

One thing Lithgow valued above everything else was his own neck. For three years, he had tried altruism. It was clear it didn't work. You had to look after yourself.

Even if that meant doing terrible things.

The phone rang, and Lithgow flinched.

It stood on a marble plinth. It kept ringing.

Lithgow drank some wine. He crossed to the phone and picked up the receiver.

"Uh... hello?"

A woman's voice said, "You are truly your father's son."

CHAPTER 51.
APOSTOL GOGA.

DURKHAM licked his thumb and counted out a thousand pounds in fifty-pound notes onto the table of his motor home, and after doing it he said, "And there's another nine grand to follow." He rubbed his one good eye.

Lawton stared at the money.

Aaliyah said, "No, Jake, don't look."

"It'll help."

"Not if you're dead, it won't."

Durkham said, "I've not had any deaths in my promotions, thank you very much."

Aaliyah glared at the promoter. "Might be one right here, if you don't keep it shut."

"Lawton," said Durkham, "can you keep her on a leash?"

"In your dreams," Aaliyah said.

"Two against one," said Lawton.

"That's right," said Durkham.

Aaliyah said, "Jesus," and walked out of the motor home.

Lawton pondered the money again. It was a lot of cash. Double his biggest purse. But they were pitting him against two men.

"It's a special challenge," Durkham had said when they arrived at the abandoned farm. Inside Durkham's motor home, they'd started to negotiate. Lawton expected the usual tussle. But the promoter had made the offer immediately:

"Ten grand. You against two blokes at the same time."

The door flung open, and Aaliyah came back inside. She said, "Jake, you can't. This is just crazy. It's a trap."

Lawton looked at Durkham, and the one-eyed man held his stare. The promoter was a liar and a scoundrel. But Lawton could read him. In that moment, Jake knew it wasn't a trap. Or if it was, Durkham didn't know about it.

"Who are they?" said Lawton.

"The boss is Romanian, I think."

Aaliyah gripped Lawton's arm. She was tense, and he could feel it, so he eased her hand away.

Durkham grinned, showing his only tooth. "What's up, Lawton? Don't like Romanians?"

"I've only met two. I just didn't like them. But I'm not going to hold that against an entire race, Durkham."

"How politically correct of you. This fella wants to meet."

Lawton nodded.

Durkham said, "I'll go get him."

The promoter walked out of the motor home.

"Jake, this is crazy – let's get out of here," said Aaliyah. "My heart's going like mad. I'm bricking it, babe. This is a trap."

"Where's David?"

"I don't know – around. Jake – "

"Keep an eye on him."

"What? Why? Hang on, I'm not his fucking babysitter."

"I know, just keep an eye."

"Why? You're scaring me. This is a trap."

"It's not a trap. I can tell when Durkham's lying. He's not lying. Keep an eye on David."

"Why do you want me to do that?"

"I don't know… something."

"Jake, you got to – "

The door opened, and Durkham entered the motor home, followed by a tall man wearing an expensive-looking overcoat and a red cravat around his throat. He carried an ivory walking stick that had a gold handle and ferrule.

The man was in his fifties. Grey flecks peppered his brown hair. He wore gold, square-framed glasses. His eyes were green. He smiled and nodded at Lawton and Aaliyah.

Durkham said, "Jake Lawton and Aaliyah Sinclair. Apostol Goga."

Goga offered a hand, and Lawton shook it. The Romanian then offered to shake Aaliyah's hand, but she folded her arms and looked him up and down.

The Romanian spoke. "It is good to meet you, Mr Lawton." His accent was thick, but his English was good. "We have heard much about you on the fighting circuit."

"We?" said Lawton.

"My people. We who follow this sport. We who must travel to places like this to enjoy it. Boxing was illegal once, was it not? Maybe one day we can be legitimate, also."

"Maybe," said Lawton.

"A two-on-one battle is one I enjoy, you see," said Goga. "But my two, they have beaten so many across Europe. No one will take up my challenge any longer."

"It's not really a fair fight."

Goga shrugged. "What is fair in life? It is what people pay to see. And those fighters who step into the ring with my boys, they do so of their own free will. Do you, Mr Lawton?"

"I do, yes."

Goga looked at Aaliyah and smiled, but he got nothing in return. "Do you fight, also, Miss Sinclair?"

"Would you like to find out?" she said.

Goga laughed. "I see what they say about you two are true."

Lawton bristled. "What do they say?"

"And who says it?" said Aaliyah.

Goga flapped his hand, dismissing their questions. "I will go to my fighters and tell them the great Jake Lawton is here. They are – how do you say? – champing at the bit?" He bowed and turned to leave.

"Aren't we talking rules?" said Lawton.

Goga tilted his head. "Rules?"

"We usually have one or two," said Durkham. "No biting. No kicking a downed fighter in the head. No weapons, obviously."

"My fighters will have no weapons," said Goga. "And my fights will have no rules."

CHAPTER 52.
A NEW IMAGE.

The Ritz Hotel, London – 3.56pm, February 14, 2011

"AND what did you make of my son?" said Bernard Lithgow. He poured tea into the china cup and then offered it to Jacqueline Burrows.

She said, "Lacks the social skills of his father. A follower rather than a leader. Malleable. Easily manipulated. Will do anything for a bit of cash and an afternoon in bed with a tart, I'd say."

Bernard Lithgow smiled. He offered Burrows a cucumber sandwich. She declined and sat down on the couch. She wore an Armani suit. She'd straightened her hair and applied more make-up than she usually wore. *A new image,* he thought. She looked very good indeed.

"He mumbled," said Burrows. "I didn't get much of what he thinks about things. What does he believe, Bernard?"

"He believes that Lawton doesn't care about him. That's his faith, now. And I do believe he is a fundamentalist. It was easy to convert him." He touched the scrap of skin that was tucked into his breast pocket in the form of a handkerchief. "My son wasn't given one of these. The question 'Why?' made him doubt Lawton."

Burrows touched the brooch on the lapel of her Chanel suit. Her gesture must have been triggered by seeing Bernard fidget with his mark. These things were so valuable. They would keep the Nebuchadnezzars alive in a world of killers.

"So Fraser deserves your love again?" she said.

"I don't think so. I feel nothing for him, sadly. He has been a disappointment."

"He'll not let us down this time though."

"Jacqueline, he did not truly let us down last time. He distributed Skarlet. He would do anything for money, that boy. It was only when Lawton got involved that my son was diverted from the true path. I've put him on the straight and narrow again."

"You can ask him to join us if you want."

"He's no good. He's fickle, you see. Once he hated Lawton. Then he adored him. Now, one hopes there's hate again. For the time being. But you can never tell with Fraser."

"But you are sure he'll do what he's told."

"I've promised him things. He cannot resist."

Burrows said, "When I spoke to him on the phone, I asked him about the flat, and he clearly adores it."

"Oh yes. Who wouldn't? You know, I believe my son might have had some kind of crush on Lawton. A father-son thing perhaps. I mean, I was not much of a dad. Not the kind he needed, anyway. Maybe Lawton is a stand-in father."

"Not for much longer," said Burrows. "The young assassin you primed will hopefully do his job. Lawton brought bloodshed to my doorstep, Bernard. He challenged me. He challenged us with his 'Vlad the Impaler' show. He won't do that again."

"And what happened to old Mr Wilson?"

"He made a good lunch for the vampires. There was a bit of him left. If Lawton makes it through tonight, we will have a little gift for him."

Bernard said, "And tonight is your night, Jacqueline."

"Our night."

"When do you intend to visit Strand?"

"When the sun goes down. With an army behind me. Blood will flow. Many will die. And we shall reign."

"You know, I am in the most excited state."

She smiled at him. "Are you, Bernard? How convenient."

CHAPTER 53.
ROUND ONE.

"WHERE'S David now?" asked Lawton

"Outside having a fag."

"Having a fag?" He stopped wrapping the bandages around his knuckles. "He's thirteen or something."

"Were you having a smoke when you were thirteen?"

"It's not the point."

"I can't see another one."

"What would his mother say?"

"I don't know, Jake. Are you going through with this?"

He began casing his fists in the dressing again. "Looks like it. What time is it?"

"Time you saw sense."

"Aaliyah."

"It's seven-twenty."

In the distance, a crowd bayed.

"The animals are in," said Aaliyah. "It's packed to the rafters out there."

"Any shit," he said, gesturing at the Remington slung over Aaliyah's shoulder, "start shooting."

"Yeah, I know the plan, man."

"And get out of here, Aaliyah. You and David."

"Oh, babe, not without you. Don't give me any of that macho shit. You're my man, and I ain't going nowhere without you. And anyway, why're you so worried all of a sudden? You said there wasn't a trap."

"You know me. Chilled out."

Lawton sat on the bench running along the wall. They were in a toilet. It had a washbasin and a loo. The smell of piss tainted the air. There were bloodstains on the tiles above the sink and on the wooden floor. A single bulb illuminated the room.

"Two guys, Jake – you're crazy," she said.

He opened and closed his fists. They felt okay. A bit sore from his previous fight. And he was tired too. He could happily lie down on the bench and sleep. But he had to do this. They needed the money – to fund the battle and to...

Yeah, whatever, he thought. *You'll never do that, Jake.*

He finished the thought.

... to escape.

It would be easy for him and Aaliyah to disappear. They could leave the country. No one would find them. Britain could fall. The vampires could have it.

Why should I care?

After all, what did Britain ever do for him?

Durkham poked his head around the door and said, "They're ready for you, Lawton. Can you hear it?"

Lawton tuned in to the crowd.

"They're in good voice tonight," said Durkham.

"Have you got the rest of our money ready?" said Aaliyah.

"Of course, darling," he said.

"I'm not putting up with any bullshit tonight, Durkham," she said.

"I never thought you did," he said.

"I have a twitchy trigger finger."

"Point taken," said Durkham.

"Okay," said Lawton. "Let's go."

He kissed Aaliyah, and they embraced, and she said, "Be careful."

He shadowboxed as Durkham led him down a corridor that was carpeted in hay. He breathed in its fresh odour. The crowd's noise increased. They stamped their feet and chanted.

At the end of the corridor, the door stood open, and Lawton could see into the main ring. The crowd bellowed. The barn shook.

Durkham stood to the side and nodded. Lawton walked through the door and into the ring, kicking up sawdust as he danced his way to the centre.

The crowd roared. They waved their betting slips.

Lawton looked for his opponents, and they stood at the far end of the circle, their eyes fixed on Jake.

The one on the left was black and built like a truck. He stood six-four and weighed around eighteen stone. He had a white-blond mohican haircut and was missing one ear.

The second fighter was lean and stood around five-six. His body glistened with sweat. There was no fat on him. He was packed with muscle. A dragon tattoo covered his shaven head.

Martial arts, thought Lawton when he saw the tattoo. He hated martial arts. All that flashy kicking and spinning.

The referee in his striped shirt called all three fighters to the centre of the ring.

Lawton stared at both his opponents in turn, and they stared right back.

The ref said, "Ready?"

All three fighters nodded.

"Fight," the ref called out.

The crowd screamed.

The black man charged at Lawton.

CHAPTER 54.
COUP D'ÉTAT.

"CHANGED your mind, Jacqueline?" said Graeme Strand. He stood in the doorway of his private quarters at No.10.

"I've come to make a deal," said Burrows.

"Not alone, though." He glanced behind her, to where a man and a woman stood.

Burrows indicated the man. "This is Phil Birch, my authorized protection officer."

Strand nodded. "And the girl?"

"Sassie Rae, my PA."

Strand looked at the girl. She was blonde and wore a T-shirt and jeans. Her skin was pale and eyes dark in the dimly lit corridor.

"She looks ill," he said.

"She's fine," said Burrows.

He moved aside and let them in. Miss Rae looked at him, and her eyes were tinted red. He shuddered, and something writhed in his belly. He felt sick. He felt doomed.

Strand shut the door and stared at Burrows for a moment.

She had rung an hour earlier requesting a meeting with him. The backstabbing bitch had offered to "save his political career". Outraged by her arrogance, Strand almost told her to fuck off. But he was a realist. Burrows had more support than him both in the party and in the country. He understood how important she could be if he wanted to remain Prime Minister.

"Are you alone?" asked Burrows.

He stared at her. "It seems so, Jacqueline."

He led them down the hallway. Family photos hung on the wall. Pictures of Irene and the kids, mostly.

While he was walking, he thought about the PA and why she hadn't got a notebook or a handbag. PAs, spin doctors, and press officers brandished BlackBerrys or iPhones. But this woman had nothing.

At least Birch had his clipboard. The other protection officers called Birch "Phil the Fuss" because of his habits. Carrying the clipboard with him everywhere was ridiculous. And no one knew what that red ribbon flapping at the metal clamp represented.

Strand opened the door that led to his study, and he beckoned them in.

The odour of the cigar he'd enjoyed earlier clung to the air. The red velvet curtain kept the night at bay. A television played Sky News with the volume down. The channel's political reporter was broadcasting live from outside No.10. The reporter's mouth moved, and Strand wondered what was coming out of it. *Shit, probably*, he thought.

Strand grabbed the remote and switched off the television.

He stood near the window and folded his arms. "Right," he said.

Burrows glanced around the room.

Strand bristled. "Checking it out before you move in, Jacqueline? Don't be so sure."

His fury bubbled. Firestarter had betrayed him. The most senior member of his Cabinet to jump from the sinking ship of his Government.

He'd called on their support yesterday. All of them. His spin doctor Luke Spofford had ticked off those they could depend on – His Chancellor and former lover, Liz Wilson, Ralph Allenby, the Foreign Secretary, and Jacqueline Burrows.

He and Spofford had gone through the whole Cabinet, and Burrows had been a definite tick, a certain "yes".

"Nothing of the sort, Prime Minister," said Burrows, returning her gaze to him.

"I'd like Luke to be here if we're discussing a deal," he said.

"There's no need," said Burrows.

Strand narrowed his eyes. The PA stood at the door. Birch lingered near the desk with his arms folded over the clipboard.

"What's going on?" said Strand.

"I want you to resign tonight," said Burrows. "If you issue a press release now, it'll make the first editions of the newspapers, and you'll catch the main news this evening."

Strand gawped.

Burrows continued:

"Announce that you are naming me as your successor."

He found his voice and it came out as a croak.

"Anything wrong, Prime Minister?" said Burrows.

"How dare you come in here with... with such an outrageous demand. How dare you. I've got a good mind to call security and have you kicked out of the front door, so all the world can see. That'll give them a headline. And that'll make the first editions. How dare you."

He shook with rage and had to look away from her because he was so angry.

"Get out, Jacqueline," he said. "You and your fucking lapdogs – before I bring in a real dog." He took his mobile from his trouser pocket and flipped it open, ready to call Spofford.

"Stop that," said Birch.

Strand froze and stared at the policeman. "What did you say, officer?"

"I said, stop that," Birch said.

Strand looked at Burrows and said, "Are you going to let your staff talk to me like that?"

Burrows said nothing. She stared at him with her cold, blue eyes.

Bloody Firestarter, he thought. *I'll...*

And then he said it: "I'll destroy you, Jacqueline."

The PA hissed, her face twisting with rage.

Strand said, "She's not your PA, is she."

Burrows said, "No, I think it's forgotten how to write – and it has very little shorthand."

Cold fear rippled through Strand. He'd never seen one face to face before. The rumours were rife that they were coming back. The police and security services had been on high alert for three years. There was that business in 2008, when hundreds of people had died. But that was a disease. A virus. That's what he and his Government had decided to call it – and he'd learned to accept that explanation. He'd learned to believe it.

Many people refused to accept the authorized account of what had taken place in London during that time. So they spread their beliefs on the internet.

Despite the official explanation, that word appeared in reports and on security documents that arrived on Strand's desk.

A word he preferred to ignore.

The word *Vampire*.

"Sassie," said Burrows, "his blood is yours."

Strand gasped with horror.

The vampire came forward, hissing and showing its fangs.

Strand backed away, horrified. "You… you'll never get away with this, Jacqueline."

"I have done, Graeme," she said.

The vampire snarled and sprang towards him.

The Prime Minister screamed.

CHAPTER 55.
ST VALENTINE'S DAY
MASSACRE.

DOWNING STREET, LONDON – 8.01PM, FEBRUARY 14, 2011

LUKE Spofford heard the scream. He jumped out of his chair and stood, listening.

Spofford, at twenty-nine the youngest editor of a Fleet Street red-top and three years later spin doctor to the British Prime Minister, had been surfing the news channels.

Now at thirty-five years of age, he faced his toughest assignment – saving Graeme Strand's career.

The news that evening had been bad. The headlines were all about Jacqueline "Firestarter" Burrows putting a rocket up the PM's arse.

Spofford couldn't believe it when she refused to back Strand. She'd been odds on to come out in support of the Prime Minister.

There were rumours that she disagreed with the Government's immigration policy. But Spofford was convinced she'd stick with Strand, if only to enhance her own career opportunities. The PM had been planning to quit before the next General Election, and Burrows had been mentioned as a possible replacement.

Her chances would be better if she stayed in the Government.

But that morning, she'd done the unexpected.

Bitch, he thought.

He turned the television's volume down and narrowed his eyes. It had definitely been a scream. Where had it come from? Sounded like the third floor, where the PM had his private quarters.

Spofford was posted on floor two, where during the day the offices would be crammed with advisors and secretaries. Newspapers and box files were piled in the corridor. The smell of coffee and sweat saturated the air. It was a busy place, even at eight in the evening.

Spofford was about to sit down again when another scream made him flinch.

"Fucking hell, what's that?"

He glanced at the television. Strand's jowls dominated the screen. It didn't help that the PM looked like a Bassett hound. The ticker at the bottom of the screen reeled out the bad news. Quotes from Labour MPs, calling Strand a "dead duck Prime Minister", had dominated the day's headlines. A former Labour Prime Minister saying, "Graeme Strand is in dire straits," hadn't been helpful. And the Opposition leader Jayne Monson declaring that "the Prime Minister's allies are stabbing him in the back," had caused Spofford to throw a coffee cup at a television that morning.

The screams intensified, snapping Spofford's attention away from the news channel.

Shouts and cries now seemed to be filling No.10 Downing Street.

Christ, we're under attack, he thought.

A shiver ran through him. He didn't like fear. He never showed it. He was brash and loud and intimidating. But there was no steel in his heart. He was a soft man. A bully spawned by bullies.

At school, they rammed his head down the toilet and pulled down his trousers. His older brother Aaron used him as a punchbag. His dad, an Army officer, always told him to pull himself together after his brother had beaten him up.

His mother mollycoddled him and told him everything was all right, and that had been fine until she walked out when he was eleven years old.

Luke Spofford was scared of everything and to hide that, he had to be strong. And that meant shouting and swearing in people's faces, swaggering down corridors, barking into his BlackBerry at MPs and journalists.

He didn't feel much like barking now. What he really wanted to do was hide in the cupboard till the screaming stopped.

Instead, he went to the door. His throat was dry with fear. He leaned forward to listen.

Feet trampled along the corridor. More shouts filled the wing. Screams seemed to be coming from all over the building.

He opened the door and peered out into the corridor.

A secretary he recognized bolted past the door and made Spofford jump.

And then a white flash shot past the door. Spofford felt cold air coming off the figure. There was a growl, and the secretary cried out, and when Spofford looked out of the door and down the corridor, he froze.

Someone had pinned the secretary to the floor and had his face buried in the woman's neck.

She was shouting, "He's biting me, he's biting me!"

Spofford slammed the door shut. The blood rinsed from his face, and he felt dizzy. His gaze skipped around the room, searching for a way out.

The window.

There was a stampede in the corridor. The screams were everywhere. Something rammed against the door. Spofford flinched and staggered into the room, and his gaze happened to rest on the TV screen.

Sky News reported a disturbance at Downing Street. Police ushered journalists away from No.10. A hand covered the camera's lens, and a voice said, "Get out of here now, or we'll arrest you," and the reporter responded with, "Don't touch that camera."

Spofford ran to the window. He whipped open the curtain. The rose garden lay in darkness two floor below. He unlatched the window and swung it open. He leaped out and landed awkwardly, his ankle bending. He screeched in agony.

Spofford moaned and got to his feet. Sweat coated his body. The pain in his leg was terrible. He could barely put any weight on it.

I've broken it, he thought, *I've fucking broken it.*

He hobbled down the garden towards the trees that lined the high security wall. There was a gate behind those evergreens. It was for emergency situations – emergency situations, just like this one.

Screams burst out of the building behind him. He didn't turn round to look.

He made it to the trees. They rustled in the wind, moving around him and brushing against him. It was pitch black, and he whined, the pain in his ankle and the fear in his chest preventing him from concentrating on his escape.

Something brushed against his leg. He froze, goosepimples racing down his back.

He hobbled on towards the back wall, moaning. The darkness was deep. The trees swayed and rustled. Anyone would think there were people running around in here. But it was only the wind.

From the corner of his eye, he saw a dark shape. He stopped and turned.

"Who's there?"

But no one said anything.

Someone hissed, though.

Someone or something.

"Oh my God," said Spofford.

Two eyes glinted in the darkness. Red eyes. Animal eyes.

Spofford's legs buckled.

And then two more eyes appeared before him, and a snarl came from whatever animal looked through them.

Spofford screamed. He bolted for the wall. His ankle gave way and he fell, shrieking in pain.

And they were on him, their teeth cold at his throat.

CHAPTER 56.
TO THE VICTOR.

LAWTON was sprawled on the bench in the toilet. Blood came from his nose and his mouth. His ribs were bruised, and his eyes were swollen.

Aaliyah cried while she unwrapped the bandages from his knuckles.

"What's the matter, babe?" he said, barely able to speak.

"You shit," she said.

"I know."

"How could you put me through this?"

"I don't know. I'm a sod."

She looked into his eyes and said, "You like to see me upset?"

He shook his head and pain shot through his neck. "You're so beautiful."

"You're babbling."

"I'm not. Honestly. Beautiful. Beautiful."

She stuffed the bloody bandages into a plastic bag and sealed it. She stowed it in the rucksack.

"Aaliyah… "

"What?" She swabbed a cut on his shoulder. It was a bite mark. "Christ, you should've said no to teeth. They could have AIDS, you know. I have to sleep with you."

"You don't get AIDS by sharing a bed."

"You do by doing what we do, babe."

He smiled, which made his face hurt. Blood dribbled from his mouth.

"But Aaliyah," he said.

"What?"

"You and me, we should... let's just – "

The door swung open and Apostol Goga entered the room, scowling.

Jake stiffened. Aaliyah sprang to her feet and faced the Romanian. But then he smiled and held up his walking stick and said, "Please, I have come to congratulate you, Mr Lawton."

"Oh, cheers, mate."

"My boys, they say they have never met such a mean, determined, never-say-die attitude. They're proud to have lost to you."

"Tell them thanks."

"What do you want?" said Aaliyah.

"I want to speak to Mr Lawton. To the both of you."

"Go on then, speak," said Aaliyah.

"You are – what's the English word?"

"Bitch?" said Aaliyah.

Goga laughed. "No, certainly not. No... feisty, I think."

Aaliyah said, "I prefer bitch."

Lawton said, "I'm fucked, Goga. You know I never sleep? I want to but I can't. And at times like this, I could really do with being out for the count. Can we do this another time?"

Goga's eyes narrowed. He looked from Lawton to Aaliyah. "This is very important," he said.

"Not interested."

"I think you would be if – "

Aaliyah stepped towards Goga and said, "I don't charge for English lessons if you'd like some, mate. Understand? 'Not interested' in English means 'fuck off', all right?"

Goga stared at her.

"Another time, Goga," said Lawton.

He guessed the Romanian was going to offer him a fight deal. It might be something Lawton would consider if it got him out of Britain. But he wasn't going to talk about it with Aaliyah in the room. She would be against him fighting any more than he had to. And he could never leave without her. So he'd have to turn down Goga's offer – if that's what he wanted to discuss.

He was about to say something when Goga spoke:

"I will leave you for now. But Mr Lawton, Miss Sinclair, what I have to say is very important, and I – "

The door opened. Durkham peered into the toilet. "All friends, are we?" he said. "There's rumours of some police activity in the area, lady and gents, so if you want to come to talk money, come with me to my boudoir."

Goga looked at Lawton. "Mr Lawton, I urge – "

"Now, Mr Goga," said Durkham. "I can sniff pig poo close by."

Goga left the room, and Lawton told Aaliyah to go and collect the rest of their money. "And shoot Durkham if he fucks about," he called out as she left the room.

After they'd gone, Lawton closed his eyes. He didn't know how long they'd been shut, but they snapped open when he felt the cold steel of a knife press into his throat.

CHAPTER 57.
THE KNIFE.

The A2, ten miles out of Dover – 8.40pm, February 14, 2011

GEORGE Fuad put his feet up on the truck's dashboard and said, "Nice to be back in England, ain't it, Alfie."

Alfred, driving the DAF heavy-goods vehicle, said, "Green and pleasant fucking land, brother."

"Soon will be. Green with a hint of red, eh?"

"Yeah, and plenty of rain, looks like."

On the opposite side of the road, traffic was heavy heading east towards Dover.

George said, "Few people leaving the country tonight."

"Let's hope they're all foreign, I say."

George's phone vibrated in the pocket of his jeans. He took it out and answered it.

The voice on the other end of the line said, "You might want to turn on the radio if you're still on the road."

"Hello, Bernie, my old mucker," said George.

"Christ, you're common, George," said Bernard Lithgow. "How we are descended from the same bloodline, I shall never know."

"Yeah, we're like brothers, ain't we. Radio, you say. What's going on?"

"Listen to the news. Where are you?"

George told him.

"We'll see you in a couple of hours, George."

Bernard Lithgow hung up. George turned on the radio and tuned it to Five Live.

The presenter was saying, "...and we are being told that a group of criminals somehow smashed their way into No.10 Downing Street and started to attack the staff and residents. The Prime Minister, we understand, faced up to the invaders, but he suffered a heart attack."

"Hey, we're in," said George.

"Jackie's done her magic," said Alfred.

The presenter said, "We now have a statement from the interim Prime Minister, Jacqueline Burrows."

"Here's our Jackie," said George.

Burrows began:

"A few hours ago, a group of men broke into No.10 Downing Street and attacked the Prime Minister and his staff. This is a major security breach, unprecedented in the history of Britain. It is clear that those involved had inside information. It's a very sad day for me, for all of us, to report that our friend, Graeme Strand, the Prime Minister, died. We have also lost the Government's communications director, Luke Spofford, and... "

She reeled off a few more names, but George's mind had wandered. His excitement grew. They were in Downing Street. Burrows was their knife, cutting a path to the door of power. Nothing could stop them now.

He listened to Burrows again:

"Also," said the Firestarter, "I am sad to report that a senior member of the Government has been arrested in connection with this security breach, but I am not going to name anyone here – that's not my job. However, I can reveal the names of individuals the police wish to speak to in connection with this tragedy. One is Jake Lawton, a known criminal who has been hunted by the authorities over the past three years, and his accomplice, Aaliyah Sinclair. Photos will be distributed, but anyone who sees either of these people should contact the authorities immediately. We believe they have information linked to this evening's terrible atrocity."

"The end is fucking nigh for you, Lawton," said George.

"He was a good doorman, you know," said Alfred.

"So they say. Tough as nails, according to the fellas down at Religion. Shame he was such a pain in the arse."

"Yeah, shame."

On the radio, Burrows continued:

"As interim Prime Minister, I shall have to make difficult decisions, and tonight I make one of the hardest. I have ordered British borders to be closed until further notice. We have suffered greatly in recent months from increased immigration to these shores. The result has been violence, with many of the refugees falling victim. My belief is that in order to investigate these crimes and prevent further attacks, we should stem the tide of migrants entering the UK. There is also good evidence pointing to a link between foreign gangs and tonight's attack on Downing Street."

George said, "Britain closed until further notice."

"Until forever."

George switched off the radio, and the brothers were quiet for while.

And then George said, "Do you think we're going far enough?"

"How do you mean, brother?"

"Haddad. Burrows. All of them. Are they going far enough? We're rebuilding the old empire here in Britain, with London as her golden city. But don't you think we should be looking further afield?"

"I'm always thinking we should look further afield, George."

"That's what I reckoned you'd say, brother."

"Absolutely. After all, why settle for this little island when we can own an entire continent – or the entire fucking world."

* * * *

"Go on, David," said Lawton, "push the blade into my throat. You'll sever my jugular. I'll be dead in minutes. Job done. Go on, kid."

Tears rolled down David's face. He was shaking, and his hand perspired around the knife's ivory handle.

The point of the blade pressed into Lawton's neck, and like he'd said, all David had to do was push.

Push.

"Have I done something bad to you?" said Lawton.

David sobbed.

"Is it about your mum? You think I've – "

"It's not about Mum."

David looked into Lawton's steel-grey eyes. They hadn't blinked yet. They stared right at him, and he could see his reflection in them.

He could see himself.

"You know I could take the knife off you if I wanted to," said Lawton. "But I'm giving you a chance – do what you have to do, or don't do it. Your call, kid."

"I don't... I don't want... "

"Tell me why I deserve to die."

"You don't, Jake. You don't deserve to die."

"Okay."

"It's just you've got to, that's all."

"I've got to die. Is it like a prophecy or something?"

After David told him, Lawton said, "And you believed him, did you? You believed Fraser's dad."

"I... I don't know... he said... "

"He's taken advantage of you, David. Michael's a vampire. You can't turn them back into humans."

"I've seen *The Lost Boys*. You kill the head vampire."

"I killed one of them already. Big ugly red thing. It was going to drink your blood. Remember?"

"Yeah, I remember."

"That didn't stop people being vampires. It didn't stop Sassie being a vampire. It's a plague, David. A disease. And the only way to get better is to die."

"No... "

"You want to die?"

He stared at Jake. "N-no... "

"Well, you got to get better at killing people, then. You've been standing there with that knife at my throat, and you haven't seen what's behind you, have you?"

David felt something cold and sharp against the back of his neck and a foreign voice saying, "Shall I kill him for you, Mr Lawton, the little traitor?"

Lawton grabbed David's wrist and eased the knife away from his throat.

He said, "You can keep it, kid – it's a nice blade."

"Shall I kill him?" asked the foreign man.

Lawton said, "No, Goga. Let him be."

David fell in a heap on the floor and started to cry.

"Get up, you little bastard," he heard Aaliyah say, and he looked up to see her tower over him. "Come on, you backstabbing little – "

"Aaliyah, leave him," said Lawton. "David, sit up. Sit up. I understand what happened, and it's okay."

David crawled to the corner near the toilet bowl. It smelled of shit, but he didn't care. He deserved to suffer. Lawton winked at him, and his kindness made David feel worse. He'd been a fool to believe Mr Lithgow. He'd been deceived. He rested his head on his arms and cried while the grown-ups talked.

"Get your money?" Lawton asked Goga.

"Thank you, yes."

Aaliyah said, "We should leave this little bastard here in the middle of nowhere."

She was talking about him again, and he didn't want to look up and see her angry face.

"Did Durkham pay up okay?" said Lawton.

"He did," said Aaliyah. "No bother."

"Now, since I did you a favour," said Goga, "by preventing this young fellow from murdering you – "

"He wasn't going to murder me."

"He had a knife to your throat, Lawton."

"Yeah, but no will behind it."

"Fine, you are not grateful. But I insist that you listen to me."

"Goga," said Lawton, "I am not going to fight for you, okay?"

"Fight for me?"

"Fight for him?" said Aaliyah.

"Yes," Lawton said. "Isn't that what you were going to say? You were going to ask me to fight."

Goga shook his head. "Not fight for me, Lawton – fight with me, perhaps."

"With you?"

"We are soldiers in the same war, Lawton."

Aaliyah said, "What the fuck do you mean?"

"We are all of us here enemies of the Nebuchadnezzar bloodline. Let me tell you how I have been fighting them all my life. Let me tell you how to stop them."

CHAPTER 58.
HISTORY LESSON.

LAWTON said, "Are you police?"

Goga shook his head. "Until two years ago, I was a member of GSPI, the Romanian counter-terrorist and interior protection organization."

"Special services."

"Yes. A soldier like you, Mr Lawton."

"But now?"

Goga said, "I am on a private mission."

"Doing what?"

"Saving the world."

"Good for you."

Goga sat down on the bench opposite Lawton.

"We should get going," said Aaliyah. "And decide what we're going to do with him," she added, pointing at David.

Goga raised his hand. "Please don't worry. My men are out there, keeping watch on things. They will warn us if we have visitors."

Aaliyah said, "Durkham said the cops were hanging around."

"A few minutes are all I ask of you," said Goga.

"You've got two," said Lawton. "I'm in a bad way, and I want to get out of here – but I'm all ears for 120 seconds."

Goga nodded. "I begin by telling you who I am."

"We know," said Lawton.

"No you don't. You don't know."

Lawton's nerves tightened. "Okay, off you go."

Goga sat up straight. "I am a descendent of Vlad Tepes."

"Vlad who?" said Lawton.

"Dracula," said David.

"I didn't think he was real," said Aaliyah.

"Dracula was not real," said Goga. "He was created by Bram Stoker, the Irish author. But Stoker based the character on my ancestor."

"Wore a big black cape and had sharp teeth, did he?" said Lawton.

"He impaled his enemies on stakes," said David. "That's what 'Tepes' means — 'impaler'. He was Vlad III or Vlad Dracula."

Goga scowled. "Perhaps you would like to tell the story, little traitor?"

David looked nervous. The boy cowered in the corner. Tears streaked his cheek. His eyes moved from Goga, to Aaliyah, and finally to Lawton.

"Go on, kid," said Jake.

David said, "Vlad Tepes wasn't killing Ottoman Turks."

Goga looked surprised.

David went on:

"He was killing vampires."

"We've got our own little Mastermind here," said Lawton.

Aaliyah said, "Is that true?"

Goga said, "It is true. My ancestor was a vampire killer. History has misjudged him." He looked at David. "How do you know, boy?"

David paused. His Adam's apple bobbed, and sweat glazed his forehead.

Aaliyah said, "Go on, David, tell us."

"My mum told me. She studied Haddad and the Fuad family carefully, studied all the Nebuchadnezzars." He looked at Goga, and for the Romanian's benefit he said, "She was a journalist."

Goga nodded.

David went on:

"The Nebuchadnezzars, they tried to resurrect Kea, Kakash, and Kasdeja in Transylvania in the 15th century. Vlad led his armies against them. He killed thousands of vampires. Impaled them on stakes and left them alive till the dawn came, and then they died."

Aaliyah looked at Lawton. "Sounds familiar."

"That was you, was it?" Goga said to Lawton. "You left those ten-foot poles in the middle of London."

Lawton raised his eyebrows.

Goga said, "The boy here is right."

"Okay," said Lawton, "the history lesson's very interesting, but why do we need to know?"

Goga said, "Tepes had the spear that you have in your possession, Mr Lawton – but he was killed for it. However, he prevented the resurrection. The vessels containing the ashes of the trinity were returned to the East. I believe they were recovered by a friend of yours, Mr Tom Wilson, while he was soldiering in Mesopotamia in 1920."

Lawton nodded.

Goga went on:

"And the skins of the trinity, which you are displaying here, which I have, also –" he fingered the cravat around his neck "– they were salvaged by a monk called Simeon, who was a Nebuchadnezzar. He left Holy Orders and sired children. His descendents stored those pieces of flesh. His descendents, Mr Lawton, were the Friniucs. You killed the last of them: Nadia and Ion."

Ion, the scarred warrior Lawton had killed in his flat in New Cross. Nadia, his witch sister Lawton destroyed only a few days earlier, in Ramsgate.

"So," he said, "you're going to help us kill vampires, then?"

Goga narrowed his eyes. "A war is coming, Mr Lawton. What you faced three years ago will be nothing compared to what they will unleash. Three thousand years of hate will fall on Britain."

"They tried it before and failed," said Lawton.

"But they will succeed."

"I feel you've got an 'unless' up your sleeve, Goga."

Goga smiled, but then his grin disappeared and he looked Lawton in the face.

He said, "Unless you abandon Britain and her people to fate and come with me. The battle here is lost, Mr Lawton. But we can still win the war."

CHAPTER 59.
A FOREST OF STAKES.

THE priest scurried down the stone steps into the pit. His heart raced, and dread mounted in his chest.

Everything was going wrong.

The battle is lost, he thought, *the battle is lost.*

The drip-drip of water was the only sound apart from his footsteps as he made his way deep into the bowels of the church. They'd be here soon. He'd seen them on the horizon. They were a cloud of dust sweeping towards the village. And the thunderous sound of their horses galloping across the plain could be heard from miles away. The smell of the fire they brought with them carried on the wind, and the odour triggered a vision in the priest's mind.

He moaned at the awful sights. He tried to push the images away, but they had stained his memory.

He went deeper. The staircase spiralled. Damp and decay saturated the air. He panted for breath. Torches burned to show him the way. Shadows danced against the stone walls as the stairs sucked him down.

The stairs ended, and an open door stood before him. He looked into the room beyond. A flame flickered. The priest shuddered, fear making his bones cold.

"Simeon," he said. "Are you there?"

A rat scuttled across the stone floor.

"Simeon," he said again.

"Father," came a voice from the gloom.

"Where are you?"

"Here."

A figure stepped from the darkness. It looked like a ghost – like one of the undead. The priest flinched and clutched his rosary.

"Why are you skulking in there, Simeon?"

"I am readying the ritual."

The priest stepped into the room, and it was colder in there.

"I prepared everything," said Simeon.

Three empty coffins filled with earth lay on the ground. Resting in the coffins were three clay vessels.

"Seal them," the priest told Simeon.

Simeon said, "But... but are we not preparing the ritual? We have – "

The priest ignored Simeon and asked, "Where are the marks?"

Simeon pointed to a trunk. It lay open. Piled into it were scraps of red material. There were hundreds of pieces of different sizes. Some were large enough to be worn as a cloak, while others were small and might be set into a ring.

"Father," said Simeon, "why do we delay?"

"He's coming."

"Father?"

"He's coming."

Simeon stared at the priest.

"Hurry, Simeon. Seal them. We have to protect the ashes. They must leave this place. They must find another home. And the marks, too. Shut the chest. Do you have a lock for it?"

Simeon put his hands together as if in prayer. "But, Father, we're so close. Everything is prepared."

The priest bristled. Panic mounted in his chest. "I know, Simeon. But the battle is lost. We will regroup. The war is still ours to win. But not tonight."

The priest's heart filled with anguish. For weeks, he'd been convinced the ancient prophecies were going to be fulfilled – and he was going to fulfil them.

His family had told the story for centuries.

Three hundred years ago, his forebears had followed Richard the Lionheart out of the Holy Land.

From a house in Acre, the English king had stolen the artefacts that were here in the pit tonight.

The Lionheart had planned to destroy them. The ashes would be thrown into the sea and the scarlet rags burned.

It would be the end.

But the priest's ancestors had caught up with Richard's knights in nearby Wallachia, just across the border. There had been a battle in a forest, and the knights were defeated. The artefacts were salvaged. All but one.

A single knight survived the battle, and he managed to escape. He took the treasure with him. For centuries it remained missing.

But now it was here. The priest had seen it brandished by the Wallachian *voivode*, Vlad III, son of Vlad Dracul.

It was the Spear of Abraham.

This two-horned weapon was the only thing that could kill the trinity the priest worshipped. The *true* trinity. Not the false one symbolized by the cross he wore, but the authentic one denoted by the cord that looped the cross around his neck.

The cord was made from the skin of his gods. It was of the same material as the rags in the trunk.

Simeon said, "We can do this, Father – we empty the vessels into the coffins and make sacrifice. Look, we have them."

Simeon pointed to a cell in the wall. Crammed in behind the rusting, iron bars were a dozen figures.

They were children taken from nearby villages.

The youngsters cried and prayed. But they wouldn't get salvation. They were going to be sacrificed to the Lords of Babylon, the vampire trinity destroyed by Alexander the Great.

And resurrected by me, thought the priest.

But it wasn't to be. He moaned and ran a hand through his grey hair.

"We have no time, Simeon," he said. "The *voivode* and his army will be here in no time. He'll destroy this church. He knows where we are hiding. He will find these treasures and destroy them. We must accept defeat and move on. Hurry."

Simeon obeyed, but he mumbled as he sealed the three jars. The priest looked at the children. He went over to the cell. Their small faces were pressed against the bars.

A child spoke:

"Please, Holy Father... "

The priest made the sign of the cross before spitting on the ground.

"What have we done, Father?" said another child.

"You've cursed God," he told them.

The children moaned and cried and were saying, "Forgive us, forgive us."

"You are forgiven. Are you done, Simeon?"

"Yes."

It was time to leave.

He watched as Simeon locked the door to the pit, leaving the children behind in the dark. As he scaled the stairs, the priest let the youngsters fade from his mind. They would be dead soon – from starvation or thirst, or madness would drive them to kill each other.

The priest carried the three jars. They had been wrapped in a sack. He clutched them to his breast. He looked over his shoulder. Simeon hauled the trunk up the stairs.

It took them a while to climb all the way back up to the church, mainly because Simeon had to stop a few times.

But they finally made it and entered the confessional through the secret door, before stepping out in the church.

The priest froze. Flames danced in the windows. The roar of an approaching army grew louder.

He handed Simeon the sack.

"There's a horse and cart in the stable," said the priest. "Take them and go, Simeon. Make sure the vessels and the skins are safe. Find allies. There is a prince in the Ottoman army. His name is Mehmed. But he is not a Mussulman, he is our brother. He wears a red mark on his turban. Go to him, and he will help you. But only him. The wars of men are not our wars, Simeon."

Grief cut the priest's heart in two. He had been so close. He so believed that he would be the first one in more than a thousand years to kneel at the living feet of Kea, Kakash, and Kasdeja.

But fate had not chosen him. Maybe it was Simeon's destiny.

"Take them, my son," he said to the younger man.

"Come with me, Father," said Simeon.

"I can't. I must stay with the church. It would not do, a priest running away."

"You are not a priest, Father – you are a Nebuchadnezzar, as I am. Your duty is with these artefacts."

The priest shook his head. "If I stay, you will be safe. If I come with you, they will hunt us down, Simeon. If he finds me here, in the church, the Dracula will think I am a genuine priest. He will spare me. I cannot run. I am protecting you, my son. What else can a father do?"

The priest embraced his child, his secret son. Simeon's mother had been a whore. The priest had been fucking her for months, trying to make her pregnant. When she conceived, the villagers thought the father was a client. The priest had done the Christian thing and taken her into the church for protection. After she gave birth to Simeon, the priest killed her. He had his son. He had the next generation of Nebuchadnezzars.

Now the priest said, "When you find the prince, send me a message. I will come to you, Simeon, and we will fulfil our destiny. Now go."

The priest watched him leave through the rear door that led to the stables. The noise outside was tremendous. Vlad's army was getting closer. He walked to the pulpit, where he opened the Bible and read from the Psalms for while.

And then he went up to the bell tower.

He stood on the creaking wooden planks and stared out over the village. Fire tore through the buildings. The locals had set their homes alight and fled. They would rather burn their possessions than see them taken by someone else.

He gazed into the distance, and what he saw nearly made him faint. He'd seen it before in Wallachia.

"No," he said, "no, no... "

217

Silhouetted against the fire-stained skyline was a forest of stakes, and pinned to each stake was a writhing figure.

Their screams washed across the land towards the priest. He clamped his hands over his ears.

A group of men grappled with someone. They lifted the figure over their heads and rammed him down on a stake. The sharpened end pierced the victim's back and jutted from his belly. The men stood the stake up and placed its base in a hole in the ground.

"No," said the priest, "no... "

All those who'd been staked would be left all night. They would scream, but they wouldn't die. They couldn't die in that way. Not unless you stabbed them through the heart. And Vlad Dracula's cruel soldiers knew that. So they drove the stakes through the bellies instead.

The victims would be alive all night.

And then dawn would break, and the sun would kill them.

"My poor vampires," said the priest, "my poor, poor vampires. Children of my trinity. Children of my lords. My poor vampires."

CHAPTER 60.
BRITAIN IS LOST.

THE M1 – 10.06PM, FEBRUARY 14, 2011

"DEAD?" said Lawton.

"Dead," said Aaliyah.

"And Burrows has taken over?"

"That's what it says."

"Shit."

"What are we going to do?" she asked.

Lawton thought about things. His eyes were fixed on the road ahead. He gripped the steering wheel tightly, his knuckles going white.

Aaliyah said, "Goga said forget about Britain."

Lawton said nothing.

She continued:

"He didn't know this had happened, though. He didn't know they were in charge. What are we going to do?"

He glanced in the rearview mirror. David slept in the back seat. Aaliyah had wanted to abandon the boy at the farmhouse.

But Lawton had forgiven him. It wasn't David's fault that he'd been tricked into trying to murder Jake. The kid was desperate. His family had been torn apart. The Nebuchadnezzars promised him everything would be all right if only he did what they asked.

"But what are we going to do with him?" Aaliyah had said.

Lawton didn't know.

Now he said, "What else does it say?"

Aaliyah studied the laptop. She'd switched the computer on soon after they left the farmhouse, and news of Burrows's takeover was everywhere. Twitter chirped wildly with rumours about what had happened. The Facebook accounts that Aaliyah followed buzzed.

"They're calling it the St Valentine's Day Massacre," she said.

"Bet it was."

"Official line is 'suspected foreign criminals'."

"Christ, that's a big bucket of shit."

"She's named us as suspects."

Lawton bristled.

Aaliyah said, "And she's closed the borders."

"How can she do that?"

"I don't know. I suppose if she's Prime Minister, she can do anything she likes."

"But you can't close the borders."

Aaliyah studied the laptop. "Says here that the police and Army are co-operating."

"That's crap. I don't believe that. She's got her people in positions of power. She's got Nebuchadnezzars everywhere."

"Jake, what do we do?"

"Switch that thing off. The glare's giving me a headache."

Aaliyah shut the laptop.

She said, "Goga says we should leave."

"I know."

"The war can't be won."

"I know."

The last thing Goga had said before driving away from the farmhouse was, "Britain is lost, Jake."

Lawton furrowed his brow. The Romanian's words came to him:

"The source of the vampire plague is not here. It is not in those old jars so valued by Afdal Haddad and the Nebuchadnezzars. The source is in Iraq, Mr Lawton."

"Iraq?" Jake had said.

"Mesopotamia. Where Mr Tom Wilson found the ashes and the Spear of Abraham."

"Hillah."

"That's right," Goga had said. "Hillah. Ancient Babylon."

"What's there that can stop this?"

CHAPTER 61.
THE BIRTH OF THREE.

THE Great Hunter fumed.

He stormed through the caverns deep beneath the tower he'd built. When he moved, it was like a wind sweeping through the darkness. General Nanshe had to lean against a pillar to stop himself from being thrown off his feet by the force of the wind.

The storm relented, and there was silence.

Nanshe shivered and tried to see into the darkness.

A voice boomed:

"My prophets said a child would be born who will wrench away my power. The one with wounds, they said. Who is as strong as I am. Three years ago, I sent you to kill him, General Nanshe."

"Yes, my lord," said Nanshe.

"I sent you out to kill the newborn children of Ur."

"And we did as you ordered, my lord."

"You slaughtered thousands. You killed them all. You killed them even in the womb. You killed all the children under the age of ten, Nanshe."

"To... to ensure your command was observed, my lord. To kill the chosen one."

The Great Hunter said, "But they didn't all die, general."

Nanshe said nothing.

"A pregnant woman fled," said the Great Hunter. "Her child was born in the desert. With wolves, they say. Born with wolves, Nanshe."

The pillars trembled.

"How should I deal with failure such as yours, General Nanshe? How should I punish it?"

The general stayed quiet. He was too scared to speak. His predecessor, Uttu, had died down here in the catacombs.

Hissing came from the shadows, and Nanshe winced. He looked around, and they floated out of the gloom...

The one hundred brides.

As pale as death, they bared their fangs.

"My lord, I... "

"Quiet, Nanshe."

The general turned towards the voice. A shape appeared from between the pillars. Nanshe gasped at the size of the figure looming out of the darkness. He craned his neck so he could look up into his master's face.

Steam billowed from the Great Hunter's nostrils. His blood-red eyes blazed, and the scarlet skin glistened with sweat. Two large horns jutted from the giant's forehead.

Nanshe quaked.

The Great Hunter spoke:

"If heaven has made a child, then I will make a child. I will make three, General Nanshe. A trinity of my own. Three immortals that no man can destroy. Only my bones shall kill them, and who will ever have my bones?"

The catacombs rumbled. Rubble showered from the ceiling, high above. The floor moved under the general's feet, and he lost his balance.

Surrounding Nanshe, the one hundred brides swayed and snarled. They were hungry for blood. If the Great Hunter told his witch-wives to attack, the general would be devoured.

The dark god stepped forward.

The sight of this monster brought alarm to the general's heart. Nanshe was a warrior who had faced many enemies and often triumphed when the odds were against him.

But only now did he know what fear was.

The Great Hunter towered above him. He glared at Nanshe and showed his fangs. Blood dripped from them. The blood of a girl brought here to be another bride. Nanshe looked quickly towards the witch-wives. He wanted to know where they were and to make sure they didn't get too close.

The Great Hunter clawed at his own chest. The odour of blood filled the cavern. Nanshe had smelled it often on the battlefield.

The monster roared. Breath plumed from his nostrils. Saliva oozed from his jaws.

The catacomb shook. Nanshe feared the whole tower would collapse. He would be trapped here in Irkalla, the land of the dead. He would never see his wife or children again.

For a moment, he thought about running.

But then something happened that froze his blood and made it impossible for him to move.

The Great Hunter tore open his own chest.

Blood exploded from the wound and sprayed the pillars and the ground. And when it splashed over the stone, the liquid sizzled, and smoke rose from it. It ate into the earth and melted the paint on the columns.

Nanshe stepped back.

With both hands, the Great Hunter dug into the wound and opened up his body, as if he were opening a gown.

Three hearts pulsed in the cavity. Each was the size of a man's head, and they were reddish-black in colour.

"My children," said the dark god.

He ripped out one of the hearts and his cry of pain shocked the general.

The monster tossed the organ on the ground. Steam rose from the pulsing appendage.

The second heart hit the ground before Nanshe could blink, and as he lifted his gaze to the self-mutilated creature, the third heart was flung in his direction.

The general gawped at the throbbing hearts.

The Great Hunter dropped to his knees and the impact made the ground shake. His chest gaped. The general looked inside the god's torso and he saw the same design in there as he'd seen inside the broken bodies of men.

The dark god panted. Blood poured from the wound.

"I... I will hide, now, and take time to heal. Watch my children, general. They will be your sword and your shield. With my children, you will be unconquerable. Clear a path for them, Nanshe, and they will be your allies for all time."

The Great Hunter crawled away. His witch-wives faded into the darkness.

The general looked at the hearts again.

He gasped and clutched his own breast.

"What is this?" he said.

The three hearts had grown. They were changing shape, each one different. Limbs sprouted from the organs.

Arms and legs, thought Nanshe.

They are becoming alive.

They continued to grow. Their limbs stretched. Heads developed. And tails, too. And one of them even had wings.

CHAPTER 62.
STAY OR GO?

THEY passed the London Gateway Service area, where six police cars surrounded a vehicle. Blue flashing lights illuminated the night. The coppers dragged someone out of the car.

Is this where they turn Britain into a police state? thought Lawton.

"Perhaps we should leave with Goga," said Aaliyah.

"If the borders are shut, I don't know how he plans to get out."

"He looks rich. I'd say he's got his own plane or boat."

"It still doesn't mean he'll get out."

"He looks like a man who'll get out if he wants to get out."

"Like the look of him, do you?"

"Yeah, he's just my type."

Lawton smiled to himself. "Maybe we should go," he said. "If we can end this, Britain just might have to cope without us for – "

"No, we should stay."

Lawton looked in the rear-view mirror, and Aaliyah turned round in her seat.

David had woken up.

Aaliyah said, "I don't think you have a vote."

The boy's eyes glittered with tears.

Lawton pulled the car into a lay-by and stopped the engine.

Aaliyah said, "What're you doing, Jake?"

"I want to know why David thinks we should stay." He turned and looked at the boy, and the youngster bowed his head. Lawton said, "Speak to me. Why should we stay?"

David looked up again. "I'm sorry I did what I did – "

"You should be," said Aaliyah.

"But... but I've lost my family and... and they said I could bring them back if I... if I killed you, Jake. They lied, but I didn't know that."

"They're the bad guys," said Aaliyah. "Lying is one of the things bad guys do to get their own way."

"Yeah," said David, "but you would've done the same thing."

"Would I?" said Aaliyah.

"I think so," said the boy.

"You still haven't said why we should stay," said Lawton.

"Because of my mum."

Lawton's stomach wrenched. Murray was still missing. She'd slipped his mind over the past few hours. But the guilt welled up again now that David had mentioned her.

And Fraser, too, thought Lawton.

"Christ," he said.

"What?" said Aaliyah.

"We can't leave them, can we?"

"Leave who?" said Aaliyah.

"Fraser and Christine."

Aaliyah looked at him. Her eyes were wide. She was confused, and he was too.

He was convinced that Lithgow and Murray had been taken by the Nebuchadnezzars. But he'd also been told by Goga that they could win this war against the vampires by killing one creature.

But would that death save his friends?

Goga's words came back to him...

* * * *

227

The Romanian said, "Three years ago when the vampires came to London, I was in Mesopotamia."

He leaned against his Mercedes-Benz M-Class 4x4. The tattooed fighter sat in the driver's seat, and the mohican fighter was in the back.

Lawton looked across to the Fiat. Aaliyah sat on the bonnet. David slept in the back seat. They had left the farmhouse and driven down a track on the Cranfield Road, where they came to a clearing. It was here they had started to listen to Goga's story.

Lawton rolled a cigarette before lighting it with a match. It was his first since the fight, and it tasted good.

Goga continued:

"I was there officially with GSPI."

"But unofficially?" said Lawton

Goga pulled the cravat from around his neck. He bunched it up in his hand. It was made from the skin of the vampire trinity and matched the rag Lawton wore around his throat.

Goga said, "This is the skin of the fathers, and their children fear it. Like your spear, Mr Lawton: the only thing that can destroy Kea, Kakash, and Kasdeja is forged from the bones of their creator."

The Spear of Abraham, thought Lawton. The weapon was in the boot of the Fiat. Lawton couldn't wait to use it on another of those giant, red clowns.

He said, "Isn't that true of every religion? The creator seems to have the right to kill, have power over what he creates. We can't look at the face of God, can we."

"Myths are enduring," said Goga.

"Myths are bollocks."

"Don't you believe anything?"

"I believe a gun kills bad guys. A stake kills vampires. That spear kills those red things. I believe that you are wasting my time. Why were you in Iraq?"

Goga said, "For three thousand years the clan of Nebuchadnezzar has been trying to resurrect these demons. Fortunately, there have been many brave men ready to stand in their way. Richard the Lionheart. My ancestor, Vlad — although his reputation was soiled by a fiction writer. And you, Mr Lawton."

"Me?"

"Yes. I was hearing stories while I was in Iraq. In Hillah."

"I know Hillah."

"It was full of Americans when I was there."

"Most places are."

"I was looking for the Great Hunter."

"Didn't Abraham kill him? That's how the story goes." Tom Wilson had told Lawton this tale three years before. Jake was starting to think that listening to Goga was a waste of time.

The Romanian said, "Abraham *defeated* him. He did not kill him. He tore the horns from Nimrod's head and, with the power of God, brought down the Tower of Babel, burying the Great Hunter and his harem."

"Harem?"

"His one hundred brides. The witch-wives of Babylon. Incubi who came up from Irkalla at night to drink human blood."

"Very nice." Lawton took a final drag on his cigarette before dropping it on the ground. It started to rain. Jake looked up at the sky. His bones ached. "So did you find this Nimrod?"

"No. There was not time. It was dangerous. But that's no reason not to try again."

"You're right. So when are you going?"

"Soon. But I would like you and Miss Sinclair to come with me."

Lawton nodded.

Goga went on:

"You are great vampire killers."

"It's what we do."

"No one, since Vlad, has killed so many vampires."

"I'll put that on my CV."

"Together we can end this, Mr Lawton. We can win the war."

Lawton looked at him. "And what about Britain? There are vampires here. The Nebuchadnezzars are coming back. They're putting up a fight."

Goga shook his head. "You can finish this in Hillah. Kill Nimrod, and it is like a chain reaction – every vampire dies. He is their source. He is their beating heart."

Lawton said, "So how do you kill him?"

Goga frowned.

Here we go, thought Lawton.

The Romanian said, "I don't know."

"Great."

"But there is a Mesopotamian legend saying Nimrod can only be killed if you –" Goga furrowed his brow "– make him one with himself again."

"Make him what?"

* * * *

THE M1 – 10.32PM, FEBRUARY 14, 2011

David wept. "I want my mum back, that's all. I know I can't have Michael or my dad, now. I know that. But I want my mum. That's why I... why I'm asking you, please, Jake, to stay here. Don't go to Iraq with Mr Goga."

Lawton looked away. They had agreed to meet Goga in London once they got back there. He stared down the motorway.

London calls me, he thought. *It needs me. And Murray needs me and Fraser needs me.* But after thinking those things, he turned again to face Aaliyah and David and said, "But what if we can end this by killing Nimrod?"

"I say we kill Nimrod," said Aaliyah.

David leaned forward between the seats. "Jake, please – "

"Shut your mouth, David," said Aaliyah, getting in the boy's face. "You tried to kill Jake, and that makes me want to kill you. I don't know why he's even let you come back with us, but I think it's because he's a good, good man. Don't ask him to do things for you."

"I'm... I'm not... I'm – "

Lawton said, "He's asking me to do it for his mum, Aaliyah."

"For... for my mum."

"No he's not. He said, '*I* want my mum' not 'Please save her from the evil people for *her* sake.' It's for him, Jake."

David sobbed. "I'm sorry for what I did; I'm really sorry – but they made me, they made me... "

Lawton and Aaliyah looked at each other. He could see that she had no sympathy for the boy. But Jake knew the youngster

230

had been deceived. He'd been desperate to see his brother and his dad again, and the Nebuchadnezzars had exploited that.

But they'd lied to him. His dad was gone. Burned bodies didn't come back to life. And you couldn't un-make a vampire, so Michael would be one of those forever – unless someone drove a stake through his heart and killed him.

So with David's dad and brother gone, Lawton could at least try to reunite him with his mum.

But there was also another reason for finding Christine Murray.

"She's our friend, Aaliyah," he said.

"Yeah, I know."

"And so is Fraser."

"Okay."

"I can't leave them out there."

She nodded, but her eyes were hard.

David's voice broke Lawton's trance:

"There's policemen walking down the hard shoulder behind us, Jake."

"Cops?" he said.

"And, Jake... they've got AK47s."

CHAPTER 63.
IN POWER.

No.10 Downing Street, London – 10.42pm, February 14, 2011

BURROWS stepped over a corpse. "Don't leave the bodies out in the corridor like this, Phil. It's disgusting."

"What do you want me to do with them?" he asked.

"I don't know. I am Prime Minister. I don't have to worry about things like this. You deal with it."

Birch grumbled. Burrows ignored him. She walked down the corridor. Her heart thundered with excitement. Finally she was here. Number 10 Downing Street. And not just as a guest. She lived here now. She would soon be named Prime Minister. "Interim" would have to do for the moment, but it wouldn't be long before she was officially in charge.

She came to a door embossed with the words "Prime Minister", and she smiled and opened it and entered the room.

Strand's paraphernalia cluttered the office. Family photos covered the walls. A Leeds United mug sat on the desk. Lying on the mantelpiece under a flat-screen TV was a DVD case. She went over and looked at the cover. It was a collection of John Wayne films. The DVD box had been signed by the US President.

What a ridiculous gift, she thought.

Heads of State often exchanged trinkets, and the gifts always had something to do with the leader's country. But Western movies? That wasn't a special gift. Strand could've easily bought the movies at HMV or off Amazon. Did the President not think that John Wayne films were available in the UK?

But Strand was such a poodle. He'd obviously been watching the DVD in case an American representative dropped by.

His own Cabinet members weren't allowed to drop by. But the door was always open to US diplomats. They seemed to come and go as they please. They thought they owned the place.

Not anymore, thought Burrows. *It's mine, now.*

She went to the desk and swept everything off it. The mug smashed on the varnished floor. The papers scattered. Pens rolled under cupboards.

Mine, she thought. *Mine.*

* * * *

Ten minutes later Burrows was sitting behind the desk and lighting her first cigarette in twenty years.

The nicotine made her dizzy. She blew smoke out of her mouth, and it formed a cloud above her head.

Burrows had never wanted to stop smoking. She started when she was twelve, stealing her dad's Marlboros. The taste had been horrible, but the feeling of being grown-up gave her confidence.

But when she was twenty-three, she became pregnant.

Her boyfriend, Ian Burrows, demanded that she quit the fags. Using books from his medical studies, he showed her what smoking could do to an unborn child. So she stopped and married the future Dr Burrows.

Simon was born healthy, but three years later meningitis killed him. Two years after his death, Adrian was born. Four years later, Adrian drowned when he fell through ice on a Cumbrian lake.

Two years on from the death of her second child, Burrows became an MP. She was 35. Within a year she was a junior minister. Soon after that promotion, she divorced Ian, and weeks later Afdal Haddad appeared in her constituency office.

Someone knocked on the door, now, and she said, "Come in."

Birch entered and said, "You're smoking."

"Sit down," she said. "I was thinking about the first time I met Afdal Haddad, and how it changed my life."

Birch pulled a face and coughed.

Burrows ignored him and continued:

"He was sitting there in my office and just asked me if I knew who I was."

"He asked me the same thing," said Birch, his face red.

Burrows wasn't interested. She was talking about her. She puffed on the cigarette, and it made her feel sick. But it was good at the same time. The itch she'd had for twenty years had finally been scratched.

She said, "I was going to have him kicked out, but when he spoke, it felt like I was the only person in the world."

"I understand that, I felt – "

"And he told me about Babylon and Nebuchadnezzar – and then, vampires."

Birch said, "If I said that he – "

"Phil. I'm telling my story. I'm telling *our* story. It's *all* our stories, so don't interrupt. This is my day to tell it. Please."

He grumbled.

She went on:

"Dr Haddad said I'd be powerful one day, but only if I embraced my ancestry. I said I was Scots-English with some Irish thrown in. He said I was a descendent of the King of Babylon. It was ridiculous. I *should* have had him thrown out. What he was saying just didn't make any sense, but it *did* make sense. I knew it was true. It felt true. It was as if I had lived before. You know, I always thought I was special. And he came along to say I was."

She stubbed out the cigarette in a shard of the Leeds United mug.

"Smoking that cigarette has made me *me* again. Taken me back to being twenty-three, searching, full of hope, full of lust for life – and now my dreams have been fulfilled. I'm Prime Minister. I am about to be ruler for life. Britain is mine – ours, ours, now."

She fingered the brooch of ancient skin.

"He showed me a vampire," she said. "Brought one into the meeting. It was winter, so dark. I was amazed. He gave me this" – she indicated the brooch – "and showed me how much power I could wield with it. How I could instil fear into the creature in my office."

She noticed Birch fidgeting with his mark, the ribbon knotted to his clipboard.

She said, "We'll make Britain great, again, Phil. No crime. No poverty. We'll be a plentiful nation. We won't have to worry about the way we're perceived. We won't have to worry about political correctness or the way we treat other people. We are chosen, and the chosen lead the way. The rest are fodder. We'll all have important roles to play. As the professional politician, I can lead. That's my job. You being an officer of the law, you'll have an important role to play too. You'll be answerable to the leaders, to me."

Birch narrowed his eyes. "And who will you be answerable to?"

"To Babylon. To its concept. The idea of it. The dream. Vampires don't want to rule. They only want to feed. We keep them in blood, they'll be happy. They will be our army. They know nothing about being in charge."

He looked at her for a few seconds, and she saw that he feared her.

Maybe I've said too much, she thought, *allowed my heart to rule my head*.

She changed the subject:

"Where's the Chancellor of the Exchequer?"

"Liz Wilson is in custody. The press is in a frenzy. Her lawyers are trooping down to Scotland Yard. I'm not sure how long they can hold her."

"It doesn't matter. If she gets out, I'll have vampires hunt her down – see how she likes that."

Birch's phone rang, and he answered it. His face reddened. His mouth dropped open, and his eyes widened. He said, "Good, good, there's a bit of luck. I'll let you know."

He ended the call and looked at Burrows and she said, "Tell me, Phil."

"A group of our police officers were driving along the M1 when they saw a car parked on the hard shoulder. They drove past a couple of times and confirmed the identities of the three individuals in the – "

"Don't talk jargon to me – tell me."

"Jake Lawton, Aaliyah Sinclair, and David Murray."

Burrows's excitement grew.

"Do you want them alive or dead, Jacqueline? I said I'd let them know."

"Prime Minister," she said. "Refer to me as Prime Minister. And how do you *think* I want them, Phil?"

CHAPTER 64.
PAIN IN THE NECK.

Westminster, London – 11.35pm, February 14, 2011

BERNARD LITHGOW grimaced when the Sky News ticker announced "Breaking News". The ticker said, "Three police officers killed on M1 near London Gateway Services."

The presenter said, "As you can see, we have breaking news coming in from the M1. Three police officers shot dead. At the moment, it is unclear if the men were actually real police officers. It may be that they were dressed as policemen, but – "

"Curse them," said Bernard.

The press and the media had better start towing the line. *Not real policemen.* How dare Sky say that. Those officers were Nebuchadnezzars. They were hired by Birch. After a few weeks, they would take over from the present police forces, which were full of do-gooders and officers who might refuse to obey difficult orders. Orders such as, *Kill them all.*

Burrows had called him from No.10 half an hour ago to say Lawton and his friends had been spotted. Although he was pleased by the news, it did mean that David Murray had either failed to kill Lawton or hadn't tried yet.

But now the fake coppers had also botched their attempt to kill Lawton. The soldier and his bitch had escaped again and left another three men dead.

"Bastard," said Bernard.

The toilet flushed. Fraser came back into the room. Bernard smiled at his son.

"Watching the news?" said Fraser.

"Seeing what kind of television set we'd given you," said Bernard, switching off the TV using the remote control. "Do you approve of the flat, Fraser?"

"It's nice, Dad."

"And the BMW we got you?"

"It's cracking."

"Very good. You loved cars when you were a boy. We'd be walking along, and you'd stop and name all the vehicles, all of them. Every car. I had no interest."

Fraser said nothing. He took a seat on the couch and flicked through a copy of *FHM*. Bernard sat in the armchair.

He said, "We'll replace the car after a year."

Fraser looked at him and nodded.

"And after this task is done, Fraser, we'd like to offer you a job."

"A job?"

"Certainly."

"What kind of job?"

"Really, any kind of job you'd like. What job would you like?"

"I don't know. Sex job?"

Bernard curled his lip. "I'm sorry, I don't – "

"Joke, dad."

Bernard laughed but he was thinking, *You little shit, I'll kill you myself when this is over.*

And then he stood up and said, "Fraser, I must make a call."

He went out into the hallway and rang Burrows. He'd slept with her that afternoon at The Ritz. It was good, and she screamed. The idea of the Prime Minister naked and flat on her back underneath him got Bernard's blood going.

When he got through to her, she was angry.

"How could three men with very big guns not kill Jake Lawton for me?" she said.

He asked her something, and she told her the answer.

238

Then he said, "I'll give George Fuad a ring and get Murray to ring her son. We need to show Lawton that we can get to him."

"Perhaps we should kill Murray, too," said Burrows.

"She's going to die, Jacqueline – she'll know what death is when our saviour awakens and feeds on her."

"Lawton is like a stain. You just can't get rid of him. He came to my door, Bernard, and left dead things for me to see. And now he kills our men once more. Is he immortal, too?"

"You'll soon see that he is not, my darling. Leave Lawton to me. You focus on running this country. The borders are closed. We should unleash the vampires tonight. Let them kill. Let the transformation begin. Let Britain be Babylon. The new blood is here, Jacqueline. The old blood is drying out. This is our time. This is the age of monsters. Forget Lawton. Forget them all."

After saying goodnight to Burrows, he called George Fuad. He spoke to Fuad for ten minutes and then went back into the living room.

Fraser lay on the sofa watching the news. The ticker still rolled across the bottom of the screen announcing the death of three "alleged policemen".

Fraser said, "Jake's still being a pain in the neck, then."

CHAPTER 65.
RUNNING INTO TROUBLE.

LAWTON ran along the treeline. Aaliyah and David followed him. Lawton carried the spear in a leather scabbard slung over one shoulder. Over the other shoulder, he carried one of the AK47s retrieved from the men who attacked them. Aaliyah had a second weapon, which she carried along with her Remington shotgun. David carried a rucksack full of stakes.

Lawton had known they were fake cops when he saw them. Real cops didn't carry AK47s, and real cops didn't open fire on you without warning.

The men had peppered the Fiat with bullets, and Lawton, Aaliyah, and David had been lucky to get out of the car.

Aaliyah fired at one of the fake cops with her shotgun, blowing him off his feet. Lawton took out the other two with his spear.

The Fiat was wrecked, so they decided to take the police car. But as they approached it, blue lights flashed in the distance and sirens wailed.

More cops on the way. And it didn't matter if they were real or fake. Either type would be bad news for Lawton and Aaliyah.

They had scrabbled up the slope and hacked through hawthorn bushes before coming out into a field. Woodland surrounded them, and the fields spread for acres. It was dark, so it would be difficult for anyone coming after them to see.

He looked behind him to check on Aaliyah and David. The rain made it hard going. Lawton was soaked through. Aaliyah's long, black hair was flat on her scalp and hung down in damp strands over her shoulders. The rain made David's face look like he'd been crying. He blinked away the drizzle.

"Everyone all right?" said Lawton.

Aaliyah and David said nothing.

Lawton started moving again, and up ahead the trees angled to the left. After they'd got round the bend, he would stop them, and they would rest for a while.

His mind drifted to the fake cops. *How did they find us?* he thought. Was it luck? *If so, why are there policemen wandering around with AK47s?* He remembered what he'd seen earlier. The cops arresting the man on the motorway. Thinking about it now, Lawton didn't believe they looked like police. Something hadn't been right about the scene.

He stopped worrying about it. Everyone was trying to kill him. Even David had had a go. He had to focus on "the now". It was pointless trying to analyze things he couldn't do anything about.

If people were coming after him and they found him, he would just have to deal with them.

He relaxed and found himself in the moment again, reacting to what was immediate and not to what had gone or what was to come.

After taking a look over his shoulder, he ran around the bend in the treeline.

The dogs barked.

Lawton stopped dead.

Before he could swing the AK47 off his shoulder, two shotguns were aimed at his face.

And then the headlights came on right in front of him so he couldn't see a thing.

CHAPTER 66.
A NEW FAITH.

THE boy was chained to the scaffold. He was hung face down by his wrists and his ankles. He screamed in pain and terror. The other children were locked in a cage. There were only three of them left. During the journey from France to England, the others had been sacrificed to the monster in the casket.

"Don't do this anymore, George," Murray said.

But she knew there was no point in begging. The Fuads hadn't listened before, so why should they listen now?

Earlier that afternoon, they had arrived in London. When the lorry stopped and the rear door was opened, Murray was shocked to discover where they were.

"No," she said, finding her voice, "not here."

George had laughed at her. "We're still the owners, you know. One day we might open it again. It can be like a church for the new faith of England. A church for the worship of vampires. And it's got a good name for a church, ain't it. Religion."

Religion.

The nightclub where it had all started three years previously.

The Fuads and their allies had tried to resurrect Kea in the caverns deep below the club, only to come up against Jake Lawton.

But they weren't going to give up.

"We're back at Religion, and this time we won't fail," George had told her as men filed into the rear of the truck and began to move the casket.

Sick with fear and exhaustion, Murray had passed out. She had woken up in the cave underneath the club. They had put a rusty collar around her neck, and a chain led from it to a corroded plug jammed into the stone floor.

The casket stood at the centre of the cavern. Surrounding it was the scaffold. The children were in the cage nearby. Alfred Fuad had gone over to the cage and opened the door. He dragged out the boy and attached him to the scaffold.

Now with Alfred about to cut the youngster's throat, George said, "Worried about the kids, Christine?"

"They're children," she said.

"Just small people, that's all."

"They are children."

"They're detritus," he said. "These kids are just street urchins. Their lives aren't worth living. They eat dog shit. They sell 'emselves for a shot of meths. Look at them."

Murray scanned the faces in the cage.

"Then why not leave them on the street?" she said.

"They're the waste of the human race, Christine," George said. "They serve no purpose. Got no point in life. But here there is a point to them. They can bring to life a great thing — "

Murray made a noise of disgust.

Fuad went on:

"They can fuel a great change in Britain. We're only a few hours away. Our girl's in Number 10, now."

Burrows, she thought. Dread leached into her chest.

Alfred stood on the plank that had been placed over the mouth of the casket. He sharpened his butcher's knife. Blood stained his apron. The boy screamed.

"Please let him go, George," said Murray. "Put me there instead. Let them all go."

He looked at her carefully, and for a moment she thought he was going to agree, and the horror of what she'd suggested made her quail.

Guilt filled her then. She bowed her head in shame. She wasn't brave enough to save these children. She could offer to die in their place. But when it looked as if that offer might be accepted, she became a coward.

But then George said, "No, we've got plans for you, Christine."

"You're mad."

He scowled. "We're mad? We're mad? You seen your country, lately? It's a mess, darling. Me and my brother, we've known what we were since we were kids. We've known that we're special. Our dad, he used to tell us all the time that we were descended from kings. But not these poncey, partying puffs you see these days. Real kings. Warrior kings. Kings who ruled over the greatest city in the world," said Murray.

"Kings who sold their people into slavery and sacrificed them to monsters."

"Those gods, they kept Babylon great. An undead army. A sewer system, cleaning up all the human debris. Only the chosen survived. Everything was good. Everything was clean."

"This isn't going to happen today, George."

"Why not?"

"Do you think the rest of the world will allow this?"

"They can try to stop us. They tried to stop Babylon, but her kings had their army, and we'll have ours. And anyway, darling, Britain's closed, now."

Murray opened her mouth.

George laughed at her. "Yeah, that's right. Jacqueline's closed the borders, see. We got out people manning the frontiers. Nothing comes in, nothing goes out. There's going to be a plague, Christine. The vampires are being unleashed on this fucking city, this fucking country. And then a new poison will do what Skarlet failed to do. It'll kill the people in their millions and then raise them up as vampires. It's over, darling. Over."

"Jake will come. He'll destroy this thing like he destroyed Kea."

"Lawton. Ha! What a joke. He's fucked. He's done and dusted. And you're going to help us get rid of him."

Murray was about to say something, but the boy shrieked.

Alfred looked down into the casket and said, "Bloody hell." He scuttled along the plank and climbed down the step ladder.

George said, "What's up?"

Alfred backed away from the casket. "Watch this," he said.

The casket began to shake. Murray stared. Alfred and George retreated. The boy thrashed about and squealed, his eyes wide with terror.

Murray said, "George, get the boy away from – "

Something shot out of the container. It looked like a tentacle, but seemed to be made from chunks of flesh and pieces of gore that had been pressed together. It was pink and as thick as an elephant's trunk, and it looped around the boy's waist.

The child shrieked.

The limb ripped him off the shackles and into the container, leaving his hands and his feet still attached to the manacles.

The boy's screams became muffled as the container quaked, and a fountain of blood came from within it to cover the ground in a crimson pool.

And then everything became still and silent for a few seconds before the children in the cage screamed, and Murray screamed with them.

* * * *

George Fuad held out the mobile phone and said, "Take it and do as I say."

All Murray's strength had ebbed away by now. Not only had her physical energy waned, but she was also broken emotionally.

Seeing the boy's death had taken away any hope she had. The monster in the casket was much worse than what they'd faced three years previously. Not even Jake Lawton could fight this thing.

"Come on, Christine," George said.

The smell of blood was in the air. The children cried in the cage. Alfred Fuad was on the phone with someone, but he was too far away for Murray to hear the conversation.

"Take the phone and make the call," said George. "I'm giving you back your phone. Take it and do as I say."

"Why should I?"

"To save your son's life."

"I don't believe you'll save him. I don't believe anything you say. You're all liars and murderers."

George shrugged. "Up to you, darling. I mean, what do you do? Not play along and see David die for sure, or do as I say and maybe just give him a chance of life?"

Murray thought for a few seconds.

"What do you want me to do?" she said.

"That's my girl." He handed her the phone and then presented her with a piece of A4 paper. "There's some words we'd like you to say."

She read the words.

George went on:

"Stick to the script, and everything will be okay. Don't even think about improvising and tossing in your own lines – these'll do just fine."

She looked up at him. "What are you going to do?"

"You just make the call, and we'll have you back with David before you can say 'Jake Lawton, you're dead,' all right?"

"I can't."

"You can't?"

"I can't say this – "

"Why ever not, darling?"

"Why are you sending them here? What's there waiting for them? Tell me. Tell me."

George bent down towards her, and his face darkened. "You make the call, doll, or I'll find that lad of yours, bring him here, and put him on a skewer with onions and peppers and turn him into a fucking kebab for my lord and master over there." He stood up straight and smiled at her. "There's a good girl."

CHAPTER 67.
POACHERS.

THE man standing in the headlights' glare said, "Put that fucking machine gun down on the ground, mate, and do it very, very carefully."

The dogs barked.

Lawton shielded his eyes from the powerful light.

The second man addressed Aaliyah by saying, "And you, tasty bird, I don't know what you're doing with two guns, but I don't like birds with guns, so you put them down, too."

Lawton said, "Why don't you turn those headlights off, mate, so I can see what I'm doing."

The first man said, "You don't need to see, chum, you only need to feel – now feel for that gun and lay it on the ground."

"You too, brown girl," said the second man.

"You shut your fucking mouth," said Aaliyah.

"Put the fucking gun down," said the second man. "And you. The kid. You, lad. If you've got any weapons, you drop 'em too."

Lawton eased the strap of the AK47 off his shoulder, and he started to think about ways they could get out of this situation.

"Do as they say," he told Aaliyah and David.

The dogs were still barking. Although he hadn't seen them, they sounded like small dogs. He guessed they were Jack Russell terriers and that the men were poachers.

He laid the gun on the grass and said, "We're not coppers."

"Good," said the first man.

"And we're not after your game."

"Our game?" said the second man.

"You after rabbits?" asked Lawton.

"None of your business," said the first man.

"Tell your mate there to kill those lights," said Lawton.

"No need for that," said the first poacher.

Lawton's eyes had adjusted to the glare. He could see the men in the light. They were three yards away. The shotguns were jammed into their shoulders. If they pulled their triggers, he would be blown to pieces.

"You're not going to give up that easy, are you?" said Aaliyah.

"I think these gentlemen mean business, sweetheart," Lawton told her.

"Are you going to let them point a gun at me?" she said.

"There's not much I can do about it," he answered.

"Here," said the first poacher, "it ain't no time to have a lovers' tiff."

His voice quivered a little, and it was just what Lawton wanted to hear.

Aaliyah came up to him, and the second poacher said, "Christ, stay where you are, you tart."

She ignored the man and said to Lawton, "You said this was a good spot for rabbits."

"Hey," said the second poacher, "they are after our spot."

Lawton said, "I told you to keep your mouth shut, sweetheart."

Aaliyah grabbed him by the collar. "You're fucking useless, you are – "

The poachers stepped forward. Aaliyah used Lawton's shoulders as leverage and swung her legs out, and he grabbed her arms and wheeled.

She kicked the second poacher in the face. The first man ducked. The dogs barked. Lawton let go of Aaliyah, and she rolled away before leaping on the second poacher, while Jake smashed into the other one. He slapped the gun away and punched the man in the jaw. The poacher crumpled in a heap.

The terriers were nipping at Lawton's ankles, and he shoved them away, but they kept barking and coming at him.

The headlights swept over the field and away from Lawton, leaving him in darkness.

An engine roared. Lawton saw the vehicle. It was a Land Rover, skidding on the wet grass as the driver tried to get away.

The second poacher cried as Aaliyah punched him three times in the face.

Lawton scooped up his AK47 and also one of the shotguns, and he fired at the Land Rover. The windscreen shattered. The noise scared the dogs and they ran off. The vehicle rolled into a tree.

A voice from inside the cab cried, "No, please don't shoot!"

Aaliyah stood beside Lawton.

"Nice acting," he said.

She picked up her weapons.

A phone rang, and Lawton and Aaliyah turned round and aimed their guns in the direction of the ringtone.

David stood there gawping, the ringing phone in his hand.

"You know who that is?" said Aaliyah.

"It... it says it's my mum."

CHAPTER 68.
NOT CHRISTIAN, NOT JEW, NOT MUSSULMAN.

TÂRGOVIŞTE, CAPITAL OF WALLACHIA – NOVEMBER 1462

SIMEON sat on a pile of silk cushions in front of Prince Mehmed. Simeon was glad to rest. The journey had taken him three days, and when he arrived at the Ottomans' camp on the Ialomiţa River, his horse had died.

He asked to see Mehmed, but at first the Ottomans wouldn't listen to him, and they wanted to cut off his head.

They forced him to his knees and were about to decapitate him when a voice shouted for them to stop.

It was Mehmed.

The prince's men helped Simeon into a tent. They brought him fruit and water. Before he started to eat, he handed Mehmed the sack containing the three clay pots. The prince also ordered his men to bring in the trunk that was full of the trinity's red flesh.

After he'd eaten, Simeon thanked the prince.

"You've done well, brother," the Ottoman said.

Simeon nodded.

Mehmed was in his twenties. His beard was forked like a swallow's tail, and his bronze eyes rarely blinked. Just as

Simeon's father had said, the prince wore a turban decorated with a piece of scarlet.

The mark of the Nebuchadnezzars.

"You saved our history," said Mehmed.

"I only serve."

"We all serve."

"As best we can, prince."

"Had the Wallachian got hold of these precious things –" he waved a hand at the jars and the open trunk "– it would have been the end of everything. And at the rate he is killing the vampires, making forests of them, there would be none left. The few remaining undead have escaped to the Transylvanian mountains. They will stay there until we rise again."

"Are you leaving, prince?"

"We are leaving. We have been foiled again. Your father was so close, this time. But it was not to be. At least you salvaged our treasure. We will return to Constantinople and ready ourselves for the next time. A battle is lost, but we will win the war. We have eternity. They have nothing. After this Vlad dies, there is no one. But my son follows me, and your son follows you –"

"Prince, I have no son."

"Your daughter then. Though women are not much use."

"I am in Holy Orders, prince. I am not permitted to marry and must remain celibate."

The prince scowled. "Nonsense, Simeon. Wasn't you father in Holy Orders? He broke his vows. You shall break yours. It is imperative that you have a son. The Nebuchadnezzar bloodline must continue. It is your duty."

"Yes… "

"We are not Christian, we are not Jew, we are not Mussulman, brother. We are the oldest religion. We come from a king. We are linked by our blood. Why would you stay true to these Holy Orders of yours?"

"I… sometimes have doubts, prince."

"Doubts?"

"That… that our faith will ever conquer the Christian empire or the Mussulman empire. I fear that our gods are not as strong as the Pope's god, and I –"

251

"I should have let those soldiers cut your head off, scoundrel."

"Prince, I – "

"All gods are pitiful before ours. Ours are living gods. They will walk among us. They shall rise from these ashes that you risk your life to bring to me, and they shall make us into kings. But you prefer the meek and mild Jesus? You prefer celibacy?"

Simeon said nothing. He bowed his head in shame. The prince was right. *I have shown fear*, he thought, *and I have shown weakness.* He looked up at Mehmed and said, "Perhaps I should die for my feebleness. But I saw my father butchered by Tepes. It made me fear that his Christian god is stronger than our trinity."

"Pah! How did your father die?"

Simeon shut his eyes, and he saw his father's murder in his mind.

After packing the treasure on the cart, he had trotted the horse out of the stables. As he rode down the track, he turned back to look at the church for one last time.

His father stood in the bell tower, gazing out over the burning village. Simeon had called out to him, but the priest didn't hear.

Then Vlad Dracula's men charged down the track towards Simeon. He managed to pull the cart into the surrounding forest before the troops could see him. They galloped past where he was hiding and raced towards the church.

"Tell me," said the prince.

Simeon opened his eyes and looked at Mehmed and said, "They dragged my father out of the church and whipped him, calling him a witch and a devil worshipper, and they… "

The memory seared his mind and his face twisted with pain. After a few moments, he mastered his anguish and went on:

"Tepes himself arrived. They… they stripped my father. He screamed and begged for mercy. But they whipped him again. And then… then they brought one of their stakes and – oh my Lord – they drove it through my father's back and it came out of his belly and he screamed and screamed – I hear it now – so dreadful, so dreadful."

Simeon shook.

Mehmed looked grim. "Tell me," he said.

Simeon said, "They lifted him up and made a hole for the stake and put it in the ground. My father screamed and writhed. He was pierced through. He begged them to kill him. But they laughed. They laughed and waited all night with him, but he didn't die like the vampires do when the dawn comes. His suffering continued. His cries will stay with me till I die. His end was terrible, prince. A long, agonizing death."

For a while, the prince said nothing. He frowned and scratched his beard. Then he spoke: "They shall pay. Tepes and his hordes. The Christians, the Jews, and the Mussulmen. They shall all pay. We shall be strong again. We shall raise armies to conquer them, and when we are ready, we shall bring life to Kea, Kakash, and Kasdeja, and we shall rule over a new Babylon."

"Yes, prince."

"Now. Stay in your Holy Orders, if you wish. But don't obey them, Simeon. I urge you to take a woman and breed with her. The bloodline is vital. You shall take this trunk-full of marks and keep them safe. Hand them down to your offspring. Teach them our history. I shall return to Constantinople with the ashes."

"What of the spear, prince? Tepes has it."

Mehmed closed his eyes and seemed to be thinking. "We will send assassins. We will send women. They are always the downfall of men."

CHAPTER 69.
THERE IS ONLY BLOOD.

SASSIE killed a man near Victoria Station.

He struggled for a while, but she held him tightly and drank the blood from his veins quickly so he grew weak.

They probably looked like lovers to anyone passing Grosvenor Gardens. Sassie was sitting near the railings and the man lay across her legs and her face was buried in his neck.

Her fangs had pierced his jugular vein. The blood flowed hot into her mouth. The taste energized her and made her feel alive.

After he died, she tucked him up against the railings in the corner. No one would notice. He looked like a drunk sleeping off a heavy session. The people would ignore him dead like they ignored him dying.

Sassie slipped out of the gardens and crossed Buckingham Palace Road. Although it was past midnight, crowds still bustled around Victoria Station.

Sassie smelled their blood. Her belly writhed, but she wasn't hungry anymore. The odour just excited her. It was the only thing that mattered.

Blood.

To go without it was agony.

That night, however, had been a good one. There had been plenty of opportunities to feed. Counting the man in the gardens, Sassie had killed three people in the past few hours.

Including the Prime Minister.

She walked over to the taxi rank and leaned on the railings. Her gaze flitted over the bus station. Passengers waited in the rain. Some of them were drunk, just like the guy she'd killed in the gardens. There were a lot of people with suitcases. Families with young children. Old people huddled in the bus shelters. It was never usually like this. Never so many people looking like they were trying to get away.

A feeling of nausea swept through Sassie. She bristled and showed her teeth. Wheeling around, she found a man standing under an umbrella. He carried a box under his arm. Sassie retched. Her eyes fell on the scarlet handkerchief in the man's breast pocket. A light seemed to come off the fabric, which made her eyes water.

"How fascinating that this piece of cloth makes you baulk," said the man. "The skin of your maker terrifies you. But there's a lesson there on how to rule, I think." He smiled. "With fear."

She hissed at the man.

He said, "Don't show your teeth here, you stupid vampire bitch." His gaze went towards the bus station. "You see those people with their suitcases and their children? They're trying to leave the country. But the borders are closed. They're trapped. They are your food. Aren't we good to you?"

He put the box on the ground. Sassie leaned down and picked it up. She sniffed it, recognizing the smell coming from inside the package. She salivated.

The man said, "You know what to do?"

Sassie nodded.

The man continued:

"Let's hope you don't botch it like everyone else. But I suppose they weren't natural killers, were they. You are."

Sassie growled.

"And remember," said the man, "he has a mark." He touched the handkerchief in his breast pocket. "I don't know how you're going to by-pass that."

"I'll seduce him. He loved me once."

The man smiled. "Do you remember what that felt like?"

Sassie said, "No."

"You feel nothing?"

"Hunger."

"Yes, hunger. We all feel hunger. For sex. For power. For money. He has another woman, now. Does that make you jealous?"

Sassie tilted her head to the side.

The man said, "Obviously not. It's just the kill, isn't it."

"Just the kill," she said. "Just the blood. I feel nothing. Human is only food. Human is only blood."

"Do you remember being human?"

She narrowed her eyes and thought about things before saying, "Yes, I remember – but I don't remember what it felt like. If I was human, I would be jealous, I would hate. I know what those feelings are, but I don't know what they would be like to feel anymore. There is only blood."

And it was thick in the atmosphere. She turned her nose to the sky and sniffed for a long time. And when the scent of blood had saturated her airwaves, that familiar sensation had returned.

She was hungry again.

Just in time for Jake.

CHAPTER 70.
IT'S A TRAP.

SCRATCHWOOD PARK, BARNET – 12.15AM, FEBRUARY 15, 2011

LAWTON and Aaliyah tied up the poachers with some rope they found in the back of the Land Rover. Lawton stuffed pieces of cloth into the men's mouths to stop them making any noise. He taped the cloth in place but made sure the trio's nostrils were clear so they could breathe.

The dogs had come back, and they were barking at Lawton. Aaliyah wanted to shoot them, but he said no. "I like dogs," he said. "It's not their fault."

"I hate them," she said. "Cats are better."

In the distance, sirens blared and a helicopter cast a spotlight over the fields.

They were looking for the killers of the fake cops.

"We haven't got much time," Lawton said. "We've got to get going."

He got into the Land Rover's driving seat. Aaliyah got in next to him, and David sat in the back.

He started the vehicle and drove towards a cluster of lights in the distance. It looked like a housing estate, so there had to be a gate or some kind of entrance.

As they drove, Lawton asked David about the phone call from Murray:

"Tell me again, what did your mum tell you?"

"She said not to say anything, just listen."

"How did she sound?"

"Her voice was shaky."

"It's a trap," said Aaliyah.

Lawton said, "Go over it again."

David said, "She... she told us we had to go to our house in Pimlico, because there was something there for us."

"I fucking bet there is," said Aaliyah.

"And we had to go, because if we didn't, she... she was going to be killed."

"Bastards," said Lawton.

David went on:

"It would save her life, she said. What was there would save her life. And we had to do it, or she... she was going to die, Jake."

"There's nothing there," said Aaliyah. "Just a lot of trouble."

"We haven't got a choice," said Lawton.

Aaliyah said, "Yes we have."

There was a gate up ahead. Lawton put his foot down, and the Land Rover picked up speed. He glanced in the side mirror. Behind them, the sky glowed. Blue flashing lights and the helicopter's spotlight lit up the night. Lawton looked ahead again and drove towards the gate.

Ten minutes later, they were racing along a country lane. It was quiet and remote, with only a few houses along the way.

"I just think we should consider what Goga's saying," said Aaliyah.

"Fine, but only after we do this," said Lawton.

"Jake, it's a trap."

"I know it's a trap, but if there's a chance I can save Christine, then I'll walk into it." He looked at her. "I'd do the same for you."

"I know. And I would, too."

"You understand, then."

"Of course I understand, Jake, I'm only saying they're setting us up. They've got her, and they're using her."

David spoke from the back. "We can't leave my mum."

No one said anything.

David spoke again:

"I know you hate me, Aaliyah, but I hate me, too. I was only trying to get my family back. I would never have killed Jake. He wouldn't have let me, anyway. But I was sad. I was upset. I... I like to think I'm grown-up, but I'm only thirteen. I'm just a kid. I want my mum and my dad and my brother. That's all."

Lawton gave him a few seconds and then said, "Good speech, David."

Aaliyah said, "Oh, fuck it."

CHAPTER 71.
VENGEANCE.

THE boy and the wolf walked alongside each other through the desert.

Far away, the tower rose towards Heaven. The structure was so high the boy couldn't see where it ended. It just went up and up and tapered into nothing.

Somewhere over the horizon lay the city of Babylon. And the tower stood in the centre in of the city. And beneath the tower was Irkalla, the land of the dead. And in the land of the dead lived the one who built the tower.

And I will kill you there in the darkness that you made, thought the boy.

He had left his home in the caves above the city of Ur ten days ago. It was his twelfth birthday. His mother had cried when he said he was going, but she knew he had no choice.

He was the only one left of his generation.

Twelve years before, the King of Babylon had sent his armies to kill the children of Ur. Thousands died, but they weren't all young.

Men and women died, too. Fathers and mothers who tried to protect their sons and daughters. Grandfathers and grandmothers, uncles and aunts, brothers and sisters.

The bodies had piled up. Blood streamed through the streets, and the ground was stained for years after the slaughter. They even said the Euphrates ran red.

"Why didn't Nanna protect us?" the boy had asked his mother.

"Gods cannot do everything, Abraham."

"One god can."

"Don't blaspheme, boy. Nanna will hear."

But Nanna didn't hear. If he did exist, he was weak.

During his childhood, Abraham often went out into the desert with his wolf brother. The days were hot, and the nights were cold. Food was difficult to find, and there was no water. But Abraham and the wolf were never hungry or thirsty. The boy felt as if someone were leading him through the wasteland, and he would come to a fruit tree that should not be in the desert, or an oasis filled with clear, blue water.

He spent more and more time in the desert, until one day he realized that Nanna was only the god of Ur, and in the wilderness he found the god of the world.

"The one true god," he'd told his wolf brother only two weeks before.

The animal lay down beside him in the cave. It was old now. Its pregnant mother had entered her cave twelve years ago to find a human there, who was also about to give birth.

The wolf and the boy were born at the same time.

The animal was one of seven cubs born that night, and over the next few months they were nursed alongside the boy. Two mothers, side by side, caring for their offspring. Months later, the wolf left with her all her cubs except one. The seventh one stayed in the cave with the humans.

Now in the desert, the wolf lay down and panted. The boy squatted next to the animal and stroked its head. "Are you tired, brother? We'll get to water soon, old man. My Lord is leading me. I can feel him in my heart. We'll drink and eat."

An hour later they were drinking from a pool in the desert. The boy killed a snake and shared the meat with his wolf. It was getting dark by then, so they settled down to sleep. The boy lay under the sheepskin coat, and the wolf curled up beside him. The animal snored, but the boy didn't sleep. He stared up at the sky. He started counting the stars, but there were too many.

"You are mighty, Lord, to make the heavens," he said to his new god. "I am Abraham, your servant. I shall bring your wrath upon the Great Hunter. I am your sword, my God. I am your plague. He shall pay for murdering the children of Ur. He shall pay for building his tower. He shall pay for his allegiances with dark things. He shall pay. He shall... "

Abraham fell asleep.

* * * *

Battersea, London – 12.56am, February 15, 2011

After handing the box to the vampire Sassie Rae, Bernard Lithgow went to B13 in Battersea.

He told Norkutt to wait outside in the car while he went inside the secret unit. He unlocked the metal gate and entered the compound. He looked around. High walls topped with coils of barbed wire surrounded the building.

He hurried over to the main entrance and unlocked the door. Once inside, he shivered. He didn't like it here. It was a place for dead bodies.

And undead ones.

It was dimly lit inside the building. Striplights buzzed. Dead insects filled the plastic casings.

He went to the door behind the reception area, pressed five numbers into the console, and gave the door a shove. It opened on a corridor.

Christ, he thought.

With his hands tucked into the pockets of his overcoat, Bernard strode down the passageway.

The corridor lit up while he walked, sensors picking up his presence and turning on the low-quality lighting.

He was cold by the time he got to the door marked MORGUE, and the temperature dropped further when he stepped into the office.

This is where they had killed Tom Wilson. The old man's blood still stained the walls and the floor. Bernard smiled when he thought of something.

But the smile faded when he caught sight of the shadows moving behind the porthole window of the door at the end of the office.

He remembered what he told Jacqueline Burrows a few hours ago:

We should unleash the vampires tonight. Let them kill. Let the transformation begin. Let Britain be Babylon.

He went to the door, and just when he was about to open it, a pale, snarling face leaped up at the porthole window.

Bernard flinched.

And then he chuckled.

He touched the handkerchief in his breast pocket.

"I'm safe," he said to himself. "I'm safe."

He opened the door and stepped back as the vampires came out.

"Go kill," he told them. "The night is yours."

CHAPTER 72.
THE MURRAYS' HOUSE.

PIMLICO, LONDON – 2AM, FEBRUARY 15, 2011

THE house had been boarded up.

"Can we get in through the back?" said Lawton.

"I think so," said David.

"I hope not," said Aaliyah.

"Well if we can't," said Lawton, "no one else can get in either, and someone's pulling our legs."

"I wish they were," she said. "I can take a joke."

Around the back of the house, they climbed over the garden wall. The three of them crouched near the hedge that separated the Murrays' house from the property next door. The hedge was overgrown. It hadn't been pruned in years.

"When was the last time you were here, David?" asked Lawton.

The boy bowed his head. "I... I've never been back since, you know... since it all started."

"Who boarded it up?" said Lawton.

"I remember Mum and Dad talking about it, saying... saying they might as well just... just pack up and leave. But they didn't sell it. Just in case things... " The boy sniffed and rubbed his eyes.

"I get it," said Lawton. "Shouldn't have asked. Come on, let's see who's home."

When they got to the house, they found that the lock on the back door had been broken. "Someone's used a wrench on it," said Lawton. He nudged the door, and it swung inwards. He peered inside the kitchen. He smelled something rotten. "Food's gone off in there," he said.

"Or something else," said Aaliyah.

Lawton said, "Ready?"

Aaliyah nodded.

"You stay here, David."

"No way, Jake. No way I'm staying here."

"Son, you've got to – "

But David didn't let Lawton finish. The boy barged past him into the kitchen. Lawton hissed the lad's name and tried to grab him, but he was gone into the darkness of the house.

* * * *

Aaliyah rifled through Murray's notebooks. They were piled on a desk in the downstairs study.

Aaliyah had a torch, so she could see that the room was a mess. Newspapers were strewn all over the floor. Drawers had been pulled out and their contents scattered everywhere.

The study smelled damp. Cobwebs hung from the ceiling and covered an old armchair. Woodworm infected the desk. The wood was rotting.

The notebooks were written in shorthand. Aaliyah had studied Teeline shorthand in college a few years ago but gave up after two weeks, when she realized that marrying a rich gangster would bring her more money. She winced at her stupidity. The fools she'd gone out with.

Christ, you were a dumb cow, Aaliyah Sinclair, she told herself. She thought about Jake. He'd gone searching upstairs with David. "You go and do that," she'd told him, "I'll have a look down here – quicker we do it, quicker we get out."

She abandoned the notebooks now and turned her attention to a corkboard hanging on the wall. She shone the torch across it. Newspaper cuttings covered the board. The clippings had yellowed with age. They featured stories about vampires. Scanning the board, Aaliyah noticed a photograph on a page.

It was Jake. She lifted the clippings on top of it so she could read the story. It was about Jake killing an Iraqi civilian.

The newspaper was dated January 2005. She read the article. It said Jake had shot an innocent man in Basra in November 2004.

But Aaliyah knew it was a lie. Everyone did. Even Christine Murray, who had first written about the killing and blamed Jake for it.

The dead man hadn't been innocent. He'd been a suicide bomber. But no one cared at the time. The war in Iraq was going badly. The authorities needed a scapegoat.

They took Jake.

He was kicked out of the Army.

Anger rippled through her. She cursed the authorities for treating him so badly. He was a hero. He would always be a hero. But then, sometimes heroes were hated.

She looked at his photo in the newspaper cutting and her mind drifted. So when the door creaked open behind her, she was slow to react.

She wheeled and swung the torch. The beam sprayed across the dark room. And as it swept past the door it showed two pale faces creeping towards Aaliyah.

CHAPTER 73.
SHE IS DEATH.

POIENARI CASTLE, WALLACHIA – DECEMBER 1476

VLAD III, forty-five years old and *voivode* of Wallachia, drank the wine without stopping. In his other hand, the prince held a torch, and the flame was hot on his bare chest.

After finishing his drink, he put the empty wine goblet down on the table and stared out of the window. Snow covered the Fǎgǎraş Mountains, and heavy clouds hid the moon. Down in the valley near the River Argeş, his army was camped.

Tomorrow morning he would join them, and they would march to Bucharest, seventy-five miles away, where the Dracula would again go to war against his enemies.

Vlad tossed the torch out of the window, and its fiery tail whipped through the darkness towards the forest below.

When the torch landed in the snow and the fire went out, one of the soldiers in the valley started to climb up towards the castle. A longbow was strapped to his back. He was too far away for Vlad to recognize him, but he would be one of the best archers in Wallachia.

Now the Dracula said, "I have killed men and women and children. I have killed young and old. I have impaled thousands. I have burned hundreds. I have tortured and I have decapitated. I see nothing but blood."

He turned to face the naked woman on his bed. She looked young, but Vlad knew she was old.

Older than Christ. Older than Moses. Older than Abraham.

Her hair was white-gold, and her red eyes never blinked. Her skin was the colour of snow, so pale she looked like death.

She is death, he thought.

But she was very beautiful.

Vlad spoke again:

"I have become a monster to kill monsters. The Saxons hate me. The Ottomans hate me. History will hate me. But I have done God's work. I have protected my people. My life has been a strongman's life." He touched his throat where she'd bitten him and drawn blood. "Until now. Until you, Ereshkigal."

She sat up, and he looked at her body and was amazed at how perfect it was. He'd never seen such a perfect figure. She smiled at him, showing her fangs. Or maybe she was snarling. He didn't know. She'd made him weak. His mind was slipping away.

She rose, and something stirred in Vlad's loins.

"One more bite, *voivode*," said the woman, "and you will be with me forever."

She came towards him. His legs felt like paper, and his vision was hazy.

"You are too weak to fight me now, prince," she said. "You have fucked my dead flesh and it's corrupted you. You'll die here tonight, and tomorrow you will become alive again. Now tell me, where is it?"

Resisting her had been impossible. She'd come to him six weeks previously, when he was bitter and angry.

Two years before he had been arrested by his former ally Matthias Corvinus, the Hungarian king.

Corvinus lied about Vlad, claiming the Dracula had promised to hand Wallachia to the Ottomans.

Vlad spent ten years in a Hungarian jail, where he ate rats and spiders and scratched curses on the walls using the bones of his dead and decayed cellmates.

When he was released, he came back to Poienari Castle and started to drink heavily. He cursed the Wallachian people for turning their backs on him.

He lived alone in the castle, apart from one servant, and he never left his quarters in the east tower.

But one night he heard singing, and it seemed to come from the walls.

He spent hours chasing after voice. Going from room to room, he opened doors that had been shut for centuries. He hacked through corridors thick with cobwebs and found human bones in a chamber deep under the earth.

And using his hands and feet to climb, he even scaled the outside walls of the castle because he was sure the voice was coming from the crevices between the stones.

When he thought he must be mad, he ran screaming to his quarters again – and there she was.

Ereshkigal, a princess of Babylon.

He knelt in front of her she said, "You will be prince again if you let me drink, Vlad Dracula."

And she drank blood from the veins in his throat. Not enough to kill him and make him undead, but enough to make him sick.

The next day, November 26, the High Council made him *voivode* again.

Two weeks later, Ereshkigal came back.

"You have spent your life killing my kind," she said.

"Ten years ago," he said, "I would've impaled you on a spear and watched while the sun burned you."

She'd slipped off her white gown and told him, "Burn me now."

While they made love, she'd bitten him again and drank more blood from his veins. It made him drowsy. She'd said, "Tell me where you keep the Spear of Abraham, my Dracula."

"I want your dead flesh again, Ereshkigal," he said.

"For your blood and the spear."

He'd somehow managed to resist. He knew a third bite from a vampire would also make him undead. And to give her the Spear of Abraham would take away the only thing that could kill their unholy gods, a trinity of vampires destroyed by Alexander the Great.

Since that time, the descendents of Nebuchadnezzar had been trying to resurrect the demons. They had nearly succeeded fourteen years before, when a priest in Tălmaciu had been ready to carry out the ritual that would bring the trinity back to life. The priest had the trinity's ashes and was going to use the blood of local children to revive the monsters.

Vlad had impaled the false cleric and waited at the foot of the spear while the man died. It took more than a day. Later, he tried to find the remains of the trinity, but they were missing. Someone had taken them from the church.

Vlad had murdered thousands over the years in an effort to find the ashes. He failed. But at least he had the spear.

Feeling weak after Ereshkigal had left him a second time, he prayed. But God didn't answer, and he cursed the Lord.

What has been my purpose? he thought. *Why have I spilled so much blood?*

For nothing.

God has given me nothing, but Ereshkigal, for a drop of my blood, has made me prince once more.

And when she'd come back again the previous night, Vlad decided she could take his blood.

Now, Ereshkigal asked him again:

"Where is it?"

He pointed to a trunk that was near the bed.

She smiled, her fangs showing. "Always next to us while we fucked, Vlad." She laughed, and it made him recoil. She called out, "Simeon," and the door opened, and Vlad's only servant entered the room.

"Princess," the servant said, his eyes raking over her nude body.

Vlad gaped. "What is this?"

Simeon looked at him. "It is betrayal, you murdering bastard."

"The spear is in the trunk, Simeon," said Ereshkigal. "Take it to Bucharest tomorrow with the army and hand it over to Mehmed. He'll return it to Constantinople. Take it, Simeon."

The servant scuttled across the room, and Vlad said, "No, you shall not – " but Ereshkigal moved so quickly she became a white blur and was at his throat before he could say another word.

She growled as her teeth sank into his neck, and the veins popped. The blood flowed out of him, and his head swam. The servant stole the Spear of Abraham and ran from the room.

Vlad tried to reach after him, but the Dracula was too weak now.

However, he remembered one thing while he was dying.

He turned with Ereshkigal in his arms. Now she had her back to the window. She gripped him tightly. There was no escape from her.

The loss of blood made him weak, but he found one last drop of strength, enough to push Ereshkigal nearer to the window.

He groaned as everything became hazy, and his life slipped away.

Now, he thought, *now*.

The flaming arrow shot from the trees and arced through the air, coming straight for the window.

When it pierced Ereshkigal's heart, she screamed and pulled her teeth away from Vlad's throat. The last thing he saw was her bloody mouth. Then the arrow jutted from her breast and punctured his heart, and just before he died he felt the fire from her burning body scorch his skin.

CHAPTER 74.
TROUBLE.

THE white faces came at her from the dark.

Aaliyah had no time to lift the barrel of the Remington, so she used the torch as a weapon.

With a backhanded sweep, she struck the first attacker on the jaw, and he fell in a heap.

The light from the torch slashed around the room.

Aaliyah stepped to the side. The second attacker ran past her and crashed into the corkboard.

Aaliyah thumped him across the back of the skull with the torch. He grunted and hit the floor.

She swung the torch around and shone it where the first attacker had fallen.

He wasn't there.

He rammed into her from the side and sent her reeling into the desk. Notebooks and papers went flying. Aaliyah kept rolling so the man wouldn't be able to get on top of her. She fell off the desk and scrabbled around, trying to find her shotgun and torch.

She found the torch and swung it round. The beam fell on a pair of legs, standing on the desk.

"Don't shine that in my face, you cow, or I'll fucking shoot you," said the voice.

She moved the beam up, and the Remington was aimed right at her. In the arc of light, she could see that the youth wore a hoodie.

"I told you, don't bring it any higher."

"Do you know how to use that?" she asked him.

"Can't be that difficult if a girl's using it."

"Sure, that's right."

"Put the light down, darling."

Aaliyah lowered the beam down over the youth's sweat pants and trainers, and then to the floor. She looked at the desk's leg. It looked unsteady.

"She hit me on the back of the head, Marty," said the second youth.

"Oh, you fucking genius, Curtis, why don't you tell her where we live as well, you prick."

"Hello, Marty and Curtis," she said.

"Now you've told her my name, too," said Curtis. "Fucking hell, Marty, you've got a gun. Is she a cop?"

They were quiet for a few seconds before Marty asked, "Are you a cop?"

"Maybe," she said.

"Maybe?" said Curtis.

"She ain't," said Marty.

"No, but I'm not alone," she said.

"Bollocks," said Marty.

"Marty?" said Aaliyah.

"What?"

"Hold on, yeah."

"What?"

Aaliyah kicked the leg out from under the desk. It collapsed. Marty squawked. Aaliyah scrabbled back and lifted up the torch to see the youth falling off the desk. He lost control of the gun.

Aaliyah sprang at him and tackled him around the waist. She drove him back over the desk. They crashed into Curtis.

Aaliyah flailed with the torch and hit something. Someone grunted.

She kept swinging and kicking. The light from the torch speared around the room giving her glimpses of the youths.

Hands grabbed her and she continued to lash out and made contact with something hard that cracked.

"She's broken my fucking leg!"

She swung the torch towards the voice.

The beam locked on the Remington's barrels pointing straight at Aaliyah.

"Kill the bitch," said one of the youths. "Kill her, Curtis."

CHAPTER 75.
OLD FLAME.

THE shotgun blast came from downstairs.

"Aaliyah," said Lawton.

He spun on his heel and shone the torch at the door – and froze.

"I will tear his throat out with my nails if you move, my love," said Sassie.

She stood in the doorway. With her left hand she held David by the neck. Her right hand was inches from his throat. Her nails were long. Her eyes glittered red in the torch's beam. Blood dripped from her fangs.

Christ, had she bitten David? The boy looked terrified.

"David, are you okay?" he said.

"He's fine," said Sassie.

"Don't hurt him."

"A rather desperate plea, Jake, darling."

"Don't hurt him," he said again.

"You look beautiful," she said. She licked her lips and made a hissing noise. "And you smell ever so lovely. Your blood is thick. Its odour saturates the air, my prince."

"Let him go," said Lawton.

"For what?" she said.

"There someone downstairs. Did you hear?"

"What do I care about guns? You have a big one, Jake. Doesn't make any difference to me, though."

Lawton's nerves tightened. Who did Aaliyah fire at? Or was it someone firing at her? He had to get downstairs to check. He was sweating, desperate to go and find her.

He and David had searched the first floor before coming up here to the second storey. David had gone into his old room. Lawton had entered this room, which was across the corridor. It used to be Michael's, David had told him.

The room smelled musty. Cobwebs hung from the ceiling. A wardrobe stood in the corner.

"Let him go, Sassie."

"Again I ask, for what?"

"Do you want me?"

She shoved David into the room. The boy stumbled and fell against the wall.

Jake was about to launch himself at Sassie when another figure shot out from behind her.

A dark blur flashed across the room and barged into David. The youngster was lifted off his feet and slammed against the far wall. Then he was thrown to the floor and the figure stood over him.

David said, "Michael."

"Hi, little brother," said the vampire Michael.

"You were a prisoner when I – "

Michael laughed and looked at Lawton. "When you decided to betray Jake?"

"N – no."

"When you promised to kill him – to save me."

"N – "

Lawton said, "Pull him off, Sassie."

"Why?" she said. "It's so nice seeing brothers reunited."

"Sassie –" Lawton whipped the spear out of its scabbard "– call him off."

Sassie smiled at him and sauntered forward a couple of steps.

Lawton stayed where he was. He had the mark around his neck – the red skin of the trinity. Sassie couldn't touch him.

He glanced over at David and Michael. The vampire lifted his brother from the floor and held him round the neck. Michael's fangs brushed against David's throat.

"Someone's going to die tonight," said Sassie. "Who will it be? Who will join us? You or the boy?"

He looked at her. "Do you remember things, Sassie?"

"I remember."

"You remember how you felt when you kissed me?"

"I remember, Jake. But it means nothing. It's only a memory." She hissed, baring her fangs. "All I feel now, babe, is hunger. Are you going to let me feed, Jake? Like you let Jenna feed?"

"Is that what you want?" he said. "You want my blood?"

Sassie said, "Weren't you sweet, falling for her little game. 'Feed me or I kill someone else,' she told you. And you let her. What good did it do, Jake?"

"I might have saved someone that night."

"But was is worth it just for one life?"

"Only someone who hasn't had to live under monsters would ask that question, Sassie."

Her face twisted. "I did have to face it. I remember loving you and standing with you. I don't know" – she put a hand to her breast and knitted her brow – "how that felt, now... how wanting you felt. It's gone. But I know I did feel it. And I faced that fear with you, I'm sure I did. Did I?"

"Yes, you did."

"But *you* let them get me, Jake."

He felt sick at the thought of her dying that night in Religion.

She went on:

"You let them savage me. Their hands all over me. Their teeth in my veins, drinking me. Emptying me, Jake. Emptying me of everything that made me human."

"I'm sorry that happened," he said.

"I'm not sure I am," she said. "I don't know. All I know is this. All I know is blood. And whose blood will I have tonight?"

"Let the boy go," he said.

Michael laughed. "My brother's going nowhere."

Sassie grinned at Lawton, and it made something cold slither down his spine. "Brotherly love, see," she said. "Michael wants to play with his brother forever. Maybe I'll play, too. He's easier than you, Jake." She moved towards Michael and David. "He's not protected. Rather careless of you, not giving him a mark."

Lawton flung the spear at her. She snarled and ducked, but it was enough of a diversion for Jake to lunge across the room towards the brothers. He ripped the red rag from his throat and pressed it into Michael's face. The boy-vampire shrieked and reeled away.

"Take it," Lawton said to David and stuffed the fabric into the boy's hand. "He can't touch you."

And Lawton turned again to face Sassie as she reared up and came for him.

"You clever bastard, Jake," she said. "But now you're unprotected."

"I'm okay," he said.

"Give me a little blood, baby," she said. "Just a few drops. Like you gave Jenna. I don't want to kill you yet. There's a little gift for you here somewhere."

His belly knotted. "What the fuck are you talking about?" He thought about the gun going off. Had they killed Aaliyah? "Sassie, what's going on? Where's Aaliyah? If you've – "

He stopped talking when Sassie's brow furrowed, and her head tilted to one side.

David was holding Michael at bay with the mark. Michael begged his brother not to come any closer.

"Blood for me, baby," said Sassie. "A little drink."

Lawton looked at the spear. It lay by the door. Too far. He was unarmed. The AK47 was useless against her.

"You're not going to let me drink from you?" she said.

"I think you've had enough."

"I never have enough, Jake. It hurts. In my belly. In my chest. Like a fire. And only blood can quench it. Let me drink a little. I won't kill you. Save a life tonight, Jake. Like you saved a life when you let Jenna drink. You remember how that felt? Did it feel good? Make you hard? I remember you hard, babe. Jesus, you got really hard, didn't you. When we kissed. I'll make you hard like that again. Let me drink from you."

While she spoke, Lawton noticed something.

A shadow moving in the corridor behind Sassie.

"Stay where you are, Sassie," he said.

"You're not going to kill me, Jake, are you?"

He said nothing.

"First Jenna and now me? You've a track record of killing women, Jake."

"You're not a woman," said Lawton.

It was too late, but Sassie had sensed the movement behind her and she wheeled, ready to attack.

Lawton said, "*That's* a woman."

Aaliyah drove the Spear of Abraham into Sassie's chest.

The vampire shrieked.

The sharp end of the tusk jutted out of her back. Black blood sprayed from the wound.

Aaliyah lifted Sassie off the floor using the spear.

The vampire thrashed about, squealing. It kicked and scratched at Aaliyah, whose face was set in an expression of determination.

Sassie looked back at Jake and for a second he saw in her eyes that she had been human once, and he'd been very close to loving her.

She called out to him: "Jake, Jake, don't let me die, I love you…"

He nearly went to her.

Sassie's hair caught fire. Her skin charred and blistered. Her face, porcelain white, blackened. She screamed and fought, but Aaliyah was too strong.

She yelled his name one last time:

"*Jake!*"

He turned away and walked over to David.

The smell of Sassie burning filled the room, and her body popped as it exploded into dust.

Behind him Aaliyah said, "I don't like it when your exes come round, Jake – I get a bit jealous."

Lawton looked at David and said, "Do you want to kill him, or do you want me to do it?"

CHAPTER 76.
WHAT THEY LEFT BEHIND.

"YOU made me kill my brother," said David.

"I didn't make you do anything," said Lawton.

"You made me kill my brother."

"He wasn't your brother anymore."

"You made me – "

"I would've killed him for you."

"That's what I mean," said the boy. "You made me do it. You didn't give me a choice."

David knelt where his brother's dust speckled the floor.

Lawton went over to the boy. "I gave you a choice," he said. "Me or you. You chose you."

"He didn't have to die, Jake."

"He was already dead. David. We've got to go."

"I'm not going. This is my home. This... this was my brother."

"Your brother is gone. Your dad is gone. But your mum is out there somewhere. They've got her, David. Those people. They've got her, and they're not going to be nice to her and let her go. Are you going to help me find her, or are you going to mope?"

"Help you."

"Come on, we can't stay here."

Aaliyah came back into the room. She had returned downstairs to check on the youths.

"One's got a broken leg, and the other one's dead," she said.

"What happened?"

"The kid aimed the shotgun at me. I kicked out at the barrel. It flipped up just as he was pulling the trigger. His head's gone."

"Jesus. We're leaving a trail of bodies behind."

"What's new, Jake?" She gestured at David and said, "What's up with Kevin the Teenager over there?"

"He's going to help us find his mum," said Lawton.

Aaliyah looked at him. "So, we're not going to see Goga."

"You think we should?"

"I think we should talk to him," she said.

"Okay, but I thought we'd agreed to find Christine."

"Where do we start?"

"Spain."

"Spain? Are we going to Spain?"

"No, but that's where she was. And I don't think she's there, now – I think she's back in Britain."

David got up. "She's here?"

"The Fuads'll be here. Haddad's here, for sure. If they were the ones who got your mum, then she's here too."

"Where?" said David.

"I'm many things, David, but I ain't psychic. Come on, let's get out of here. We've been hanging around far too long."

"Wait," said Aaliyah. "You remember what that bitch said before I killed her?"

Lawton creased his brow. "What are you talking about?" he said. And then he remembered Sassie's words:

There's a little gift for you here somewhere.

He said, "Bullshit – it was bullshit."

David said, "No, it's not. My mum said something when I spoke to her. She said… she said there'd be something here that could help her, didn't she."

"That was a lie," said Lawton. "They made her lie, David. Just to get us here."

"I don't know," said Aaliyah. "I got a feeling."

"Oh fuck," said Lawton.

"Where were you when Sassie caught you, David?" said Aaliyah.

* * * *

In David's room, a poster of Frank Lampard still clung to the wall. The edges of the picture were frayed, and Lampard's England shirt was stained yellow.

Apart from the image that had been pinned up by David five years before, the only thing left in the room was the walk-in wardrobe.

"She came from in there," said the boy.

"She was hiding in the wardrobe?" said Aaliyah.

"Not really hiding, I suppose," said David. "More like waiting."

Lawton strode over to the wardrobe and started to open it, but then stopped.

"What is it?" said Aaliyah.

He looked over his shoulder at her.

"Babe, you look scared," she said.

"I can smell something."

"Smell what, Jake? What's going on?"

"Don't come any closer." Lawton mastered his fear. There was something unpleasant in the wardrobe, he just knew it. He could feel it in his belly. Sassie *had* left something here. And whatever it was, it smelled dead.

He opened the doors. The smell grew stronger. He looked around the wardrobe. It was empty apart from a box. A cardboard box with a lid. The type you'd have if you'd brought a hat.

But Lawton knew it wasn't a hat.

Shit, he thought, *shit*.

A sweat broke out on his back.

"Jake, what's going on? What's in there?" said Aaliyah.

"What did she bring?" said David.

Lawton crouched and looked at the box. He shone the torch over it just in case it was wired. But it wasn't a bomb. He knew that. It was worse.

"Stay there," he told David and Aaliyah.

Aaliyah said, "Jake, what – "

He glared at her and said, "Stay where you are, Aaliyah," and she recoiled.

He went back to the box. His throat was dry. He tried to slow his heart, but it was pelting against his ribcage.

Okay, he thought, *just do it. Get it over with.*

He lifted the lid. The smell hit him and he winced. Red paper lined the inside of the box. Lawton nudged the lid aside. He pointed the torch into the box.

His breath stopped.

"Jake... my God... what is it?" Aaliyah was saying.

He tried to say something, but no words came out of his throat, and his legs wouldn't move so he could get up and run away from this thing.

His rage volcanoed. He found his voice. The noise that came out of him was one an animal would make.

And as the fury came out of him, he couldn't take his eyes off Tom Wilson's head.

PART TWO.

RETRIBUTION.

CHAPTER 77.
THE FIRST DAY.

No.10 Downing Street, London – 7.22am, February 15, 2011

"HOW many dead last night?" said Jacqueline Burrows.

Birch checked his clipboard. "Thirty-seven that we know of. That is according to media reports this morning. Their sources are the police. Oh, and that figure does not include our three guys Lawton killed on the M1. And the headless robber we found in Pimlico. Named as Curtis Lehman – like the bank – which is also no more."

"That bastard Lawton got away again," said Burrows. "Where's the other youth? The one with the broken leg?"

"We have him under arrest. His name is" – he checked his clipboard – "Martyn, known as Marty, Potter."

"Has he talked?"

"He's screamed a lot."

Burrows lifted the coffee cup and held it under her nose. She smelled the odour – strong and rich.

Birch said, "I don't know what he'll be able to tell us. We know it was Lawton and Sinclair because we'd lured them there."

"We should've sent humans – just had them shot."

"But you wanted to send Lawton a message. Wilson's head. A 'we can get to you and your friends' message. A head-in-the-bed, Godfather-style message."

"I also hoped that he and Sinclair would die. We should've sent humans." She looked up at Birch. "We can get them on murder, though. Our men on the M1. And the little yob they shot from last night. Throw in kidnapping charges for what they did to those poachers, and it'll put more pressure on Lawton and his lot."

"Shall I distribute photos?"

"Yes." She got up from the table and gathered up her box files.

She'd been in the office since 5.30am.

Bernard Lithgow had released the vampires from B13 in the early hours of the morning, and then he'd driven to her flat.

It was about 2.00am when he knocked on her door. Birch, flanked by an armed police officer, had answered the door and let Bernard into the flat.

He wanted to sleep with her, but she was tired and wanted to be alone. He begged: "Please let me stay."

Being surrounded by so many vampires had scared him, he said. He needed company, so they went to bed together and had sex again.

After only a couple of hours' sleep, Burrows had been driven to No.10. There was a lot to do. A country to steal. A democracy to dismantle. A population to crush.

The Nebuchadnezzars had members in politics, in the police, the Armed Forces, banking, showbusiness, sport, the law, and many other professions.

They numbered only a few hundred, which didn't sound like enough to take over a country of more than sixty-million people.

But the Nebuchadnezzars were organized. They had been planning a takeover like this for thousands of years. And they had determined and ruthless leaders such as the Fuad brothers and Bernard Lithgow.

And me, thought Burrows.

"I have a Cabinet meeting in ten minutes," she said. "Walk with me, Phil, and tell me about last night's vampire attacks. Cheer me up with some death notices, will you."

They walked out of the office and along the corridor to an elevator. On the way down in the lift, Birch told her about the killings.

Burrows knew that the ones who died would become vampires themselves that night. And they would hunt and kill. Tomorrow evening, their victims would come back from the dead, also hungry.

The vampires were multiplying.

But it wasn't enough.

Lawton was still out there, and he would do everything he could to destroy the creatures.

"And we also had instances last night," said Birch as the elevator reached the second floor, "of the general public fighting back."

"Resistance," said Burrows. "We'll soon put a stop to that." She stepped out of the lift and strode along another corridor towards the Cabinet room. "We need to get moving on resurrecting our new prince. People need to see what they're dealing with. They need to be fearful. They need to be awed. They need to know their place, Phil."

They reached the Cabinet room. Members of the Government lingered outside in the corridor. They saw Burrows approach. Some of them bowed their heads. Others sneered. She saw them and marked them for death.

I'll have prison camps built, she thought. *You can spend your lives there, you bastards. You'll be put to work. You'll be made to breed, and your offspring will be food for the vampires.*

"Good morning, ladies and gentlemen," she said. "Thank you for coming so early. We need to make a start. There's a lot of salvage work to do. Britain needs healing. Please, do go in…"

She waited while her Cabinet filed into the room, and after they were inside, she turned to Birch.

"And we need to get moving on the Haddad project as well," she said. "How are we doing with our stocks of drinking water?"

288

CHAPTER 78.
RETURN TO RELIGION.

GEORGE Fuad drove through London. The traffic was heavy. He knew it would be at that time of the morning. Vehicles crammed the Bayswater Road. The four-mile journey from the Holland Park lock-up, where they'd stored the HGV the previous evening, to Soho was taking more time than he thought.

But he wasn't worried or stressed. Everything was going to plan.

As he approached the Marble Arch Roundabout, traffic slowed again and finally came to a stop.

Fuad looked around. Other drivers had worried faces. Pedestrians looked terrified. He turned on the radio. Reports of deaths in London overnight dominated the news programmes. The headlines also mentioned Burrows becoming interim Prime Minister, and how the borders had been closed.

Good, he thought.

No more over-population. No more mass immigration. No more scum filling the estates. Those places would be destroyed, or they would become ghettos where the human waste would just about survive.

There would be no drugs – unless you were rich like him and indulged in a line of coke a couple of times a week.

No drunkenness in the streets. Only in your own home. Some champagne. Good wine.

No violence. Unless you were the bottom feeders, whose lives would be plagued by brutality. They would be born to die. Maybe after dying, they would rise again as vampires. Or they might just get slaughtered.

Everything would be better. These streets would be clean. He would have power. Unlimited power.

Britain is mine, he thought.

"There are now only a few flights departing and arriving at UK airports," said the radio presenter as he introduced a clip of people complaining about the situation.

George curled his lip when he heard them moan. *Count yourselves lucky to be alive*, he thought.

Someone who was identified as a spokesman for the European Union then came on the radio, warning the British Government that it was breaking laws by shutting the borders.

"This will have grave consequences," said the spokesman.

Fuck your laws, thought George. *If I'd had my way, we'd be razing Brussels to the ground, too.*

But Haddad and Burrows didn't want to do that. Britain was their target. If the vampire plague happened to spread across the English Channel to the continent, then fine. But it wasn't part of the plan.

And fuck the plan, thought George.

The traffic started to move again. George took the A40 off the Marble Arch roundabout.

Along Oxford Street, people looked scared. They were huddled in groups, studying copies of the *Evening Standard* and *Metro*. They were talking and waving their arms around and shrugging.

Some of the shops along Oxford Street had been boarded up. A mobile phone store looked as if it had been on fire. The front of the building was charred, and smoke billowed from inside the shop.

When he got to Soho, he made his way to Religion. He and his brother had bought the club years ago. It became successful, with quite a few celebrities being photographed falling out of the nightspot in the early hours of the morning.

But then Jake Lawton got involved. In the caverns below Religion the ex-soldier killed Kea. During the mayhem, the club caught fire. It was badly damaged. The Fuads had to shut it down. Now it was boarded up and appeared derelict.

But Religion hadn't been abandoned.

He squeezed the HGV down the alley that ran down the rear of the club. Once he'd stopped the engine, he made a phone call.

After completing his call, George got out of the cab — although there was hardly any room for him to open his door and get out.

The alley was a dead end, and black bin bags were piled high at the bottom of the lane.

He waited. Five minutes later, a metal door in the building creaked open, and half-a-dozen men filed out.

George spoke to one of them, and he then led the others to the rear of the lorry.

They opened the back door of the truck. George heard them gasp and curse. Murray whined. George smiled at her agony as he strolled to the end of the lane.

From a skip, he removed a sign saying PRIVATE ROAD: NO ENTRY TO VEHICLES OR PEDESTRIANS and placed it at the mouth of the alley.

While the men emptied the lorry and carried what was inside it into Religion, George continued to block off the road using yellow tape marked with the words POLICE: DO NOT CROSS.

He went back down the alley and locked the truck before entering Religion and shutting the metal door behind him.

* * * *

Inside the club, it was cold and dark. George walked down two sets of stairs and came to a lift that had scissor-style doors.

He rode down in the lift, and it clanked and groaned, and the lights flickered.

"Christ," he said.

He blew into his hands to warm them up and shivered. He was relieved when the lift reached its destination, and he flung open the doors.

It was even colder down here. Voices echoed in the cavern.

The odour of a dead fire hung in the air. It was the effects of the blaze that had almost destroyed the club. The smoke had saturated the walls and made them black. The ground had been seared and the wood charred.

Inside the cavern was the container he'd ferried from France. Murray was also there, tied up and lying on the ground, exhausted. All the kids were dead. Their blood had been fed to the monster in the tank and their bodies discarded.

George walked towards the men. They all wore luminous jackets and hard hats. A drill churned into the earth and made the ground shake under George's feet.

The man George had spoken to outside a few minutes before said, "Morning, sir."

"Morning, Meadows."

Soot and dirt stained Meadows's face. His white eyes stood out. *Just like a Black and White Minstrel*, thought George.

Meadows said, "We're down into the tunnel now – "

The drill roared.

George waited for the drill to stop, and when it did he said, "How long before we can lower everything down there?"

"Tonight, sir," said Meadows. "Definitely before dawn."

George said, "That's what I like to hear."

He turned away and strolled over to the wall. As he walked, he kicked some bones out of the way. Human bones. A skull. A femur. A couple of ribs.

Ash layered the ground, and within it were the remains of maybe a thousand vampires. Burned to cinders by Lawton and his gang.

The remains of Kea, the first vampire god they resurrected, were also here somewhere. There was no chance they could recover his ruins as the Nebuchadnezzars had done when Alexander the Great killed the trinity.

He looked over the ashes and thought, *Gods from dust.*

He looked up. High above him, what remained of Religion's ceiling was now a skeleton of charred steel.

The drill started up again, and the earth shook. George glanced over at the men. They were all private contractors hired on high wages.

"You'll see things you shouldn't see," George had told them. "We expect you to be quiet."

Meadows had said, "For the kind of money you're paying, you can glue our lips together, sir."

At the time George had thought, *I might just do that for fun.*

The men had not been told why they were here. They were being paid very well, and the money was enough to stop them asking questions. They had no idea what was inside the now-sealed casket, and they didn't want to know. And neither did they ask about Murray, although one or two glanced at her with concerned eyes.

The power of money, thought George. *Everyone has a price.*

And the price they were paying was death. The men would be dead by dawn. A dawn that would mark the beginning of a new age.

An age of monsters.

CHAPTER 79.
"WHITE CLIFFS OF DOVER."

WITH his hood pulled down to hide his face, Max Abbott waited outside the Post Office on the estate for a victim.

He felt sick. He'd only slept for two hours. Lemon's brother had come round again last night and asked about Max's girlfriend – or *ex*-girlfriend, since those people had killed her.

This is an ex-girlfriend, he thought, Monty Python's parrot sketch somehow appearing in his confused mind. *This girlfriend is no more.*

Lemon's brother had been a pain. He'd been distributing leaflets on the estate and in the town centre and stuck some on lampposts as well.

That meant Lemon's face was everywhere, and seeing it made Max feel sick.

"She's fucked off," Max had told him. "I keep fucking telling you."

Lemon's brother was queer, so Max didn't feel threatened by him. He was thin, and his hair was bleached blond. He had tattoos of naked men on his stick-thin arms and a ring through his nose.

"She not the type to fuck off, Max," her brother had said.

Max said, "You better stop harassing me or… or I'll have you fucking wasted. I… I fucking know people."

"My mam's worried."

"So's mine," said Max.

"About what?"

"Fuck off."

"When did you last see my sister, Max?"

"Christ, son."

"Just tell me."

"Last week. We had a shout, okay. She kicked off about some pills she needed. I told her we didn't have any. She called me a wanker and fucked off. Not seen her since."

"I still don't believe you."

"I still don't give a shit. Leave me alone, or I swear to God I'll kick the shit out of you."

"I been to the cops."

A cold sweat had broken out all over Max's body. "Oh yeah, and what did the pigs say?"

"To wait a while," said Lemon's brother. "She might've just run off. They treat her like lowlife. The druggie she was. She's not from a nice home. Otherwise they'd give a shit. But they don't. There's only me and our mam who gives a shit."

Max said he didn't know where she was – for the hundredth time.

Lemon's brother had gone away crying again. But Max knew he'd be back. And that could turn out to be awkward. Eventually, the police would become interested. And that meant they'd come round to his flat, and he didn't think he could shrug them off as easily as he'd shrugged off Lemon's brother.

And there was no way he could tell the police anything. If he did, those men would be back, and he really didn't want to see them ever again. Not after that bloke with the gaucho moustache had come back yesterday and showed Max a video of what they did to Lemon.

It kept him awake most of the night.

He needed to get away from Nottingham, and for that to happen, he needed money.

So he went out and waited near the Post Office.

His face itched. He needed a shave. He looked up. The sky was grey. Rain in the air. Always rain these days. The cold bit into his bones. He only wore a vest underneath his hoodie.

A humming made him look over towards the Post Office. An old woman walked out of the building. Short and thin, she wore a woollen hat and a fur coat. She had blue wellington boots on her feet, and she carried a large, brown leather handbag.

Stashed with cash from her pension, thought Max.

Old people were funny. For a few years now, the Government had been paying pensions directly into people's bank or Post Office accounts. The money was safe there. A pensioner could take a few quid out using their bank card and pop down to the shops to buy their bread and milk.

But the oldies didn't do that. They tottered down to their banks and emptied their accounts. Every penny of their pension.

Max's gran did it. "It's an old-fashioned thing," she'd told him one day when he went to her flat to steal a tenner. "It's nice to have the money in your hand."

It sure is, he thought now as the old woman walked down the road and hummed "White Cliffs Of Dover".

Max followed the pensioner.

He stayed about twenty yards behind her, and he stopped a few times to light a cigarette or pretend to speak on his phone.

Then he'd catch her up again, and then stop, and do the same thing until she came to the tower block where she obviously lived.

Max looked around for any potential have-a-go heroes. There were some kids about, but they were busy smashing up a car with slabs of concrete and pieces of two-by-four.

The old woman walked into the subway, which led to the elevators and the stairs. Shadows filled the alley and the dimly lit passage excited Max. No one would see him attack the pensioner, and because of the gloom, it was unlikely that she'd be able to describe him to police or vigilantes.

He quickened his pace and entered the walkway. He froze and looked up, sensing someone above him in the stairwell. He blew air out of his cheeks. Nothing up there but shadows.

Up ahead, the old woman stood out as a thin, dark shape against the white light of the exit. She continued to hum that wartime song.

He gained on his victim. He clenched his fist just in case he needed to hit the old girl. He planned to jerk the bag off her shoulder and run. But if she did fight, he would punch her. He'd have to. He needed the money.

He was five yards behind her when she turned and looked at him. Her mouth opened, and her eyes were wide with fear.

That fired Max up.

He lunged for the woman and said, "Give me your fucking —"

The shadow came from above. It must've been lurking in the stairwell. The figure landed between Max and the old woman. It blocked off the light coming from the alley's exit and made everything dark.

Max tried to scream, but a hand locked around his throat, and he was lifted off the ground and slammed against the wall.

CHAPTER 80.
FRASER'S TASK.

"YOU take them down to the water," said Afdal Haddad. "You remove the stopper, thus. You pour the contents into the reservoir. You do this at three different venues. Your father will be with you."

Lithgow looked at his dad, who smiled at him.

"How do you feel about that, Fraser?" said Jacqueline Burrows, also grinning. "Do you feel that you understand, now? Do you see how this is for the good of the country? Do you see how Lawton doesn't care for you? Do you see where loyalty truly lies? Do you see how that very lovely apartment will suit you nicely, and also the BMW? And the girls we have provided? The money? Do you see?"

Lithgow thought for a moment. "Yes, I see."

"He sees," said his dad, embracing him. Lithgow trembled in his father's arms. He smelled his dad's aftershave. He closed his eyes, and his mind reeled back to childhood.

He was five again. Kids screaming. He and his mates playing in Battersea, where Fraser lived with his mum and dad.

Keith "The Teeth" Thomas, aged seven, shoving Fraser against a wall before slapping him across the face.

Fraser racing home, wailing. Crashing through the front door, calling out for his dad.

His dad there scowling at him saying, "Wipe your feet before you enter the house, Fraser."

Fraser crying and telling his parents that he'd been struck by Keith Thomas. Fraser hoping his dad would embrace him and tell him it was all right and they'd go and sort out the bully.

But all his dad did was tut and shake his head before telling his wife, "We've got a coward for a son, dear."

Now, twenty years later, Fraser cried again and held on to his dad.

Applause burst out in the room. Lithgow snapped out of his daydream and blinked. He looked around at the people.

They were in a house in Holland Park. It was filled with antique furniture. Lithgow sat between his father and Burrows on a daybed.

Afdal Haddad sat in his wheelchair opposite them. A briefcase lay open on a low, varnished table. In the briefcase's foam inlay sat three glass vials.

Lithgow stared at the vials and remembered the old man's words:

You remove the stopper, thus. You pour the contents into the reservoir...

He looked up again, gazing around the room. A huge painting hung over a large fireplace. The painting showed an ancient king in a chariot. Behind him were three monstrous, red demons at the head of an army of fanged soldiers.

A vampire army led by Kea, Kakash, and Kasdeja.

A vampire army helping King Nebuchadnezzar conquer and rule Babylon.

Lithgow shrugged off his father's arm and looked at him.

"Good to have you back, son," said his dad.

"I never went away."

His dad nodded and shook his hand.

"Wonderful," said Burrows. She rested a hand on Lithgow's knee. "Your father will be with you."

Lithgow said, "Why me?"

He scanned the room again. There were about twenty people looking at him. He made eye contact with a man in military uniform. He'd been introduced earlier as General Howard Vince, Chief of the General Staff. That made him head of the British Army.

A man in a Navy uniform had been introduced as Sir Mark Wakeford, the First Sea Lord. Also there was Air Chief Marshal Bob Ospring, Chief of the Air Staff.

"Are they your lot as well?" Lithgow had asked his father.

"General Vince is a Nebuchadnezzar. Sir Mark and Air Chief Marshal Ospring have seen the light, Fraser. They are collaborating for the sake of the country."

"And their own necks," Lithgow had said.

Now Burrows raised her eyebrows and said, "Why you, Fraser?" addressing his earlier question.

"Yes. Anyone could do this. You could."

"Yes, I could," she said, "but I have my role to play."

"What about you then, Dad?"

"I'm passing this on to you. This is an opportunity to make a difference. I told you. Be great. Be famous. Be someone. Show Lawton you mean something. I might not have been a good father, but I'm trying to make amends. This is a great thing you will do."

Lithgow furrowed his brow. He thought about Lawton. He felt anger towards him. His dad had been right – Jake hadn't protected him. And now he hadn't even bothered to come and save him.

Lithgow said, "And what will this stuff do when I pour it into the water?"

His dad smiled. "Well, if it's anything to do with homeopathy, bugger all."

A man who'd been identified as Alfred Fuad stepped forward. "Excuse me, Bernard," he said, "but I made a fortune out of homeopathy – "

"Doesn't mean it works, Alfred," said Lithgow's dad.

Alfred Fuad went on. "This'll work, mate. There's power in them little tubes of water, I'm telling you."

"What kind of power?" said Fraser.

"A power to heal," said Haddad. "It will make things better, young man. This will re-humanize everyone who has been infected by vampirism. It will heal. Do you want to heal? Do you want to make right your error?"

"Yes, I do."

Haddad went on:

"The only thing your friend Jake Lawton wants to do is kill. He burns the bodies of innocent people."

"Only when they get attacked and killed by vampires," said Lithgow.

"But they can be healed, we are telling you," said Haddad. "This is a cure. This will undo vampires."

"Why would you want to undo vampires? You made them in the first place."

Haddad said, "Because we did it wrong."

"Wrong?" said Lithgow.

Haddad struggled to stand. Alfred Fuad helped him up by holding his arm. The old man grimaced. He addressed Lithgow:

"This is not about death, boy. This is about life. This is about rejuvenating. Vampirism is about birth. It is about invigorating the nation. New blood. New life. You understand?"

"What about the deaths?"

"There won't be deaths this way. You can save lives by doing this, you see. They will be healed, and they will stronger. They will be better humans for it. Healthier humans."

"This will heal Britain, Fraser," said his dad. "What an opportunity to right your own wrongs."

"You make it sound like it was my entire fault."

Burrows touched his arm. "We don't think that, Fraser, but we know that you do. You have a good heart. You have been manipulated over the years. Now we give you a chance to make your mark. To stand as a man. Do you see? Do you see, Fraser?"

"I think so... "

Haddad said, "With a new Prime Minister and many talented, able people – such as you father and Mr Fuad, here – Britain will be great again, young man. We don't want to destroy this country. We want to make it strong. It will be a place where you can do what you want. What is it that you want? To have fun?"

Lithgow shrugged.

Haddad said, "Then you will have fun. You are part of us, Fraser. You are a Nebuchadnezzar. You are of his bloodline. You are important. Be with us, young man. Be with us and heal this nation. Heal it and thrive. Heal it and live freely."

Haddad went to the table and shut the briefcase. He picked it up and came over to Lithgow.

"Take it, Fraser," said the old man. "Take it and heal. Be the healer. Be the one who made a miracle happen. Take it and be magnificent."

He took it.

CHAPTER 81.
PERSUASION.

LAWTON slammed his hands down on Max's shoulders to stop him getting up off the chair.

"Fucking hell, who the fuck are you?" Max said.

"Me? I'm fucking hell on earth, son, that's who I am. Hell on fucking earth."

Without any sleep, Lawton had driven up to Nottingham soon after opening the box and finding Tom Wilson's head inside.

The discovery had lit a fire in Lawton's chest. It made him realize that he had to find Fraser and Murray.

He couldn't wait any longer.

After leaving Pimlico, Lawton, Aaliyah, and David had gone to the hotel in Earls Court that Goga and his men had hired out. It was a dingy place. It smelled of damp and the rooms were cold. Goga said it was better to stay in a spot like this rather than pick a more upscale venue.

"The people here are poorly paid and if you give them good money, they will keep quiet for you," the Romanian had said.

When Lawton told him he was going to Nottingham to find Lithgow, Goga had frowned and urged Jake to come with him to Iraq.

"Britain is doomed, now," said Goga.

"My friends aren't," said Lawton.

The plan was that Aaliyah and David would try to find Murray. After finding her, they'd let Jake know, and he'd come back down from Nottingham – hopefully with some information about Fraser.

But Aaliyah shocked Lawton by saying, "Perhaps we should think about what Mr Goga's saying, darling."

Lawton couldn't speak for a few seconds after hearing that. But then he found his voice and said, "I can't deal with what you've just told me right now, Aaliyah, so I'm going to Nottingham. I'll speak to you when I know something about Fraser. You ring me when you find out about Christine."

She nodded at him, but her eyes showed that she didn't agree with what he was doing.

And that broke Lawton's heart.

He drove north and reached Nottingham before dawn. He parked in a city centre car park and sat in the Land Rover, thinking about the conversations he'd had with Fraser over the past few weeks.

Jake knew his friend was here in the city. But whom had he come to see? Fraser had told him, but he couldn't remember. He was so tired. He was wounded. His mind wasn't working properly.

At 7.00am, Lawton got out of his vehicle and found a café, where he drank three cups of coffee. His gaze had wandered to a noticeboard covered with posters and flyers.

He looked straight at a leaflet showing a photo of a blonde-haired girl. A message written in black felt-tip pen under the photo said, "Missing: please help us find our daughter and sister, Alice Barley, known to everyone as Lemon."

He remembered who Fraser was meeting.

Outside the café, Lawton had phoned the number on the poster.

"Who are you?" the voice had asked.

Lawton said his name and said, "You?"

"I'm her brother. Do you know anything?"

"A friend of mine met her last week. Fraser Lithgow. We've not heard from him since."

"Lithgow? Is he... is he some kind of creep?"

"Some kind, but not the kind you'd worry about."

"Is my sister in danger?"

"I don't know. I'm trying to find Fraser. You're trying to find your sister. Maybe we can both get a result, here."

Lemon's brother said his sister had met this guy who had been asking about Skarlet.

He added that Max, Lemon's boyfriend, had some of the pills.

"Where does Max live?" said Lawton.

Lemon's brother told him. "He says he doesn't know anything. If he does, he won't tell me."

"Don't worry," said Lawton. "He'll tell me. What does he look like?"

"I'll text you his photo."

Lawton gave him his number, and then Lemon's brother asked, "Do you think my sister's all right?"

"I don't know, mate," said Lawton. "And I don't know if Fraser's okay, either. We've got to hope, I guess. If you're able to."

"Yeah, I'm able to. I'm... I'm kind of psychic, see."

Lawton had rolled his eyes but said nothing.

Lemon's brother said, "I've... I've seen that she'll be okay and that she'll be with me and our mam at Christmas. I just had this dream of us together the other night, and I woke up sweating. I knew it was a message, you know."

"Yeah, sure," Lawton had said. "You keep hold of that."

Then Lemon's brother said, "Do you think this has something to do with what's going on?"

"What do you mean?" said Lawton.

"I mean, Britain turning into Nazi Germany. Closing borders. People dying in London last night. Everybody's scared. Really scared. Do you?"

"I don't know."

"Anyway... you'll phone me when you find my sister?"

Lawton had said yes. But he knew Lemon's brother would probably never see his sister again.

* * * *

305

Now Max said, "What do you want? Leave me – "

Lawton slapped him on the head.

Max said, "I haven't got anything, honest. Is it about those pills I got last week? I gave him the cash. He was called Will. He was a student."

"You know someone called Lithgow?" said Lawton.

The look on Max's face told Lawton that the answer was yes.

Jake grabbed him by the throat. "Where is he?"

Max gurgled and tried to pry Lawton's hand away from his neck, but he wasn't strong enough.

Jake released his grip on the man's throat and said, "If you force me to ask the question again, I'll squeeze harder next time – and every time I have to ask it, my hand'll get tighter and tighter. That's how it'll work. I ask a question, I squeeze. I ask it again, I squeeze some more. Got it?"

Max got it.

Lawton had found Max after going to the address Lemon's brother had given him. When Jake was pulling up outside the tower block, a man matching the photograph Lemon's brother had texted him scurried out of the stairwell.

He'd looked like a creepy, greasy little shit.

From the tower block, Lawton had followed him on foot. Max had walked for about fifteen minutes before coming to a row of shops: takeaways, mini-supermarket, off-licence, Post Office, dole office.

Lawton had waited in the mini-supermarket while Max idled outside the Post Office.

I know what you're up to, Lawton had thought at the time.

And when Max had started to follow the old woman from the Post Office, Lawton had tailed him. He was ready to protect the pensioner whenever the time came. But Max didn't make his move until they'd reached a tower block.

After ambushing Max in the subway, Lawton had tossed him through a door into a room that appeared to be a storeroom.

Lawton had slammed the door and wedged the handle with a broom. With Max lying in a heap on the floor, Jake raced around the storeroom, pulling down shelves and throwing things about. His tantrum did the job. Max was terrified. The guy thought he was trapped with a psychopath.

Lawton had grabbed a chair and hauled Max to his feet.

"Sit the fuck down, cunt," he'd told Max.

Max obeyed. Lawton punched the wall. Max tried to get up, which was when Lawton slammed his hands on his shoulders.

Now Lawton said, "I know you're Lemon's boyfriend."

"Who?"

"Don't bullshit me, Max. I'm fucking mean."

"You're... you're... oh, shit... "

"You know me?"

"N-no – fuck, no!"

He did. Lithgow must've told him. He always told them.

My mate, Jake.

"Tell me about Lithgow," said Lawton.

Max said, "What are you talking about?"

Lawton grabbed him round the neck and squeezed. "What did I say about asking a question more than once?"

Max choked. His face turned red. He tried to push at Lawton's wrists, but he was too weak.

Lawton let him go. Max panted.

"When you're ready," said Jake.

CHAPTER 82.
THE GREATER GOOD.

"I'M not going anywhere till Jake gets back," said Aaliyah.

Goga sighed. "I do not understand. This is grave. Our enemy is strong, now. Soon, there will vampires crawling all over this city, all over this country."

"You said we should abandon Britain," she said.

"For the greater good, Miss Sinclair. Turn your back on today to save tomorrow. Yes, people will die. Thousands. They will become vampires. But if we find and kill Nimrod, his death will extinguish all vampires."

"But they won't come back as human, will they."

"No, they will be dead. But not undead."

Aaliyah was sitting on a chair at the desk. Names and messages had been scrawled into the tabletop. She gouged into the wood with her thumbnail. Jake was in her mind, and without realizing it she scratched the letter "J" into the desk.

"Mr Lawton wastes his time looking for his friends, and now you've let the boy go to look for his mother," said Goga.

She glared at him "What would you do?"

"I would persuade them that my mission is most important. Always the greater good, Miss Sinclair. Can't you see?"

She bowed her head. She *could* see. And earlier that morning, she had made it clear to Jake how she felt about things.

Perhaps we should think about what Mr Goga's saying, darling.

Now she wished her mouth had stayed shut. Jake had been hurt by her words. She'd betrayed the trust they had in each other.

But then she thought, *Isn't it better to be honest?*

She looked at Goga.

Yes, it was better. But only in private. In public, you supported each other.

Goga went to the window. There wasn't really a view. You could see the back of the Victorian tenements that had been turned into modern-day bedsits.

Grey clouds shrouded London. Aaliyah's heart was heavy. She pined for Jake.

Goga said, "England is not the end, Miss Sinclair. This will spread. It must spread. Plagues always do. France. Germany. The Netherlands. Spain. Europe will fall. Then Africa. Into Turkey, and from there, Asia. And in Asia lies Babylon. Once they have Iraq under their control, we will not be able to enter the country. We will not be able to hunt down Nimrod. While we loiter, they grow strong. We must act now. It is fine to have friends, but allies are better. It is a good thing to care for our companions, but humanity as a whole is more important. The few must sometimes be sacrificed for the many, Miss Sinclair. It is the way of war."

Aaliyah looked at the portable television. The volume was turned down, but the pictures on screen relayed the bad news.

Britain was in trouble.

A "News Special" was being broadcast on BBC1 at that moment. Like every other channel, the Beeb had replaced their normal programmes with news.

A worried-looking Archbishop of Canterbury was on the TV. He nodded his head as if he were making an important point. A ticker running along the bottom of the screen displayed highlights of what the cleric was saying.

The ticker said, "Archbishop of Canterbury: PM must announce immediate election. Free movement of peoples must be restored. Unofficial security organizations removed from streets, airports, ports."

Jesus, thought Aaliyah.

"It is a dictatorship," said Goga, finishing what she was thinking.

"Jake saved my life," she said. "I was in a hole in the ground surrounded by blood and gore and some fucking red-skinned angel of fucking death coming to life six inches from my face. I've seen death and anguish and more than you have of these vampires. I understand what you're saying, and part of me agrees with you. I want this over and done with so Jake and me — so we can be together, normally. But another part of me says we've got to stick by our friends. We've got to do our best here."

He looked her in the eye. "In Iraq, beneath the ruins of the old city of Babylon, lies a terrible monster. The god of vampires. It is still alive. I went there to kill it and end the plague, but I failed. Now I am here, hoping for your help. And Mr Lawton's help. The world is in peril. Do you understand?"

"I understand. But Fraser's in peril, too. So is David's mum. And Jake's trying to save them, Goga."

"You are tenacious, Miss Sinclair, for sure."

"You could say that."

He slumped on an armchair. "I am telling you this, if you want a life with Mr Lawton, you shall not have one if you continue this fight. How are you going to kill thousands of vampires, Miss Sinclair? How will you do that?"

She shook her head. "I don't know."

"I do. I know. And I've told you how. I also know it is the only way you can be with Mr Lawton 'normally', as you say. This is what you want, yes? This is what you wish. Good. Let that wish be 'the greater good' for you, Miss Sinclair. Do you understand?"

CHAPTER 83.
ENEMIES WITHIN.

THE Leader of the Opposition, Jayne Monson, stood up, and the Speaker called for order.

Monson said, "It is the people of Britain who choose their leader, not some cabal hidden away in a darkened room... "

"Here, here... " came the calls from both sides of the House.

Monson went on:

"So I ask, when will the unelected Prime Minister call a General Election?"

The MPs roared.

Phil Birch, watching from the public gallery, said to Bernard Lithgow, "The sooner we put an end to the pantomime, the better."

Bernard said, "It'll be over soon. The country is ours."

Burrows stood up to a mixture of cheers and boos.

She answered Monson's question by saying, "When the time is right," and then she sat down again.

More howls. More cheers.

"They're like animals," said Birch.

The public gallery was packed with people. Journalists, campaigners, and members of the public had swamped the viewing area to witness Burrows's first appearance as Prime Minister – or *interim* Prime Minister, as the Opposition was so keen to point out.

Monson had another opportunity to speak.

"What has happened in this country since the sad death of the Prime Minister has been disgraceful," she said. "The Right Honourable Lady must re-open our borders. We on this side of the House believe that certain curbs should be in place on immigration, but denying everyone entry – and making exit very, very difficult – is wholly undemocratic."

Jeers and roars filled the chamber.

"Bitch," said Bernard. "That's what you get when you put women in charge."

Birch glared at him. "Don't tell Jacqueline that."

Burrows was back on her feet. "I think it is a shame that the Right Honourable Lady is playing politics at a time of mourning. The measures we have taken are in place to protect this country. We are under attack, as the incident yesterday in which my Right Honourable colleague – and friend – died."

"Here, here," cried MPs.

"We are in mourning as a nation," said Burrows, "but we are also on high alert. I am sure that the public understands that at times of peril, we must be watchful. When we have enemies within, we must occasionally sacrifice certain liberties we enjoy. It is not pleasant, but it is necessary."

Monson stood up. "This is a democracy. We cannot overnight turn into a dictatorship – "

Just watch us, thought Birch.

He looked at Burrows with pride. His heart swelled with admiration for her. Sometimes he didn't feel worthy to be in her company. He felt like that about most of the Nebuchadnezzars. But there was no reason to feel inferior to people like Bernard Lithgow, Afdal Haddad, and all the others.

The cabal was egalitarian. Everyone was equal. They were there to serve the vampire trinity who would protect their new Babylon.

Burrows was under great strain, but she was coping well.

No thanks to idiots like this Monson woman, he thought as the Opposition leader spoke again.

Monson said, "We as members of Her Majesty's Opposition realize the nation is under attack. The terrible incident in Downing Street last night made this abundantly clear. But it is no reason for us to play into the hands of our enemies. This is what they want. They want democracy to fail. They want to show how weak we are. We are not weak. We are strong. And what make us strong are the freedoms that we have. Don't take away those freedoms."

Cheers erupted.

Burrows scowled.

The Speaker then called on Daniel Colyer, the leader of the Liberal Democrats, who rose to jeers and boos.

"He looks pasty," said Birch.

"He's scared," said Bernard Lithgow. "They're all scared."

Colyer spoke. "All our church leaders, most of our political leaders, our allies in Europe, in the United States, the G8 nations, and even China, have called on upon the Right Honourable Lady to roll back these draconian measures she has taken since becoming *interim* Prime Minister yesterday. She is unelected and what she and her Government have done is undemocratic – and if I am to be honest, the country lives in fear."

Burrows rose to speak again. "There will come a time when I, as interim Prime Minister, will consider matters of democracy. For the time being, I suggest we contemplate the life of a wonderful man, a great politician, and a kind friend. And contemplate also the security of the country he served."

"Here, here," came the calls again.

Burrows went on:

"Governance will continue, in the meantime, and we shall persist in fulfilling the pledges made in our manifesto at the last election – "

Monson, with her face red and her eyes wide with rage, leapt to her feet uninvited and said, "While turning Britain into a hell on earth with your damn creatures!"

MPs stood and shouted. They waved order papers. They booed and yelled at each other. And some even started jostling.

Monson had sat down, and her colleagues on the Opposition's front bench clustered around her, trying to comfort her.

In the public gallery, Birch said, "She's going to need all the protection she can get."

* * * *

Twenty minutes later, Burrows was sitting behind her desk in the small House of Commons office she had kept since she first became an MP.

As Prime Minister – even interim Prime Minister – she could've been allocated a larger, grander office. But throughout her career, even when she joined the Cabinet, she had been happy here. It was cosy and dark. Coffee mugs lined the windowsill. Personal photos hung on the wall. Newspapers were piled in corners. The room smelled musty.

Birch and Bernard Lithgow sat on a couple of old, wooden chairs that creaked when they moved.

Also in the office was General Howard Vince, Chief of the General Staff.

He was speaking:

"Soldiers will follow orders to a degree, but they will not fire on their own people – they will not."

"They might have to," said Bernard.

Vince said, "They won't."

"It's very simple," said Burrows. "In these days, you are either with us or you are not with us. If you are not with us, you are nothing. Those men and women who choose not to follow orders will be stripped of their ranks, and they can join the civilian population – as food and workers. Phil, give me a state of the nation, will you."

Birch checked his clipboard. "It's creaking, Jacqueline. Britain's falling apart."

"The old order disintegrates," she said. "A new one is ready to take its place. Howard, do you trust that sailor and that pilot?"

"Wakeford and Ospring?" said Vince. "Certainly not. But they don't have a choice. We should be using collaborators, of course. There are many in positions of power across this country. They will not want to relinquish their authority just because of regime change. We can use their greed and their ambition to manipulate them. Naturally, some will have honour or some such nonsense. Many military men, for sure. But as you say, they will pay a heavy price."

Burrows narrowed her eyes. "They will. As will fucking Jayne Monson. What was that nonsense she spouted about our 'damn creatures'?"

Bernard said, "Everyone knows, Jacqueline. It's just they won't use the word 'vampire', that's all."

Birch said, "It's everywhere, though. You hear it in the canteens. You hear it in the pubs. The other PPOs talk about it."

Burrows said, "What do they say?"

"They talk about vampires. They talk about conspiracies. They... they talk about Lawton as if he were some kind of superhero."

Burrows bristled.

General Vince said, "The men love him. Ex-soldier, you see. And highly respected among the rank and file. They regard him as being badly treated when he was dishonourably discharged. He's a hero to the boys and girls in uniform."

Birch said, "There is a world out there that's never mentioned or written about in the mainstream press and media. The internet fuels it. It's superstition. It's fable. It's conspiracy. But to have someone like Monson, today, voice that concern... it'll fuel the panic. I've already seen the mention of 'vampire' increase on the Twitter feeds." He glanced at his BlackBerry and without looking up from the screen said, "The political blogs have picked up on Monson's comments, already."

Burrows thought for a while.

"If they want vampires," she said after a few moments, "we will give them vampires. Let them feed. A frenzy. And by tomorrow, the poison will be in the waters. Nothing can stop us, now. Not Monson. Not Lawton. Our time is here, gentlemen. Babylon is rising again."

CHAPTER 84.
THE HEIGHTS OF HEAVEN.

BABYLON, SUMERIA – 3,208 BC

GENERAL Nanshe gave the man a bowl of fruit, and the stranger ate.

When the man had eaten the food, Nanshe told him, "You are the one they said will come – you are the one with wounds."

The stranger looked at Nanshe with a confused expression. "I don't know," he said. "I have no wounds. I am pure in God's spirit. I am clean and holy."

"You are the one; I'm sure of it," said the general.

The stranger was aged around twenty-eight or twenty-nine. He had a long, black beard and shoulder-length hair. His face was dirty, but his sky-blue eyes glittered through the grime.

Nanshe said, "What are you called?"

"Abraham."

"How long have you been in Babylon?"

"Three years. But I have been travelling here since I was twelve – fourteen years in the desert."

"And you've lived like a pauper since you've been here?"

"No other way to live."

"How have you eaten?"

"The Lord my God provides."

"Who is your god? Not Marduk?"

The man called Abraham sneered. "There is only one god, and he is Yahweh. He led me through the desert. He provided me with food and water."

Nanshe shrugged. "He must be a strong god to let you live out there for twenty years. Perhaps I should worship him."

Abraham's eyes narrowed. "You *must* worship him. He is above all other gods."

"You didn't come to my house to convert me."

Abraham shook his head. "They said you lead a rebellion."

Nanshe leaned back on the seat and laughed. "Not much of a rebellion. Twenty years ago I led the armies of Sumeria. I was Nimrod's general."

Abraham looked at him coldly.

"What is it?" said Nanshe. "I am no longer his soldier. I am his enemy now."

"Ur," said Abraham.

Shame filled Nanshe's heart. "Look at my hands. I can't wash the blood away. It stains my skin. It always will, no matter how much I scrub. We slaughtered children. It was genocide. It was – "

" – my city."

Nanshe looked Abraham in the eye. "What did you say?"

"Ur was my city. The people were my people. The blood is my blood."

There was a knife on the table. Nanshe snatched it before the stranger could reach for it. "That's why I left Nimrod's service," he said. "What we did was not within the rules of engagement. We committed a war crime. I committed a war crime."

"Then you should pay."

"I *am* paying."

"With your life."

"You are not my judge, stranger."

"No, the Lord is your judge."

"I don't worship your god. You came to my house. I gave you my food. Show me respect."

Abraham stared at him. He was an intense young man. He might be the one to challenge Nimrod. The one, as the prophecy said, who could bring down the Great Hunter. The one with wounds.

Nanshe spoke again. "Nimrod ordered the slaughter of innocents at Ur. Yes, I obeyed him. But I was his general. And I feared him. He is mighty."

"Only the Lord is mighty."

"No, Nimrod is mighty. You clearly don't know. He tore three hearts from his chest, and they became demons before my eyes. For years, I worshipped them, and they protected me from all my enemies. But since Ur, guilt had plagued me. I saw the evil in Nimrod, then. I couldn't serve him any longer. Some of my men left with me. We are in hiding. We live in these slums, now. With dogs and rats. Every night, Nimrod's hundred brides sweep through these streets and take blood from people's veins. I stay inside after nightfall. It's safer."

"So do you fight? Do you lead a rebellion?"

"There is no rebellion. We gather at my house to plot the Great Hunter's downfall, but we don't have the power to defeat him. He has his brides. He has his trinity, too. And he, himself, is immortal. How can you kill immortality?"

"I can kill him."

"You *are* the one."

"I don't know. I'm here for vengeance. All I need is a way into the tower – a route to Irkalla."

Nanshe looked at the stranger and thought about things. Then he said, "Come with me."

A few minutes later, they were standing on the roof of Nanshe's house, looking towards the centre of the city, which was five miles away from the slums.

"It is a terrible structure, don't you think?" said Nanshe.

Abraham shielded his eyes from the sun. His head tilted back as he stared up towards the top of the tower. It climbed from the heart of Babylon to the heights of heaven.

"You can't see where it ends," said Nanshe. "It's too high. It goes to the door of God."

"No it doesn't."

"But that's why Nimrod had it built. So he could touch God, and mock him while living down in the dark depths of Irkalla. He wanted to rule the high and the low. Heaven and the abyss."

"How do I get past the guard?" said Abraham.

Two hundred soldiers known as the Death Legion surrounded the tower to prevent any citizen from approaching. Not that anyone would want to. It would mean death. But Nimrod and his priests feared an uprising.

"Bribe them," Nanshe said. "They are poorly paid and will do anything for money."

"And how do I enter the tower?"

Nanshe took a bunch of keys from his belt and removed one. It was large and rusty. "There is a door at the base of the north face. It is covered in foliage. You won't see it immediately. Here." He gave Abraham the key. "Why is your god special to you?"

"One day, my God will show me a land where I must go. Out of me, he will make a great nation. He will make my name legendary. And those who curse me, he will curse."

"All gods promise these things."

"But not all gods deliver them."

"You will face Nimrod?"

"I will face him; I will destroy him – and I will bring down his blasphemous tower.

"I tell you, he can't be destroyed."

"We'll see."

Nanshe shrugged. "But if you are the one they said will come... maybe you can destroy him... the prophets said that the one with wounds would kill the Great Hunter."

"Your prophets are false prophets."

"If that's true, you're doomed."

"Not with God as my sword."

"You religious people... I don't know what to say to you." Nanshe turned and went to the stairs to walk back down into the house. He turned. Abraham continued to stare up at the tower in the distance. "Come with me and have some bread," said Nanshe. "Then you can go. And I will pray to the idols that you are the prophecy. Because if you are not... I pity you."

CHAPTER 85.
THE DEPTHS OF THE EARTH.

THE tunnel smelled of decay. The protective mask George Fuad wore over his mouth and nose filtered out a lot of the stench, but the odour still seeped into his airwaves.

And it was sweltering. Perspiration oozed out of his pores. His hair was soaked, heavy on his head. The heat made the smell worse. Christ, he was going to puke.

The tunnel was twelve feet high, and it was half the width of a football pitch. Hanging from the ceiling were rows of 100-watt bulbs, and they twinkled like stars far down into the tunnel.

"We'll take a break," said George.

The men slumped.

George knew they were about halfway to Westminster. The journey by road was just over a mile and a half. It was a little less under the earth.

The only thing that delayed them was the cargo.

The container carrying Haddad's monstrous creation weighed nearly a tonne. It was now on wheels, but pushing it through the tunnel was still hard work.

George had asked for Meadows and three other men to carry out the work. The rest of the workers who'd been digging through into the tunnel from the basement in Religion had been told to leave. They took Christine Murray with them so she could get hospital treatment.

Some of them had been eyeing her anxiously while they worked. The men looked worried. They spent their water breaks muttering to each other. George could tell they were desperate to ask about the blood-soaked woman. He gambled that their wages would moderate their curiosity. He lost. Three of the men had come over to him and said they were worried about her.

"I've been so busy down here, I've not had an opportunity to take her to a doctor," he'd told them. "She got hurt in a rock fall. Would you guys take her to hospital when you leave?"

They agreed, not knowing they'd never reach a hospital. Actually, they didn't even get out of Religion.

Alfred and a couple of hitmen had been waiting for them when they came out of the elevator.

George had decided that it was necessary to kill the men.

"Better safe than in the shit," he'd told his fellow conspirators.

Just in case this gets fucked up again, he thought. *Just in case we don't succeed, and the new authorities look for witnesses. Just in case.*

Now, Alfred and the hitmen, with Murray in tow, were somewhere behind them in the tunnel. George looked back down the passageway and imagined his brother back there in the gloom.

After George and Meadows's team reached their destination in the next couple of hours, Alfred and his killers would arrive soon after. And there would be more shooting.

"I'm a Londoner," said Meadows now, "and I'd've sworn on my mother's grave that I knew every inch of this old town. I'm damned, I really am. Never knew this tunnel was here."

George said, "It was built in the 19th century by the owners of Religion."

"Was it a den of iniquity back then, too?"

"Kind of — it was a church. They called themselves the Church Of The Event Of Resurrection. I hear there's a bunch of them still around. Hornsey Park Road area, I'm told."

"Mad, these religious folk, ain't they."

George said, "They thought the end of the world was coming, and that the devil was arming himself to fight God."

"So they dig themselves a bunker? Or an escape route?"

"No, they dug themselves down into hell, so they could stop the devil at the border."

"You're joking."

"Ain't no joke, Meadows."

"They went down here thinking they'd find the devil?"

"That's right. And some say they did find him."

"I don't believe all that stuff."

"Who does? Okay, let's get our boots on."

They started heaving the crate again. Two men in front, pulling on ropes attached to the container, and three at the rear, pushing. It was hard work. And to ignore the strain on his body, George tried to think about the future.

They were so close to achieving their aim of a new Babylon in Britain.

But why stop here?

And why stop with Kea, Kakash, and Kasdeja?

Meadows, pushing the crate alongside George, said, "So what's this all about again? Why're we shoving this thing two miles underground when we could take it in a truck?"

George glared at the worker.

Meadows said, "All right, I know we're not allowed to ask questions — "

"You're getting paid a lot of money to keep your mouth shut, Meadows."

"I understand, Mr Fuad, but I'm curious. We all are, you know."

"You know what happened to the cat, don't you."

"All right. Understood."

They were quiet for a while.

But then George said, "We're taking this to the cellars of the Houses of Parliament."

Meadows stopped pushing. It didn't make much difference. The crate rolled on.

"The Houses of Parliament?" he said. "Like Guy Fawkes? You know, trying to blow up the place. Is that right?"

George said, "That's a question too far, Meadows. Your pay's being docked. You moan about it, or ask me anything else, I dock your men's pay, too – and then I tell 'em why their wage packet is lighter than was agreed. Clear? Now fucking push, you lazy sod."

Meadows pushed.

CHAPTER 86.
SAVE MANY OR SAVE A FEW.

WEST CROMWELL ROAD, EARLS COURT, LONDON –
12.06PM, FEBRUARY 15, 2011

GOGA said, "This man, Bernard Lithgow – you say he is allied with your enemies. He is of the Nebuchadnezzar bloodline?"

Lawton nodded and drank the coffee.

"So that means his son, your so-called friend, is also of the bloodline."

"He's not his father's son," said Lawton.

"Whose son is he?"

Lawton looked at the Romanian. "It's an expression. Fraser is Bernard Lithgow's son, but they've never seen eye to eye. You understand?"

Goga nodded.

Lawton had returned to London and arrived at the hotel minutes before. He found that Aaliyah and David had gone, and only Goga and his men remained.

"Your lady will be back soon," Goga had told him, "but I think the boy has gone looking for his mother."

Lawton was exhausted and made himself a coffee. He wished he could sleep properly.

Insomnia had plagued him since he left the Army. At best, he could only rely on an hour's shut-eye. At worst, he would go days without sleep.

He made another coffee and told Goga, "His dad tried to persuade Fraser to join them three years ago."

"And what happened?"

"Fraser chose the good guys."

"You don't have children, Mr Lawton?"

"Not that I know of."

"If you were a father, and you had attempted what Mr Lithgow had attempted three years ago, would you try again? As a father, now. Would you try? If you believed it would save your son's soul?"

"I don't believe in souls."

"Life, then. If it saved his life."

Lawton pondered. "I guess I'd have to try."

"You would. And Bernard Lithgow has tried."

"He'll fail. Again."

"We don't know."

"Fraser wouldn't do that."

"You have not heard from him in days. And your Mr Abbott in Nottingham confirmed that he'd gone with his father. They are in London, Mr Lawton. They are plotting."

"No – not Fraser."

"What drives him, this Fraser?"

Lawton thought about Lithgow. They hadn't been friends three years before. They had been enemies. Lithgow was a drug dealer who'd sell his own grandmother for cash, drugs, or a good time. That's all Fraser wanted – the right to party.

Maybe if someone offered him that right, he'd support them.

Something twisted in Lawton's chest, and he rested his hand on his heart. He answered Goga's question: "The same thing that drives us all. Survival."

"Then he is dangerous," said Goga. "He is with them."

"I don't accept that."

"Lawton, you must listen to me. London has fallen. Did you see the streets? There is fear. And the night will bring more terror. It is over. Britain is doomed."

"Not while I breathe."

"You must listen. You can save your country. But you must leave her to fate for now. You must come with me to Iraq."

Lawton looked at him. "Been there."

"You must come and help me find Nimrod. We destroy the Great Hunter, we destroy all vampires. And we save your country."

"But what about my friends?"

Goga turned away from him. "You can save many, or you can save a few," the Romanian said. "It's your choice."

"When I have my friends, they can help me."

Goga faced him again. "Can they? They are not like you, Mr Lawton. They are not warriors. They are not killers like you and I. What can they do?"

Lawton fumed. "What they can do, Goga, is stand with me."

"I will stand with you. I will fight with you. I will hunt and kill with you. But only if there is salvation. Staying here is death, Lawton. You have no hope. Britain is lost. She is swamped. The Nebuchadnezzars rule. Only the death of Nimrod can save your country."

Lawton stood and drank down his coffee before saying, "And only I can save my friends."

CHAPTER 87.
DERINGER MODEL 1.

HOLLAND PARK, LONDON – 12.59PM, FEBRUARY 15, 2011

"KILL your son after this is finished, Bernard," said Burrows. "I don't know how committed he is to us."

He looked at her. "If I have to, I will."

"You will have to." She got up from the couch and went over to an antique chest-of-drawers, and from it she took a velvet pouch. She returned and sat down and gave him the bag.

He tipped the pouch, and out of it, into the palm of his hand, slid a small handgun.

She said, "It's an American Deringer Model 1. John Wilkes used a Deringer pistol to assassinate Abraham Lincoln in 1865. My father gave it to me. It's recognized as a woman's gun, these days. Weighs fifteen ounces. But it kills. Kill your son with it. For me."

"Why have we asked him to do this thing for us if we're going to kill him, Jacqueline?"

"We're giving him an opportunity to show he is committed. His blood tells me that he's one of us. But I don't know if he believes that in his heart."

"We lied to him about his task. He thinks he's going to heal people. He thinks he's going to make things better."

"It'll test his mettle when he finds out the truth. And then you can shoot him though his weak, little heart. Can you kill your child, do you think?"

He said nothing.

"Obey your god?" said Burrows.

He stayed quiet.

She went on:

"Like Abraham obeyed his god and showed he was ready to kill Isaac?"

Bernard took a deep breath.

"I will kill my son if it is necessary," he said.

"Where is he?"

"Downstairs, ready to leave. He's waiting for me, I assume. Norkutt will drive us." He took her hand, and she flinched. "I think we should marry, Jacqueline."

"You're already married."

"I'm divorcing her."

"Are you?"

"I promise you."

"You told me that twenty years ago, Bernard."

He mumbled.

She went on:

"Before we even knew about this. About who we were. You promised me."

"I was young. A fool."

"A fool to say you loved me?"

"I was thirty. I was fifteen in my head."

"I still think you're still fifteen in your head, dear."

"Jacqueline, I... "

"Love me?"

"No. No, I don't. But you... "

"It's the power that gets you going, isn't it, Bernard."

"You and I, we can be magnificent, Jacqueline."

"Bernard, I have used you for sex. I find you relatively appealing, but that's about it. I cannot become romantically involved."

"Marriage doesn't have to be romantic. But if you want romance, what is more romantic than a man offering to kill his own son for the woman he admires?"

"Can we not talk about this?" she said.

His face reddened. "So I was just a fuck, was I?"

She looked at him coldly.

"Who knows?" she said.

"My God, you're a bitch."

"I didn't get to where I am today by being a darling, Bernard."

He got to his feet. "You intend to be first among equals, don't you? *Primus inter pares*."

"The Prime Minister usually is."

"In a democracy, Jacqueline, only in a democracy. We'll not have a democracy."

"I will be *primus inter pares* among the humans. I will be Nebuchadnezzar. I will be queen."

He kneeled and took Burrows's hand in his. "So let me be king."

"There won't be a king, Bernard. I shall be a virgin queen. I'll bow to my vampire god. He will protect me, and I will protect you and the others of the bloodline. But I rule. On my own."

He sprang to his feet. "You'll regret this."

"No, I won't," she said. "If you want to show me how strong you are, kill your son. Then... then I might make you my regent. Now go and do this. I have to be interviewed by Jeremy Paxman." She stood up. "And if he pisses me off, I'll have him fed to vampires."

CHAPTER 88.
FIREWORKS.

"JESUS, so this is why we have bonfire night and fireworks, then," said Meadows. The workman's voice echoed through the catacombs. "Thought it was fairy tales. Legends and myths. Dungeons and dragons, you know."

George said nothing. He scanned the cellars. The room stretched into the distance. It was too dark for George to see. The ceiling was arched and held up with joists. The wood was charred, and you could smell burning here, just like at Religion. Striplights clung to the walls. They cast a dim glow across the cellar, and their weak light made shadows dance. The temperature had also dropped. It was a relief to be out of the tunnels, but George was a little shivery, now. He said, "Rumour has it that these cellars burned down in 1834."

"There was a fire, you can see that – and smell it," said Meadows.

"It was around the same time as the church built the tunnels to hell."

Meadows furrowed his brow. "You saying it was them religious chaps burned it down?"

George shrugged. It didn't matter that Meadows was

asking questions now. They were here. They'd reached their destination. Meadows and his men would be dead in the next few seconds.

A groan came from behind them, and he turned. The container squeezed through the hole in the rear wall, just making it. The three workmen came after it, sweating and puffing.

"Take it easy, fellas," said Meadows. "We'll be done in a while. You all right with it here, Mr Fuad?"

"It's fine."

A clanking noise echoed out of the distance, and George turned towards the sound. A shiver ran down his spine. He was about to ask one of the workmen to take a look when Meadows spoke again:

"This ain't some modern-day bonfire night business, is it? You're not planning to do what Guy Fawkes tried to do and blow up them MPs?"

"Why would we do that?"

George ignored any worries he had about the noise.

Rats, he thought. *Or something.*

Meadows continued: "It's a mess now, ain't it. That woman in charge. Closing the borders, an' all. Mind you, can't say that's a bad thing. Keep them foreigners out. Taking our jobs and the like. But my lad, he's working out in Cyprus on the building sites, and he was due home tomorrow for his mum's birthday, but – "

The gunshot blew Meadows's head off his shoulders.

The other three workmen leapt to their feet but were mown down before they could do anything.

The smell of cordite hung in the air.

"Perfect timing," George told his brother.

Smoke plumed from Alfred's gun. "Better late than dead, brother," he said.

The two men who came with Alfred went to deal with the dead bodies.

"Where's Murray?" asked George.

Alfred went back through the hole that led into the tunnel, and after a few moments he appeared again with Christine Murray.

George grimaced. "She looks great. You look great, Christine."

"Bastards," she said.

"She looks barely human. You look barely human."

"Bastards," she said again.

"Don't worry, Christine, you won't be human for long."

Alfred said, "This is it, then," and craned his neck to look around.

George said, "We are directly under the House of Commons."

"This is how Guy Fawkes felt, eh?"

"Bet he had a fucking hard-on."

"You would, wouldn't you."

George said, "Traditionally, before the State Opening of Parliament, beefeaters will symbolically check down here – just symbolically. It's a throwback to the Guy Fawkes plot."

"You would want to check, symbolically or fucking literally, if someone tried to blow up the Houses of Parliament."

The brothers wheeled the container forward. They chained Murray to the tank.

She looked up at George. Her lips were chapped. Dirt and blood covered her face. Wounds peppered her body. She was a mess.

She said, "Jake'll destroy you."

The Fuad brothers laughed.

"She cracks me up," said Alfred.

George kneeled in front of her. "Christine, darling, our mighty vampire prince here" – he rapped on the tank with his knuckle – "will soon rise up", and in a scene worthy of any Hollywood movie, it will tear itself up through the flimsy ceiling above you, claw through mud and concrete, the foundations of your democracy, before bursting out into the House of Commons, where his presence will be announced to the world."

"You're crazy," she said.

"I like to think so."

"The end is nighty nigh, Christine," said Alfred. "It's over."

The brothers stood over her and laughed.

Murray said, "Not until Jake Lawton says it."

CHAPTER 89.
LUCK.

LAWTON said, "I'm sitting here doing fuck all while they're taking my country and killing my mates." He got to his feet. "Enough. Enough of this. This is a time for fighting. This is a time for standing up for your mates. This is Queen and fucking country stuff. They are not taking this place without a loss of blood. They are not taking my friends. They've killed Tom. Christ, he's been through more wars than you've had shits, Goga, and they... they cut off his head. Jesus. And we're sitting here while they've got Christine, while they've got Fraser – "

"One last time, Lawton," said Goga. "You can end this war by coming with me."

"One last time, Goga," said Lawton. "No."

"Look at your television. The news is bad. People are out on the streets. Some of your citizens are rioting. The police are shooting at them. The Armed Forces are patrolling your cities. The Nebuchadnezzars' own private security teams are prowling this nation. Tonight, vampires will rise. There will be more deaths. You are not Canute. You cannot stop the tide by staying on the shore."

Lawton said nothing. He rubbed his hands together, thinking.

Come on, he told himself, *you're a soldier – do something*.

But he didn't know what to do. It was like being surrounded. There was nowhere to go. The enemy had hostages. You were outnumbered. You were in a bunker. And you had one offer on the table. A chance to end the war. But it would mean your comrades would die. And civilian casualties would number thousands, perhaps more.

What do you do?

Was this how the Americans felt when they were thinking about dropping nuclear bombs on Hiroshima and Nagasaki?

He looked at Goga.

What I need is a bit of luck, he thought. He waited a few seconds, but nothing came, and then he said, "I'm going to get Murray and Lithgow. I'm not letting these people get away with it. If I die, fine. But I cannot abandon those two. I cannot. Do you understand?"

"No, I do not," said Goga. "I should leave, then. You are a warrior, Lawton, and a proven killer of monsters. You would have been a good ally."

"You looked for this Nimrod before, and you didn't find him."

"I will keep looking. It is the only way to save humanity. You cannot see this, and it makes me angry and sad."

The door flew open, and Aaliyah entered, her face red and glazed in sweat.

Lawton's nerves tightened. "What's happened?"

"It's David," she said.

* * * *

Houses of Parliament, London – 1.55pm, February 15, 2011

"And this is what you saw," said Jayne Monson.

Nigel Thomas bowed and said, "Yes, ma'am, this is what I saw."

Monson said, "Don't call me 'ma'am', Mr Thomas; I'm Leader of the Opposition, not Queen."

"Sorry, ma'am."

They were sitting in Monson's office in the House of Commons.

"I didn't know the cellars were accessible," she said.

"They're not, really. There is a trapdoor from the kitchen."

"Oh, there would be, wouldn't there — trapdoors, secret passages."

Thomas went on: "It leads down some stone steps to a metal door, and behind that lie the cellars."

"What were you doing down there, Mr Thomas?"

"As Yeomen Warders, we traditionally check the cellar before the State Opening of Parliament — due to the Guy Fawkes business, you see. It's a bit of a tradition. I mean, of course, we don't expect to find anything. Not these days, you know. We took it more seriously during the Second World War. And, well..."

He tailed off and blushed.

Monson said, "Go on, Mr Thomas."

"Well, you see... what with this terrorism business and poor Mr Strand being killed — that awful attack on Downing Street, I just... we just thought we should... we didn't expect to find anything ... well, I didn't..."

"Thank God for the Beefeaters," said Monson. "Why did you come to me, Mr Thomas? Why not your superiors or the Prime Minister's office?"

Thomas stared at her. He was in his fifties. He had bushy eyebrows and thinning grey-red hair. His uniform was dark blue with red trimmings. The Yeomen only wore the more recognizable Tudor State Dress of red and gold on State occasions.

He spoke: "I know what's going on in this country, Mrs Monson. My grand-daughters are always on the internet, you see. It's there you get the truth these days. I know about vampires."

Monson flinched. She didn't like to hear the word. She wanted a more rational explanation to what had been going on in Britain for the past few years. But she wasn't going to get one.

Thomas said, "And I know about conspiracies, too, and that Mrs Burrows is not all that she seems. I love this country, ma'am. I served in the Army, you know. Twenty years. I don't want to see Britain fall into the hands of... of evil people. I don't want to see it fall into the hands of monsters, ma'am."

They looked at each other for a few moments before Monson asked, "What do you suggest, Mr Thomas?"

"Well... there's this man... ex-soldier... "

CHAPTER 90.
WHAT DAVID SAW.

WEST CROMWELL ROAD, LONDON – 2PM, FEBRUARY 15, 2011

LAWTON said, "Tell me what you saw, David."

On the other end of the phone, David said, "It was a black Mercedes. It was parked outside a house in Holland Park. There were a lot of policemen around – with guns."

"What did the driver look like?" said Lawton, striding down West Cromwell Road. Aaliyah walked with him.

"He had, like, a gaucho moustache."

Lawton stopped walking. Max Abbott had told him a few hours earlier about a man with a gaucho moustache who'd accompanied Bernard Lithgow.

And David then confirmed Lawton's fears: "You know Fraser's dad?"

"Yes, David, I know Fraser's dad."

Aaliyah stood in front of Lawton, waiting. She shrugged her shoulders, as if to ask, *What's going on?*

Lawton shook his head.

David spoke again:

"Well he came out and got into the car, and they waited."

"Waited?"

"Outside the house."

"Okay. Then what?"

"Fraser came out of the house, Jake."

A cold feeling spread across Lawton's chest.

David went on: "He was carrying, like, this briefcase."

"How did he look, son?"

"He... I don't know, kind of glum, I suppose."

"A briefcase."

"Yeah, a briefcase."

"You didn't endanger yourself, did you?"

"Well, I guess I did, but I had to find out."

"What made you go there?"

"Mum was... was a reporter, right? Well, she always said if you get stuck on a story, go back. Like, go back to the scene of the crime or whatever. I... well... this place was where a lot of it started, wasn't it. Holland Park. So I came to look."

"Clever," said Lawton. "What did Fraser do?"

"He got in the car."

"Okay." Lawton was beginning to feel sick. A dull ache throbbed in his breast. Maybe Goga was right. Fraser had joined the enemy. "What then?"

He listened to David. After a minute, he put the phone back in his pocket and Aaliyah said, "What do you think?"

"I think 'shit' – that's what I think. Shit, shit, shit."

He looked around. Traffic was heavy. Horns blared as drivers lost patience with the gridlock plaguing London that day. Armed police patrolled the pavements. Lawton bowed his head. "We need to get out of sight – and we need a car."

"Where are we going?"

* * * *

A305, MIDDLESEX – 2.40PM, FEBRUARY 15, 2011

"West?" said Aaliyah.

"West."

"What's west?"

"I don't know," said Lawton. "But that's what David said. I can't believe that he nicked a car. I said, *You're thirteen*, and he

338

said, *So what?* He and his brother have been 'Taking Without Consent' since the Murrays became nomads."

"Is it irony that you're shaking your head at a kid who steals cars while you're actually driving a stolen car?"

Lawton said nothing. His eyes were fixed on the road ahead. They were travelling along the A305 – in a Lexus he stole from Earls Court.

Aaliyah said, "David lost them."

"Few miles back near St Margaret's Pub."

"Where is he now?"

"Gone back to the hotel."

"He's a brave little sod, I'll give him that."

"He is."

"He tried to kill you, though."

"That's forgiven."

"Not forgotten?"

"Never forgotten."

They were quiet for a while, looking at traffic and trying to spot the black Mercedes.

"But where's it going?" said Aaliyah.

Where? thought Lawton.

"Christ," said Aaliyah.

Lawton jumped in his seat. "What?"

"Four cars ahead."

They were on the Hampton Road, now. And there it was. The black Mercedes.

"Jesus," said Lawton. He felt a surge of energy shoot through him. The exhaustion and the aches plaguing him dimmed for the moment. He was tempted to accelerate and overtake the cars in front, but he controlled his eagerness. "Okay, we'll just hang back... hang back and wait."

They drove down Creek Road. Red-brick buildings lined the street. They passed a Chinese restaurant, and Lawton's stomach rumbled. He couldn't remember when he last had a proper meal.

Where are they going? he thought.

"Maybe they're going to kill Fraser," said Aaliyah. "Take him out somewhere, execute him."

Lawton said nothing.

He followed the Mercedes onto Walton Road. He saw the sign and gawped. *No way*, he thought. What was in the briefcase David had seen Fraser carry? *No way*, he thought again.

"Why the fuck are they going there?" he said.

"Where?" said Aaliyah.

He pointed at the sign that said they were a couple of miles away from a cluster of reservoirs owned by Thames Water.

CHAPTER 91.
A BROTHER'S FAREWELL.

GEORGE Fuad rubbed his hands together. It was cold. His breath came out white when he blew air out of his cheeks.

"I think you should get going," he told his brother.

Alfred looked at his watch and then said, "Shame, 'cause I'd like to stay for the match, you know."

"Bruv, you're heading off to do something much more important."

"*This* is important, Georgie. We've been waiting a lifetime for it. It's what being a Fuad is all about. We missed the last resurrection, and I just don't want to miss this one."

"Alfie – the bigger picture, mate."

"Yeah, yeah."

George scanned the cellar. Floodlights had been set up here now. He could see better. Damp made the walls glisten. The place smelled old.

Alfred laid a hand on the container. "Christ, it's warm."

"Something coming alive in there," said George.

"That's what I want to see."

"You'll see. You'll be back in a few weeks. Burrows is on the way down. You should be gone when she arrives."

"She'll ask questions."

"Sod her."

"She's PM now," said Alfred. "Ain't that scary."

George said, "Not as scary as Maggie Thatcher. Remember when we met her?"

"Eighty-eight. Bit of wine. Canapés. Lots of us flashy entrepreneurs having a chin-wag with the old girl. Nice. She was very small. Big presence, though."

"Yeah, some people have that, don't they. Some people." George looked down at Christine Murray. "Not you, Chrissy, girl. You don't have a presence at all, do you. You'll be nothing soon, love. Nothing at all."

She whimpered.

"She dying?" said Alfred.

"She will be."

"No, I mean now."

"Don't know."

"You should feed her. Be a shame if she dies before our prince here wakes up. He'll be starving. She's food."

"Yeah," said George, "maybe you're right."

"Do we need any more blood?"

"No, I think he's awake in there. Just bubbling nicely, I'd say."

Alfred said, "You can smell it. The decay. The old, old smell."

A clanking noise drew George's attention further down the cellar. It reminded him of something, but he couldn't remember what. "Get going, Alfie; she's here."

The brothers hugged. George said, "Take care. Make sure you got muscle with you. Lots of muscle. It's dangerous out there."

Alfred slipped through the hole that led into the tunnel. It was a mile-and-a-half walk underground to Religion. George shivered, thinking about his brother on his own in the deep darkness. But he'd be all right. He'd be out in about thirty minutes. Then he'd head out to Biggin Hill Airport in Kent, where the chartered flight was waiting for him. From there, Alfred would travel to France, where he would catch a Lufthansa flight to Frankfurt, and then on to Erbil Airport, Baghdad.

"How should we be addressing it?" said Burrows. Her voice echoed through the cellar, and George turned round to face her as she strolled towards him. "After all, it is three in one. A true trinity. Kakash, Kasdeja, and also Nadia Radu. What kind of fantastical beast will we have leading our armies?"

"It don't matter what we call it – it's coming," said George. "And let's not mess it up this time, all right?"

Burrows frowned. "Excuse me, George, but who do you – "

"It doesn't matter who I think I am, Jackie."

She bristled. She hated being called Jackie. And he knew it. George continued:

"What matters is what we're doing. There's no one in charge here, you know that. We're working together – all of us. We're making Babylon again, Jackie. All I'm saying is we should try not to fuck up like last time."

Burrows glared at him and smiled. "You're right, George. We can't let our own egos get the better of us. We should act for the greater good. We have an opportunity to change Britain, to achieve what our ancestors have been trying to achieve for centuries. It is within our grasp. Nothing should be allowed to stand in our way. And nothing will." She looked down at Murray and her brow furrowed. "Soon, this trash will be gone. And so will Jake Lawton and Aaliyah Sinclair. And after Lithgow releases the substance into the water, London will become vampiric."

CHAPTER 92.
HEARTBREAK.

B369 WALTON ROAD, SURREY – 3PM, FEBRUARY 15, 2011

LAWTON followed the Mercedes along Walton Road.

"Is it them?" asked Aaliyah.

"That's Fraser in the back seat."

"Who's in the front?"

"Can't see. Fraser's dad, is my guess."

His heart pounded. Questions rifled through his head. He had to drive carefully. *Don't get too close*, he kept telling himself, *don't get too close. And don't lose them, either.*

"Do you think Fraser's joined them?" she asked.

"No, what are you talking about?"

"But what if?"

"Then I'll deal with it."

"Why are they headed for the reservoirs?"

Lawton said nothing.

"We are wasting time, Jake."

He nearly crashed. "Wasting time? Wasting time trying to save our friend's life?"

"He's left us. He's with them, now."

"No way."

"And Goga's right, we're losing the war."

He bristled. "Aaliyah, is this you? Is this you?"

She put her head in her hands. "I don't know."

He glanced at her before fixing his eyes on the road again, and asked, "What's going on?"

Thoughts streamed through his head. He felt himself redden and grow angry. Had Aaliyah teamed with Goga? Had she –

"Have you slept with him?"

"Jesus, Jake – no!"

"Why's his fucking voice coming through your mouth, then?"

"His voice?"

"Yeah, you know – his doubts, his misgivings about this – about saving our friends, Aaliyah."

"It's not about that, it's... it's about something more."

Lawton was torn between wanting to stop the Lexus to argue with Aaliyah, and following the Merc. The car was two vehicles ahead now. They were driving down Walton Road, a tree lined B-road. Beyond the trees on either side of the street, the land sloped upwards. Lawton guessed the reservoirs were on the other side of the slopes

"Something more?" he asked.

"Jake... "

"What more is there?"

"Us," she said.

He pulled up on the side of the road. The car behind swerved and blasted its horn.

Lawton looked at her, and she was crying.

"Aaliyah," he said.

"I just want to be with you, Jake," she said, fighting her tears. "You understand that?"

"Yes... but... "

"Sorry, I might be selfish – I might be self-centred and thinking about me, or us, but I've seen a way that this can happen, okay – and I'm going for that."

"And that is?"

"That is putting an end to this, Jake. Killing this Nimrod – "

"If he exists."

"Christ, vampires exist – anything's fucking possible."

He looked away. "You want to go with Goga?"

345

"For us."

He thought for a few moments, and then he looked at her again. The words he was about to say were already hurting him in his mind, but he said them anyway: "I can't leave, babe."

Her shoulders sagged.

"It doesn't mean I don't want to be with you," he said.

"Yes it does."

"No it fucking doesn't."

"Oh my God… I've made a fool of myself."

"Aaliyah, no… how can I leave Christine and Fraser?"

"I don't know… for us… I said so… I… Jesus, I'm coming apart, Jake… shit… fuck this – " She opened the door and got out. "Get them, Jake. Go on, get them. Save them. That's a good thing, but… but I'm going to save us. And if you want to be with me after all this, find me. I'll love you always."

Aaliyah ran back down the road.

He shouted her name. He jumped out of the car and nearly got hit by a 4x4, which had to veer out of Lawton's path.

He looked at Aaliyah run and wanted to go after her, but then he thought, *I can't let Fraser die.*

The 4x4 that missed him had stopped, and a heavy-bellied man with tattooed arms had got out of the driver's side. "What the fuck are you doing, mate? Eh?" He bounded towards Lawton.

Jake's fury exploded.

He faced the man, who kept coming.

"Come on then, you bastard," said Lawton. "Come on."

CHAPTER 93.
DREAMS AND NIGHTMARES.

KWAN Mei looked at the television screen. She sat cross-legged on the carpet. She was eating *man tao* and fruit. She'd only got up half an hour ago.

The previous day had been terrifying. She'd managed to escape from Mr Wilson's flat just in time. She'd heard the front door splinter while she was clambering out of the window and onto the fire escape.

After running for an hour, she collapsed and looked around, not knowing where she was.

She asked someone, and they said, "You're in Piccadilly."

Across the road stood an amusement arcade. And out of it came Mei's saviour.

The old woman was called Liao Bo.

At first she stopped and stared at Mei, and it looked like she was going to walk away.

But she shook her head, as if berating herself, and then crossed the road.

Mei had told the woman her story while they walked. They came to Faulkner Street, and Mei gazed around her, and felt like she was nearly home.

It was Chinatown.

Liao Bo lived above her son's bakery, and she made a bed for Mei on the sofa.

Before Mei went to sleep, the old woman said that she was going out in the morning at 10.00am to work at the arcade and wouldn't be back till 5.00pm.

Mei thanked her for being kind, and Mrs Liao flapped a hand dismissively.

Now as she watched television in the old woman's flat, the fear grew in Mei.

She was watching a Chinese satellite news channel that showed London in turmoil.

They had Chinese people talking to the reporter and saying how terrible things were in the city.

"We've lived here for twenty years," said a man, "and it's never been so bad."

Police sirens blared. Helicopters swooped through the air. The TV reporter looked scared. He stood with Big Ben behind him.

Mei bit into the *man tao* and chewed without tasting the steamed dough.

Watching the carnage, she thought about Mr Wilson. Did the attack on him have anything to do with what was happening in London? She started weeping again and cursed herself for being weak, for leaving the old man.

Why couldn't I help him? she thought.

Jake Lawton wouldn't have left. Aaliyah Sinclair would've stayed and fought.

But I'm not a hero, she thought. *I'm not brave.*

She was only a girl from a place no one knew, a small Chinese village that meant nothing to anyone.

She had come to London to look for dreams and found nightmares.

Just like her mother had warned.

Mei watched the TV report.

Another man being interviewed said, "There are vampires in London, and they are killing people at night."

Mei's mouth opened.

She stared at the screen.

"London today is a very dangerous city," said the reporter. "If you live here, the advice from our embassy is to stay at home. Earlier, I spoke to Mr Wu."

A man with glasses was pictured outside the Chinese Embassy in Portland Place. A caption came up on screen saying the man was Mr Wu from the embassy.

Mr Wu nodded as if he were listening to a question and then said, "All citizens of the People's Republic living and working in the UK, particularly London, should stay at home until further notice. Our government has expressed concern with the UK government that the borders are now closed and no one is able to leave this perilous country. We are working closely with the authorities, and our citizens should keep in touch with the embassy."

A number appeared on screen.

Mei thought about scribbling it down. She was scared, and a yearning to go home burned in her chest.

But then the fire dwindled. She watched the chaos. She thought about Lawton and how he'd rescued her.

"I am your only hope," he'd said.

He was right.

The door opened and Mrs Liao marched in, shouting.

Her boss had shut the arcade early. Everyone had been told to go home before nightfall. The authorities were worried about people being attacked in Manchester. Although it wasn't as bad as London, the newspapers and the local TV news said there had been nine deaths in the city overnight.

Mei said, "It's vampires."

Mrs Liao waved her hands in the air. "I want to go back to Hong Kong," she said. "This is a terrible country."

"But we must help," said Mei. "We must save England."

CHAPTER 94.
180LBS OF BASTARD.

QUEEN ELIZABETH II RESERVOIR, SURREY – 3.09PM,
FEBRUARY 15, 2011

LAWTON pulled the Lexus into the parking area. The Merc
was there, empty.

Before getting out of the car, Lawton looked around. Trees
hid the car park from the road. A steep bank of yellowing grass
led up to a ridge and a low fence.

Beyond the ridge, Lawton guessed, was the reservoir.

He leaned his forehead on the steering wheel. Exhaustion
overwhelmed him. His chest ached, and he felt a dull weight in
his belly.

Aaliyah, he thought.

He got out. He flexed his fist. His knuckles hurt now, after
he'd knocked out the 4x4 driver. He rolled a cigarette and
smoked it. He got his backpack, which contained a knife and
the Spear of Abraham. He didn't have a gun. They'd left them
at the hotel, and now he regretted that decision.

He looked up towards the slope. Why were they here?

Lawton's nape prickled with fear.

He tossed the cigarette aside.

He slipped the knife into his belt and hoisted the scabbard
containing the spear over his shoulder before making his way
towards the slope.

He started to scramble up the bank, still thinking why Bernard Lithgow had brought his son here.

* * * *

Fifty yards away in the trees, Norkutt waited for Lawton to scale the bank, and then he followed him.

On the way here, Bernard Lithgow had said, "I've got a pain in my gut, and it's either the curry I had last night or someone's following us, so when we get there, Mr Norkutt, hang back and keep an eye for a few minutes."

Bernard Lithgow's gut was a good indicator.

Ten minutes after Norkutt had driven into the parking area, Lawton pulled in.

Bernard Lithgow had said, "I know you'll do a good job if someone is following us, Mr Norkutt; you always do. Catch us up after you deal with it, and you can see history being made."

Norkutt's pride swelled. This was good money. But no cash felt as good as praise.

Earlier, Bernard Lithgow and George Fuad had been squabbling over him.

"I want Norkutt with me," Fuad had said.

Norkutt felt even better then. These people respected him. They knew he did a good job. He was good muscle.

Wait till I get home and tell Janet, he'd thought at the time, and then remembered he wasn't allowed to tell Janet.

He wasn't allowed to tell anyone.

Norkutt never realized he was related to royalty. He'd never heard of Nebuchadnezzar till Bernard Lithgow and Afdal Haddad turned up at his flat seven years before.

At first he thought they were DSS inspectors, but Haddad was too old. He was on a zimmer frame and complained about the disabled access into the flats.

The men had come in and sat down with him in his kitchen and told him who he really was and where he came from.

"Bollocks," he'd said and told them to get out. But they didn't. And when Haddad gave him two thousand pounds in fifties, he started to accept their story. Money was sometimes persuasive.

After all, Norkutt was a mercenary.

Well, two years in the Territorial Army. It was fun to be a "weekend warrior". But then came the wars in Iraq and Afghanistan. The TA toughened up. They fought on the frontline. They became warriors all week, then.

But Norkutt didn't fancy it. He preferred to go down to the Hound And Fox, get drunk, and smash some students.

He was big and he was a bully and what were you going to do about it?

He trudged after Lawton and looked up the slope.

Norkutt blew air out of his cheeks. He'd be knackered by the time he got up there. But he had to do it. Bernard Lithgow'd asked him to look out for anyone suspicious.

There was no one more suspicious than Lawton. The guy was an ex-soldier. A real one.

So fucking what? thought Norkutt. *So was I.*

Rumours had spread about Lawton making his money these days in bare-knuckle fights.

The grapevine said he was undefeated. It said he was unbeatable. But what did the grapevine know? The grapevine was just drunks in pubs, tramps on street corners, and geeks on the internet.

I'd take you on, you bastard, thought Norkutt. *I'm going to fucking have you right now.*

He made his way up the bank. The grass was wet. He dug his heels into the soil and used his hands to claw himself up.

Lawton was so dim. He hadn't spotted a tail. He hadn't accounted for Bernard Lithgow's dodgy tummy.

Norkutt liked Bernard Lithgow. Not because he gave him cash and got him off a couple of assault charges. He'd given him a BMW, too. And he let him do anything he wanted to people.

"No one will judge you ever again, Mr Norkutt," Bernard Lithgow had told him. "We are the law."

It was great. Free to torture. Free to kill. He thought about that bird Lemon up in Nottingham and what he'd done to her. That prick Max pissed himself when Norkutt showed him the video.

Nearly at the top now. His chest felt heavy. He should've kept in shape. He was a big fellow, and the muscle he pretended to have was mostly fat.

He straightened. He could see over the ridge to the other side of the reservoir.

Norkutt clenched his fists. He'd smash Lawton today. Attack him from behind before he could do anything.

It was all about hitting first with Norkutt. That's how you won a brawl. Punch first. Glass first. Stab first. Kick first. Always get in there before they do.

And with Lawton, he'd have to do that. The man was mean. 180lbs of bastard.

Norkutt got a surge of energy and jogged up to the top of the ridge and was blinded by the white sun when he got there. And as he threw up his arm to shield his eyes a dark shape popped up in front of him.

Norkutt gasped.

A voice said, "I smelled you coming," and Norkutt felt a punch drive into his ribs, and after that things got hazy.

CHAPTER 95.
SEE ME.

GEORGE Fuad, in the cellars of the Houses of Parliament, watched as Christine Murray troughed up the soup. She slurped like an animal, and it ran down her chin and splashed on the ground.

Burrows said, "You should've fed her on the way."

"Humanitarian of the year, are we?" said George.

"No. It's to ensure that she is decent meat for his –" she pointed to the container "– coming."

George scowled. "She'll be all right."

"Are you counting on that?"

"I am."

"She's the first meal, George. Good blood is imperative. It will nourish the creature on its birth."

"Yeah, yeah." George shivered. The cellar was cold, but it was fear that rippled through him. He didn't want to piss off the vampire god that would spring from that container. He wanted to serve it. He was desperate to worship it.

He didn't understand why he felt like that. Maybe it was genes. The Nebuchadnezzar DNA.

Or perhaps the need for religion – any religion – was evolutionary.

Humans just *had* to make up gods. They wanted to believe in something more. They craved the security of salvation.

The smell wafting from the crate was terrible. Steam oozed from beneath the lid.

"We should have a look inside," he said.

"Not without Haddad," said Burrows.

"Where is he?"

"Asleep."

"I say we look – we've got as much right as he has."

Burrows creased her brow. George looked at her.

"Come on, Jacqueline," he said.

She nodded.

"Christ," he said ten minutes later, after he'd got the lid off. He stood on the step ladder and leaned on the side of the container,

"Oh my God," said Burrows. "The smell... "

The cellar filled with the odour of death. It made George dizzy. He put a hand over his nose and mouth and peered into the tank, and his eyes widened.

"What do you see?" said Burrows. "Is he alive?"

A bipedal form was being fashioned in the gore. It was nearly ten feet in length. It had two heads on its shoulders and another growing out of its thorax. The skin was red. The chest rose and fell. The swollen, black heart, which lay outside of the body at the moment, pulsed and glistened. A transparent substance that looked like glue coated the whole figure.

"It's living, and we need to feed it," said George. He looked at Murray. "Her."

"No," said Burrows. "She's the first meal. I want her to look my lord in the eye. I want her to see how worthless her war has been. She's an enemy, George. She's one of Lawton's. Let her feel what real power is. Let her regret her tiny, pointless life as she stares into the eyes of an immortal."

"Okay. Hold back on the melodrama, darling. But we need blood."

"That's fine. The vampires can bring back prey tonight."

Shit, thought George, *I never imagined such a creature.*

He couldn't take his eyes off the monster that had been forged out of three vampires.

Open your eyes, he thought, *open your eyes, great one, and see me first as your servant. See me so I can reign. See me so I can wield you as a weapon. See me as I conquer the world.*

The creature's six eyes snapped open.

CHAPTER 96.
INTO THE WATER.

BERNARD Lithgow said, "All you have to do is pull the
stopper out, Fraser, and pour the liquid into the water down
there."

He had to shout over the churning water. He and his son
stood on the metal bridge overlooking the water below. It
swirled and gushed.

"What is this place?" said his son.

"This is the Queen Elizabeth II Reservoir, son. It treats river
water and supplies it as drinking water. You see? It holds 4,300
million gallons. The tiny samples you have in that briefcase
will… will spread throughout the system. It'll heal the infected,
Fraser. We can start again. You can be part of this healing.
Like… like Jesus."

Fraser lingered. All he had to do was empty the tubes
containing the ashes into the water.

Bernard pictured it seeping into the supply. In his
imagination, he saw a woman in Bermondsey turn on her tap
and fill a bottle for her toddler. He thought of a youth in West
Ham taking a shower, the water in his mouth as he idled under
the spray. He envisioned a chef in the West End pouring water
into pastry as he screamed at his staff.

Water everywhere, he thought.

Poisoned water.

"You've got to do this now, Fraser."

"I've got a question," said his son.

Bernard flushed. He looked around. They had walked around the reservoir and entered the underground treatment works through a metal door.

Once they were inside, it was difficult to hear anything over the noise. The jet mixing system roared as it controlled the chemicals in the water. Bernard and his son stood on a metal walkway spanning a tank in which the supply gushed and churned.

He sweated. "Pour it into the water, Fraser," he said.

"Yeah, but I've got a question."

"All right."

"If this stuff −" he held up the capsule "− is meant to cure vampires, how do we get vampires to drink it?"

Bernard opened his mouth, but nothing came out. The gun in his pocket seemed to throb. He put his hand in there and felt the weapon.

Then a voice boomed over the noise of the water:

"Put those capsules back in the briefcase, Fraser."

Bernard wheeled.

Jake Lawton loomed at the top of the stairs leading down to the walkway.

Panic made Bernard quake. He turned back to Fraser and said, "Don't listen to him, son. Remember that he abandoned you, Fraser. He didn't give you protection, did he. He didn't give you what I gave you − the red mark of the Nebuchadnezzars. You are one of us, my boy. One of us.""

"Fraser," said Lawton. "I've come to get you."

"Why didn't you protect me with a skin?" said Fraser.

Lawton said, "Is that what this is about? You're sulking because you didn't get a fashion accessory? I don't have one anymore, Fraser. Look. Do you see? Courage gets you through, not trinkets like that."

"You… you were happy to put him at risk, Lawton," said Bernard. He saw the plan falling apart. He was losing control. Lawton came down the stairs.

358

Bernard's belly grew cold.

Lawton had that look about him. He had evil in him. He had iron bones. A concrete will. The man had been shot five times during his military career. They said he still had the bullets in his body. He had scars. He had wounds. But he was still strong and dangerous.

Where was that idiot, Norkutt?

But then Fraser pulled the stopper out of one of the capsules and held it over the side.

Bernard said, "Do it, son, and save lives. Save this country. Don't forget the apartment. The car. The money and the women. Don't forget what we're giving you and what he's never given you."

"Is that what they've offered you, Fraser?" said Lawton.

"They care about me, that's what."

Fraser was crying. Bernard thought this was a good thing. His son was obviously angry with Lawton.

"They don't give a shit about you," said Lawton.

"And you do?" said Fraser.

Lawton jumped off the stairs and landed on the walkway.

Bernard gasped with fear.

"I do," said Lawton.

"Funny way of showing it," said Fraser.

Lawton folded his arms. "What do you want? Apartments? Flash cars? Wads of cash? I can't give you that, mate."

Fraser said, "What can you give me? You've given me nothing. You put me at risk, Jake. You really did. Aaliyah was protected. So were you. And Christine. But not me. I didn't think at the time, but now I see. I wasn't as important as you lot. Was it because I started all this by selling Skarlet? I know you hated me back then, but I thought we were friends, now."

Lawton said, "We are."

Fraser said, "I can't see that, Jake."

Bernard said, "Fraser, don't forget what we're giving you – "

"I don't give a shit," said his son.

Lawton said, "That's more like the Fraser I know. Put the stopper back in that tube, stick it in your pocket, and walk towards me. We'll leave together."

"No you won't," said Bernard. He took the gun out of his pocket and aimed it at Lawton, who flinched.

Seeing such a menacing figure cringe gave Bernard some confidence and he laughed. "I'll kill you here and now, Lawton," he said. "I'll be a hero of the Nebuchadnezzars. The man who killed the great Jake Lawton. See? I'll bloody shoot you in the heart, you bastard."

"You wouldn't be the first to put a bullet in me," said Lawton.

Now he looked like he didn't care, and Bernard's arm felt heavy as he tried to continue pointing the gun at him.

"Put it away, Dad. Or I won't do it."

Bernard swivelled. Fraser's hand had dropped to his side. The capsule, still uncorked, looked far less threatening now.

"Toss it over the side, Fraser."

"I don't know."

"Toss it over the side, or I'll –" and he glanced towards Lawton "– kill your darling Jake."

"If you kill him, I won't do it," Fraser told him.

"You're a fool," said Bernard. He was panicking. His skin goosefleshed. He sweated, and his heart raced. Everything was going wrong.

Lawton shuffled forward on the walkway.

Bernard glanced at him. "Shall I kill him, Fraser? Then your infatuation with this thug ends, you see?"

Tears streamed down Fraser's face.

"Bloody hell, Fraser," said Bernard, "you're still such a baby."

Behind him, boots clanked on metal. He knew what was coming. Lawton was coming. He cried out and wheeled, off balance. Lawton strode towards him, brow furrowed.

Bernard stumbled backwards.

He turned to ask Fraser for help and saw the uncorked capsule between his son's thumb and forefinger and made a decision.

He aimed the gun at Fraser and pulled the trigger.

The shot cracked and deafened Bernard.

Lawton shouted, "No, Fraser!"

Fraser wavered on the walkway, a look of shock on his face.

The capsule slipped from his hand. It clinked on the walkway and rolled. Bernard watched, open-mouthed.

Lawton barged past him, knocking the gun out of his hand. Fraser fell in a heap.

The capsule tipped through a gap in the walkway.

Lawton dived for it, but he was too late.

Bernard howled with laughter.

Blood spread across Fraser's chest. Lawton went to his side and crouched next to him. "Fraser," he was saying, "Fraser." But Fraser looked pale, and blood came from his mouth.

Bernard looked around for the gun, but it had slipped down into the churning water.

He headed for the staircase. He felt dizzy, and his legs were unsteady, but he'd soon be out of here.

He never heard Lawton come up behind him. He must've moved like a panther. But he felt the ex-soldier grab his hair and spin him round.

Dread filled Bernard's chest. "You... let me go, Lawton."

The brute shoved him backwards, towards Fraser's body.

Bernard's assailant looked terrifying now. He looked like he was made of cable, taut and sharp. His muscles corded. The scars on his face gave him a thuggish look.

"You should've shot me, Bernie," said Lawton.

"What are you going to do?" He backed down the walkway. He had to get out of here. The water churned. "Don't you dare. We're the law, now. We are in charge. Don't you dare. Oh my God. Lawton... Lawton... you can join us. A man like you. Strong and brave. Imagine the money, the power. You could be head of security or something. Yes? Oh, please."

Lawton forced him backwards.

"Lawton, don't break any of my bones. Hit me if you want but not hard. I'm an old man. Norkutt! Where the hell are you?"

Lawton stopped. "Was that your friend outside?"

"What... what did you do?"

"He wasn't very good, was he. I saw him come, Bernie. I killed him. Stabbed him through the throat."

Bernard screamed. Fear squeezed his heart. His chest hurt. "I'm having a heart attack, I'm having —"

361

Lawton grabbed him by the collar and lifted him off his feet and tipped him over the side.

Bernard's vision swam. He was upside down. The water raged beneath him. He screeched.

Lawton dropped him. His belly came up to his throat. His bowels loosened. He shrieked and flapped as the water rushed towards him and sucked him under where the jet mixing system rolled and mangled and twisted him till he was broken.

PART THREE.

RAMPAGE.

CHAPTER 97.
THE TOWER.

ABRAHAM slipped into the tower and shut the door – and everything became dark.

It was cold, and his teeth chattered.

"Protect me, oh God," he said. "Be my sword as I avenge my people. Be my shield as I face the abomination. Be my light in the abyss."

General Nanshe had told him there was a basket of torches near the entrance where he'd come in. Next to the basket was a barrel of oil.

Abraham sniffed the air and smelled the fuel. He followed his nose and grabbed the rim of the barrel. The odour was very strong. He reached to his left, and his hand patted air, but after a few attempts he found the basket and drew out a torch.

After dipping it into the oil, Abraham took the flints from his belt and tried to make a spark by hitting them against each other.

Nothing happened for a while. He grew fearful. The darkness closed around him. He heard scuttling noises and was also convinced that there were voices whispering to him from the gloom.

He ignored them and prayed – prayed for light.

And God answered.

Sparks flew from the clashing flints and fell on the oil and a fire ignited, illuminating the hallway where Abraham was crouching.

He stared at his surroundings.

As he waved the torch from side to side, it made shadows. If he weren't such a faithful man who knew that God protected him, he might have believed they were being cast by his enemies.

But they weren't. And even if the passageway ahead crawled with demons, they would not be able to hurt him.

He walked into the corridor. It was narrow, and he had to bend slightly. He held the torch up.

The fire showed the path ahead, which sloped down into the earth.

The walls were damp, and as he dragged his light over them, spiders as big as his hand scuttled away from the glare. Their webs hung like drapes in the passageway. He eased them out of the way as he descended.

The deeper he went, the colder it got. He grimaced, trying to ignore the temperature. But he shivered and goosepimples raked his back and arms.

After a while, he reached a fork. Two passageways faced him. He shone his light on the left one. A human skeleton hung on the wall. Nails had been driven through its hands.

Abraham swept the light towards the right passageway.

He reared back and gasped.

The bones of a huge animal blocked his way. It was larger than a camel. It had three horns coming out of its skull, and a long nose. The ribs were like armour, and the tail like a cedar tree.

What kind of creature was this?

Abraham could pass if he were careful, but he thought the left-hand route might be better. He cast the light into that passage again and considered the skeleton on the wall. Then, once more, he illuminated the right-handed fork, and the light showed the monster.

Left, he thought. *Where evil lies.*

He fanned the torch to the left again and was ready to walk down the passageway.

But a hundred white-haired women with sharp teeth had appeared there to block Abraham's route.

CHAPTER 98.
ALLIES.

LAWTON sat on the bed and looked at his hands. Outside the hotel window, the rain pelted down. Lawton was soaked, and he'd made the carpet and the furnishings wet. But he didn't care.

"I failed him," he said. "I failed you all."

David came from the window and said, "No, no you haven't."

"I let Fraser down, and they tempted him."

"It's not your fault. Jake. It's hell out there. London's dying. Please. Please, my mum's out there."

"I should've treated him better."

"You treated him good."

"So why did he think the grass was greener?"

David stood in front of him pleading. "I don't know. There's no green grass, Jake. There's just concrete and... and vampires taking over England. Jake, please."

Lawton shook his head. "What they offered him was better. Maybe it's a sign."

"Sign of what?"

"That we're going to lose this fight. Maybe Goga was right. Maybe I should've gone with him. Lose the battle, win the war. For the greater good and all that."

"But what about my mum?"

Lawton looked at him and opened his mouth to speak. He was about to say, *Perhaps it's better if I don't stick my nose in, seeing as when I did, Fraser got killed.* But he didn't say anything.

"Everyone depends on you," said David.

"Everyone shouldn't."

"They do anyway."

"What's so fucking special about me?"

"You fight, that's what's special about you. You fight, Jake, and you never give up."

"Maybe I should."

"Please don't. I don't know what I'd do."

Lawton looked at him. The boy cried. Jake felt responsible for him. The gloom lifted. His head cleared. And then he thought about something and said, "Where's Aaliyah?"

"Gone with Goga."

Lawton's blood froze. "Goga?"

"Yeah, she came back here in a state. Said you'd gone to rescue Fraser and you'd had a row. What about?"

Lawton thought about Aaliyah gone, and it left a hole in his heart. He felt alone without her. But he'd always been alone. He'd fended for himself for most of his life, until he signed up for the Army.

And that's where he found a family.

Until they also took that away from him.

But now he had Aaliyah. And it was the strongest bond he'd known.

He was furious with himself for arguing with her and letting her get out of the car.

"What about?" David said again.

"Nothing, David."

"Oh, you're going to tell me I'm just a kid, now, and what you argued about was grown-up stuff?"

"No, I'm going to tell you it's none of your business — whether you're thirteen or a hundred-and-thirteen."

"Okay."

"So where have they gone? Have they 'gone' gone? Or are they just gone from here?"

"Um, I think... think they might have 'gone' gone, because Goga was saying they had to get to Kent or somewhere. He'd hired a plane – chartered, that's what he said. Chartered."

"Kent somewhere?"

"Yeah, sorry."

Lawton was about to say something, but then Fraser's death played out in his head again.

And the capsule rolling along the walkway and dropping through the gap and –

Lawton leapt to his feet. "You've got to ring the papers, the TV."

"W-what?"

"You've got to tell everyone, David, not to drink water from the taps – not to use tap water at all – for anything."

"W-why?"

He told David why and the boy gawped. "I-I-I drank some earlier."

Lawton looked him in the eye. "When?"

"A-a-about three hours ago."

"You'll be okay. But everyone else won't be. You've got to do this, okay? This is your job. This is your part in the rescue mission."

"O-okay. Where do I get the numbers?"

"You got a phone? Ring enquiries. Use the phone in the room. Spend as much money as you want."

"Where are you going, Jake?"

Lawton grabbed the backpack containing the Spear of Abraham. "To war."

* * * *

Mei said, "Look at the city."

And they looked. The television showed footage of London. People rioted. There was panic on the streets. Armed police patrolled areas like Westminster and Victoria Station.

Mrs Liao's son said, "This is not our business."

Mei said, "It's our country, so it's our business."

"Since when has it been your country?" he said.

"Since I arrived here."

A dozen of them were crammed into Mrs Liao's flat above the bakery. The smell of fresh bread hung in the air. It mingled with the odour of tobacco and tea. Three of the men here, including Mrs Liao's son, were coated in flour. They worked at the bakery.

Mei looked at Mrs Liao's son. He had two names. A Chinese one, which was Jin, and an English one, Jon. Mei kept her eyes on him until he looked away and shook his head.

"We can't help," said a man with yellow fingers who was smoking his tenth cigarette of the hour.

"I have to help," said Mei.

"You're crazy, girl," said Jon.

The woman who ran one of the restaurants on Faulkner Street said, "I should've stayed in Hong Kong. England is dangerous."

Mei continued to beg. "We have to help, or this country will be run by monsters, by demons."

"It's already run by monsters," said the smoking man.

Jon said, "How can we help? What can we do? We are nothing, Mei."

"We are something." She looked at the screen. "We are here."

"Who do you want to help, then?" said Jon. "This country? This country does nothing for us. We are dirt. 'Chinky,' they say to me. 'Go back to Chinky-land, you slanty-eyed bastard,' they say. 'Flied lice, Ho Chi Minh,' is what they say to my son on a Saturday night in the takeaway. He's sixteen. He was born here. He's British, and he wants to play football for England. And that's how they treat him. Let them die, I say."

"If they die, Liao Jin, we die, too." She gestured to the TV screen, and he looked. They all looked. It was bad. There was fire coming from a building. The reporter looked scared and warned people that they should stay at home.

Mei said, "My mother told me there were monsters. She warned me. I came anyway. To look for something better."

"And you didn't find it, Mei," said Jon.

"I did find it. I found a reason to fight. I found a reason to stand up for this country. I found a reason to fight and a reason to hope."

"What did you find?" asked the smoking man. "Booze?"
Laughter rippled through the room.
Mei ignored them. She said, "No, I found Jake Lawton."
And she told them about him.

CHAPTER 99.
NIGHT OF THE VAMPIRES.

THE rain soaked Luke Spofford to the skin. But he didn't care. He didn't feel the cold at all. He didn't feel the wet. Not in the way he felt them when he had been human. All he felt now was hunger. And food was nearby. He could smell it. Rich and thick and warm.

Blood.

His jaw ached. His heart punched at his ribs. There was also a pain in his chest, and instinct told him it was a signal.

Luke's maker was coming. Something was being resurrected that he feared and loved. It excited him and gave him more strength, made him bolder as he started hunting humans,

He stood in the middle of the parking ground and waited.

The rain fell heavily. Lightning sliced the sky. Thunder growled.

"Hey, dickhead," said the voice. "You're in the wrong fucking place – this ain't no zone for men in suits, fuckface."

Spofford turned towards the voice.

Three youths swaggered over. Two of them wore hoodies, and the third had on a baseball cap studded with fake diamonds.

Spofford sniffed.

He smelled the rain and the diesel from the cars, and he smelled the blood coming from the teenagers. It raced through their veins. They were excited, so their heartbeats had quickened.

The trio was energized by the possibility of robbing and beating up this mug they'd found on their patch.

"Yo, City boy," said the baseball-capped youth, "you out of your depth, boy. You in the wrong place, tonight, yeah?"

Spofford looked around. He wasn't sure where he was. He remembered dying the previous night, and he remembered waking up a couple of hours ago in the cold room that was made of steel and smelled of disinfectant.

And then someone had opened the door, and Spofford and the other vampires had spilled out of the room.

Instinctively, he went for the human who'd opened the door, but she wore a red scarf that blazed like fire and burned Spofford's eyes when he got too close.

He ignored the woman and went with the others and found himself out in the rain.

And then he ran, following his nose, arriving at the tower block and standing in the car park.

He thought he might've lived here when he was human. Or maybe someone he knew had lived here.

One of the youths approaching him clambered over a car and stomped on the roof.

The boys laughed.

Spofford wondered what they would taste like. He salivated, his gums turning liquid.

"You look sick," said one of the hoodies.

"Yeah, we put you down," his fellow hoodie said, "like we put down a dog, bitch."

The boy in the cap shoved Spofford in the chest.

Spofford backed away and looked the boy in the eye. He curled back his top lip and snarled at the youth.

The kid flinched and said, "Shit, man, he's got – "

Spofford pounced. He was like the lightning. The youth didn't stand a chance. Spofford sank his teeth into the white throat and blood sprayed, hot and thick, and it filled his mouth and he swallowed.

The boy screamed and struggled, but Spofford held him tightly.

The other boys were shouting. Spofford swung his victim round so he could keep an eye on the other two.

"Hey, man," said the first hoodie, "hey, man, he's a vampire, man – he's a fucking vampire."

Spofford growled. The blood pulsed into his mouth and down his throat. It filled him and he grew stronger and the taste of it made him want more.

The boy dying in his arms moaned.

Spofford saw them coming. They swept in down the alley leading to the car park. The first four hurdled over the cars.

He dropped the boy, and the youth slumped to the ground, twitching.

"Oh, Jesus, man," said the first hoodie.

"We need to split, man," said his mate.

Spofford licked his mouth and hissed. "You're fucked – *man*."

The vampires bolted towards them, leaping over cars.

The boys heard them come and turned, screaming when they saw the creatures.

As the undead mobbed the youths, Spofford laughed. Blood ran down his chin. Blood ran down his throat. Blood filled him.

This is better than politics, he thought. *This is life*.

CHAPTER 100.
THE SHOW MUST GO ON.

ROYAL ALBERT HALL, LONDON – 5.48PM, FEBRUARY 15, 2011

GOGA removed the gold ferrule from the end of his walking stick to reveal the metal spike.

He looked around the auditorium. The singer on stage sang "Don't Cry For Me, Argentina". She was halfway through the song.

Goga was in a box at the back of the theatre. It was directly facing the stage. He had a good view of the whole auditorium.

He'd rushed in twenty minutes earlier and bought his ticket with cash. The place was only half-full. Normally the hall would've been heaving for an event like this. Music from the Broadway shows always pulled in the crowds.

But this wasn't a normal evening. The streets were dangerous. People were dying. The country was changing.

Most theatre-goers had decided to stay at home. But there were a few hundred at the hall that night who'd risked their lives to come out and listen to some music.

And it was a risk.

But the show had to go on. And to make things safer – but only a little – the organizers had brought the start time forward to 5.00pm.

It didn't do any good. It was winter, and darkness came early. And with darkness, came vampires.

Goga had been driving past the hall with his men, and a tearful Aaliyah Sinclair, when he spotted two of the creatures scuttling up the side of the building.

He'd told Rush to stop the car. Aaliyah had wanted to come inside with him, but she'd been too emotional. It was because of an argument with Lawton. Goga was irritated that they were squabbling over personal matters while the Nebuchadnezzars' grip on power increased.

He had told Aaliyah, "Come with me to Iraq. You can fight for your country and for your man over there. The real enemy is in Babylon, Miss Sinclair. It is buried beneath the rubble of the tower it built. It lives, Miss Sinclair. And while it lives, vampires will reign."

Goga knew she was a good fighter and would be a useful ally in Iraq. But the real reason he asked her to come was because he knew Lawton would follow.

Many courageous men had faced the Nebuchadnezzars and their vampires over the centuries.

Richard the Lionheart and Saladin had joined together to fight them in Jerusalem. Goga's own ancestor, Vlad III, had risen against them in Romania. And the settlers killed in Roanoke in the 16th century, in what would become the United States, were not innocent pilgrims murdered by local tribes – they were vampires destroyed by Goga's predecessors.

But none of these vampire killers had surprised Goga more than Lawton.

The former soldier knew nothing about the power he fought against – but he still fought. Brutally and without fear.

Goga battled the Nebuchadnezzars because he had a duty to fight. Vlad went to war against them for the same reason. And Richard the Lionheart and Saladin were also driven by an obligation to their gods.

But Lawton's only incentive seemed to be his friends.

And that was the problem. He would never see the greater good. He could not see the value in sacrificing one or two people to save many.

Why wouldn't he understand that finding and killing Nimrod could end this vampire plague for good?

Winning a battle was pointless if you lost the war.

Every time the Nebuchadnezzars had been beaten back over the centuries would mean nothing if they finally triumphed.

And looking at London, Goga knew they were very close to winning – unless he could do something.

The woman sitting next to Goga in the box said, "That's a wonderful walking stick," as she applauded the end of the song.

Goga said, "I'm sorry, I was concentrating so much on the music. Thank you, it has been in my family many years."

"Isn't this music cheering at such a terrible time?" said the woman.

Goga nodded.

"We did consider staying home," she told him, "but we were determined not to be intimidated."

On stage, the performer thanked the audience and introduced the next song as a tune out of *Les Miserables*.

And then the audience craned their necks.

Goga chilled. His grip on the walking stick tightened.

"What in heaven's name is that?" said the woman next to him.

Gasps and shrieks rifled through the auditorium.

Goga stared at the ceiling.

Two vampires clung there, upside down.

Some people thought it was part of the show and started to applaud. Others were less convinced. A few leapt to their feet. Staff scurried down the walkways. The orchestra was up on its feet. The singer due to perform looked up and gawped.

And then the vampires dive-bombed the audience.

And panic tore through the Albert Hall.

CHAPTER 101.
PRETEND DRUNK.

Victoria Station, London – 5.55pm, February 15, 2011

CHARLIE Sandford, twenty-seven and with a few Friday afternoon cocktails sloshing about in his stomach, told his wife not to hassle him.

"I'll see you when I see you," he said into the phone.

"You be on that fucking train, you bastard. Telly says London's dangerous. Get home, you shit. Don't be an idiot all your life. You're taking the kids swimming at 6.00am tomorrow. It's their Wednesday morning lesson. You be on that fucking train. You get home to us, Charlie."

"Don't fucking swear at me – "

"You're slurring, Charlie. You're drunk. You'll do something stupid. Don't think you can sort this out, Charlie. Please. Leave it to the cops. You're pissed."

"I am not pissed."

He was. He'd been drinking since mid-day.

Charlie worked in the investor relations department of a private equity firm. The markets had crashed since the PM's murder the previous day. Britain was headed for the scrapheap. No one was interested in buying anything. Charlie's boss had come in that morning and said, "All of you might as well go home – or get drunk."

Charlie and his colleagues chose the "get drunk" option. They spent the afternoon at All Bar One on Chiswell Street, which was five minutes from the office.

He had drunk a lot. He drunk so much he bought a packet of fags. He hadn't bought a packet of fags in three years. He'd stopped when Grace was born. A promise to his wife.

Now he fished in his pocket for the Silk Cuts. Using his mouth, he plucked a fag out of the packet. He lit the cigarette and took a drag and felt sick.

He retched.

"You're puking, you pig," said his wife.

"I... I'm ill... flu coming... "

"Sir, you cannot smoke in the station – *anywhere* in the station."

Charlie looked up. A copper glared at him. He smiled. She was a girl. Twenties, her blonde hair tucked into her cap. His eyes raked over her body. She wasn't a real cop. She was one of those community ones. *A pretend copper*, he thought.

Charlie told the pretend copper, "It's all right, darling..."

"Who's there?" said his wife. "Who are you calling 'darling', you bastard?"

"Don't call me, 'darling', sir," said the pretend cop.

Another cop came up to Charlie. A tall black man. Built like a truck. *Size of an elephant*, thought Charlie, mimicking a character from a cartoon called *Arabian Nights* he loved as a kid. The character could change into any animal by saying, *Size of a...* and then whatever animal he wanted to change into.

Charlie looked up at the black cop. "All right, mate?" he said. "You're a big fella."

"Who are you talking to?" said his wife.

"You must leave the station if you want to smoke," said the girl copper.

"You come with me, doll."

"Charlie, who are you talking to?" said his wife

"If you call me 'doll' again, I'll – "

"What, darling, what will you do?"

His wife in his ear again: "What's going on, Charlie?"

"It's okay, babe," he told her. "A couple of pretend PCs giving me hassle."

The black copper said, "And are you a pretend drunk, sir? Being pretend tough?"

Charlie winced. "What d'you say?" And then something caught his eye. Up in the rafters. He swayed and blinked. "What's that up there?"

"Don't be stupid, sir. Please leave the station if you are going to smoke," said the female officer.

"No, look," he said.

"Charlie, what's going on?" his wife said again.

"Fuck," said Charlie.

The officers looked up.

Other commuters were seeing the same thing. And they pointed and screamed, while some of them ran.

"Are they acrobats?" said Charlie, because the dozen or so people skittering along the rafters were agile.

But when they dropped down onto the concourse, Charlie didn't see any wires.

It was like they'd floated down. Or fallen without suffering injury.

"Christ, they're good," he said as the acrobats, or whatever they were, pounced on commuters.

One of them landed on the concourse five yards away from Charlie. By this time, his heart was racing and dread grew in him.

But it was only when the acrobat crouched like a panther and glared at him through red eyes that Charlie realized this was no circus.

When Charlie saw fangs, he tried to run. But too many Friday afternoon cocktails made him easy prey. He died screaming, "I've got to take my kids swimming, I've got to... "

CHAPTER 102.
DON'T DRINK THE WATER.

VICTORIA STATION, LONDON – 6.08PM, FEBRUARY 15, 2011

JAKE said, "Don't drink the water."

He barged through the crowds filling Buckingham Palace Road.

"Don't use or drink the water," he said again.

He was shouting but no one listened. There was too much noise. Many people were yelling. Sirens whined. Horns blared. Up above, helicopters swooped.

He kept yelling:

"Don't drink the water – it's infected – the water's infected – "

He elbowed his way through the crowd. Someone had said, "There are vampires in the station," and if there were bloodsuckers nearby, Lawton was going to kill them.

As he forced his way through the crowds, drinkers spilled out of The Shakespeare pub opposite the station. Fights broke out. Glasses were thrown. Beer spilled. A bus skidded to a halt as it came round the corner.

Lawton broke through the throng. He vaulted a black cab. The driver poked his head out of the vehicle's window and swore at Lawton, who ignored the insult.

Commuters spilled out of the station. Police herded them to safety. But unfortunately they directed them towards the fight going on outside the pub.

Lawton pressed himself against the wall of the station, near one of the entrances.

A young Community Support Officer fell against Lawton. She looked up at him. Her eyes showed how scared she was. She had no hat on, and her blonde hair hung messily down to her shoulders.

"God, what's going on?" she said. "I was just telling someone to stop smoking in the station, then this happened."

Lawton grabbed her arms and looked her in the eye. "You have got to tell people not to drink or use tap water," he told her. "You have got to make it clear that the water is poisoned. If anyone drinks, or uses it, they will become like those things in there."

She started to cry.

"Listen," he said, "listen... what's your name?"

"Na-Na-Nancy."

"Nancy – you have got to do this. You have got to tell people, or millions will die."

"They won't – they won't listen – "

"They won't listen to *me*," said Lawton.

"Who... who are you?"

"It doesn't matter."

"Who?"

"You've got to do this."

"W-who?"

"Jake Lawton."

"You're... it's vampires, isn't it."

"It's vampires, Nancy. And there'll be more of them if you don't tell people not to use the water – any water. They should only drink and use bottled stuff, right? Tell them, Nancy. And get your colleagues to tell them." He left her and went through the archway into the station, looking back at Nancy as he went. "Tell them."

CHAPTER 103.
HONESTY.

BURROWS watched television with some of her colleagues in the offices of a Labour peer at the Palace of Westminster.

She drank from a bottle of water. Her head swam. She couldn't get the image of the monster out of her mind. It was coming alive. She wanted to go back down to the cellar and stay with it. She'd told George Fuad to ring her if the creature awakened.

Her excitement grew. But it was tinged with fear.

Bernard was missing. No one could contact him.

She looked up at the television. Sky News showed the panic gripping London.

Three senior members of her Government were with her. The Home Secretary, the Justice Secretary, and the Security Minister. The peer had excused himself and headed off to an emergency meeting with other members of the House of Lords. Before leaving, he told his guests that they should stay and finish their tea and coffee.

Now, Burrows eyed her three colleagues. They didn't know who Burrows really was and what she was planning. They didn't know what was going on.

The Home Secretary, once Burrows's job, said, "I can't get a hold of the Commissioner of the Met – he's unavailable."

The Justice Secretary said, "He's on the streets with his officers – that's why you can't speak to him."

"They're not doing a very good job, are they," said the Security Minister.

Burrows looked at Phil Birch, and he nodded at her. She walked over to her protection officer and asked if he'd heard from Bernard Lithgow.

Birch said no.

Footage from Victoria Station was now being broadcast. The reporter grabbed a frantic woman and pulled her in front of the camera. Her eyes were red with tears, and her make-up was smeared.

"Can you tell us what you saw?" said the reporter.

"Oh my God! They came from the sky. From the rafters. They fell on the people. Swooped like birds of prey. It was awful. They... they were drinking blood... vampires... vampires again... my husband... "

The woman staggered away.

The reporter stared into the camera. Her eyes gaped and she licked her lips.

"There you have it, Jeremy – "

Burrows picked up the remote control from the arm of a couch and changed the channel, selecting BBC News.

The Home Secretary said, "Not too keen on Murdoch's view of the world, Jacqueline?"

"I like a different perspective sometimes," she said.

But it wasn't different. It was the same. Footage from Hyde Park of stampeding crowds. A West End theatre spilling out its audience. The Arsenal vs. West Ham Premiership football match abandoned because of crowd trouble outside the ground.

Burrows's heart pounded.

It was wonderful. It was happening.

But then her belly tightened.

Where was Bernard Lithgow?

She'd received a text from him saying he'd arrived at the reservoir. But since then – nothing.

She walked over to the desk and opened another bottle of water. She was thirsty. This was how the people of London would feel tomorrow. Parched. But they wouldn't be able to drink unless they'd stocked up on bottled water.

She looked at her three Government colleagues. They were drinking coffee. Made in the kitchens of the House of Commons. She pictured the staff opening the taps and filling the kettles.

Was the poison in the water? Had Bernard succeeded? And if so, how long would it take for the infection to stream through the supply?

Not long, Haddad said. The fragments of Kakash and Kasdeja were potent, he'd assured her.

The three ministers sipped their coffees.

If Bernard had been successful or not, these men would be dead by dawn. Dead or caged somewhere, ready to be farmed as vampire food.

Burrows felt torn. On the one hand she was happy that their plans were working out, but she was also fearful because Bernard was missing.

Where was he?

She didn't love him, but it was good to share a bed with someone again.

"Prime Minister," said the Home Secretary, "I recommend we call out the Army. Not just a few troops here and there. I mean everything. Roll out the tanks."

"I understand what you're saying," she told him, "but we can't turn the streets of London into a battleground."

"It already is a battleground, Jacqueline. Get the Army out there. People are dying."

"It would give the wrong impression," she said. She swigged from the bottle of water.

"Do we have more water?" said the Justice Secretary.

"There's a jug of iced water with a lemon on the desk over there," Burrows told him.

Burrows sat down. She wanted to go back down to the cellar and be with her god again. But there was an emergency sitting of the House of Commons planned for later that night.

The Justice Secretary poured out a glass of water.

"Anyone else?" he asked.

The other men shook their heads.

He drank.

His face reddened.

Burrows stiffened.

The man coughed.

Burrows leapt from her seat and said his name.

The man spluttered. He wafted a hand.

"I'm... I'm fine," he said. "Wrong way, that's all."

Burrows looked at Birch. Sweat glazed the policeman's brow. She sat down and looked at the TV.

"It's carnage out there, Jacqueline," said the Home Secretary. "Please reconsider."

"No," she said. "No tanks on the streets."

"Your statement to the House tonight," said the Security Minister, "will need to explain why you don't think it is necessary to go to war against this invasion."

She glared at him. "Invasion?"

His face darkened. "Shall I say the word, Prime Minister?" he said.

"I think you'd better," she answered. "Because I'm not clear what you mean."

He narrowed his eyes and said, "Vampires, Jacqueline. Everyone knows. There are vampires in London. We have to stop this. We should have stopped it three years ago."

"It looks like it's too late," said the Home Secretary.

He was looking at the television.

The screen showed a photograph. It showed the chalk-white face of a vampire snarling at the lens. Its fangs were stained red. Someone lay under the creature, their throat torn.

"Shall I use the word in the House, gentlemen?" said Burrows. "No member of Government has used it, yet. Some backbenchers, of course. But no member of the Government. What do you think?"

The three men looked at Burrows.

The Home Secretary said, "We have to recognize what's happening. It's been well known on the internet for years. But we've always ignored it. We've connived with the mainstream media to cover this up. It's about time we were honest."

"It might be too late," said the Security Minister.

Burrows ignored him and said, "All right, gentlemen, I will be honest. I think it's about time."

"Good," said the Home Secretary.

"You are all going to die," Burrows told them.

CHAPTER 104.
KILLING FOR PLEASURE.

GOGA leapt over the balcony. He landed on the seats below and hurt his leg.

The audience scattered. They poured out of the auditorium. Some of them fell as they escaped, and they were trampled. Others tripped over them. The bodies piled up in the aisles, and screams filled the hall.

The two vampires attacked. They bounded through the theatre and pounced on members of the audience. Some of the humans were killed by having their necks broken. Others had their throats ripped open, and the vampires would then drink the blood that gushed from the wounds.

Goga strode over the seating.

"You... you can't stand on the chairs, sir," said a voice.

Goga turned. A young woman in a white blouse and black skirt stared at him. Shock had bleached her face.

"Get out of here or die," he told her and carried on stepping over the chairs. He made it over four rows, but then the panicked audience blocked his way. He started to force his way through them.

His leg hurt, but he ignored the pain. It was easy. You focus on something else. You roll the pain up in a ball and squeeze it till it's tiny. Even when someone accidentally kicked him in the shin, he took no notice of the soreness.

One of the vampires, a red-haired youth in a hoodie, moved away from its most recent kill. The creature's mouth was bloody. It snarled and showed its fangs before darting after the crowd and ploughing into them.

The attack sparked more panic. The escaping horde shunted forward. Those near the doors were barged ahead. Some were crushed to death against the walls, because the exits weren't wide enough for everyone to spill through.

Goga gritted his teeth. He didn't like to see them die, but he couldn't help. You always expected casualties. And he wasn't a medic; he was a soldier. He pushed through the crowd.

The red-haired vampire had dragged down another victim. She was a blonde woman in a white evening gown. Three men tried to kick at the creature when it tore the woman's throat away with its fangs. The vampire ignored the men and opened its mouth to catch the spray of blood.

The second vampire came from nowhere. Goga failed to notice the creature. It barrelled into the men and fell on one of them, tearing at his throat.

Blood jetted from the man's open veins. The vampire clamped its mouth on the wound. After a few seconds, it lifted its head. Blood covered its face and smeared its bald head.

It snarled at the people who were trapped in the auditorium.

Outside, sirens blared.

The bald vampire turned to its companion and said, "You done? Let's kill 'em all." And it laughed.

The red-haired vampire came up from the dead woman's throat, and blood poured from its mouth.

It sprang away from the corpse like a cat and smashed into the humans.

They screamed. It caused more panic, more stampeding.

The vampires were beyond feeding, now.

They were killing for pleasure.

Goga had never seen that before.

Whoever they caught, they killed. They tore at the people with nails and with teeth. Blood flowed. The dead and dying piled up. The killing was done quickly. The killers moved like lightning.

If only two vampires can do this, thought Goga, *what could two hundred do? What could two thousand do?*

Goga finally got through the crowd. He stumbled over a row of seats, nearly dropping his cane.

The red-haired vampire fixed on him.

Goga snarled at the creature.

The vampire flew at him.

Goga whipped the red handkerchief from his breast pocket and waved it at the creature.

In mid-flight, the vampire's face stretched in horror.

It dropped from the air and fell in a heap.

Goga bounded towards the creature. Before the vampire could get up, the Romanian plunged his cane into its chest.

The blood-drinker screeched.

The other one stopped killing for a moment and stared.

Goga smelled burning. It was a good smell. The vampire gave one last howl before fire burst out of its eyes and lapped over its face. In seconds, flames washed over its entire body, and then it disintegrated.

The smell of roasted meat filled the air.

The other vampire cried out. It rushed at Goga but then noticed the protective red skin the Romanian had used to deflect its partner's attack.

"You are not a Nebuchadnezzar," said the vampire. "How do you have the flesh of my fathers?"

Goga said nothing. He marched towards the vampire. The creature screeched and wheeled, ready to leap and sail over the audience and make its escape.

But it tripped over a corpse.

Goga swooped on the vampire and thrust his cane through the creature's chest.

He watched it turn to dust and then turned to the crowd.

"Leave calmly," he said. "The vampires are dead."

The crowd swarmed out, and he followed them, and more screams greeted Goga as he stepped out of the Albert Hall.

He looked for the car where Aaliyah, Rush, and Trojan would be waiting. There was no sign of it. The road was packed with traffic and people.

Goga held his breath. People were screaming and running – some heading east into Knightsbridge, others going west towards Hyde Park Corner.

Seven double-decker buses stood at the stop opposite the Albert Hall. They were crammed with people and tottered under the pressure of their load.

Sirens and horns blared. Blue, flashing lights from police cars and ambulances bathed the crowds.

Goga looked for the car. The crowd swept past him, shoving. Panic had gripped London. He started to run into the street, but what he saw at the bus stop made him stop dead.

Vampires fell from the trees and landed on the coaches, squatting there menacingly.

His phone started to ring. Without taking his eyes off the vampires, he reached into his pocket and answered the call. It was Lawton, and he shouted in Goga's ear:

"Don't drink the water! Where's Aaliyah? Tell her not to drink – what the hell's going on there? Where are you?"

"I think the same as what is happening where you are, my friend," said Goga, hearing the screams filtering down the phone line. He told Lawton where he was, and Lawton said, "I'm at Victoria Station. You've got to stay. You've got to help."

"It's too late, Lawton. We have to get out. Come with us. Find Nimrod and destroy him. England can't start again. There's no hope here now. Come with – "

Lawton had cut him off.

CHAPTER 105.
"YOU'VE GOT TO HELP US, MR LAWTON."

VICTORIA STATION – 6.25PM, FEBRUARY 15, 2011

LAWTON used his phone to smash the vampire in the face. The creature reeled away. Lawton looked down at the girl whose life he'd saved. The vampire had been attacking her while Lawton was on the phone to Goga.

He scanned the station concourse.

Commuters were running around everywhere. They were trying to escape. Some staggered down the rail tracks with vampires chasing them.

Lawton put his phone away. He'd failed to change Goga's mind. The Romanian was going to Iraq – and Aaliyah was going with him.

Lawton shouted out in anger and brandished the Spear of Abraham. Because he'd given David the red mark that he always wore around his neck, he wasn't protected anymore.

And the vampires knew it.

Another one barrelled towards him, baring its fangs.

Lawton cut the creature's face open with the spear and then drove one of the tusks into the vampire's chest.

It came apart, and its ashes wafted away.

"Are you all right?" he asked the girl. He crouched next to her. She was about ten. He lifted her chin to see if she'd been bitten.

A voice said, "What are you doing?"

Lawton looked up. "Ar you her mother?"

The woman nodded.

Lawton said, "Get her out of here. Jump in a taxi. Anything. Leave London." He lifted the girl to her feet and shoved the child towards her mother.

The vampire Lawton had smashed in the face with his phone came back at him now.

"Come on then, see if you can bite me," he said to the creature.

The vampire pounced.

Lawton stabbed upwards with his spear.

The point went through the creature's chest, and it shrieked in pain before disintegrating, the remains showering Lawton.

Even before the vampire was dead, Lawton looked for his next kill. All around him, vampires attacked humans. Some humans fought back. A group of men smacked a vampire around the head with their briefcases. A woman jabbed at a creature with her umbrella. A member of staff sprayed a fire extinguisher over a pair of vampires, and they flapped around, covered in foam. Police officers maced and batoned the undead.

Lawton surveyed the battle.

He started shouting again: "Don't drink the water, okay? It's infected. Use bottled water. Don't drink the water." He thought for a second and blushed, but went ahead with what he planned to say: "I'm Jake Lawton" – people stopped and turned to glance at him – "and I'm telling you, the water is infected. Only use bottled. Do not drink tap water."

He felt embarrassed that people knew who he was. Aaliyah always said he was a folk hero, but he didn't care. He hadn't chosen to live like this.

The wail of a horn broke Lawton's concentration. A train was coming. Lawton gawped with horror. It mowed down the commuters who were fleeing the station.

Someone crashed into him. He spun round, ready to hack and stab with the spear.

The British Transport Police officer raised his hands and said, "You're Jake Lawton?"

Lawton stared at the cop.

"What do we do?" asked the bobby.

"Tell the people not to drink the water."

"They won't listen — not everyone — not the whole of London."

"Try."

"What else can we do?" said the policeman.

"I don't know," said Lawton. "Ask your bosses."

"They don't know, either. It's chaos. Order's gone, sir. There's nothing but panic. What do we do? You've got to help us, Mr Lawton."

Lawton looked the officer in the eye. "Kill as many of them as you can. That's all you can do. Kill them. Everyone you see. Kill them. You know how?"

The officer nodded. Lawton dashed past the constable to drive his spear into the chest of another vampire.

He had his back to the WH Smith store. The grille had been pulled down. There were people inside, and Lawton could see the fear in their eyes. They looked like prisoners. He turned from them and scoped the concourse.

Vampires hunted the terrified commuters. He tried to count the creatures. Maybe two dozen. Not many, but enough to cause panic and death. They moved quickly after killing, targeting the next victim.

A group of youths had surrounded a vampire and were kicking it. But the creature leapt out of the circle and sailed across the concourse. The youths raced after it.

Lawton saw other battles taking place. He felt pride. The humans were fighting back. But it was a losing battle; he knew that.

Maybe Goga was right. Maybe Aaliyah was right. They had to go to the source.

To Nimrod.

He gritted his teeth. How could he turn his back on these people, on this country?

Easily, he thought. *What have they ever done for me?*

Portcullis House, Westminster – 6.29pm, February 15, 2011

Jayne Monson, Leader of the Opposition, walked into the Attlee suite and said, "Have you found it yet?"

The three women and two men working in the room looked up at her and continued to either speak into their telephones or study their computer screens.

The five Tory Party workers sat around the long oak table. Monson had been careful when she picked them. It was difficult to trust anyone these days. She'd gathered them at Portcullis House, the office block built for MPs in the 1990s, after speaking to the Yeoman, Nigel Thomas.

He'd seen something terrible down in the cellars, and when he told her, Monson knew the country was at risk.

Thomas had mentioned someone who might be able to help. Monson recognized the name the Beefeater had given her, but the individual was more myth than man. However, she had to contact him if she could.

Monson glanced up at the annunciator. The monitor was fixed to the wall with a brace. It showed what was going on in the House of Commons and House of Lords. In a few hours, it would broadcast the emergency sitting of Parliament called by the new Prime Minister earlier that day.

"Well?" she said, glaring at the five workers.

A young man with blue-framed glasses said, "It's very difficult, Mrs Monson."

"I know it's difficult, Mo, but people are dying."

The young man called Mo flushed and went back to his computer screen.

A young woman with her dark red hair in a ponytail said, "His name is everywhere on the internet, but contacting him is difficult. Some people think he's actually dead. They think he died in the fire that destroyed the Religion nightclub three years ago. He's a ghost, Mrs Monson."

"Be like Bill Murray then, Carmen – find him," said Monson.

Carmen furrowed her brow.

"Never heard of the film *Ghostbusters*?" said Monson. "Oh, never mind – find this man's number. How difficult can it be?"

A phone rang. Mo answered it. He scribbled something down on a piece of paper. He put the phone down and handed the paper to Monson.

CHAPTER 106.
BUILD A BONFIRE.

"WE have to burn the bodies," said Lawton.

"You're joking," said the British Transport Police inspector.

"Why would I fucking joke?"

"You... you can't burn them."

"You know what'll happen to them if we don't?"

The inspector, in his forties with a red face and his belly hanging over his belt, said nothing.

The station had emptied. Staff had locked the doors. Outside, the screaming continued. A riot had kicked off.

Lawton stood near the ticket offices with the inspector, some of his officers, members of Network Rail who managed the station, and staff from the various franchises that ran trains from Victoria.

Everyone looked scared. They looked around at all the bodies. Many were dead. Fifty or sixty. Others were badly hurt. Paramedics and Community Support Officers looked after them.

Lawton said, "What'll happen is that they'll wake up and become what attacked them. They will become vampires."

The inspector blew air out of his cheeks.

The young policeman who'd spoken to Lawton earlier said, "Inspector, this fellow's Jake Lawton."

The inspector looked Lawton up and down. "Is that supposed to mean anything to me?"

"You remember three years ago, those attacks? The dead people disappearing? All those rumours of – "

"All right," said the inspector, cutting the copper off, "let's have no more talk of... of whatever. We aren't burning anything."

Lawton said, "You might not be, but I am," and he strode off, hoping to find some fuel.

The inspector called after him. "Lawton, I'm ordering you to – "

Lawton wheeled. The inspector flinched.

"See this look on my face?" said Lawton. "See it? This look is my 'fuck-off' look. Fuck off, mate. I know how to kill these things. I know how to stop them. I've been killing them for years. Any of you stand in my way, you'll feel my fucking wrath. Any of you willing to help, it'd be appreciated."

The inspector said, "I will have you arrested, Lawton, I'm – "

"You and whose fucking army, Dixon of fucking Dock Green."

The inspector's mouth fell open. Lawton turned and strode away. He heard footsteps following him.

Without turning he said, "I hope whoever's following me is following me in a good way."

"We are following you in a good way, sir."

He turned. Coming up behind him was the young policeman and Nancy, the CSO he'd met earlier outside the station. Some station staff were also coming along.

Lawton faced them, and they stopped and waited. He said, "We need some fuel."

Nancy said, "Do we have to burn them?"

Lawton looked at her. "They will change. Tomorrow they will get up, and they'll have fangs and a thirst for blood. They will kill more people, and those people will then be resurrected – and they'll have fangs, too. Lots of fangs. Lots of blood. Let's make a bonfire."

"I can't allow this."

Lawton rolled his eyes. It was the inspector. He was marching towards them with his red face and his fat belly.

"Mate," Lawton said to him, "if the smell of burning flesh turns your stomach, there's something really important you can do that might save a lot of lives."

The copper asked what, and Lawton told him about the water.

The inspector said, "You can't stop people using the water."

"Okay," said Lawton, "but that means you're going to be attending a lot of bonfires."

Lawton's phone rang.

He answered it by saying, "Aaliyah?"

It was a woman but it wasn't Aaliyah.

The woman told him who she was before saying, "Mr Lawton, you're our only hope."

CHAPTER 107.
PORTCULLIS HOUSE.

LAWTON pushed through the crowds that choked the streets. He looked in people's eyes, which were white with fear.

Screams and shouts filled the air. Sirens blared, and flashing blue lights illuminated the darkness.

Lawton kept moving. His brow furrowed. He was headed for Victoria Street, which would take him down to the Houses of Parliament.

The phone call had excited him.

The woman was called Jayne Monson, and she was the Tory Party leader. "But this has got nothing to do with politics," she'd told him. "There are members of my own party who are part of this, I'm sure, and members of the Labour Party who stand with me."

She was right. It wasn't about politics. It was life and death.

Sweat coated his body. Adrenaline pulsed through his veins and slammed into his heart. He kept himself under control. The urge to scream, to shout, to fight his way through was overwhelming.

A helicopter swooped overhead. The rotors' backdraft made Lawton stagger. The people around him cried out.

He pushed on, his mind fixed on Victoria Street. The road led down to the Thames. People were hurrying down the road towards Westminster.

His phone rang again, and it was Goga.

Lawton told him where he was going and then asked, "Where's Aaliyah?"

"We are on our way to Kent," said Goga.

"Okay, but is she with you?"

"She is fighting vampires. She is a great fighter. You are too. We need you in Iraq, Lawton."

"I'm needed here."

"Can't you see? Britain is doomed. We can salvage something of your country if you come with me and we destroy Nimrod. Can't you see? The greater good, Lawton. Remember? There has to be a sacrifice."

"Fine... let me be the sacrifice."

"You fool, you're too valuable."

Lawton looked around at all the people and thought about things. "I'm nothing," he said.

"You are a symbol, Jake."

"I'm a soldier, that's all. A soldier doing his duty."

"And what is that duty?"

"Protecting my country."

"You don't understand."

"Tell Aaliyah... just tell her."

He switched the phone off and tried to stuff it back in his pocket, but people kept bumping into him. He stumbled. Steadied himself again. Shoved the phone into his pocket. Someone barged him again. He cursed and got moving again.

As he made his way through the crowd, fights broke out around him. He ignored them and pushed on. Police heaved into the crowd with batons. People screamed and cursed.

Feedback squealed from a loudspeaker before a voice bellowed for the crowd to calm down.

"Proceed slowly down Victoria Street," the voice said. "Please disperse. There's no need to panic."

Lawton quickened his pace. A man shoved into him. Lawton moved on. The man wheeled. His face was red with anger. He snarled at Lawton, and his fangs dripped blood.

The vampire lunged.

Lawton punched the creature in the mouth, and it reeled away.

See a vampire, kill a vampire, he thought.

He chased after the creature. He whipped a stake from his backpack and stabbed the vampire in the heart.

It shrieked and evaporated.

"Vampires!" someone shouted

Lawton tensed.

"Vampires!"

The crowd stampeded and swept Lawton off his feet, knocking the wind out him.

He swam against the flow of the mob. They were screaming and shouting. Panic spread like a virus.

Lawton elbowed his way through the throng. It was heavy going. He sweated, and his body ached. His ribs still throbbed after the fight with Trojan and Rush. He could've happily found an alley to lie down in and go to sleep.

But he kept going forward.

Finally, he came to Parliament Square. The place was packed with people. On the green, tents had been flattened by the stampede. Banners and placards emblazoned with anti-war slogans lay strewn on the grass and on the road. They were the remnants of a protest that had been camped outside the Palace of Westminster for a few months.

Traffic had come to a standstill here. Up ahead stood Lambeth Palace, official residence of the Archbishop of Canterbury. Lawton wondered if he was inside, praying.

Behind Lambeth Palace were the Houses of Parliament and Big Ben. Portcullis House stood to the left, and that's where Lawton was headed.

He clambered on the roof of a parked car so he could see over the crowd.

He started to run over the cars. Their roofs buckled under his weight. Drivers popped their heads out of their windows and cursed at him.

He was out of breath by the time he got to St Margaret Street.

Parliament stood right in front of him. A line of riot police protected the building. TV crews were filming. Reporters interviewed members of the public and MPs. Vampires ambushed people.

Lawton asked a dark-haired woman with a microphone what was going on. She looked at him, and her eyes narrowed as if she'd recognized him. Maybe she had. People did seem to know who he was. It made him uncomfortable.

The woman, who was in her early twenties, said, "Parliament is having a late sitting. Excuse me, can I interview you? I'm Sarah Demeter. I'm freelance."

"I don't talk."

"You don't talk? I'm doing a vox pop. Will you be a vox pop for me?"

He shook his head and walked away, heading towards Portcullis House.

A young Asian man with blue-rimmed glasses loitered outside the building. He looked nervous, and his gaze flitted around.

Lawton jogged over to him.

"Are you Mo?" he said.

"Bloody hell," said Mo, "thank God you're here – I'm scared shitless being outside."

CHAPTER 108.
SARAH DEMETER.

SHE said, "I – I think I've just spoken to Jake Lawton."

George stared at Sarah Demeter. "Say that again, babe."

She rolled her eyes and said, "I think I've just spoken – "

"Right, that *is* what you said. Just wasn't sure I heard you right, sweetheart. How do you know it was him?"

She blushed. "He was just... just... meaty and manly. I could smell it coming off him. And... and I'd seen his picture, too. He's, you know, very male."

"Stop quivering, you tart."

"Excuse me – "

"Where did he go?"

"He was headed for Portcullis House."

George furrowed his brow. *Fucking Lawton*, he thought. *You just can't fucking kill the bastard.*

"Why Portcullis House?" he said.

"I don't know," she said.

"I wasn't asking you, Sarah; I was thinking out loud."

"Don't be rude to me, George, or I'll tell my aunt."

"Oh, I'm scared."

"You should be. She's Prime Minister. And when this is over, she'll be queen of this country."

"You think so, sweetheart?"

"She's going to be in charge, whether you like it or not."

George looked her up and down. She was a tasty little object. Nice body. No brain. "You want to see who's really in charge, doll?" he said.

Sarah had come down the stairs at the far end of the cellar. They led from the Commons' kitchens. She had a pass that allowed her access to everywhere in the Parliament buildings.

Now George led her along the cellar towards the container.

"Oh Jesus, it stinks in here," she said. "And it's freezing."

"I'd warm you up, but we ain't got time," he said.

They came to the big, clay tank.

"Christ," she said.

"As good as, darling. It's a second coming." Steam rose from the container. You could hear the liquid inside bubbling. The creature was alive now. George had looked it in the eye – in all six of its eyes. It was a terrifying sight.

"Oh my God," said Sarah, "what is that?"

"Oh, that," said George.

The figure lying against the wall groaned. It was covered in blood and gore.

"That's one of your colleagues, doll," said George. "Meet Christine Murray. Or what's left of her. Here, you want to see our prince?"

Sarah swallowed. "Sort of."

"You should. Just up that little stepladder and take a peek inside."

George looked up her skirt as she perched on the step. She stood on tiptoe and leaned over the edge of the container. He was tempted to hoist her over the edge and into the gore.

"What do you see?" he said.

"Ugh… monster… I feel sick… "

He helped her down. She looked pale. He said, "Your Auntie Jackie's not going to be in charge of nothing, darling. *That's* what's going to be in charge. That monster in there. That god."

Sarah swayed.

George went on:

"Humans don't mean anything. Humans are over. The world's done with humans."

Except for me and Alfie, he thought.

CHAPTER 109.
INTO THE PALACE OF
WESTMINSTER.

LAWTON, dressed as a policeman, followed Jayne Monson through the underground passage leading from Portcullis House to the Palace of Westminster.

Without looking at him, Monson asked, "What's going on, Mr Lawton?"

He told her everything.

After listening, she said nothing.

When they got to a staircase she turned and looked at him. "You'd make a good copper, Mr Lawton."

He pulled a face.

Monson said, "Didn't you kill someone once?"

"I've killed a lot of people once," said Lawton. "I've killed some of them twice. But that's vampires for you."

She reached into her pocket and handed Lawton a laminated pass. "That's yours. It'll give you access to all areas in the Palace of Westminster."

"How do I get into the cellars?"

She told him.

He started up the stairs, but she called his name.

"I'm sorry you're not the hero you deserve to be," she told him.

"I'm not a hero," he said. "And I don't want anyone to think I am."

"Is there anything I can do?"

Lawton said, "Tonight in the House, tell everyone about the water. Tell them not to drink it or millions will die – and then they'll get up again tomorrow, craving blood. Tell them, or we are more fucked than we already are."

* * * *

Lawton stood in the Central Lobby. Corridors decorated with murals led off from the octagonal hall.

Hundreds of people milled around. Lawton guessed they were mostly MPs, but there were also children. Perhaps some of the members had brought their families here for safety.

Dozens of police officers stalked the place. The cops looked tense and nervous. Some of them were armed, and Lawton imagined one or two had twitchy trigger fingers – any suspicious movements, they'd spray the lobby with bullets.

His throat was dry. His gaze skipped around. He'd done undercover work before. He had no problem fitting in.

What made him nervous were the cellars and what waited there for him.

Much of his strength had drained away over the past few days. The bare-knuckle fight with Goga's men had left him with injuries that really needed time to heal. He'd already been damaged in his win over Stoke John. And added to the constant battles he had with vampires, Lawton's body was wrecked.

A fight with whatever lay below the Houses of Parliament might be a battle too far for him.

He left the Central Lobby, taking one of the hundreds of staircases the building contained, and descended to the ground floor again.

Lawton had initially entered the building through the passageway, which led him to the Members' Entrance on the south side of the New Palace Yard. Now he looked at

St Stephen's Entrance on the building's west front, where members of the public came in.

The area was crammed. Outside, the night had darkened. Rain fell. Police clustered around the entrance. They kept people back, urging them to stay inside. They also probably prevented anyone from coming in.

Following the instructions Monson had given him, Lawton headed for the kitchens.

A commotion made him stop and tuck himself behind a pillar.

Voices were saying, "Prime Minister, Prime Minister... "

A crowd of MPs were trotting through the hallway. They were bunched around someone.

"Prime Minister, you have to make a statement," said a voice.

Burrows, thought Lawton.

And when the crowd of MPs parted, she was there.

She pushed Afdal Haddad in his wheelchair ahead of her. Her nose was in the air, and she looked as if she'd spit on all these MPs if she could.

Phil Birch flanked her. He carried his clipboard.

Lawton grimaced. He remembered smashing Birch in the face at Religion three years before.

He might just do it again.

A group of men in suits blocked the MPs, preventing them from following Burrows and her companions.

The trio slipped into a corridor.

Lawton followed them.

CHAPTER 110.
NO HUMAN POWER.

DOWN in the cellars, Burrows breathed in the decay.

"The stench of tomorrow, friends," she said. "The odour of immortality."

She looked around the dimly-lit cellar. Fuad leaned against the tank containing the vampire god. Birch stood over Christine Murray, laughing. The journalist was covered in blood. She was barely recognizable.

Afdal Haddad peered into the tank and whispered to himself. They'd wheeled him onto a platform that Fuad had raised using a hydraulic system he'd set up.

Sarah, Burrows's niece, was also here.

She'd seen Lawton.

"Where, Sarah?" said Burrows.

The young woman told her.

Burrows asked, "And have we heard anything from Bernard Lithgow?"

Birch said they'd heard nothing, but he'd been saying that for hours. Burrows wanted to hear something different. Or hear someone else say the same thing.

"George, have you heard from Bernard?" she said.

"Why would I hear from Bernard?"

"What about Mr Norkutt?"

Birch told her no, while Fuad said, "I refer you to my previous answer, Prime Minister."

Burrows bit her lip. Her belly squirmed.

Phil Birch said, "If Lawton's around, maybe... " He trailed off.

Fuad finished the sentence for him: "Maybe he got to them. To Bernie and knobhead. Sorry, I meant Norkutt."

"No," said Burrows. "I shan't have that thinking."

"Jacqueline, you can 'shan't' all you like – the thing is it's very likely," said Fuad. "And I think it's time we make it clear who runs things around here."

Burrows glared at him.

He went on:

"No one, Jacqueline. No one runs things. Our power comes from that god in there. There's no human power, you understand? You don't make decisions. I don't, neither. Nor does Afdal."

The tension rose. The god forming in the container sizzled and bubbled. Steam rose from the gore and filled the air. The stench still lingered. There was something beautiful about the pestilence.

"George, you are right," she said. "There is no human power. Our authority comes from Kea, Kakash, and Kasdeja. Just like Nebuchadnezzar's power did. He was only a symbol. I will only be a symbol."

"You," said Fuad.

"I've found myself in the position I am, George. We have to use the authority I've acquired for our own means. It may mean little, in reality. Only human power, not godly powers. But this is what we must do. We have to get ourselves into these situations, these positions of power – and then activate our project. This is what we have been doing for the past decades in Britain. This is what we are doing today. Are you with me?"

George scowled. "You know I am, Jacqueline. I just don't want people to get too big for their boots, that's all."

"I have very small feet, George," she said. "All I want to do is serve my gods."

"As we all do," he said.

"Then let's serve them," said Burrows. "How long before he rises?"

Haddad, speaking from the platform, said, "Soon, very soon. A little more blood, I'd say. Just a little. Isn't this wonderful? The age of monsters is here. Babylon is rising. The streets are in chaos. The people are dying. A golden age is coming. We have done what we set out to do three thousand years ago."

"Not quite yet," said Fuad.

"Close enough to touch, George," said Haddad. And then the old man furrowed his brow. "Where's Alfred? I've not seen him in hours. Where's your brother?"

A cold sweat broke on Burrows's nape. "Where is he, George?"

Before Fuad could answer, a police officer came striding down the cellar towards them.

"Who's this fellow?" said Fuad and moved towards the officer.

It was gloomy, so Burrows couldn't see the policeman's face. But something in the way he walked, in the shape of his body, sent a chill down her spine.

And when he knocked George Fuad out with a vicious elbow strike, Burrows recognized the trespasser.

CHAPTER 111.
THE PRESS WON'T LISTEN.

WEST CROMWELL ROAD, EARLS COURT – 8.10PM, FEBRUARY 15, 2011

DAVID said, "You've got to tell people not to drink the water."

The reporter said, "Why?"

David told her why.

The woman said, "Is this some kind of joke?"

"It's not a joke. Don't you know what's happening?"

"Don't give me cheek, you little shit."

"But don't you know London's falling to bits?"

"I can see that. We're doing stories on it. But what's that got to do with not drinking the water? Is this you and your mates messing about?"

"No, it's not."

"Your parents know what you're up to?"

"My dad's dead and my mum's being held hostage by the people trying to destroy this country."

He slammed the phone down. He wiped tears from his eyes.

He phoned another newspaper and asked for the newsdesk. After talking to the reporter David said, "You've got to report this. The water is poison. People will die. Jake Lawton says so. You've got to listen."

"How do you know all this?"

"I told you, Jake's my friend. You've heard of Jake Lawton?"

"Maybe. But how do you know?"

"Please tell people. Please write a story about it."

"We're very busy tonight. You know it's a war zone out there."

"I know, and this is part of it – the water is part of it."

"Part of what?"

"Conspiracy."

The reporter sighed. "You think you're the first one to call up with a crazy story tonight? You're not. And you're not the first one to claim to be mates with this Lawton character, either. We've had some people claiming to be him. We have to check things, you know."

David felt angry. "Check, then – make yourself a cup of coffee with water from the tap and see what happens."

He put the phone down.

No one believed him. But he was just a kid. They thought he was messing about. He felt drained. He slumped on the bed in the hotel room.

"They don't believe me, Jake," he said to the empty room. "They don't believe me, and everyone's going to die – everyone's going to become a vampire."

What would Jake do? He wouldn't give up. He'd keep trying. David took a deep breath.

The noise of London dying could be heard from the room, despite it being at the back of the hotel.

"He wouldn't give up," said David. "Jake wouldn't give up."

He picked up the phone and checked the list of numbers he'd taken from the Yellow Pages.

He dialled.

"Associated Newspapers," said a man and David asked for the newsdesk.

"Which newspaper?" said the man.

David said, "Any newspaper."

"We've got *The Independent, The Daily Mail, The Evening Standard, The Metro* – "

"All of them," said David. "Put me through to all of them."

CHAPTER 112.
RESCUE MISSION.

WHEN Lawton saw Murray, he stopped dead.

The man on the floor behind him groaned. He probably had a broken jaw after Lawton elbowed him.

"It's you, you bastard," said Jacqueline Burrows.

Lawton looked at her. "You bitch."

Burrows screamed.

Lawton's blood boiled. He scanned them all. Birch was there, fear in his eyes. The reporter he'd spoken to earlier. She was also part of it. And the old man, Haddad. Their holy man. Their priest. Their mad professor.

"You killed Tom Wilson," he told them.

"Do something, Phil," said Burrows. "You're my bodyguard."

Lawton sneered. He wished he had the spear. He would've killed them all. But he'd had to leave it in Monson's care. He didn't have a choice. There was no way he could've got it through Palace of Westminster security, even though he was disguised as a policeman.

"I should've brought you Bernard Lithgow's head in return," he said.

"No," said Burrows. She paled. "What have you done?"

"What was in those test tubes?" he said.

Haddad spoke:

"Death, Mr Lawton. Death to millions. You're lost, now. London is doomed. Britain will follow. Tomorrow, many will die. The water will kill them. And later, they will rise. Vampires, Mr Lawton. Virtually the whole population of London will be vampires."

"You see?" said Burrows. "It's over for you."

Lawton charged. He barrelled through Birch, sending him reeling into the side of the container. The reporter shrieked and ran away. Lawton went for Murray.

"Someone stop him," said Burrows, but there was no one left. Only her, Haddad, and the young reporter left standing. "Phil, you useless oaf, get up. George, where are you? What are you doing lying over there?"

"I think the bastard broke my jaw," said the man named George.

"Come on, Christine," said Lawton, "we're getting out of here." He crouched next to her. She was covered in blood. She looked thin and very sick. Her chest heaved as she struggled to breathe. "Fuck, what have they done to you?"

She opened her mouth. For a second he thought she was saying his name, but a reflection sparkled in her eyes.

He spun round. Burrows tried to smash his skull with the piece of wood. He raised his arm and took the blow on his bicep. Pain shot up into his shoulder. With his free hand, he shoved Burrows hard in the belly. She flew backwards and fell in a heap, moaning.

Birch rose and he was on the phone. "Get down here, now. We've got trouble," he said.

"You're a fool, Lawton," said Haddad.

"What's in the big tank, old man?"

"A nightmare for you, soldier."

"Another one of your Coco the Clown impersonators? Remember what I did to the last one, Haddad? I'll do the same to this one. Smash his ugly red face in."

Haddad laughed. "Fool. Fool, Lawton."

Lawton was tempted to stride over to the old man, hoist him up, and tip him into the container.

But when Birch said, "Bring your weapons," he decided it was time to go.

He said, "I'll be back for you all."

"Bastard," said Burrows.

Lawton picked up Murray. She felt fragile and was light in his arms. She stank of sweat and blood. She raised a hand and pointed in the opposite direction from which Lawton had come. He saw an entrance had been gouged into the cellar's wall. Beyond it, a dimly-lit corridor snaked into darkness.

"That way?" he said.

She nodded.

A scream of rage made him stop. Burrows charged towards him. He laid Murray down. Burrows rammed into him. He grabbed her by her lapels and gave her a shake.

"I should kill you," he said.

"But... but you can't?"

"Maybe not," he said, "but I know someone who can."

He shoved her away, and as she reeled back, Lawton snatched the red brooch from her jacket.

It came away in his hand.

Burrows looked horrified. She tripped over Haddad and hit the ground.

She screamed, "Give it back, Lawton, give it back to me."

Lawton pocketed the brooch. He picked Murray up again.

She said something. Or maybe it was just a grunt. Lawton didn't know. But then words came from her:

"You... you came for me."

CHAPTER 113.
WARRIOR WOMAN.

A232, West Wickham Common, Bromley, Kent –
8.28pm, February 15, 2011

"GET back in the car," shouted Goga.

He lifted the child-vampire off its feet and slammed it on the bonnet of the car before driving his cane through the creature's chest. The boy shrieked. Its skin withered and crumpled, and it became dust on the hood of the 4x4.

Goga said again, "Get back in the car."

The vampires were everywhere. They had poured out of the trees surrounding West Wickham Common. Traffic clogged the A232. Vehicles had crashed. Drivers had panicked. Now they and their passengers fled the area. But they were being hunted by the undead.

Goga watched the vampires attack. They darted after the fleeing humans and pounced on them. They attacked in packs, dragging down their prey before starting to drink their blood.

Goga couldn't do anymore. The plague was spreading out of London. He and the others had to leave this dying country. The plane was waiting at Biggin Hill Airport, only ten miles away. But Aaliyah had insisted they stop.

"We've got to help," she'd said. "Jake would help."

A vampire came at Goga, baring its fangs.

Goga whipped the red rag from his breast pocket and said, "You know what this is, creature, so scurry away – but if you want to die, come at me and I'll gladly drive my cane through your black heart."

The vampire snarled and ran away.

Aaliyah, armed with a rucksack-full of stakes, killed vampires one after the other.

She was a remarkable warrior. An Amazon.

Trojan and Rush returned to the vehicle, both of them breathing heavily.

"Get in," Goga told them, "get the car started."

The men got in.

This mad woman, Goga thought as he watched Aaliyah.

She caught his eye and ran over. "Help me," she said.

"There's too many," he said.

"They're killing people."

"We have to go."

"No."

"We can stop this," said Goga. "But not here. On the other side of the world. That's where the secret lies. That's where we finish it, Aaliyah. You can have your romantic story, then. You can have your life with Lawton."

She looked around at the chaos. Goga could tell she wanted to dive back into the fray. He said, "We have to go – *now*."

Aaliyah said, "The dead ones, we should burn their bodies."

He furrowed his brow. "What did you say?"

"Like me and Jake do. Burn the dead. Stop them becoming vampires."

Goga scowled. The Englishman was clever. He was practical. The Nebuchadnezzars must have hated him. He thought about what Aaliyah had said for a moment but then said, "No time," and he leapt into the car. "No, Aaliyah, we must go now."

From inside the car he watched the killing continue.

Ten yards away, a vampire pinned a woman to the road. Two more creatures dragged down a man who was with her.

Aaliyah strode over.

Goga said, "No," but she was gone.

419

Aaliyah drove a stake through the vampire's spine. It screeched and arched its back and turned to ash, the debris raining over the woman like confetti.

"Help me," came the shout, and Aaliyah responded, dashing towards the man who tussled with two vampires.

One was biting the man's arm and drinking his blood. The other was trying to bite into the man's neck.

Snatching two stakes from her backpack, Aaliyah killed both vampires and then stood over the remains. She looked around.

Goga knew what she was thinking. He leaned out of the window. "You can't kill them all tonight, Aaliyah," he said. "But you can if you come with me now."

She looked at him. Her dark eyes blazed.

* * * *

WESTMINSTER – 8.32PM, FEBRUARY 15, 2011

BURROWS showed them why she was nicknamed Firestarter.

Red in the face and hot in the blood, she paced the cellar.

She came to a stop and glared at Phil Birch. "How did you allow this to happen?" she said.

Birch nursed his arm. "I... he didn't... I didn't... it's not my fault..."

Fuad wandered over. He was holding his jaw and flexing it. A bruise stained the right side of his face. Burrows ignored him and fixed her attention on Birch:

"You're my protection officer. You protect the Prime Minister. How can someone get so close to me, Phil? He could've killed me."

Sarah Demeter moaned. Haddad tutted. The old man said, "He broke though our defences. He can get to us, Jacqueline. This Lawton. We kill his old friend, Tom Wilson, and he kills Bernard Lithgow. We kill his young friend, Fraser Lithgow – now who will he kill? He will be back. This has to be finished tonight. Did Bernard spread the plague?"

Burrows said, "We don't know, do we?" Now she looked at Fuad as he cupped his chin. "Is it broken?" she asked him.

Fuad shrugged.

"My ribs are," said Birch.

"Oh shut up," said Burrows. "This is your responsibility."

"You idiots," said Haddad. "All of you, how could you let this happen?" The old man shook. "This man, this cursed man, you let him in. He comes dressed as a policeman, and you" – he jabbed his stick at Birch – "you are head of the police."

"I'm… I'm not head of… I'm… I'm just…"

Fear gripped Burrows. She patted her jacket, looking for something. And then she remembered. "Lawton stole my… my mark. He stole my mark." She stared at all of them. "You're all to blame. What am I going to do?"

Haddad said, "Take his." He pointed at Birch.

The policeman said, "What? No, no, you can't."

"Someone has to pay for this," said Haddad. "I've decided it is you, Mr Birch."

Birch held the clipboard to his chest. The red ribbon dangled from the metal clip. "This is outrageous, you… you… can't… "

Fuad circled behind Birch and punched him in the back of the head.

The policeman fell.

Burrows rushed over and picked up the clipboard. Birch moaned and tried to get up. Fuad crouched and punched him again, twice in the face. Birch crumpled.

Burrows snatched the ribbon from the clipboard and bunched it in her hands, gasping.

She said, "I have to go back up. The Commons is sitting at 10.00pm, I have to make a statement. Will our Lord of Blood be ready by then, Afdal?"

The old man said, "Soon, very soon. It might need another dose of blood, although it could come alive at any moment. It will need nourishment when it rises. We should leave food."

Burrows looked around. She glanced at George Fuad and nodded. His gaze drifted over to Sarah Demeter.

"We have to leave," said Haddad.

"Where are we going?" said Birch.

"Chain him where Murray was chained," said Burrows, nodding in Birch's direction. "He can be the first meal."

Birch screamed.

Fuad dragged Birch over to the tank and cuffed him to the chain attached to the container. He slapped the policeman across the face and laughed at him.

Burrows smiled at her niece. The girl looked pale. "Are you all right, Sarah?"

"No, I'm scared, Aunt Jacqueline."

"Never mind. Chain her up, too, George," said Burrows before striding away.

Sarah cried out. But George shut her up with a whack to the back of her skull.

CHAPTER 114.
LAWTON THE WRECK.

LAWTON sat on the floor with his back against the couch, smoking. He was drained. It felt as if all his strength had seeped out of his body. He was a broken man.

Sky News played on the 42-inch flat screen TV in Jayne Monson's flat. The pictures showed anarchy in London. A yellow ticker ran along the bottom of the screen declaring:

> BREAKING NEWS: VAMPIRE ATTACKS SPREAD
> ACROSS LONDON AND OTHER MAJOR CITIES.

Lawton blew air out of his cheeks. The smell of tobacco filled the air. Fortunately, Monson didn't mind him having a fag. She was a smoker herself. He was glad he didn't have to debate the issue with her, because he'd really needed a smoke when he got back here with Murray.

Christine was in a bad way. Monson had to help her bathe, because she was too weak to keep herself from slipping under water. They'd had to use bottled water after what Lawton had learned. David had tried to warn the newspapers and television reporters about the water supply.

"But they didn't believe me," he'd said.

The boy had cried when he saw his mother. Maybe from relief, maybe from distress. Maybe both. Now, he and his mum were in Monson's spare bedroom. Murray was tucked under the sheets while David lay on the bed next to her, glad to have his mother back alive.

On TV, the Sky News reporter said, "Police in riot gear have cordoned off Parliament on the orders of the Prime Minister. We are on the verge of having a curfew called. It would be unprecedented in a democracy."

Lawton leaned his head back and looked at the ceiling.

The reporter went on. "Some people are already describing Britain as a police state, while the Government insists this is only a short-term measure. There's still no official comment but we are hearing that some ministers and shadow ministers are using the word 'vampire'."

Lawton turned his attention back to the screen.

The reporter said, "Interim Prime Minister, Jacqueline Burrows, will make a statement to the House at ten o'clock."

The broadcast cut to a tape showing two young girls in Parliament Square speaking into the camera. They looked scared.

They talked over each other: "We've seen vampires – people being killed – blood-drinking – blood everywhere – things with fangs like this – long and sharp – and they're not nice, like in *Twilight* – it's scary, so scary – "

The presenter asked them if they'd been drinking.

"Everyone here's not drunk, are they," said one of the girls. "Everyone's not on drugs. But we've all seen them. This happened three years ago, but, like, the Government and all the official people just denied it was happening."

The programme cut back to the live feed from Westminster. The reporter looked cold and tired. "We know what people think; we know what they're saying. But it seems the authorities are not thinking, or saying – or perhaps even seeing – the same things."

Lawton stubbed out his cigarette and muted the TV. He wanted a drink, but that would be no good. In the past, drink had made him rotten. He'd been clean of it for a few years.

A photograph of him appeared on the screen. He straightened and turned up the volume. The reporter said, "... the Religion nightclub three years ago. Lawton disappeared and has been on a 'most wanted' list since then. But he is also a Robin Hood character among bloggers and Tweeters – "

Robin Hood, he thought, muting the TV again. He didn't want to hear. He shut his eyes and yearned for Aaliyah. If she were here, he'd feel strong. But Goga had persuaded her to leave.

Lawton thought about going after her. He should. He was a man in love. That's what you did. You fought for your woman.

He was desperate to hear her voice. He checked his pockets for his phone again, hoping to find it tucked in there somewhere. But it was gone. He knew where he'd lost it: headed down Victoria Street, bumping and shoving through that crowd.

He folded his arms. His heart sunk.

Let her go, he thought. He felt sulky. He felt angry. He felt lost without her. *Maybe I should go. Beg her to come back*. He was willing to do that. Go down on his knees if he had to and ask her to stay with him.

But then he thought about the monster in the cellar.

Christ, he said to himself.

The journey back through the tunnel, out into Soho, played out in his mind. Murray had told him to enter a passageway. He had no idea where he was. He followed the route. A string of bulbs, stretching off into the distance, illuminated their escape. It was stale and damp under the earth.

"Where does this lead?" he'd asked her. He was exhausted, carrying Murray over his shoulders. She didn't answer. She couldn't. Death skulked in the shadows, waiting for Christine.

You're not having her, Lawton thought at the time. *You're not having any of them again*.

When they came out in the basement of Religion, Lawton gawped with astonishment.

Out in the street, he hijacked a car, apologizing to the man by saying it was an emergency: "My friend's dying – I have to take her to hospital."

Poor Christine, he thought. She'd suffered so much. Her son and husband dead. Her future bleak.

All our futures bleak.

"You should sleep," said a voice.

He lifted his head. Jayne Monson stood in the kitchen door. She wore a blue suit. Her face was grey.

Lawton said, "I don't do much of that."

"It would replenish you. We need you strong, Mr Lawton. This country needs you strong."

His shoulders sagged. "Why do people put this on me? Why should I be responsible?"

"I don't know," she said. She came into the living room and sat down on an armchair. "Will you tell me about this monster that's in the cellar?"

He told her what he'd seen and what he'd learned about Haddad's plan to poison the waters. "You've got to tell them tonight in the House," he said. "Tell them the waters are poisoned. We've tried, but they're not listening. You tell them."

She said, "This is like a film. *The Lost Boys*. Do you remember that?"

"It's much worse than Hollywood – it's fucking real."

"You see, that's why we need you. Pretend heroes would be no good. We need someone without foibles, Mr Lawton. Someone ruthless in ruthless times."

He leaned back his head. "I wish people wouldn't expect me to save the world."

"We don't. Just save your friends, for a start. David in there. The boy's life has been awful for the past three years."

"Mostly down to me. I dragged his mother into this."

"I don't think so. But you are the only light in their lives. You're his father figure, and boys need fathers."

Lawton thought about his own childhood. A father would've been good. As a kid, he'd been ferried from foster home to foster home. His mum died when he was two. His dad had fucked off soon after he was born.

The authorities had turned Lawton into a nomad. Move him here, move him there. But he was a rebel. He never settled. At sixteen, he went in search of his dad. He found him in Birkenhead and turned up on his old man's doorstep.

His dad had come to the door wearing a stained vest and smoking a roll-up. "Who the fuck are you?" he'd said.

426

"I... I'm your son," the sixteen-year-old Jake said.

His dad's mouth fell open, and the fag dropped to the ground. The man's steel-grey eyes widened with shock. "My... my... whose kid are you?"

"Yours?"

"Who's your mum, dickhead?"

The young Lawton flinched. "Debra Lawton."

His dad's brow creased. His mind was churning, the teenaged Jake could see that. The man was looking into the distance, searching out the past.

Then his eyes, hard and cold, came back to Lawton.

"That fucking barmaid slag?"

Lawton bristled and bunched his fists. He'd been a fighter since he was a boy, but he wasn't sure if he wanted to fight his dad. It didn't feel right.

"She kick you out?" said his dad.

"She died when I was two."

"Drank herself to death, eh?"

Lawton said, "I came to see you, D – " He nearly called him "Dad," but it didn't sound right just yet. "I came all the way from London to see you. I thought – "

"You thought wrong, lad. What the fuck are you to me? I got dozens of kids. Tarts opening their legs to me all over the fucking place. What am I supposed to do? Fuck off back to London, you southern softie cunt."

His dad slammed the door.

Lawton had stood there staring at the house. Tears welled. Anger flowered in his chest. He didn't know what to do. He looked up and down the terraced street.

He went to knock on the door again but stopped himself.

He unzipped his pants and pissed through the letterbox.

After pissing through his dad's door, he went back to Liverpool city centre and stood shivering in the bus stop.

The rain hammered down on him. Lawton, lost in a strange city.

He slept on the street that night and had to fight off three drunks who tried to nick his backpack. He fought like a wolf. They were bigger than him, but he was strong for a scrawny lad. Strong and tough and determined.

He held one of the drunks down by the neck and said, "I'm going to be around for a while, mate, so remember my face, right? Don't fuck with me, and tell your mates not to fuck with me."

They didn't fuck with him much after that. He was young. He was a good-looking lad. He could've been prey. But he made it clear from the start that he was more of a predator.

Mess with him, he'd fight them. He'd hunt them. He'd hurt them.

And he had to fight. There was always someone ready to have a go. The streets were wild. But he'd been around them since he was small, so once he got his bearings he was okay.

He travelled back and forth between Manchester and Liverpool, sleeping rough. On people's couches. On people's floors. In hostels. He did odd jobs. Cleared people's gardens. Washed cars. Cleaned toilets.

And then one morning he saw the poster.

The King's Regiment.

He went into their recruiting office in Bolton and joined up.

He loved it. His first real family. His first proper mates. True brothers. Men who would die for you – after they'd taken the piss out of you, of course.

He saw combat. He fought in a war. He lost mates. He killed men. He did his duty.

And then they kicked him out.

Not the Army's fault. The politicians. People like Jacqueline Burrows, who send others to fight and die for them. At the time, they wanted a scapegoat, because the war in Iraq was going badly.

Lawton fitted the bill.

He seethed now, recalling his shame.

The woman who had triggered his demise was sleeping in the other room.

Christine Murray.

She broke the story of Lawton killing a suicide bomber in Basra. But in the reports, the guy wasn't an insurgent who was planning to kill hundreds of innocent Muslims in a mosque. According to Murray at the time, he was civilian.

428

But the truth didn't matter. The story did, And "soldier kills innocent man" sounded better than "soldier kills suicide bomber".

More newspapers picked up on Murray's story and added a few more details that never happened, and Jake's career was over.

They booted him out and called him a murderer.

He stared at the door of the bedroom where Murray now slept.

He and that reporter had come a long way. They were enemies teaming up at the beginning. Now they were friends who would die for each other.

Just like the Army.

Comrades in arms.

Monson spoke. "You are our only hope, Mr Lawton. You're the only one with the courage to face up to this."

"I'm the only one stupid enough."

"You are admired, you know. I've seen what they say – Facebook, Twitter. That world. The world that's more important than the real one, these days. You're wanted, Jake. You're needed."

He stayed quiet for a few seconds, thinking.

Then he said, "Where's my spear?"

CHAPTER 115.
ANOTHER TRAVELLER.

"HE might be dead," said Aaliyah. "My man could be dead, and I've abandoned him."

Goga tried to ring Lawton again, but he got no answer.

"You see, he's gone," said Aaliyah. "He's dead."

She slumped on the bench.

Goga said, "You think Lawton would die this easily? When he was a soldier, they tried to shoot him. He has five bullets in his body. He lived. They have tried to burn him. He has the scars, but his heart still beats. How have they killed him?"

Aaliyah shook her head.

"He is alive," said Goga. "Our plane is nearly ready."

She looked up. The plane, a CitationJet 525 that carried four passengers, sat in the middle of the hanger. Next to the aircraft, Trojan and Rush spoke to a man in a suit. Mechanics checked out the jet. It would fly them to Spain. From Madrid they'd catch a flight to Istanbul. A Turkish Airlines flight would then take them to Erbil Airport in Iraq.

"I have to find him," said Aaliyah. "Without him, I'm lost."

"Britain is doomed," said Goga. "Come with me. Help me, and you might be able to salvage your country. Do you understand?"

"I understand. I do. But… "

"You want to be with him, I see this. You love this man. But he is strong. He will fight as long as he can. But unless Nimrod is destroyed, there is no hope for England, no hope for Lawton or you. It will always be war. And you will always lose."

Trojan and Rush walked over and called to Goga. The Romanian went to them, and the three men huddled together, talking.

Aaliyah couldn't hear what they were saying. But when Goga approached her with his face red and his brow creased, she knew he had bad news.

He said, "The gentleman over there who has booked this flight for us tells my men that someone we know left this airport earlier today."

Aaliyah looked up at him.

"Alfred Fuad," said Goga.

She mouthed the name and then said, "Where was he going?"

"France, they said."

"Okay. Why France?"

"I don't think France was his destination, Aaliyah."

She said nothing.

Goga went on: "Accompanying Fuad was General Howard Vince, head of your British Army."

"Why would the head of the Army go to France?"

"France is not the destination. Iraq is the destination. General Vince is a veteran of the Iraq War. He led British Forces there. He is one of them, Aaliyah. Vince is a Nebuchadnezzar."

"Are they going to kill Nimrod?"

"I don't think so. I think they are going to resurrect him. That would truly be the end of us. If the Nebuchadnezzars are planning to dig him up, it is not only Britain that faces annihilation – it is the whole world."

Aaliyah looked at Goga, but she didn't know what to say.

The Romanian said, "Now you see why we must get there before Fuad and Vince. Now you see why our mission is the most important in the history of humanity. You must come with me, Aaliyah."

CHAPTER 116.
FIRST HUMAN.

BURROWS fumed. The evening had gone badly. And the reason for that again was Jake Lawton.

Why couldn't they kill this man? Why couldn't they get rid of him?

Sitting at her desk in the Houses of Parliament, she looked at the sheet of paper in front of her. It was her speech. She'd be giving it in a few minutes. But first she had to calm down.

She was furious with Phil Birch and George Fuad. How could they have just let Lawton march into the cellar, overwhelm them, and rescue Murray?

They were Nebuchadnezzars. They were supposed to be the chosen humans.

But it didn't mean they weren't weak.

Take Fraser Lithgow, for example. Part of the bloodline. A descendant of the ancient king. Just like she was.

But Lithgow denied his heritage, despite his father's efforts. The young man could never have been one of them – despite his genetics.

And Burrows feared his lack of commitment to the cause may have resulted in Bernard Lithgow's death.

Bernard dead, and now Birch.

She took the ribbon snatched from the policeman's clipboard out of her pocket. She laid it on the sheet of paper. It was Phil's protection. The mark that kept the vampires at bay. The scrap of skin salvaged from the vampire trinity's destruction three thousand years before.

Now he wasn't protected.

But someone had to pay for Lawton's invasion.

It was going to be Phil Birch. He'd been a friend and an ally. Always faithful and ready to protect her, he'd got her out of Religion three years before, when the place was burning down – when Lawton had again scuppered their plans.

She put her head in her hands. She wanted to cry. All her life she'd waited to be Prime Minister. A lust for power had gripped Burrows for years. But now that she had power, it was all going wrong.

She straightened and let out a cry.

"I will be triumphant," she said. "I will see this through, and paradise will be mine. Get a grip, Jacqueline," she told herself. "Get a grip."

The monster would be resurrected. Britain would be a vampire nation. Babylon would thrive. And she would be queen. Seated on a throne of blood. Protected by an army of undead.

She felt excited again.

She stood up and switched on the TV that was on the office wall. The BBC News channel reported that London was in ruins. Eyewitnesses made claims about vampires. Experts suggested it was delusional. Others said it was possible. No one really knew for certain.

The confusion tasted like honey to Burrows. She would appear from the chaos like an angel, and she would bring order again.

She would walk with monsters.

In the age of vampires, she would be First Human.

* * * *

Birch said, "Jesus Christ, George, let me go." Next to him, Sarah Demeter cried and yanked at the chain.

433

They had both been bound to the container.

Fuad perched on the stepladder and peered into the big, clay tank. Something was alive in the gore.

A god.

A three-headed hell-thing.

The smell was awful, but Fuad didn't care.

"Shut up, Phil," he said.

"You can't let Jacqueline do this to me," said Birch. "She hasn't got the right."

"Phil, someone's got to pay."

"Not me," said Sarah, tears streaming down her face. She shrieked, which made George wince. "Please," she continued, "I've not done anything wrong. I'm the PM's niece, for Christ's sake."

"Makes no difference if you're the Queen's grannie, darling," said George. He looked at her for a few moments and liked what he saw. "Shame about having to kill you. You're very pretty."

Her eyes widened, and hope blazed in them. "Oh God," she said, "fuck me, then... fuck me... or whatever you want... anything... I'll – I'll do anything if you let me go."

George pondered. "You are delicious, ain't you."

"Yes, yes I am. And willing. Very willing. Please, Mr Fuad. Please. Oh God."

Birch said, "No, what about me? George, we're old friends."

George furrowed his brow. "Maybe, but you wouldn't do things with me, though, would you. Dirty stuff. Fuck stuff."

Birch gawped. "What the hell are you talking about?"

"You wouldn't do what she's offering to do."

"George, you can't... "

"Mr Fuad," said the girl. "Please, Mr Fuad. I'll do what you want me to do. I'll... I'll be your girlfriend. You're really handsome."

"Aw, shucks," said George.

"Christ, George," said Birch. "I'll be your fucking girlfriend, if it means you get me out of these chains."

George was enjoying this. He loved inflicting pain. Seeing people suffer made him happy. Torture was fun.

And he needed some fun after Lawton's attack. His jaw still throbbed. He didn't think he'd broken it, but the side of his face ached. Because Lawton had hurt him, he was going to have to hurt someone else. That's how it worked. Pain passed down the line.

As top dog, George couldn't let people push him around without showing that he was still strong. So when Lawton got the better of him, he was going to have to be twice as brutal to the person below him in the chain.

And that person was either Phil Birch or Sarah Demeter.

He said, "I'm not sure I'd want you as my girlfriend, Phil, 'cause I don't know what you'd look like in a dress, mate."

"Jesus, George. I'm a copper. Let me go."

"A copper?" said George. "What difference does that make?"

"You can't kill a copper."

"We killed coppers before. What's the big deal?"

Demeter started crying. "Please, Mr Fuad, you can do anything you want... I'll do anything... "

George bit his lip and tried to look like he was thinking. "I suppose I've got three options, ain't I. I could save you both."

Demeter and Birch nodded.

"I could let you both die."

They shook their heads.

"Or I could go 'eeny meeny miny mo'." He tapped his nose with his middle finger, thinking. "Who should I choose?"

While Demeter and Birch begged, George stood there in the cellar, enjoying their anguish.

After a couple of minutes he said, "All right, I've made my choice."

CHAPTER 117.
LAST CHANCE.

GOGA leaned out of the aeroplane and said, "We must go now," his voice nearly drowned out by the jet engines.

Aaliyah waited on the tarmac. The wind from the plane's engines whipped her hair. Rain made her face wet – and hopefully hid the tears running down her cheeks.

Would she ever see Jake again?

The thought went through her mind. She didn't even know who Apostol Goga really was. He might be one of them, and all this could be a trap.

Goga spoke to the pilot and nodded.

He then looked at Aaliyah and said, "Now or not. This is hurting you, but it is the right thing to do – you know this. Aaliyah, you can save him. You can save the world."

"I don't want to save the world."

"Him, then. Him and you. Your last chance."

Goga's face turned red. He was leaning out of the plane, and it started to move, rolling down the runway.

"I have to shut the door," he said. "Come with me to kill Nimrod."

Aaliyah got out her phone. *One last try*, she thought and called Jake again. No answer – again. She texted him once more, this time saying, *Decided to go with Goga*.

But she still wasn't sure. Maybe Jake didn't want her anymore. He was angry after they'd argued. He must've considered her petty and stupid. He was ignoring her calls.

"Jake," she shouted, but her voice was drowned by the plane's engine. It rolled down the runway. Goga beckoned her to follow. Aaliyah watched the jet trundle away.

She looked at the text she'd sent seconds ago to Jake.

Goga's voice came through the engine's roar:

"Now or not."

* * * *

9.59PM, FEBRUARY 15, 2011

"No," Sarah Demeter said, rattling the chains. "No, please," but George Fuad released Birch.

"Burrows won't be too pleased with you," said Birch.

"Oh, maybe I should leave you tied up in this fucking cellar, then?"

"N-no, mate, please. Thanks."

Demeter wailed. She begged Fuad not to let her die. She offered herself to him again.

He ignored her and unshackled Birch. The policeman rubbed his wrists. They were red-raw.

Fuad grabbed him by the collar and hauled him to his feet.

The girl kept screaming.

"Thanks, George," said Birch.

Fuad grinned at him. "Yeah."

"Burrows shouldn't have done that, should she. I mean, tie me up like that. Steal my mark. That's out of order."

"Yeah. You can tell her that. I'm off to see her now. Before she addresses the House of Commons and tells them they're no longer fit for fucking purpose."

"That's great. The end is nigh, eh, George?"

"Yeah, nigh."

"But she's treated me badly, is what I'm saying."

437

"Poor you."

"We're all in this together, aren't we? I saved her life countless times, you know."

"Sure you have, buddy."

"Why – why are you grinning like that, George?"

"Why am I grinning like this, Phil?"

"Uh, yeah."

"Because, my little Philip, you made a promise. Don't you remember?"

Birch blushed. "Yeah, but… you've got to be joking, right?"

George pulled the knife out of his jacket and put the blade under Birch's chin. "How far will people go to survive, Phil?"

"Jesus, George, you're crazy. I… I can't… I'm not…"

"Get on your knees, Phil. Amuse me down there. Or I'll put you back in chains. Let you be meat for the mighty one in there."

The girl cried.

Birch shuddered. "Christ, you can't be – "

"Down, boy," said Fuad.

And Birch went down.

CHAPTER 118.
I'M THE BOSS.

"PHIL'S my bitch, Jacqueline," said George Fuad.

"You disobeyed me," said Burrows.

"Disobeyed you? You're not my boss, darling."

"There has to be some semblance of order, George."

"So long as they're your orders, eh?"

Burrows fumed. "You've made me late, George – fifteen minutes late already."

"Big deal."

"George, I can't be late to a sitting."

"'Course you can. Who gives a fuck what they think."

Bastard, she thought. He was right. It didn't matter anymore. Not after tonight.

She looked at Birch. He stood near the door in her office and looked dreadful. His hair was greasy and hung in rats' tails over his forehead. His face was pale, and his eyes were staring into the distance.

"What's the matter with him?" asked Burrows. "He doesn't look like he's with us. He looks ill. What did you do to him?"

She felt uncomfortable with Birch in the office. After stealing his mark for herself and leaving him in the cellar, she didn't expect to see her old friend again. She expected him to die.

"He's had a mouthful from me, so he's contemplating life," said Fuad.

"I left him there to die, George."

Fuad shrugged.

"What are you doing?" she said.

"What do you mean, Jackie?"

She cringed but didn't say anything about him calling her "Jackie". She just said, "Going against me."

"I ain't going against you, love."

"Don't 'love' me, you fucking half-Arab – "

"Oh, racist, racist."

"Shut up, George."

"I ain't half-Arab, anyway. I'm a quarter. More English than you, you Scottish tart."

"What's the matter with you? We're so close to achieving our goals, and you're behaving like a schoolboy."

He shrugged. "Maybe I never grew up."

She pointed at Birch and told Fuad, "Get... get him out of here; he's making me queasy."

Fuad folded his arms.

"What is it, now?" said Burrows.

"After tonight, what are you planning?"

"What do you mean?"

"I mean, are you going to be PM?"

"Someone has to be."

"Why?"

"Why? Because we have to keep up appearances, George. There will be conferences to attend. There will be nations to deal with – and for that, you need a leader."

"I think Haddad should be our leader. He's brought us to this point, ain't he."

Burrows reddened. "Professor Haddad is, if you like, the... the spiritual leader of our new world order. He is our priest. Our link with our gods."

Fuad laughed, but she ignored him and went on:

"Whereas I, for the moment, George, am the political leader."

"And what happens if we don't obey you, Mrs Leader?"

She felt confused. "What's going on with you?"

"I want to be leader, that's what's going on."

"You?"

"Yeah, me."

"You can't be – "

"Why can't I be, darling? I'm a businessman. I've run firms all my life. Big companies. I know how to manage. And I know how to lie and cheat, too. I'm top of the class at that."

"But this is politics; it's different."

"No it's not. It's leadership."

Anger burned in Burrows. "You're not having it. I've worked all my life for this."

"Fight you for it," he said, smiling.

"You're an idiot, George."

"I want what you have."

"You want me to relinquish the office of Prime Minister and announce you as my replacement?"

"Something like that."

"You fool, that's not going to happen."

He slapped her across the face.

The pain made her gasp, and she couldn't breathe for a second. She felt dizzy and stared at him, not sure if what happened had been real or not.

She tried to say something, but no words came out. Tears burned her eyes.

Fuad smiled. "You shut up, Jackie."

She found her voice. "I can't believe you did that."

"Believe, baby, believe."

"And in front of him," she said, gesturing at Birch.

"He don't care. You should've seen what I did to him."

She glanced at the policeman. "How dare you, George."

"Oh shut up. Again."

"You will pay for that."

"No I won't. I won't pay, darling. Look, you've got very few allies now. You've lost Bernard. You lost Birch, here, after you threw him to the lions and I rescued his sweet little hide. And many others, too. They ain't too confident in your abilities, either."

She was in shock. "Who?"

"Never mind who."

"What does Haddad say?"

441

"Never mind Haddad, either."

Burrows sat down at her desk. "You can't do this."

"I am. Look, girl, you can stay as PM, but only in name, right. I say what's what. Me and Alfie."

"Where is he, George? Where's your brother? Where's your pit bull?"

Fuad grinned. "He's digging for victory."

CHAPTER 119.
THE REPORTER.

POLICE packed Westminster. They looked threatening. Riot gear. Guns. It was like a battlefield. It was like the night of an England football international.

Only those already in the area were allowed to stay. If you were coming in, you had to have a pass.

The reporter had one.

He approached the checkpoint that blocked off the junction into St Margaret Street.

He badged the officers who were checking IDs. They scowled at him. He smiled. "Open your bag," said one of the coppers. He opened it, and the copper trawled through it. After he was done, he looked the reporter in the face again and after a five-second stare he said, "All right, go through."

The reporter studied the scene. It was like a military camp here. Tents emblazoned with Metropolitan Police logos and Red Crosses peppered the area. Paramedics treated the injured. Scaffolding climbed up the face of Big Ben. Armed police manned the clock tower, leaning over the metal poles to look down across the square.

Nothing was coming in here, and nothing was going out.

Vampire attacks in the area had dwindled. Reports were coming in of killings on the outskirts of Central London, but apart from the panic and the riots, there were no bloodsuckers here. For now. The police might look tough, but they wouldn't stand a chance against a full-scale assault by a vampire army.

The lockdown had been ordered by Jacqueline Burrows. Her record hadn't been good since she took interim power the previous day. During that time, she'd closed the borders and now closed the streets. Only a fool would say that it was all just precautions.

Burrows was due to make a statement in the House of Commons at 10.00pm, but it had been announced that she would not be in Parliament until 10.30pm.

It was good news. The reporter was running late. And he didn't want to miss Burrows's announcement.

But first he had to get into Portcullis House, the office block next to the Palace of Westminster. He'd been there before, so once he got inside, he knew where he was going.

The reporter turned up his collar. The rain fell heavily.

"Hey, mate, you got ID?"

The reporter wheeled.

An Armed Firearms Officer carrying a Heckler & Koch MP5 submachine gun with a red-dot sight glared at him.

"I've shown it once, but..."

"You can show it again, Clark Kent."

The reporter smiled and reached into his coat pocket.

"Easy, tiger," said the copper.

The reporter held up his hand. "It's... it's fine."

"I'm sure it is, but you just take it easy, okay?"

The reporter nodded. He slipped his hand into his pocket and retrieved his pass. The officer took it and studied it for a while.

The reporter stayed cool, but his hand was in his pocket, where it rested on a shiv he'd fashioned earlier from a Swiss Army Knife's blade, taped to a five-inch length of dowling.

"Who d'you work for?" said the cop.

"I'm freelance," said the reporter. "But I'm doing an interview with Jayne Monson. You know who she is?"

"'Course I fucking know, you pony."

He looked the reporter up and down and, handing him the ID, said, "Off you pop then, Clarky. Got your Y-fronts on under that suit?"

The policeman walked away.

The reporter headed for Portcullis House. He was stopped twice more, but after having the piss taken out of him for a few minutes by each copper, he was allowed to go on.

He reached Portcullis House and lit a cigarette. He wished he had his phone, but he'd lost it earlier.

He thought about something that distressed him – and not many things made him feel like that.

He shook it off. *Job to do*, he thought. *Let's do it.*

He shoved through the revolving doors and entered Portcullis House. MPs were being interviewed in the foyer. They were warning about a police-state Britain. One said the water was poisoned, and no one should use it.

The reporter, with five bullets in his body, stepped into the elevator.

CHAPTER 120.
THE "V" WORD.

JACQUELINE Burrows rose.

The chamber quietened as MPs on both sides of the House looked at the Prime Minister in her red jacket and white shirt.

Pinned to her lapel was a scarlet ribbon that looked frayed and worn.

She spoke:

"Outside this ancient, venerable building tonight, fear and violence stalk the streets. We do not know yet what sparked this situation – "

A murmur went through the chamber.

"Order, order," called the Speaker.

Burrows continued:

"We do not know, as yet. The police are doing their best to contain the situation. They will make the streets safe; don't be in any doubt. Members of the Armed Forces are also patrolling in certain areas. We know the violence has been triggered by a few troublemakers. It then spreads like a plague. Panic takes over. There is anarchy. As Interim Prime Minister, I would urge every citizen to be calm. If you are out tonight and are caught in a dangerous situation, leave the area calmly. Walk away, is the advice. Return to your homes. Wait for news."

"It's the immigrants," said the jowly old Tory, Shackleton.

His comments caused shouts to erupt around the House. MPs, including his own colleagues, told him to sit down.

Opposite Burrows, Jayne Monson, Leader of the Opposition, sat grim-faced. She looked straight at the Prime Minister. Her eyes were cold and hard.

Burrows grinned at her.

The shouting continued. The Speaker tried to restore order.

This is wonderful, thought Burrows. *Good old Shackleton – a brave and outspoken Nebuchadnezzar.*

She let the bedlam wash over her. She loved it. Confusion and conflict. The seeds of hate being planted. Fury blooming all around her.

The nation was close to falling.

Soon, thought Burrows, *Britain will be mine.*

The MPs roared and hollered for a while longer, until finally the Speaker managed to quieten them.

Burrows waited for silence. She had no intention of responding directly to Shackleton's comments. But when calm returned she said, "I repeat, we do not know as yet the reason for this situation, but the police are out there, maintaining control and investigating. The message, once more, is don't panic."

"What about vampires?" shouted a Liberal Democrat MP who was known to advocate conspiracy theories. The woman had been convinced that Diana, the Princess of Wales, had been murdered and claimed that some of her constituents had been abducted by aliens.

All nonsense – apart from the claim she was now making.

She wasn't the only one who'd mentioned the "V" word, as the press called it. Everyone was using it. Before, people had been embarrassed. The online community used it, but the word wasn't often spoken in mainstream society.

The Lib Dem MP refused to sit down, despite being shouted at by other members.

She spoke over the noise:

"Three years ago, hundreds of people died and many disappeared. The Religion nightclub in Soho was a haven for this activity, and it burned down. Why are the files pertaining to the incident closed for seventy years? Cover-up, I say. Cover-up."

Other MPs joined in the chorus:

"Cover-up! Cover-up!"

"Order, order," called the Speaker. "The Honourable Member must be seated. Please. And please, Honourable Members must remain quiet. Prime Minister."

Burrows went on:

"We will not allow chaos, rumour, and lies to win the day. We will not allow hatred to rule our streets. This is Britain. We have a tradition of tolerance and reason. We embrace difference, here. We embrace change."

"Here, here," said the members behind her, and some on the Opposition benches. Others scowled at her. Some stood and said, "Rubbish! Nonsense!" as they waved order papers. Her gaze roved the chamber.

The excitement grew in her. Soon this theatre would be her playhouse. There would be no challenge. Decisions would be made elsewhere. The ancient seat of democracy would only be symbolic. There would be no power here again.

The House filled with noise once more. It took a while for the MPs to calm down, and when they did, Burrows spoke again:

"In the interest of security, we will, from tomorrow evening, be operating a curfew — "

Shouts rose up again.

Burrows spoke over them:

"From 6.00pm until 6.00am every night, citizens will be expected to stay in their homes. If anyone is found out between those times, they will be arrested."

Cries of "Shame! Shame!" filled the House.

Jayne Monson got to her feet. Anger was etched on her face. She pointed at Burrows and said, "Tell the House how you've poisoned the water supply, Prime Minister. Tell them how you intend to turn London into a city of death. Tell them... "

The House erupted with noise. MPs bellowed. They stamped their feet. Fights broke out.

Burrows looked Monson in the eye. She leaned on the dispatch box on her side of the table. The box contained the Bible and the Koran, among other religious books. Burrows had thought of getting rid of the box when the new religion was in place. But for now, it was a good place from which to glare at the Leader of the Opposition.

As the noise grew louder around her, Burrows said to Monson, "You'll be dead by morning, Jayne."

CHAPTER 121.
ZEALOT.

THE smell hit Lawton first. Decay. Death. It was gut-frazzling. Vomit-making.

Hours ago, when he'd rescued Murray from this place, he'd not noticed the stench so much. He probably had other things on his mind. Surviving. Saving Christine.

He crept down the passageway. Up ahead lay the container. Steam rose from it, forming a mist that rolled along the basement's arched ceiling.

He stopped and squatted down. He slipped the backpack off his shoulders and opened it and pulled out the Spear of Abraham, which was encased in its leather scabbard. He removed the spear. It came out in two pieces. Tusks of ivory with leather hilts. The hilts slotted into each other to form a two-pointed weapon.

Along with sunlight, it was the only thing that could kill the vampire trinity. Three years previously, Lawton had used it to destroy Kea, the first of the undead princes.

He'd stowed it at Jayne Monson's office in Portcullis House while he'd entered the Palace of Westminster earlier. He didn't want to risk bringing it into the building and being stopped by security, despite his being dressed as a copper.

450

But he had to risk it now. He needed the weapon to kill whatever was coming to life in that container. And he'd already made it through the checkpoint, disguised as a reporter. Anyone seeing him wandering around Parliament with his backpack would know it had already been inspected. His hope was they'd leave him alone. They had. With so much panic inside the Palace of Westminster, he was ignored.

Down in the cellar now, he fixed the two tusks together to make the spear.

A cry came out of the darkness.

Lawton froze.

Murray, he thought.

But then he realized the noise came from a different woman. He peered into the gloom up ahead. A figure lay crumpled near the container.

He looked around and saw there was no one here. It was safe. He stood and moved towards the tank and the figure.

He recognized her. She'd been chained to the spot where he'd found Murray.

Lawton looked at her and she looked right back at him.

"Why did they leave you here?" he said. "You're one of them."

"Help me," she said.

"One minute," he said and scaled the stepladder so he could peer into the tank.

"Oh fuck," he said.

Words he'd spoken to Tom Wilson a few days before came to him:

What can be worse than a seven-foot red vampire?

This is worse, he thought.

The creature taking shape in the gore shot out a tongue of blood from the head growing out of its chest. Lawton reared backwards and fell off the stepladder, dropping the spear. He grabbed it and held it up, ready to defend himself.

The bloody tongue swished in the air before flicking back into the container.

Lawton went over to the girl and laid down the spear. His nerves jangled. The monster coming to life in there was terrifying.

451

She said, "Get me out of here, please."

"Why did they do this to you?"

"Please get me out of here, that thing's – "

"Why are you here? You're one of them."

The girl started to cry. "I'm Sarah Demeter. George Fuad chose between me and Mr Birch. He chose Mr Birch, and he made him... "

She told Lawton and he said, "Why did one of you have to die?"

"Burrows was mad that you got in and you stole her brooch – that thing – you're wearing it. They've taken mine, too. Please help me. I don't want to die."

"If you're one of them, I should leave you here for that thing," he said.

"No, please, I'll – "

"Don't make me any offers I'll be able to refuse, darling."

"Don't leave me."

"No, I won't. But you owe me, okay?"

"Yes, Mr Lawton."

"You know who I am, then?"

"Everyone does."

He nodded. "You tell me what's going on, clear?"

"Clear... please... please."

Lawton started to pick at the lock of her handcuffs with the tip of his homemade shiv.

"You're.... you're like a... a folk hero, you know," she said.

He worked the lock, focusing. "That's what they say."

"I mean, we all hate you. Or people like Burrows and Fuad hate you. But you're... you're a legend with friends of mine."

"Am I?"

"I hated you, of course. I'm a Nebuchadnezzar."

"You are – that's it, you're loose."

"Thank you." She rubbed her wrists. "And I really can't help being a Nebuchadnezzar."

He rose and turned his back to retrieve the spear.

"It's just in my DNA, you see."

"I understand – "

The pain went through him like acid. He stiffened and gritted his teeth. He wheeled and pushed Demeter away. She reared back.

452

He yelled out, angry that he'd let her catch him out.

His shoulder pulsed, and he clawed at the point of the pain and found the stiletto knife stuck in his back.

She came at him, her eyes wide.

"I can't help myself," she said.

She lunged, latching on to him. Her nails searched for his eyes. He spun around, Demeter holding on to him and scratching at him. She bit him, her teeth breaking the skin on his shoulder.

He shouted in pain. He rammed his head sideways and caught her on the cheek. She grunted and loosened her grip, and he managed to toss her away.

He reached behind his shoulder to try and pull the stiletto-knife out of his back.

"They fucking abandoned you," he said. "They left you to die, and I'm saving you... why would you want to help them?"

"If I can kill you, if I can kill Jake Lawton, they'll – "

She ploughed forward again.

Lawton yanked the knife out of his shoulder and dropped the weapon. He gritted his teeth against the pain. He dipped his shoulder and tackled the advancing Demeter around the waist, lifting her off the ground.

She screamed and fought back, slapping and scratching his back and his head.

"What's wrong with you?" he said. "I'm helping you."

"You're Lawton. They'll let me back in. I have to kill you. I want to be part of it."

"You fucking stupid girl." Lawton's shoulder ached. The strength drained out of him. The knife had scratched bone, penetrated muscle. He felt blood run down his back.

He threw Demeter to the ground.

"Stay here, then," he said.

He went for the spear again but once more she attacked him, biting his calf muscle.

He cried out and went to kick her in the head, but hesitated. He couldn't boot a woman in the skull.

Her teeth sank deeper. She thrashed her head from side to side. She tore through his skin.

Lawton grabbed her by the collar and prised her away from his leg. He hoisted her over his head.

She struggled and frothed at the mouth, his blood bubbling in the spit.

Her eyes blazed. She looked crazy. She looked unstoppable.

He threw her against the container and she slumped to the ground.

"Stop this," he told her. "I don't want to hurt you."

"You'll have to hurt me. I'm sorry. I have to kill you. They will love me if I kill you."

"I'll help you."

A growl came from the container. The smoke rising from it became thicker. The smell brought tears to Lawton's eyes.

"He's coming alive," she said.

There was awe in her face. Love. Lust. Desire.

"Christ," said Lawton, "we need to get out of here, come on – "

"I'm here, my god," she said. She scooped up the stiletto-knife and climbed up the stepladder. "I'm yours. Come alive. Our enemy is here. Take me. I give you life."

She laughed and with the knife, stabbed her own throat.

Lawton gawped. *They're mad*, he thought, *they're zealots*. Moments ago, she'd been saying how she didn't want to die. Now she was willing to sacrifice herself to whatever was coming alive in that container. *Religious maniacs*, he thought.

"I'm yours," said Sarah as the smoke rose up around her.

"Sarah, no – "

"My blood… " She stabbed herself, and blood started to jet from her torn throat. She gurgled and laughed and stared at Lawton. In a croak, she said, "He's rising, Lawton, and he'll kill you – and they will recognize my sacrifice."

Her blood gushed out.

A tongue of flesh shot up from the tank and looped around Sarah's head. It lifted her up and whipped her about, her neck snapping, her arms and legs flailing. It yanked her into the container. Blood and gore splashed up in a fountain.

Lawton staggered away, holding on to the spear. He had to get out. He was weak. Blood poured from the wound in his shoulder. He felt sick.

If this thing came to life, he wouldn't stand a chance.

The tank shuddered and clanked. The metal buckled. A split ran from the bottom to the top. Gore seeped out.

And then a tower of viscera burst out of the container, drenching the ceiling and raining down.

Lawton stumbled and fell to the ground. He scrabbled away. But it was too late.

Out of the gore came the monster.

Its two heads rose from the tank. They swivelled, searching for its first meal as a living thing.

And the four scarlet eyes fixed on Lawton.

CHAPTER 122.
THE END OF BRITAIN.

JAYNE Monson was up on her feet, shouting over the noise and telling anyone who would listen that the Prime Minister had threatened her.

Burrows smiled. It didn't matter. Time was running out for people like Monson.

The Speaker battled to bring order back to the House. But he was failing.

MPs fought. They argued. They shouted. And in the middle of it all, Burrows sat quietly, thinking about the death of England and the birth of Babylon.

She reached into her pocket and sent a text.

Thirty seconds later, ten men dressed in black and armed with submachine guns swept into the chamber.

They fired into the air, and the MPs threw themselves to the floor, while others tried to flee through the exit behind the Speaker's chair.

Silence fell.

The Speaker stood. "This is outrageous," he said. "Leave immediately. Leave this House. Call the police."

Burrows stood. "Be quiet," she told the Speaker. He slowly sat down, his mouth open. Burrows looked around. The MPs cowered. The men with guns had spread out, half of them mingling with MPs on the right of the chamber, the other half doing the same on the left.

"Listen to me," said Burrows. "Tonight sees the end of Britain. Her days are finished. A new age is coming. A golden time. The era of humans is at an end. The era of vampires now begins."

Gasps raced through the chamber.

Monson stood up and said, "You can't do this."

"I just have," said Burrows.

"I'll not allow it."

"Jayne, tomorrow you will either be dead or in a concentration camp, ready to be harvested for the vampire nation that is rising. All of you, you have a choice. Serve the new regime, or be her slaves. Free will, ladies and gentlemen."

A few MPs seemed to forget the armed men and they stood up, jeering Burrows.

But she made a signal and bullets raked the ceiling again, silencing the members.

"You have brought guns into the heart of our democracy," said Monson. "Shame on you, Mrs Burrows."

"Some of you," said Burrows, ignoring Monson, "are with me tonight. You are Nebuchadnezzars. Your hearts sing with joy at the coming of Babylon."

"About time," said jowly old Shackleton. "This country's in need of disinfecting. And those of you who are against us, you'll be flushed away with the rest of the shit."

Burrows smiled at her co-conspirator. "Below us, at this moment, a god is awakening. Many of you know of a similar attempt at resurrection three years ago. Yes, of course there were vampires. We had a vampire plague in Britain. But our plot was scuppered by traitors. Not tonight. Tonight, we are victorious."

Rubble rained from the ceiling.

Burrows looked up.

The ground trembled.

She smiled at Monson.

"It's coming, Jayne," Burrows told her opponent. "Prepare to look into the eyes of a god."

Great Cambridge Roundabout, Enfield, London – 10.45pm, February 15, 2011

Kurt Ellis, forty-eight and having been around the block a few times, had never seen anything like it in his life.

Thousands of them. And they had torches. The beams slashed the night sky. They looked like lightsabres from the Star Wars films.

Because it was dark, Kurt couldn't see their faces. But as they swung their torches, their faces were illuminated now and again.

"They're Chinese," said Kurt.

"And there's like some Afghans or Iraqis there, too," said his wife.

Kurt and his missus had been stuck on the roundabout for two hours. This was where the North Circular and the A10 met. It was the end of London, and thousands of people were trying to get out of the city. The traffic jam stretched for miles both ways.

Kurt and his wife had witnessed vampire attacks during the evening. The creatures had appeared when it got dark and assaulted anyone who'd got out of their cars.

They tried to break into vehicles, but most drivers managed to lock their doors in time.

"Who are they?" said Kurt's wife now, watching the foreign throng.

"How should I know?"

"Are... are they this immigrant gang, you think?"

"Shit, I don't know." He squirmed in his seat. Some newspapers had been warning people about foreign mobs. According to the tabloids, more and more migrants were flooding Britain. That's why the Government had closed the borders.

But then it seemed the papers had been lying. Now it wasn't immigrants who were getting the blame, it was vampires.

Maybe the immigrants are vampires, thought Kurt.

No one knew whom to blame anymore. But Kurt knew one thing for certain –

Britain was in turmoil. And like many other Londoners, he and his wife had decided to head for the hills. "We can pick up cheap property in Wales somewhere," he'd said. "Plenty of nice houses up in the hills that the local hicks can't afford."

The immigrants streamed towards them. They were headed for London.

Crazy, thought Kurt. *Everyone with half a brain is headed out.*

"I'm scared," said his wife. "What if they... what if they kill us."

But the foreigners didn't seem to be taking any notice of the cars trapped in the traffic jam. In fact, they were very careful when they walked between the vehicles. They obviously made an effort not to clip any wing mirrors or dink any doors. And a few even smiled and bowed at Kurt as they passed his window.

"I didn't think there were so many foreigners in England," said his wife.

"Well, you know what the papers say – they're everywhere."

"Do you think they're going home?"

"They don't look like it. They look to me like they're on a mission," he said.

CHAPTER 123.
THE OLD WAYS ARE GONE.

10.50PM, FEBRUARY 15, 2011

THE smear of blood running up the wall showed where Lawton had leaned against it as he staggered up the stairwell.

His shoulder throbbed. He felt as if he were falling to pieces. His head swam, and pain seemed to fill every inch of him, from his hair down to his toenails.

He reached the top of the stone stairs and felt sick. He took a second to steady himself before shoving the door open.

The noise of panic hit him. Steam billowed from boiling pots and pans. The smell of food made him salivate. Kitchen staff ran around, screaming.

And then Lawton noticed that the whole building was shaking, with utensils being thrown about and clanking on the tiled floors, sauces being spilled, and people losing their balance.

He stumbled through the kitchens.

The Palace of Westminster rumbled.

Lawton raced along some corridors. He barged past people as they tried to escape. Climbing another set of stairs, shouldering through the crowds that raced down towards him, Lawton came out in a lobby.

Panic here as well. Everyone heading for the exits. Police trying to hold back the wave of people but being swept up in it.

Lawton, weak and nauseous, asked someone how he got into the Commons chamber. The man told him.

Ten minutes later in the Central Lobby, Lawton stopped and looked around. Down the south corridor lay the House of Lords. The north corridor led to the Commons. Along the south passage now came old men, trundling as fast as they could go.

The building quaked. Some of the old men fell.

A statue of 19th century Prime Minister Gladstone toppled over and smashed, scattering itself into thousands of pieces across the floor.

Rubble rained from the ceiling seventy-five feet above Lawton. Glass cracked. The floor trembled. Ornaments fell.

Lawton gripped the Spear of Abraham. He headed down the corridor to his left. A door set in an archway stood before him. Flanking the arch were statues Lawton recognized as Winston Churchill and David Lloyd George.

The thought, *What would they think?* flashed through his mind and was then gone when he was confronted by a woman leaning on the doorframe with a terrified look on her face.

"Let me inside," he said.

"I... I can't, it's... it's the... members of the public can't... "

"Who are you?" he asked.

"I'm... I'm the Serjeant-at-Arms," he said.

"You're responsible for security, aren't you?"

She nodded.

He said, "But you're traditional, aren't you. Your role, I mean. You're not really security. You're not real."

She nodded again. "Tradition," she said. "It's tradition."

The door buckled. Screams came from inside the chamber.

"Tradition's over," said Lawton. "Bureaucracy's dead. The old ways are gone. They can't protect us anymore. Only I can protect you, now. Let me in. Let me inside, or I'll smash my way through."

* * * *

BABYLON, SUMERIA – 3,208 BC

Abraham broke through the great wooden door leading into the abyss. The stench of death swept up towards him, but he

461

didn't flinch. He stayed strong, standing in the archway and glaring down into the pit.

Into Irkalla.

I shall not fear, he told himself, *I shall not fear, because the Lord my God is with me, my shield and my sword.*

Abraham had already face Nimrod's witches. The Great Hunter's one hundred brides. The harlots of hell.

They'd filled the passageway and bared their fangs, but he stood his ground. He showed no fear. The light of Yahweh came from him, and the brides trembled.

"In the name of God," he said, his voice booming through the catacombs, "I command you, die... "

The caves rocked. The witches shrieked. Shafts of light sliced through the splitting stone, even though it was night outside. The beams speared into the brides and they scattered, trying to escape the radiance.

Abraham strode down the passageway.

All around him, the witches moaned. The light burned them. Their bodies aged rapidly. Their youthfulness withered, and they became old, and then they became bone and soon after, dust.

A bony hand had grabbed his ankle as he passed. He looked down. The face staring up at him went from young to old. The witch said, "You will not win. You will never destroy us. We are immortal. One shall live. One shall live."

Abraham raised his foot to stamp on the witch, but before he could crush her, she had disintegrated.

He had marched on, and the dark became darker and the cold, colder.

And the deeper he went, the closer he got to death.

Now, he walked down the stone steps into hell. He scanned the abyss. Great pillars rose from the earth and stretched up into the gloom, further than Abraham could see.

Irkalla, he thought. *The foundation of the Tower of Babel. I will bring it down and kill its architect. The old gods will die. After tonight, there is only Yahweh.*

And Irkalla trembled.

* * * *

Ereshkigal, bride of Nimrod, reached the door through which the trespasser had entered.

Outside it was dark. She looked back. The noise rumbling up from the deep sounded like an earthquake.

Her sisters were dead. The trespasser was a magician. He had split open the rock and light speared through, destroying the brides.

How had he done that? It was night. Where had the light come from?

Ereshkigal pined for her sisters. Now there was only her left. She had to survive. One day, she would have a purpose.

Her black heart told her that was true.

There would be days when Nimrod's cult would come again to the earth – and she had to be ready as one of its priestesses.

She peered out of the door. There was enough of the night left for her to be safe. With hunger gnawing at her gut, Ereshkigal got ready to sneak out.

"Wait," said a deep voice.

She turned.

They came crawling through the falling debris.

"Take us with you," said the one with wings.

"Hurry," she told the red-fleshed trinity.

CHAPTER 124.
THE GREAT BEAST RISING.

11.02PM, FEBRUARY 15, 2011

THE floor of the Commons chamber erupted. Wood, concrete, and soil volcanoed. Debris buried the table separating the Government and Opposition benches. The whole room trembled. Rubble showered from the ceiling.

MPs screamed and cowered. They tried to flee the chamber. But there was no way out. The doors were guarded by the armed men.

Burrows rose. Dust covered her clothes and her face, but she didn't care.

"The world is changing," she called out. "Your days are numbered."

Steam rose from the hole in the middle of the chamber. Burrows smelled the decay. It was beautiful. The odour made her feel lust.

A front bench colleague grabbed her arm. She turned to look at him. His face was grey with concrete dust. Blood ran from a wound on his forehead.

He said, "What the hell's going on, Jacqueline?"

She smiled at him. "A change of Government."

A roar came from the pit.

Burrows's heart quickened.

He was coming. The great beast was rising. Her vampire king coming to sit beside her on the throne of Britain.

A flash of red rocketed from the earth.

Screams filled the chamber.

Burrows stood still at the dispatch box, gazing upwards.

The vampire god clamped itself to the ceiling high above. It flapped its wings.

Burrows gasped at its beauty.

Then the creature swooped down, screeching. It landed on the table, splitting the wood and scattering the debris that covered it.

"My lord," said Burrows.

The vampire looked at her with its two heads – the heads of Kakash and Kasdeja.

And then the third torso that was growing from the monster's chest turned towards her. The red flesh of the face couldn't hide the creature's former identity – it had been Nadia Radu, Haddad's companion, a high-ranking Nebuchadnezzar in her time.

The Radu vampire looked as if it was buried up to its waist in the Kakash-Kasdeja vampire's chest.

The thing that had been Nadia bared its fangs and pointed at Burrows. It said, "We are hungry."

"Feed," said Burrows. "It's all for you."

The three-headed abomination flung itself into the Opposition benches. MPs were crushed under its weight. It slashed at them with its four arms. Blood splashed the benches of the Commons chamber.

The monster scooped up a man and its Kakash-Kasdeja mouths bit into his flesh, causing him to scream.

The Radu beast grabbed at a female MP and locked its arms around the woman. The vampire's fangs sank into the prey's throat, tearing the flesh away.

Burrows laughed at everything.

"Now we rule," she called out. "Now we rule. The Lord of Blood is here."

The chamber's door flew open.

Burrows's mouth fell open.

No, she thought and then screamed the word:

"NO!"

Jake Lawton, armed with the Spear of Abraham, charged inside. In the time Burrows had run out of breath after screaming, Lawton had killed two of her armed guards. And now he was coming for her.

PART FOUR.

RETREAT.

CHAPTER 125.
DEATH IS EVERYWHERE.

ROCKY Chalfont sat in the CCTV viewing room. A bank of monitors showed him images from Oxford Street.

He felt sick. Probably because he'd been out with his mates that afternoon. It wasn't meant to be a session. Just a pint at lunchtime.

But when Nate said, "Have another one... just one more... the world's going to end, you might as well enjoy yourself... " Rocky couldn't say no. And one more pint became two more, and soon he was drunk.

He had to come straight to work. No time to go home to have a nap and a shower.

The streets were crazy. Police everywhere. Fighting and rioting. People running around, barging into Rocky, saying, "There's vampires loose in London."

He rubbed his forehead and sweat dampened his hand. He flicked the sweat away and cursed. He shouldn't be as sick as this. Boozing at lunchtime was nothing new for Rocky. He should be feeling okay by now. He'd downed three pints of water when he got in at 6.00pm, which should have hydrated him.

But his insides burned. He felt dizzy, and his mouth was dry.

He looked up at the monitors. Pedestrians stampeded down Oxford Street. The images blurred. Rocky blinked.

The first monitor showed an incident. An ambulance was parked near an HMV store. A crowd clustered around a body. No, there were three bodies lying on the pavement. Paramedics shoved their way through the throng.

"Weird," said Rocky to himself. "Have you seen this, Nick?" he asked his colleague.

Nick Root said nothing. Rocky stared at the screen.

The people who were gathered around the bodies then started to collapse. They went like dominoes. Some of them vomited as they fell. Others writhed on the floor as if in pain.

"What the... " Rocky tensed.

The paramedic stared at the bodies surrounding him. He looked up at the CCTV camera and waved, making the signal for the operator to dial the police.

Rocky's heart raced.

"What's going on?" he said. "Nick, what – "

His eyes ranged the monitors. Corpses peppered Oxford Street. People were running and then slumping to the ground.

Buses crashed into shops. Cars weaved across the street.

There were twitching bodies everywhere. Twitching and dying. Dying and dead.

Rocky grimaced. The pain in his belly blazed.

"Nick," he said, turning to find his colleague slumped in the chair. Froth bubbled around Nick's mouth.

"Nick. Nick." Rocky tried to get up and see if his colleague was okay but his legs gave way. "Oh God," he said, falling in a heap.

He reached for Nick and nudged his chair, which spun round.

"Christ," said Rocky as Nick turned slowly in the chair to face him.

Nick was dead.

Rocky's heart exploded.

He screamed, and his throat clogged. He couldn't breathe. Panic raced through him. He clawed at the control desk, trying to get up, scrabbling at buttons and switches.

The monitors flashed. Death came back at him from the screens.

He moaned and gasped for air. His chest burned. Saliva filled his mouth, and he dribbled. Blood came from his nose. He tried to scream but only managed to retch.

Water, he thought, *water...*

His vision swam. His body felt like it was being torn apart. Now he couldn't breathe at all. His lungs were tight. Blood filled his throat. And death made everything go black.

CHAPTER 126.
THE NEBUCHADNEZZAR
MODEL.

FROM the window of his flat in Westminster, George Fuad watched people dying.

They were falling in heaps on the streets below.

They've been drinking the water, he thought.

The fifth-floor apartment gave him a good view of things. It was the property Bernard Lithgow had pretended to give to his son. In reality, George owned the apartment. He and his brother owned most of the Nebuchadnezzars' properties in London.

We are *the Nebuchadnezzars*, he thought.

"What's happening?"

George didn't turn round. "Bernie Lithgow must've been successful," he said, "because people are keeling over by the hundred out here."

Haddad clapped his hands.

George turned to face the old man. "Makes you happy, Afdal?"

"Of course it does. Tonight they die, tomorrow they rise. Our vampire nation is finally coming, George."

"Yeah, and Britain will be mine – ours."

Haddad glared at him. "George, temper your ambitions."

"I only want what's best, old chum."

"What's best is a reign of blood. The Nebuchadnezzar model. Rule with strength and fear. Not with chaos and anarchy."

"I had no intention of it being anarchic. But in the Nebuchadnezzar model, you need a Nebuchadnezzar."

"You were always pushy as a boy."

"We're all pushy, Afdal. We're doing this for power, ultimately. We're not doing it for the good of the country."

Haddad said, "I want a golden age. This is the only way. Freedom and democracy can only get you so far. You can't do what's best when you're encumbered by liberal capitalism."

"That's why," said George, "we're getting rid of it. That's why we're making Babylon again. The streets will be gold and we'll build grand palaces. We'll claim the great houses and the castles, and we'll have a kingdom. But I'm not kidding myself – I ain't doing it for Britain. I'm doing it for me."

"George," said Haddad, "what you are doing is dangerous. I do not care which one of us leads. It doesn't matter. Our goal is to resurrect Babylon. The great age of the world. A city of gods. London will be wonderful again. We have lost many in that pursuit. We should be dedicated to the cause in remembrance of the friends we have lost."

George shrugged. "I don't care about who's died and who's not died."

"Nadia sacrificed her life. Ion did too. Do not insult their memory, George. You anger me now." Haddad's eyes narrowed. The old man was thinking. Then he said, "Where's your brother; where's Alfred? What did you mean when you said 'digging for victory'?"

George smiled.

Haddad asked again where Alfred was. "I've not seen him in hours. Where is he? Have you sacrificed your own brother?"

"He's gone to Hillah," said George.

Haddad spoke slowly: "Why has he gone to Hillah?"

George poured himself a whisky. "What's happening in London tonight is all fine and dandy. A Britain ruled by vampires and their human allies. But I just don't want to stop at Britain."

"We won't," said Haddad. "It was never the plan. We would build an empire. But empire-building takes time."

George shook his head. "I don't want to wait. We've got the upper hand. I say we hit the world, now. A vampire shock-and-awe attack."

Haddad studied George for a few moments. George drank and waited for the old man to say something, and finally he did:

"Alfred's gone to find Nimrod, hasn't he."

George nodded.

"Nimrod is buried," said Haddad.

"Well, we can unbury him."

"You can't control him, George," said Haddad.

"You can control Kea, Kakash, and Kasdeja."

"They are minor gods. Not... not the creator. He is the unseen god of vampires, and like all gods, he is best left unseen."

George said, "I'm going to put a leash on the Great Hunter."

Haddad tried to rise from his wheelchair. "You are a fool."

"No I'm not; I'm a visionary, Afdal, old fella."

"You'll kill us all," said Haddad.

"I've got an empire to build. Let's watch the show." George picked up the TV remote control from the arm of the leather couch and switched on the 50-inch screen on the wall.

He was smiling when he turned the TV on, but his smile evaporated when the picture appeared.

Haddad gawked at the screen as well and it was the old man who said, "What is going on?"

The Sky News channel showed the House of Commons. Smoke made it difficult to see what was going on, but the ancient chamber appeared to be in ruins.

And in the smoke, a red giant wheeled violently.

"It is him," said Haddad. "Risen."

"Yes, but what's that on its back?" said George.

Haddad struck the arms of his wheelchair in anger.

"Lawton," he said. "Lawton again."

CHAPTER 127.
THE FALL OF THE TOWER OF BABEL.

ABRAHAM rode the Great Hunter.

He stood on Nimrod's shoulders and grasped the god's horns. The beast slashed its head from side to side, trying to dislodge his attacker.

But Abraham held on.

Nimrod ran through the abyss. He smashed into pillars. They cracked and toppled. Irkalla trembled. Great stones crashed down from the ceiling and exploded when they struck the ground. Rubble piled up.

Abraham pulled at the horns. Sweat coated his body. He gritted his teeth.

Give me strength, Lord, he prayed, *give me strength to destroy this false god.*

Dust blinded Abraham. He blinked, and tears rolled from his eyes. He was in pain. His arms and his legs felt like pieces of straw that were about to snap.

But he wouldn't let go.

God would not let him.

If he let go, God would curse him.

Nimrod whipped his head from side to side. As he did so, Abraham's grip on the horns loosened. Sweat from his palms also made it harder for him to hold on.

The Great Hunter barrelled through Irkalla. He shouldered pillars and pounded the ground with his fists and his feet.

The whole of Babylon could probably feel his anger.

But his wrath was nothing to God's fury.

And Abraham knew he would pay terribly if he failed his Lord.

"Let me go!" said Nimrod, his voice booming through the caverns of the underworld. "How dare you – I am a god, and you are nothing."

"There is only one god, and he is Yahweh," said Abraham.

By now his body felt weak, but his spirit was strong. He would kill the Great Hunter. He would have his vengeance. Blood for blood. Life for life.

"You destroyed my people," said Abraham. "You wiped out Ur's children in one day."

"But my foolish generals didn't kill you."

"I am nothing."

"You are the prophecy – the one who would come to kill me – the one with wounds."

"There are no prophets, only God's prophets. Your holy men are liars and fools, Nimrod. They see nothing."

"They saw you."

"They saw nothing. I am not the one. I am God's chosen."

Abraham's grip slackened. His arms had no strength in them.

Nimrod's power remained. He shook his head and clawed at Abraham as he hurtled through his dark house.

The caverns quaked. Pillars toppled and loosened masonry from the ceilings. The walls began to crack.

Abraham couldn't hold on for much longer.

He prayed to God for strength, and Yahweh told him what he had to do.

Suffer for me, said the Lord's voice in Abraham's head.

Suffer.

Quickly, Abraham lifted his hands from Nimrod's horns and brought his palms down flat on the pointed ends.

They pierced his flesh.

The pain exploded in Abraham's head. A flash of white light burst before his eyes, and in that moment he saw everything — all the demons of Irkalla, all its cities and its kings.

He felt himself grow more powerful.

He cried out Yahweh's name.

Abraham closed his hands around Nimrod's horns again. Blood ran down the ivory stalks and coated the Great Hunter's skull. Abraham's shoulders filled with the wrath of God, and he pulled on the horns.

Nimrod roared, thrashing violently to get rid of Abraham.

But his attacker wouldn't budge.

Abraham wrenched at the horns. He heard bone crack. Nimrod shrieked.

Blood gushed over the Great Hunter's head.

Had it come from Abraham's wounds, or was the Lord of Irkalla coming apart?

Wherever it came from, the sight of it spraying encouraged Abraham, and he yanked at the horns.

They loosened. Nimrod's skull cracked.

Around them, the tower started to collapse. Heavy stones plummeted to the ground and formed craters on impact. It seemed as if the whole earth were shaking. Pillars toppled, crashing into others pillars.

Abraham pulled on the horns.

Nimrod cried out and ran into a wall. The stones shattered. Abraham was tossed, head over heels. But the horns were attached to his hands.

And they came away from Nimrod's skull.

Fountains of blood shot from the gouges left by the amputated tusks.

Nimrod keeled over, bellowing.

Abraham fell in a heap, the horns nailed through his palms.

He sat up and pulled his hands free of the tusks. It was agonizing. He stared at his palms. They weren't there anymore. They gaped bloodily. His skin hung in ribbons around the punctures in his hands. His fingers drooped because all the bones and tendons had been destroyed.

He struggled to his feet and stood over Nimrod's horns.

The Great Hunter cowered. Blood masked his face. He moaned. His tower rained down on him.

Abraham said, "I shall hunt your witches and your children for eternity, Nimrod, and with your bones, I shall kill them."

He scooped up the tusks using his elbows and hurried away, praying that Yahweh would guide him through the chaos.

Behind him, the tower buried Nimrod.

CHAPTER 128.
BROKEN THRONE.

THE creature unfolded its wings and flapped them. They smacked Lawton around the head.

He held on, his fingers buried in the eyes of one of the heads. With his other hand, he slashed with his spear.

As the creature wheeled, Lawton caught glimpses of the Commons.

The MPs were in panic. They clambered over the seats trying to get away. They spilled through the doors Lawton had thrown open. Fortunately, they stampeded the armed men, two of whom Lawton had killed when he came inside.

The chamber itself was in ruins. Furniture had been wrecked. The Speaker's chair was splintered. But standing on its remains was Burrows. She looked down on the battle like a queen from her throne.

A broken throne, thought Lawton.

But he shouldn't really have been thinking about her.

The creature reached up and grabbed his head. Its claws sliced his face. Lawton was tossed across the chamber. He sailed into the seats, falling in a heap.

Burrows's laughter boomed.

He groaned, pain tearing through his body. When he got up, the creature was bounding towards him.

The Radu-vampire, growing from the monster's chest, snarled at him and said, "We'll tear you apart, Lawton. We'll open you up and feed on your heart, you bastard."

Despite feeling weak, Lawton never shirked a challenge.

"Come on then, bitch," he said. "I've killed you twice already – let's make it third time lucky."

With its wings flapping, the three-headed monster charged Lawton.

"Kill him," shouted Burrows from her throne.

Lawton readied himself.

He tried to look fearless. He could always manage that. But in his heart, he knew he didn't have much strength left. And this creature was stronger than the one he'd killed at Religion.

The monster came at him.

* * * *

"We must go down there," said Haddad.

"Perhaps we're better off in here for now," said George.

"No," said Haddad. "Take me out of here."

"We're staying in the flat. We'll watch it on TV. Much safer."

"I want to see Lawton torn apart."

"And you will, Afdal – in glorious HD, on this 50-inch flat-screen."

"Jacqueline is there. Can you see?"

"I can see."

The footage showed Burrows perched on what remained of the Speaker's chair. She was the only MP left in the chamber now. The only living one, at least. Bodies were strewn everywhere. And she was there among the dead. Lording over them like a queen.

George hoped she'd get caught in the crossfire. Then she wouldn't be queen. And it would be easier for him to take control of the Nebuchadnezzars.

The battle continued. The monster went after Lawton. The man tried his best to evade the vampire's attacks, but he looked weak.

"It won't be long," said George.

"We must go down there."

"We're not going anywhere."

"You are a disgrace, George."

"Shut up, Afdal."

Haddad scowled at him. "You and your brother, you are fools."

"So you say."

"Attempting to resurrect Nimrod is madness."

"So we're mad."

"Do you think you can control him?"

George shrugged.

Haddad said, "He is not the trinity. He is not appeased by blood. He is appeased by power. You don't make treaties with him, George. You don't make bargains. You beg for your life."

George ignored him. Outside, gunfire barked. Helicopters churned. Screams came up from the streets below. London was in turmoil. The country was in ruins. The people were dying.

"Why are you doing this, George?" said Haddad.

"I'm doing it for my ancestors. I'm doing it for my bloodline."

"You're doing it for yourself."

"I'm replicating Nebuchadnezzar."

"Nebuchadnezzar never resurrected Nimrod."

George said nothing. He walked to the window. Vampires were spilling through the streets now. They'd sensed that their god was awake. It sent them into a frenzy.

They scaled the spires of Westminster Abbey and dive-bombed civilians below. They came up from the drains and grabbed people by the legs, pulling them underground.

He nodded at the carnage and then returned his attention to the TV screen.

"Let's relax and watch the fight," he said.

CHAPTER 129.
THE MARCH.

11.16PM, FEBRUARY 15, 2011

"MUM, they're everywhere," said David.

"Oh my God," said Murray, not listening to her son but watching the television in Jayne Monson's flat.

It showed Lawton fighting a terrifying creature. A two-headed creature, with a third monster growing from its chest.

Lawton scurried through the House of Commons chamber, trying to avoid the beast.

But the angel of death flapped after him like a red-skinned pterosaur.

Murray sat on the sofa, wrapped in a blanket. She still felt weak and ill. She wanted to go and help Lawton, but knew she'd be more of a hindrance to him.

She gawped at the TV.

David looked out of the window.

"Mum, you've got to come and look."

"It's Jake, he's… "

David came away from the window. "Shit," he said. "Is that the monster they've made?"

Murray said nothing.

David said, "It's worse than Kea."

She was quiet again.

"Mum, there's an army of vampires out there. They're attacking everyone. It's much, much worse – all of it – than three years ago."

Now she looked up at her son, and the first thought that came to her head was how grown-up David appeared.

He'd been ten when all this started. But she hadn't noticed him getting to thirteen. They'd been parted for many months after she burned Richard's corpse, after the vampires took Michael.

She started to cry.

"Mum," said David, sitting next to her, "what is it?"

"Everything... everything... oh, I'm so sorry."

"For what?"

"For getting you involved in this."

"I'd've been involved, anyway. Look out there. The vampires would've come. I'm safer because you got involved, Mum. Safer because you've been around Jake and Aaliyah."

"It wasn't safe for your dad or Michael."

David looked away. "I know."

"I'm sorry, darling," she said.

They hugged.

Murray watched the TV over David's shoulder. The footage cut away from the Commons chamber, where Lawton battled the monster.

Murray sat up.

"What is it?" said David.

"Look at that," she said.

The pictures came from a helicopter. In the darkness, a wave of people moved through the streets. They carried torches and the beams sliced into the darkness.

The TV reporter said, "There are thousands of them, it seems, and they appear to be foreign – there are a lot of Chinese, other Asian people, a number from the Middle East, and also hundreds of Eastern Europeans."

The news presenter in the studio asked, "Do we know where they're going, Peter?"

"They seem to be headed for Central London. They've travelled from all over Britain, today. The immigrant community has been under a lot of pressure recently. They have been the targets of attacks, and they've also been blamed for violence. Of course, the suggestion was that a foreign gang attacked No.10 yesterday, which resulted in the former Prime Minister's death."

"Do we know what they want?" said the news presenter.

The reporter said, "Well, it's not entirely safe to be down on the streets tonight, but correspondents have been asking a few of these people that question, and also why they're doing this. One man called Rashid, originally from Iraq, told reporters he'd come to stand with his brother. Most said they've come to fight for Britain. We shall see. I'm sure the police won't look kindly on this kind of march."

* * * *

Kwan Mei's heart thundered. More than a thousand people marched behind her. Mei couldn't believe how quickly she and the others had gathered everyone together. A few e-mails and phone calls, and it seemed as if the whole world had come to London with them.

They had travelled in cars, trucks, coaches, motorbikes, mini-buses, taxis – anything with an engine and wheels.

Because London was virtually under curfew, they'd had to stop their vehicles at the Great Cambridge Roundabout and walk from there. Their abandoned transport had blocked the A10, but Mei and the others didn't care. They'd tramped out along the road, entering London.

She glanced over her shoulder. Seeing everyone energized her. She had felt so alone when she left China.

Being a foreigner here was always going to be difficult, she thought.

But now she knew she would never be lonely – or alone – again.

Together, they would fight – for Jake Lawton and for Britain.

Along the way, vampires barrelled into the marchers. But Mei and her army had come prepared. They were armed.

They dragged down the demons and staked them, then marched on.

After a while, the vampires kept their distance. They attacked easier prey. These night creatures weren't stupid. They were animals, after all, and had hunters' instincts.

A lion wouldn't attack an elephant when there was a gazelle nearby. A vampire wouldn't attack hundreds of people when there was one available to kill.

Mei held the torch ahead of her. The beam stretched out. It was eleven miles from the Great Cambridge Roundabout to Westminster. The army marched quickly. Another half an hour, and they would be close to their destination.

I am coming to help you, Jake Lawton, she thought. *I am coming to stand with you.*

CHAPTER 130.
FIGHT TO THE FINISH.

11.21PM, FEBRUARY 15, 2011

THE monster wouldn't stop. Lawton grew tired.

"Let it kill you, Lawton," said Burrows.

The creature swooped down towards him. Lawton lay between the benches on the Government side. There was blood on the floor.

The monster perched on the seats and clawed at Lawton, trying to grab him – but he slashed with his spear.

The Radu-vampire said, "You're dead, Lawton – you and your country."

The creature ripped away the seating. Wood cracked and splintered, showering Lawton. He crawled along the floor.

Burrows laughed.

The creature followed Lawton and tore away the furniture, trying to get at him. But he kept moving.

Jake reached the aisle and got to his feet, wheeling to face the monster.

Without thinking, he swung the spear. It clipped the beast on the thigh and sent it spinning.

Lawton didn't wait. He bounded down.

"You'll not get away, Lawton," said Burrows.

He looked up at her and stopped.

Behind him, the creature righted itself. Lawton glanced at the monster, then fixed on Burrows again.

He smiled at her.

"You find your death funny?" she said.

"I find yours funny."

He lunged down from the benches and clambered up towards the Speaker's chair.

Burrows screamed.

Lawton grabbed her and ripped away the red ribbon attached to her lapel.

"Got you again," he said.

Burrows shrieked. Lawton got behind her and wrapped his arm around her neck. The creature came towards them. Burrows begged Lawton to let her go. But he held her tightly.

The monster stopped a few yards away and the Radu-creature spoke:

"You're not protected, Jacqueline."

Saliva spooled from the monster's three mouths.

Burrows said, "Nadia, please… "

The Radu-creature said, "I'm sorry, Jacqueline, we can't help ourselves – if you've not got the mark, you're blood to us."

"Yeah, sorry, Jacqueline," said Lawton.

He shoved her.

She shrieked.

The monster embraced her. Its mouths clamped on Burrows's body, two on either side of her neck, and the Radu-thing's jaws on her arm.

Burrows screamed.

"Help me! Help me! Don't let this happen to me!"

Lawton lunged forward. He drove the spear into the space between the beast's two heads.

The monster screeched.

It threw Burrows aside, and her body slammed against the benches on the left of the chamber.

With the red ribbon gripped between his teeth, Lawton perched on the Radu-beast's shoulders and pushed the spear down into the creature's body.

It shrieked.

"No! No! Lawton, no!" bellowed the Radu-monster.

The vampire tried to dislodge him but he held on to the spear. He growled as he drove the tusk downwards, tearing through bone and muscle.

The creature flapped its wings and took off with Lawton holding on. It swooped through the chamber. Lawton clutched the spear tightly. The beast thrashed about, trying to throw Lawton off.

But he wouldn't let go.

Desperately, the monster clawed at Lawton. Every time it brushed the ribbon, its flesh charred, and it screamed. But it wanted to live. Its talons tore through Lawton's flesh.

His vision became bloody.

He weakened and knew he would be unconsciousness soon. He leaned down hard on the spear, putting all his weight on the two-pointed weapon. And because he was pushing down so hard, the other tusk pierced Lawton's shoulder. But he ignored the pain, ramming the spear deeper into the monster.

They tumbled through the air and came crashing to the floor, toppling down into the hole through which the creature had exploded.

They plunged.

Lawton's head swam. He saw nothing but blood.

I'm blind, he thought, *I'm blind.*

But he could feel the monster beneath him. It struggled and thrashed about and shrieked, and then another odour filled Lawton's nostrils.

Burning.

CHAPTER 131.
MAKING AN ESCAPE.

11.30PM, FEBRUARY 15, 2011

"NO, this cannot be happening again," said Haddad.

Bastard, thought George, *that bastard Lawton*.

"Jacqueline," said Haddad, "Jacqueline… "

The footage from the chamber showed Burrows's twisted body lying across the Opposition benches.

She's dead, thought George.

Haddad started crying. "Why does he do this? Why does he destroy us?"

"He's not a big fan of ours, Afdal."

"This man is a curse. He killed my Nadia. He killed Ion. Now he's killed Jacqueline."

"Afdal," said George, "I don't think hanging around here is a good idea."

Haddad stopped crying and glared at George.

"What I mean is, Afdal, it'll get a bit hot. Seems people are fighting back, see. We've got an army of migrants, apparently, marching through London – headed our way. They're killing vampires, says the telly. I know this country's ripped open, now, and I know we can salt the wound – but I think we should let it fester a bit first."

"You want us to scurry away like rats?"

"It's my suggestion, yeah."

"You go. I shall not."

"Lawton's killed it, Afdal. The monster's dead. You saw it burn. You ain't got no other monster, have you. That's Kea, Kakash, and Kasdeja dead – all killed by Lawton. The god killer. The Lord of Hell."

Haddad's shoulders slumped.

"But I've got a god," said George. "The one who made the vampire trinity. The one who ripped out his hearts and created life."

"You haven't got him."

"We will have."

"You're an idiot, George. You and Alfred."

"So you're not coming along, then."

Haddad shook his head. "Show me what's going on outside. I want to see."

"You want to see?"

George went to the window and opened it. He went back to Haddad and wheeled the old man over to the window.

Haddad leaned forward.

"What can you see?" said George.

"A war down there."

"Want a closer look?"

"No, I – "

George tipped the wheelchair, and Haddad fell out of the fifth-floor window.

CHAPTER 132.
AN ARMY LED BY A GIRL.

BOB Muncey, armed response officer with the City of London Police, got up and groaned. His face ached and he felt dizzy. Someone had smashed him over the head from behind.

Oh shit, he thought.

They'd stolen his weapon.

He looked around. Chaos reigned in Parliament Square. There was a riot going on. People were fighting for their lives. Vampires attacked humans, targeting individuals.

Stay in groups, had been the order. *Stick closely together.*

But the number of vampires was increasing. Soon they wouldn't be worried about attacking crowds of people. There would be enough of them to take on an army.

There were also piles of bodies. Hundreds of them. People had been collapsing. There had been a warning issued by Muncey's commander not to drink any tap water. The bosses hadn't said why. They never did. Just, *Don't use tap water. Repeat, don't use tap water – use only bottled water.*

"Muncey," said a voice.

He turned, and coming towards him were Nickerson and Blythe, two colleagues. They still had their weapons.

"What's up with you?" said Nickerson.

"I... I got attacked," said Muncey.

"Where's your weapon?" said Blythe.

Muncey shook his head.

"Shit, Muncey," Blythe said. "You better find it."

Bullets raked the grass ten yards away.

Nickerson and Blythe dived behind an overturned car.

"Muncey, Muncey, find cover," shouted Blythe.

The gun went off again.

Then fire came from the Palace of Westminster. Flames danced behind the windows.

More gunshots. Screams and shouts. The smell of cordite. The smell of burning.

We're not trained for war, thought Muncey.

He didn't know what to do. He had to stay here and help. But there was no control, anymore. No one to give orders. No one to co-ordinate. Everything had broken down.

He was about to join Nickerson and Blythe when he saw the throng approach.

They came down Whitehall.

"What the hell's this?" he said.

No one answered him. He stared at the horde. There had to be more than a thousand. They crammed the road. They marched forward as if they were an army – disciplined, under control.

When they were close, Muncey saw they were being led by a Chinese girl. She was maybe eighteen or nineteen. She had a torch and a wooden stake, darkened by blood.

She ran ahead of her army before turning to face them. They slowed down and stopped.

The girl shouted something, and voices rang out in different languages.

Muncey realized they were passing her orders down the line.

The girl faced front again. She raised the wooden stake above her head. She yelled out and charged towards a group of vampires.

Muncey laughed at her courage and raced to help her.

* * * *

12.24am, February 16, 2011

Kwan Mei was covered in blood. Vampire blood. She had killed dozens of them with her stake.

All around her, the army she had led to London battled the undead. Both sides had lost many fighters, but Mei felt as if they were winning. There were more of them, and they were brave.

She walked along the road towards the Houses of Parliament. Bodies lay everywhere. There had been many dead people on the way here. She'd seen hundreds just fall over and die. As they travelled towards London, a message had been passed along the convoy about the water being poisoned.

"Only drink from bottled water," Mei had told them.

Maybe it was the water that had killed these people.

She thought about Jake Lawton and Aaliyah Sinclair. She'd formed this army to help them.

Are you alive? she wondered.

The Houses of Parliament burned. Flames lit up the night. The building crumbled. It looked like it had been torn apart by an explosion.

A figure staggered out of the ruins.

Mei held her breath.

It was a man, and he was covered in blood. Every inch of him was crimson.

She recognized his shape. She knew who it was.

No, she thought. *It cannot be.*

The blood-covered man loped forward. When he stepped into the light, she saw he was carrying something.

A weapon.

The Spear of Abraham.

"Jake Lawton," she cried out, "Jake Lawton."

And she ran towards him.

PART FIVE.

RESURRECTION.

CHAPTER 133.
SANDSTORM.

ALFRED Fuad wrapped the black-and-white chequered shemagh around his mouth and nose and pulled down the goggles over his eyes.

"We stay where we are, gentlemen; it'll soon pass," said Colonel JJ Laxman, managing director and team leader of the mercenary operation called White Light Ops. He wore a tan-coloured shemagh. The Arabic headdress had been issued to the British military for decades. Laxman was a former Royal Marine.

The sandstorm swept in. Alfred hunkered down. They'd camped up twenty miles north of Hillah. It was desert here. But the closer you got to the city, the greener the landscape became. The land was irrigated by water from the Euphrates and farmers grew cereals and fruit.

"You all right there, Alfred?" said General Howard Vince.

The Chief of the General Staff also wore a tan-coloured shemagh, along with his fatigues.

"I'm fine, Howard."

The storm whistled. The desert undulated. Waves of sand washed across its surface, sweeping towards them. The tent flapped. But Alfred stayed calm. He wasn't worried.

Everything was under control. His brother would soon have London wrapped up. He looked at his watch. In fact, the city should already be crawling with vampires.

He looked around the tent. Apart from himself and Vince, there were seven men. Mercenaries from White Light Ops. Vince had hired them. The general knew Laxman well. They'd fought together during the first Gulf War in the early 1990s.

The soldiers-for-hire understood where they were going and what the mission was. But they didn't know they would be dead at the end of it.

If Alfred found what he was looking for, there would have to be a sacrifice. And these men, these seven burly killers-for-cash who would protect him, would also die for him.

They would die so he could bring back the greatest gift of all.

He would return to England with Nimrod.

The god of all vampires.

Maker of the undead.

The Great Hunter who had torn open his chest to give birth to Kea, Kakash, and Kasdeja.

With Nimrod at their side, Alfred and George would not only rule Britain, they would control the world.

"They think small, see, brother," George had told him five years ago, when they'd started planning all this.

"So what are you saying?" Alfred had asked.

"I'm saying we should go find the source."

"Don't we have the source? Kea, Kakash, and Kasdeja?"

"They ain't the source, Alfred. There's a greater one. There's the original. The one who made them. Nimrod, the Great Hunter."

"But ain't he a myth?"

"He's no more myth than they are. He's no more myth than the dust in those missing pots. We should go find him."

But that was 2006, when Iraq was dangerous. Not that it was entirely safe now. But it was better. Arriving in Baghdad yesterday, Alfred had already witnessed a car bombing. But he felt safe with Laxman and his team.

Despite having Arab blood, Alfred knew little of the desert. England was his home. He was English through and through, and the only other heritage that really made him proud was his link to Nebuchadnezzar.

Laxman huddled near a heater. It was cold at night in the desert. The mercenary was in his fifties. He had crow-black hair and a beard. A scar ran along his forehead. It was a strip of white against his tanned skin.

"Where d'you get that?" said Alfred.

Laxman ran his finger along the scar. "During the worst battle I've ever fought."

"Which one was that?"

"The divorce battle with my wife. She threw an iron at me. Clonked me right here. Sliced me up. My brains nearly fell out."

"Dangerous things, women."

"You married?"

"No, not at all."

Laxman nodded.

Alfred said, "You heard of a fella called Jake Lawton?"

"Yeah, I've heard of Lawton."

"You knew him when he was a soldier?"

"A bit. They say he's made of flint. Been shot five times, and he's still got the bullets in him. Tough guy."

"Would you have him?"

Laxman's brow furrowed. A smile broke out on his face. "I'd have him for tea, then snack on him before bed, Mr Fuad."

Alfred nodded. He was pleased to hear that but wasn't sure if it was true. Lawton had been virtually unkillable. He might even have been immortal himself. He'd messed up their plans the last time, and he was also doing his best to fuck things up this time.

He'd probably killed Bernard Lithgow, but fortunately he failed to stop the vampire virus from spreading into the water. News from London suggested people were dying by the hundreds.

And that was good.

A victory over Lawton.

Laxman said, "So you want Lawton seen to, Mr Fuad?"

Alfred thought for a moment before saying, "No, I think you're busy enough with this job for the time being, Colonel."

"We'll have this done in no time."

"Well, maybe once we've found what we're looking for, you can persuade me."

"I'm sure I can do that."

The storm rose. Alfred bowed his head. He shut his eyes and drifted off to sleep.

CHAPTER 134.
FIRE AND DEATH.

"HE will not live," said Mei.

"You don't know him," said Murray. "He'll definitely live."

"He has lost his eye."

"We'll make him another one."

"He has lost blood."

"We'll give him blood."

The boat rocked. It was a 28-footer called *Flower Of The East*. It had a varnished wooden mast and cabin. The hull was painted white. An outboard motor hung off the stern.

When Mei had found Lawton stumbling out of the Palace of Westminster, she'd helped him down Millbank and then through The Victoria Tower Gardens, to the Thames.

Across the river, on the Albert Embankment, vampires and humans fought.

Lawton had been close to death. He was soaked in blood. His face was a red mask. Mei saw the boat and waved at the man sailing it. He had looked around, obviously deciding if he were going to help or not.

He did. He had said his name, but Mei didn't remember it. He was a strong man, and he helped carry Lawton to the boat.

"Where are you going?" the man had asked Mei.

She'd shaken her head, not knowing.

Then he said, "I'll try Kent. Maybe head for France. I don't know if it's safe over there, but it's better than England."

After a while, Lawton had woken up and spluttered. Blood sprayed from his mouth. He spoke:

"Murray... tell... Murray... " He'd asked for a piece of paper and pen and somehow scrawled down a number. The man who owned the boat had phoned the number and spoken to the person called Murray. They picked up her and her son, David, at the Savoy Pier.

Murray had helped Mei clean the blood from Lawton's body. While doing this, they found he'd lost his left eye. They'd bandaged the wound and his other injuries.

Mei slept, and when dawn came, they were out of London.

"This is the Thames Estuary, where the Thames flows into the North Sea," the man who owned the boat had told her. His name was Gavin. While Mei had been asleep, they had picked up a friend of Gavin's called Neil. "There's Canvey Island." Gavin pointed to his left. "It doesn't look good."

It looked very bad. Hundreds of bodies lay on the grass that sloped down to the water. Smoke rose from the buildings.

Fire and death, thought Mei. She remembered Lawton burning the bodies of everyone who had been killed by vampires on the first night she met him. The night he'd saved her life.

After seeing the dead on Canvey Island, she went down below and spoke to Murray and David, who had just woken up. She learned more about Lawton from Murray. They had been enemies once; now they were friends.

"How can we give him blood?" Mei asked Murray now.

"We will. We won't give up on him. He wouldn't give up on us. He never gave up on me. I was as good as dead, and he came for me."

Murray was right, and Mei felt ashamed.

"Don't worry, Mei," said the woman. "Lawton's not like other men. You'd be right to think he might die if he were someone else – but he's not. He's got steel in his veins. He's got an iron will."

Mei wondered what the woman was talking about. How could someone have steel in their veins and a will of iron?

Murray smiled. "Don't worry – he's strong, is what I mean."

Lawton sat up.

Mei and Murray flinched.

"Where am I?" he said.

They told him.

Then Murray said, "London's lost. Thousands dead. It's anarchy."

Lawton sat up and groaned.

"You lie down," said Mei.

He waved away her instruction and then touched his face. He looked at Murray through his one eye. "Am I blind?"

Murray nodded. "One eye. I'm sorry, Jake."

He shrugged.

Murray said, "What do we do? Do we go back? Do we fight?"

For a few moments Lawton appeared to be thinking.

"Hillah," he said.

"What?" Murray said.

"We go to Hillah to kill a god."

END.

The Vampire Trinity trilogy will conclude with KARDINAL

ACKNOWLEDGMENTS.

I'd like to thank Snowbooks for their continued support, particularly Emma Barnes, who is always there when I've got an issue, and Anna Torborg for her wonderful editing. Also my agent Mariam Keen of the Whispering Buffalo Literary Agency for all the work she's done on my behalf. Thank you as always to my family, in England and Wales (and New Zealand, for a while), for their continued support, particularly my wonderful wife, Marnie, who has enabled me to fulfil my dream of becoming a writer.

ABOUT THE AUTHOR.

As well as *Krimson*, and its prequel *Skarlet*, Thomas Emson has written *Maneater, Prey,* and *Zombie Britannica*. Formerly a journalist, he has also been a singer-songwriter and is an award-winning playwright. Originally from Wales, he now lives in England. He is married to the writer and journalist Marnie Summerfield Smith, and they reside in Kent with a deaf American Bulldog named Mac and two house rabbits who answer to the names Teddy and Mabel. His website is thomasemson.net, and you can follow him on twitter.com/thomasemson